The Lost Patrol

(Lost Starship Series 5)

By Vaughn Heppner

ISBN-13: 978-1535377874
ISBN-10: 1535377879
BISAC: Fiction / Science Fiction / Military

The oldest Methuselah Man in existence—Strand—was too bitter and too apprehensive to gloat. Better than anyone else, he knew the risks in being here.

The Solar System swarmed with Star Watch vessels, with sensor buoys and hidden tracking devices. If the sub-men, those who called themselves humans, knew he was here, a system-wide alert would send every spaceship, every orbital laser station hunting for his cloaked star cruiser with extreme prejudice. The sub-men wanted him dead. Before they committed the heinous deed, they would try to drain his brain of every particle of information, data they desperately wished to learn but which he would never give them.

Strand sneered as he hunched in his command chair. He was a wizened little man with hellish embers for eyes.

Around him at their stations sat tall, golden-skinned New Men. In every way, they were superior to the Earthlings. Strand should know. His genius had created the super-race through careful genetic selection and modified gene-splicing.

The Methuselah Man curled the fingers of his left hand into a fist. The ungrateful Emperor of the New Men had escaped from Strand's control, taking the majority of the golden race with him. The New Men of Strand's crew would never do likewise. He'd seen to that long ago. Everyone aboard the star cruiser had undergone brain surgery. Strand had implanted control fibers into their gray matter, leaving hairline scars on their scalps. He should have done that with *all* of the New Men

1

from the beginning. He would never make such a mistake again.

"Master," the leanest of his New Men said.

Strand eyed the fellow. What was his name? Yes, yes, it was Dar Estevan. Did he detect a stubborn trace of free will in the man? What other reason would Estevan have to speak without his leave?

Dar Estevan kept his gaze downcast as trained. Strand wondered what caused him to think the golden-skinned one had become rebellious.

I've taken too many stims, Strand told himself. He'd been awake for a long time. *The stims are starting to alter my perceptions.*

Slipping into the Solar System several days ago with his modified jump drive had been a harrowing experience. Tiptoeing while cloaked toward Neptune—three days and nights of careful maneuvering—had taken its toll on him. He was full of nervous energy.

Under such conditions, Strand knew that his normal suspicions could turn into delusional paranoia much too easily. It had happened before, causing him to kill those closest to him. It was ludicrous to believe that Dar Estevan could act independently. The brain surgery had seen to that.

"Report," Strand told Estevan.

"The targeted space yacht has begun inserting into an orbital pattern, Master."

Strand almost accepted the report with a nod. Instead, a last suspicion caused him to study Estevan more closely. One of the man's eyelids twitched. Did that indicate more than simple exhaustion? Might it be nervousness? Why would Dar Estevan be nervous?

Strand scanned the bridge. The other New Men were alert at their stations, watching their monitors. Yet...the weapons specialist inhaled deeper than normal. Surely that was a signal. The comm specialist scratched his right shoulder, although he never took his eyes off his panel. Could the bridge crew be planning mutiny, secretly signaling each other?

Strand refocused on Dar Estevan. The offensive eyelid continued to twitch, almost as if it was a tic. He destroyed imperfect specimens. It was why, after one hundred and fifty years, the New Men were so superior to the Earthlings.

Strand held his breath, and the next second seemed to stretch into timelessness. For a long moment, it felt as if the bridge crew watched him with hidden cunning, observing his reactions with furtive sidelong glances.

I'm noticing now, Strand told himself. *I can see your tricks. I realize you're trying to lull me. To put me off my—*

Strand shook his head. What was wrong with him? He had to get a handle on this growing paranoia.

"Show me the luxury yacht on the main screen," he said.

Dar Estevan swiveled back to his panel. With a tap, the New Man activated the screen.

Strand took a moment to rub his face. It felt gritty, his eyes heavy. He needed to sleep for a day, maybe two, and recuperate.

Neptune appeared on the screen, a gem of an ice giant with an exotic blue color. Red triangles began to appear, each of them representing an orbital station or spaceship. Like all the outer planets, Neptune had many moons. Many of those moons boasted science stations, Star Watch outposts or industrial factories. Scattered among the moons were more spaceships, some of them Star Watch cruisers and destroyers.

"Highlight the target," Strand said.

Dar Estevan tapped his panel.

A green circle grew around a speck against the ice planet's blue background. Immediately, data began running across the left edge of the screen concerning the targeted vessel.

Strand glanced at the specs. The tonnage, carrying capacity, hull strength, and engine size told him the "speck" was a *Giaconda*-class luxury yacht, very expensive and posh. There were only three in existence. One of those had once belonged to Octavian Nerva.

"Ahhh," Strand said, rubbing his hands together. He'd gone to extreme lengths to engineer this moment. For a while, he hadn't believed he would succeed. Star Watch's Hyperion security had been too tight, too cautious. Finally, though, they had made a mistake, one he'd exploited to create today's possibility.

3

Even so, coming here alone like this was a terrible risk. If his desire for vengeance had been even one iota less powerful, he might have let it go. He had not let it go, however, because he was Strand, the wisest, smartest, *best* man in the universe. Those who had thought to sideline him would soon learn a harsh truth.

"Range?" Strand asked.

"Twenty-five thousand kilometers and closing," Dar Estevan answered.

Strand rubbed his hands again, saying, "Ready the stasis field."

Dar Estevan tapped a control. A buzzing sound commenced inside the star cruiser.

Strand's stomach began to churn. This was true daring. Who else could slip into the most fortified star system in Human Space? Who else would dare to pluck the prize right off the dinner plate and expect to do so unnoticed?

He used Builder technology that no one else possessed. The cloak, the stasis field, the stealth materials used to construct his star cruiser—

"Begin now," Strand said.

Dar Estevan tapped a control.

The buzzing sound intensified as an invisible beam radiated from the star cruiser. It started narrowly and expanded rapidly in a triangular fashion until the entire space yacht was caught in a stasis field.

"Launch," Strand whispered.

A different New Man tapped a code on his panel.

The star cruiser shuddered.

On the screen, a dark torpedo made of sensor-resistant material slid into view. The torpedo held four New Men in the nosecone.

Strand froze, his gaze riveted on the screen. As the torpedo sped toward the "speck," it dwindled in size. All the while, data played on the left corner of the main screen, the distance between torpedo and target changing rapidly.

"Comm?" Strand asked.

"Neptune area communications remain consistent," the comm specialist said. "No one has reported any unusual activity."

Strand sneered. For all their technical sophistication, the sub-men were unimaginative and dense, unable to recognize a stealth raid happening right before their eyes.

"Three, two, one, zero," Dar Estevan said.

The commando missile began dumping gravity waves, slowing its velocity as it neared the stasis field-captured yacht.

"Second report, Comm," Strand said.

"Still no unusual comm activity," the specialist said.

"Zoom in," Strand said.

A New Man tapped a panel.

Strand watched as three dark pods launched from the torpedo's nosecone. The seconds ticked away. Then, blackened hydrogen thrust caused the pods to ease near the yacht. Like a night moth breaking from its cocoon, a space-suited New Man squeezed from a hatch of the first pod. He jumped, sailing through the void. Two others—one from pod two and another from pod three—also sailed for the yacht. The three landed on the hull, using suction cups to grip tight. Because of special fibers in each suit, the commandos were immune to the stasis field. Each activated magnetic boots, clomping on the hull toward an entry hatch.

Strand snapped his teeth together as his stomach continued to churn. Time was critical, as people quickly died in a stasis field.

"*Sir*," Dar Estevan said.

Something about the tone alerted Strand. He stiffened, looking left.

Dar Estevan swiveled around, staring in Strand's direction but keeping his gaze downcast. That eyelid still twitched, though. It did so more than before. That seemed ominous somehow.

"A Star Watch vessel is hailing the yacht," Dar Estevan reported.

A thrill of fear shot down Strand's spine. "Range and type," he snapped.

"The vessel is approximately five hundred thousand kilometers away," Dar Estevan said while studying a wrist screen. "It is a destroyer-class ship."

Strand thought fast. Why did a destroyer so far away react while other, nearer spacecraft continued to remain oblivious to the situation? The destroyer was in orbit around one of the farther moons...

Strand shook his head. He must act with smooth concentration, not asking himself useless questions. He considered the problem, soon saying, "Continue the extraction."

As Strand finished speaking, the odd sensation from earlier returned. Time seemed to stretch once more, and his senses became heightened. He narrowed his focus upon Dar Estevan and his eye tic.

The subject's lips twitched in what might have been a sneer of amusement. That was ominous, indeed. Then, with seeming arrogance, Dar Estevan began to swivel back to his panel, as if he could do whatever he pleased.

"Hold," Strand said.

Dar Estevan froze.

"Why did you just smile?" Strand asked.

Dar Estevan blinked slowly, perhaps trying to gain time to marshal his thoughts. "I did not smile, Great One."

Strand heard deceit in Estevan's tone. "Your lips twitched, then."

If there had been a sneer, it had vanished. Instead, the subject's mouth tightened, as if he disapproved of the questions.

Strand had seen enough. This was rebellion. Without hesitation, he depressed a button on his wrist monitor.

Dar Estevan sharply sucked in his breath. His eyes bulged outward and his entire body spasmed. A moment later, he collapsed onto the deck, dead.

Strand leaned back in his command chair. He studied the others, gauging their reactions, trying to determine if this was supposed to have been a full-scale mutiny.

One or two glanced at the dead Dar Estevan. Then, each resumed studying his own controls. None frowned. Their

6

conditioning forbade them to react during punishments. Still, Strand wondered. Did a secret rebellion stir in his mind-controlled crew? Had he just stamped out the single spark, or was there a hidden cabal planning to unseat him?

After a few more seconds of study, Strand bared his teeth. His eyes hurt. He was tired, truly exhausted. The sooner he could leave the Solar System, the better. Commando raids in a heavily fortified star system were among the most wearying of military actions.

"Master," a New Man said.

Strand looked up sharply.

On the screen, three suited individuals stood on the hull of the space yacht. Two leaped for the nearby torpedo. The third lay limply in the grip of the two. He was the subject of the raid; the reason Strand had risked so much. Gaining the subject would change everything.

"Release the stasis field," Strand ordered.

A New Man rose from his station, went to Dar Estevan's board and tapped a control.

The stasis field vanished. So did the buzzing on the bridge. That allowed the yacht to operate normally again. The ship's engines glowed orange. The last commando to enter the luxury vessel piloted it. In seconds, a long tail grew behind the yacht. The ship plunged toward Neptune's upper atmosphere.

Strand rechecked his crew. Watching one of their own commit suicide—the New Man pilot plunging the yacht into Neptune—could have adverse effects on their conditioning. Several of them stiffened. He noticed the way they held their shoulders. One stared too fixedly at the main screen. If any dared to comment, he would kill that one instantly.

"The destroyer's comm-officer has become urgent," a New Man reported.

Strand barely checked himself in time as his hand twitched to make another kill before realizing the New Man had reported correctly. The words weren't part of a secret plot. Likely, there was no plot to unseat him. He might have needlessly slain Dar Estevan. That was unfortunate. He was more worked-up than he'd realized. He needed to relax. Yet, how could he at a critical time like this?

"The destroyer's comm officer wants to know what's wrong with the yacht," the New Man explained. "She's asking why they're heading into the atmosphere. Don't they know Neptune's gravity will crush the craft?"

Strand ingested the news in silence. Despite the distant Star Watch destroyer, no one had seen the stealth torpedo or guessed the existence of the cloaked star cruiser. He would leave the sub-men a grim mystery.

"The Star Watch destroyer is increasing velocity, Master. It is breaking out of the moon's orbit and heading toward Neptune."

Strand thought furiously. If the destroyer was fixated on the luxury yacht, its sensor officer might notice the stealth torpedo if it began accelerating.

"Instruct the torpedo pilot to remain in drift mode," Strand said. "We will go to them. Once we've retrieved everyone, we will jump out-system."

The next fifteen minutes proceeded flawlessly. The star cruiser reached the three floating individuals, hooking them with a tether line. Five minutes after that, the torpedo's former pilot floated into a hangar bay.

Now, the automated empty torpedo expelled gravity waves, heading down into the gas giant. The yacht had already imploded, crushed by Neptune's killing gravity.

"The destroyer has issued a red alert," the comm specialist said.

Strand stood up, stretching his back. He had his prize. Star Watch had a mystery. What did he care now about red alerts?

"Inform me when you're ready to jump," Strand said. "I'm going to greet our new guest."

The Methuselah Man headed for the hatch, debating whether he would operate on the subject's brain or leave the person intact. It was an interesting dilemma. One thing he knew for certain was that everything was going to be different now. Oh, yes, with the subject in his possession, the universe would learn what it meant to anger the greatest man in existence.

-2-

TWO MONTHS LATER

Maddox's earpiece crackled. He shook his head. The ancient Adok AI wasn't going to give it up so easily, it seemed.

"Captain," Galyan said in his robotic voice. "Surely, you realize this is rash. I beg you to reconsider. You mustn't injure yourself."

Maddox, in a pressurized suit and helmet, was strapped to a seat inside a tiny capsule. The one-man capsule dangled from a stratospheric balloon that climbed rapidly for near-space. He had entered the capsule in a wheat field in Normandy, France. At that point, the helium balloon had stretched fifty-five stories tall, a thin, gangling thing. As the balloon rose, it expanded into a rounder shape. At thirty-seven kilometers from sea level, the balloon would be almost completely round.

"You graduated yesterday," Galyan said. "Think of the time and money the Patrol people took in retraining you. You must not throw away the costly training in this…this absurd stunt."

"Relax," Maddox said. He wore a skin-colored pad on his throat. It was a sub-vocalization unit, allowing him to communicate with Starship *Victory* in its high orbit above him.

"You suggest I relax," Galyan said, "but I fear the coming danger you are needlessly courting. I wish I could say I do not understand why you are doing this. But I understand very well. My analyzer has determined the issue troubling you."

"There is no *issue*," Maddox said. "That's all in your circuits. I've become bored. The Patrol training was tedious, particularly the last few weeks where it was all review. Before I begin a year-long voyage into the Beyond, I want to live a little."

A little over a year ago, Maddox had transferred out of Star Watch Intelligence into the Patrol. Since the discovery of the Swarm—an entire Imperium of them that apparently included ten percent of the Milky Way Galaxy—High Command had dedicated a greater number of ships to exploration. If the Swarm Imperium was nearby, humanity needed to know it. If the Imperium was far away, humanity needed to know that, too. The expanded Commonwealth of Planets also wanted the coordinates to the New Men's Throne World…just in case hostilities were renewed with them. Altogether, that meant a fifty-seven percent increase in Patrol voyages into the Beyond.

"I do not accept your 'tedium' explanation," Galyan said. "You have a self-destructive side to your nature. When you are agitated, you tend toward extreme actions. This is a case in point."

"That's quite enough, Galyan."

"But Captain, your life is at issue. I cannot ignore that. Without you at my helm—"

"I'm going to cut communications," Maddox said.

"That is illogical. I can easily appear in the capsule as a hologram, continuing the conversation. You will listen to what I have to say. It is for your own benefit."

"Good," Maddox said.

"I beg your pardon?"

"The correct idiom is, 'I'm doing this for your own good.'"

"Oh. Yes, my data banks agree with you. I have made the correction in my speech center. Thank you, Captain."

Maddox checked a monitor. The balloon approached its float height. He'd felt a decrease in the rate of ascent. He was in near-space, although he was still in Earth's atmosphere. The outside air was thin, but still generated enough drag to prevent anyone from deploying satellites at this height. The infinitesimal drag would soon slow any satellite so it plunged to Earth.

10

Leaning forward, the captain glanced out a tiny porthole. It was dark outside, with the great blue of Earth spreading below. If he went outside in a shirt, the low pressure would turn the liquids in his body tissues to gas. It would be like the time he'd sprinted through a vacuum from a shuttle in one of *Victory's* hangar bays to a pressurized corridor. Those few seconds had almost killed him.

"Admiral Fletcher's discovery regarding the New Men has troubled you for over a year already," Galyan said. "This is simply the latest manifestation."

Maddox ignored the comment, although he knew the AI referred to the dirty secret learned in the Thebes System of "C" Quadrant.

"The New Men do not sire girls," Galyan said, "only boys."

"How fascinating," Maddox said.

"Sarcasm only proves my contention," Galyan said. "The implications of the news are obvious. Since the New Men do not sire girls, they kidnap normal women as breeders. But that creates a problem for you, Captain."

"Nonsense," Maddox said.

"By necessity, that means every son is genetically half New Man and half regular human, what you refer to at times as a half-breed."

Maddox studied the monitor. He'd reached maximum altitude. With great care, he rechecked his equipment, making sure the chutes were in place and ready to deploy. The experts considered this dangerous, calling for perfect body control. Ever since hearing that, Maddox had been determined to try.

"I have studied your medical records," Galyan said, "paying particular attention to your psychological profile. Your mother's impregnation by a New Man has always troubled you, as you have hated the label of half-breed."

Behind the visor of his helmet, Maddox's blue eyes hardened. His mother had escaped from an experimental facility while he'd been in her womb. The event had cost his mother her life.

"My analyzer has played out all the possible scenarios," Galyan said. "The one with the highest probability is this: You abhor the New Men, but have adjusted to the reality that you

11

have one half their bloodline. Now, with our new data, you believe that you might be a run-of-the-mill, Throne World New Man, as they are all half-breeds. Because of this, you have become more reckless in your choices, the self-destructive issue raising its head."

"That's a nice theory," Maddox said in a bland voice. "But there's a problem with your analysis."

"I see no problem."

"It's obvious," Maddox added.

"I can play that game, too, Captain, and I must say that is nonsense."

"Well *played*, Galyan."

"Why, thank you, Captain. Your abrupt change in attitude causes me to hope you finally see the wisdom of what I'm saying and will end this madness."

"I suppose it doesn't matter to you and your analysis that a New Man has golden skin and that mine is white."

Galyan fell silent.

"What causes their golden coloration?" Maddox asked.

"A simple—"

"There's a second problem with your theory," Maddox said, talking over the AI. "After several generations of interbreeding with genetically regular women, the New Men would have become normal humans themselves, their genetic uniqueness diluted of its so-called superhuman qualities. Unfortunately for your analysis, that isn't the case. In fact, it's the reverse. The New Men have become increasingly 'superior' to regular humans."

"It is strange," Galyan said, "but I had not considered that issue. I find it telling, however, that you already have. You have proved my point. You are worried about being a normative New Man and have already carefully thought out the various possibilities."

"Wrong," Maddox said. "My reasoning was a simple matter of quick detective logic. It was elementary, as they say."

"My analyzer says there is a nineteen percent probability that you are telling me the strict truth."

"As high as that?" Maddox asked with a hint of sarcasm.

"I see the problem in greater depth now—the idea that there would be genetic dilution given continued breeding with normal women. I am analyzing…Oh. There must be another process involved during the pregnancies. The New Men must modify each fetus in the womb with some type of invasive method."

"Precisely," Maddox whispered. Had his mother escaped the test facility soon enough, before he'd received any *Frankenstein* modifications? The idea troubled him. Dwelling on it these past months had brought an old curiosity to the surface. Who was his father? He wanted to know and wasn't sure why he did.

As if reading his various thoughts, Galyan said, "You must not trouble yourself over these useless concerns. One should only worry about situations he can actively change."

"I'm not troubling myself," Maddox said.

"I would like to believe you, Captain. But my analyzer's highest probability is that you just lied to me again."

Maddox had heard enough. He unbuckled his straps and rose from his seat. "I'm approaching the hatch," he said.

"Your capsule is still pressurized," Galyan warned.

"After I depressurize, of course," Maddox said.

"In your agitation, did you forget about the pressurization?"

Without a word, Maddox depressurized the compartment. If he'd opened the hatch before doing so, the capsule's departing atmosphere would have launched him through the opening like a cannonball.

"On further review," the AI said, "I have decided to bring you up on my own initiative. Your sullen behavior—"

"Galyan," Maddox said. "You will refrain from such action. Your concern is noted and, in a roundabout way, appreciated."

"Will you admit that I am right concerning your mother and that your tainted heritage troubles you?"

Maddox hesitated a fraction before he said, "You are an Adok. Thus, you don't realize that you've crossed a line. Please do not do so again."

"But—"

"That is all," Maddox said.

13

A *ping* in his helmet told Maddox it was safe to open the hatch. He waited a half-second before pulling a lever unlocking the wheel. He began to turn it. After the wheel clicked into place, he pushed the hatch, swinging it open and poking his head outside. The Earth spread out below in a glorious panorama. From this height, he noticed the curvature of the planet. Far below him was Europe. If everything went right, he was going to land down there in Normandy.

The moment reminded him of the emergency landing onto Wolf Prime. That had been an adventure. Recalling it, the captain laughed with exultation. It was good to be alive, even despite the...*concern* over his identity this new knowledge about the New Men had brought him, and the desire to find his father.

Maddox didn't want to think about those things anymore. He grabbed the edges of the opening and propelled himself out. He dropped from the capsule, the balloon quickly fading from sight.

This was more than glorious. It felt as if he hung in space, at peace with the world. That was not the truth, though, the hanging, the floating out here. He gained speed as he dropped.

During the fall, the darkness lessened and he could no longer see the curvature of the Earth. Finally, the sky became normal-colored as he reached denser air.

He'd assumed a skydiving position, subtly moving his limbs and body to stay that way. The G-meter remained green the entire time, a good sign. If he began to spin, the induced gravity might stop the blood flowing to his head and he'd either pass out or die. He had stabilization chutes for such an event, but so far hadn't needed to deploy them.

Checking a gauge, Maddox saw that he was supersonic. Now, he kept a close eye on his height meter.

"Get ready to deploy your main parachute," Galyan said shortly.

"Roger," Maddox said. He'd been ready to do just that, but had decided to throw the AI a bone and let him feel needed.

At eighteen hundred meters, with a Normandy plain below, Maddox gripped the deployment handle. At fifteen hundred meters, he pulled it.

A loud clapping sound and a vicious yank against his shoulders told him the parachute was out. His speed slowed considerably. Soon, he floated toward the ground.

He spied a road and a French tractor moving on it. Then, he spied an air-car. It didn't belong to his drop team. That one would have had a red flag on the top. This car skimmed over a wheat field, heading toward his landing area.

Maddox readied himself. The ground rushed up, and he hit and rolled, with the billowing silk floating down on top of him.

By the time Maddox climbed out of the silk, the air-car had grounded. A door opened. A uniformed Star Watch officer approached. It was Major Stokes from Intelligence.

Maddox double-checked. Stokes' hands were empty, neither of them holding a gun. The captain remembered all too well the time Stokes had tried to murder him in the Greenland prison complex.

The major halted as his left leg shivered. The man grabbed his left thigh, clutching it for a long moment before finally, almost experimentally, letting go. He resumed his approach, dragging the left leg.

Maddox found that odd, even a little sinister. He twisted his helmet, detaching it and tossing it to the ground. Afterward, he unzipped the pressurized suit, stepping out of it. The captain was tall and lean, with angularly handsome features.

The major's left leg shivered once more, but the man ignored it as he advanced.

"His movements are odd," Galyan said in Maddox's ear.

Maddox said nothing, watching the approaching major. There was a hole in the left thigh fabric. Had something just happened to Stokes?

Stokes slowed and took his time pulling out a pack of cigarettes. He stuck one in his mouth and sucked it alight so the tip glowed, while slipping the cigarette pack back into a pocket.

"I'm here to collect you," Stokes said as smoke trickled from his mouth.

"I am analyzing his speech patterns," Galyan said.

Maddox wondered why the major smoked a cigarette. Usually, the man smoked a stimstick.

15

"The brigadier would like a word with you," Stokes added.

"I'm no longer in Intelligence," Maddox replied.

"I'm afraid it doesn't work like that, old son. Once you're in Intelligence, you're *always* in Intelligence."

"There are Patrol officers who would disagree with you."

Stokes' left leg shivered again, but the major continued to ignore it.

Uneasy now, Maddox noted that the major wore a sidearm. For once in his life, the captain was unarmed. What could he do about that?

"It appears you have us in visual," Maddox sub-vocalized to Galyan.

"I do," the AI said.

"It's time to test the new sniper beam the Kai-Kaus installed in you. Target the major."

"Captain," Galyan said, "the sniper beam is experimental. While atmospheric conditions are good, you are far too near the target for me to attempt a laser shot."

"I accept the risk."

"I could as easily hit you as the—Captain, that is not the major. I am seventy-four percent certain you are addressing an android."

"So some slipped through our net, eh?" Maddox muttered.

"Are you well, Captain?" the thing that looked like Stokes asked. "You're talking to yourself."

"Why are you smoking a cigarette?" Maddox asked.

"I'm downwind of you, so it shouldn't be a problem."

"You misunderstand. Major Stokes smokes stimsticks, not cigarettes. Your programming is off."

The two stared at each other. The major's leg shivered again. Maddox finally noticed a dark substance smeared under the hole.

"Did someone shoot you in the leg?" the captain asked. "Now, Galyan," he sub-vocalized. "Shoot it now."

"You've interfered once too often, Captain," the pseudo-major said. "This time, you will die." Without another word, the thing reached for the gun holstered at its side.

At the same time, a narrow, nearly invisible beam slashed down from Starship *Victory* high in orbit. It produced a faint

16

haziness in the air. Then, midway between Maddox and the major, a spot of grass the size of a dime curled up, smoked, burst into flame and disappeared as a hole deepened.

Maddox raised his hands to shield himself from the radiating heat, but that proved futile. So, he threw himself backward, rolling across the ground.

The pseudo-major shuffled back from the smoking hole. In a blur of movement, he drew the gun and fired—the bullet passing where Maddox had stood a moment before.

A second faint haziness appeared, burning a new tiny circle of grass and ground. This beam was much closer to Maddox than the first one.

It caused Maddox to scramble madly across the ground to escape the radiating heat. Behind him, the major fired twice more, the last bullet clipping Maddox's shoe.

After the third shot, an invisible beam struck the major's head. It burned through, turning the head and neck into blue-sparking, molten slag. The android toppled onto the ground, more of its pseudo-flesh melting. A second later, the beam quit.

Maddox panted from his sprawled position on the ground. The Kai-Kaus chief technician who had told him about the sniper beam had spoken about it in glowing terms. The captain did not want to rely on Galyan's single-person shooting skills again.

He heard a whine. Maddox turned as he climbed to his feet. Another air-car flew low over the ground. It was identical to the first one.

"I will beam it," Galyan suggested.

"No!" Maddox said.

"It's far enough away so—"

"No," Maddox repeated. He glanced at the android's fallen gun. It looked too hot to pick up yet.

"I would like to apologize for the first two shots," Galyan said.

"Don't worry about it," Maddox said. "It's results that count. The thing is incapacitated. Well done, Galyan."

"I would like to point out that I warned you about the sniper system—"

"Let's concentrate on the issue at hand, shall we?" Maddox said, interrupting. "The air-car is slowing down."

"As you wish, Captain," Galyan said.

The air-car grounded hard, as if the occupant was in a hurry. The door opened, and out stepped Major Stokes. This one had a gun in his hand.

"Lower your gun!" Maddox shouted.

The major hesitated, his gaze taking in the scene. Slowly, he lowered his weapon so it aimed down.

"Better yet," Maddox said, "holster your sidearm."

"Don't you trust me, Captain?" Stokes asked.

Maddox pointed at the smoldering android. "Starship *Victory* has you in sight, Major. The thing over there was a replica of you. Perhaps you can understand my caution."

Stokes blinked several times before pitching his sidearm onto the ground.

"Thank you," Maddox said.

Stokes nodded. "It looked like me?" he asked, bewildered.

"With a gimpy leg," Maddox said.

The major absorbed the news. It seemed to take an effort of will for him to collect his thoughts. Finally, he said, "I found your drop team a kilometer from here. They're all dead, shot in the head. The android must have killed them."

Maddox had been afraid of that.

"It was actually *me*?" Stokes asked.

"The last of the androids," Maddox said.

"You hope," Stokes said.

The two men looked at each other.

"The brigadier sent me," Stokes said. "She and the Lord High Admiral wish to speak with you."

"Good," Maddox said, "Because I'd like to speak to them."

"We can use my air-car," Stokes said.

"Don't go, Captain," Galyan said. "This could be an elaborate trap."

"Is that your highest probability?" Maddox sub-vocalized to the AI in orbit.

"No," Galyan admitted, "but it is *a* possibility."

"I suppose," Maddox said, "but let's take the chance, shall we? It could prove interesting."

The captain pulled out a cloth, folding it twice as he approached the android's fallen gun. He gingerly picked up the revolver by the butt. He waved it in the air to cool the metal faster as he hurried to the major's air-car.

The air-car rapidly gained height as Stokes set the coordinates for Star Watch Headquarters in Geneva, Switzerland.

The major was an older, nondescript man with dark hair except for two patches of white on the sides. He was the Iron Lady's chief confidante.

"This is upsetting news," the major said. "We were sure we'd eliminated every android. How could this have happened?"

"It makes sense that a few escaped the dragnet," Maddox said. "I wonder why it targeted me, though."

"Maybe the better question is how it knew where to find you." Stokes glanced at him. "How did you know it was an android?"

"It smoked a cigarette for one thing."

"I smoke cigarettes sometimes. That couldn't have been the only giveaway."

Maddox shrugged. Did he sense a hint of insistence in the question? He wasn't sure.

"How did you destroy it?" Stokes asked.

"I already told you," Maddox said. "Starship *Victory* shot it."

"That doesn't make sense. Are you implying the starship used a beam from orbit?"

"Precisely."

Stokes glanced at him again. "I would think a starship's laser would have burned you at the same time."

"Hmm," Maddox said.

The major frowned. "Are you suggesting *Victory* has an antipersonnel laser that can target an individual from orbit?"

Instead of answering, Maddox checked the android's gun. It was a regular gunpowder revolver but of an extraordinary caliber. This one looked to be a .55 Magnum. It was a hand cannon, with three bullets remaining. He hadn't thought to grab extra ammo from the android. That might have been an oversight on his part.

"That's a big gun," Stokes said, glancing at it.

"Indeed," Maddox said, becoming thoughtful. The major was more talkative than normal. Usually, the man was sarcastic toward him. Today, Stokes was positively chatty.

"How did you signal *Victory* to smoke the android?" Stokes asked.

"I used Builder tech," Maddox said, which wasn't true. He was just curious as to the major's reaction.

Stokes looked at him sharply. Then he laughed. "You just made a joke."

"Did I?" Maddox asked.

"Now, see here, Captain—"

Maddox aimed the hand cannon at Stokes. "Take us down."

"What is this?" Stokes asked. "What are you doing? Put that down this instant."

Maddox did not repeat himself as he targeted Stokes' mid-torso.

"This is a poor joke," Stokes said.

"I will fire unless we begin to head down immediately."

"Why, man? What did I do to upset you?"

Maddox remained silent, watching, waiting. He did not sub-vocalize to Galyan, as the major would hear that. The captain was surprised Galyan hadn't spoken to him yet. That was the last giveaway that something was wrong. In some manner, Stokes had cut his communications with the starship.

The air-car headed down. Stokes guided the vehicle as he frowned. "Do you care to give me a hint what this is about?" the major asked.

"Call it a precaution."

Stokes glanced at him again, at the gun, and then lunged at Maddox.

The captain had been expecting something like this. Under normal conditions, with a regular person, the major might have succeeded. Maddox had faster-than-normal reflexes, though. He pulled the trigger as Stokes grabbed his arms.

The major had irresistible strength, more than a regular human should possess. The first shot went wild, striking the bubble dome and cracking it. The discharge was deafening, making the captain's ears ring as he winced with pain.

Maddox now gritted his teeth as he strove against the obvious android. There had been *two* Major Stokes androids, this one more like the man than the first one had been. What did the android-controllers want with him anyway?

"Surrender," the android said.

"Do you wish to kill me?" Maddox panted.

"No. I want to talk."

"Yes, I'll talk."

They spoke as the major grappled and Maddox tried to align the hand cannon at the torso.

"Release the gun," the android said.

"I can't. You're gripping me too hard for that."

"I will not fall for such an obvious tactic, Captain. Until you release the gun, I will continue to pin your arms."

"Look," Maddox said. "We're going to hit a mountain."

The android looked forward. Maddox knew there was nothing. They were still high in the air and there were no nearby mountains. As the android looked, though, Maddox tried a new maneuver, twisting the other way. The android's split-second inattention allowed Maddox to aim the barrel at the thing's torso.

BOOM!

As Maddox's ears rang painfully once again, the android slammed backward with a hole in its side. Black gunk poured out. Electrical discharges sparked farther within.

BOOM!

Maddox fired his last round into the wound. Once more, the force slammed the android back. Its eyelids fluttered as it pulled its arm back. Then it shot a fist into the control panel, smashing electrical and computer equipment.

That caused an emergency procedure in the air-car. The dome ejected, tumbling away. Cold air almost ripped Maddox out of his seat. The android's hand yanked out of the dash, holding sizzling wires.

"The seats will no longer eject," it said, staring at Maddox.

"Why do this?" Maddox asked. "What are you attempting to achieve?"

"It will delight my controller to know that you're confused seconds before you die. Good-bye, Captain Maddox. This is your final mission."

Maddox slapped the control to his seat restraints. They popped off.

"What are you doing?" the android asked.

Maddox grabbed an emergency cord and leaped upward. He pulled a parachute bundle free. The air-car had many emergency redundancies. As the slipstream caught him, jerking the captain away from the forward-moving but slowing air-car, the android lunged at the rising chute-bundle. The dying android clawed at the straps, its fingers hooking one. That ripped the cord out of the captain's hand.

A second later, the android exploded. Perhaps it had been intending to do that all along, taking Maddox into oblivion with it.

The cord jerking out of his grip caused the captain to tumble head-over-heels in the air. The burning air-car headed down, shedding debris along the way.

"Galyan," he sub-vocalized. "I hope you can hear me."

There was nothing but the rush of wind from the earpiece.

Maddox pressed the skin-pad on his throat. "Come in, Galyan. Can you hear me? I repeat. Can you hear me?"

There was no response from the Adok AI.

Maddox looked down. The distant ground rushed up all too fast. He would hit soon. The terrible realization that he would soon cease to exist welled up through him.

Maddox took a deep breath as his stomach tightened with fear. He hated the sensation. To combat it, he strove for rational thought. The fear intensified, however. This was an awful feeling.

Maddox closed his eyes so he wouldn't have to look at the ground. That helped enough so he could think again.

Was there a Creator as the Builder had believed? It was time to make his peace with Him. Maddox strove to formulate more thoughts.

He opened his eyes instead, staring at the waiting ground, causing the fear to reassert its hold.

-4-

Lieutenant Keith Maker—he'd been promoted from Second Lieutenant—whooped with delight as the new catapult system launched his jumpfighter into near-orbital space.

The small Scotsman was pressed against his cushioned seat, the Gs testing his stamina.

"You're not making me go unconscious," he said.

"Lieutenant," Galyan said over the fighter's intercom.

"I'm right here, mate, wide awake and ready."

"We must accelerate the rescue attempt," Galyan said.

"Eh? There's a problem?"

"The captain has jumped out of the air-car."

"Say again," Keith said.

"The captain is plunging to the Earth. He has less than thirty seconds to impact."

"Now, why he'd go and do something like that, eh?"

"The air-car exploded," Galyan said.

"Oh. Okay. That makes sense. Give me the coordinates."

"They are already in your flight computer."

Keith tapped the main screen. "Right, I see it. This is going to be tricky. I need more time—"

"This is no time. You must fold now or the captain dies."

"I know, I know. There's no time when you're falling to your death—unless an angel of mercy named Keith Maker is ready to rescue you. I hope you know jumpfighters aren't normally used in atmosphere."

"Please, Lieutenant, more action and less talk."

"I always talk, mate. But you need not worry."

The entire time he'd been talking, Keith had been tapping controls and readying his "tin can" for its incredible ability. It could fold space for short hops, moving from one location to another in the blink of an eye. It was a space fighter meant to be used in a vacuum. Under extremely limited conditions, it could function in atmosphere…as long as it didn't remain there long or attempt to fly. It was not aerodynamic in the slightest.

"Hop in, hop out," Keith said under his breath. Louder, he said, "I hope you're recording this, Galyan. Trainers will want to show recruits for many years to come what I'm about to do."

"The captain has twenty seconds left," Galyan said.

"That's a pity," Keith replied. "It means I have no margin for error. I have to do it right the first time. Come on, Keith, this will be a piece of bloody cake, eh?"

He pressed a switch, and with a hum, the jumpfighter's special mechanism activated. One second, the tin can was in near-orbital space less than ten kilometers from *Victory*. The next, the jumpfighter appeared in Earth's lower atmosphere, barely above the deck of Normandy.

Keith blinked once, twice—"I see him," he said. Maddox was on the screen, falling toward the jumpfighter.

"You are too close," Galyan said. "He will impact too hard."

"Wrong, boyo, I'm perfectly positioned."

Keith's fingers played over the controls. The jumpfighter shook badly in the dense air. Smoke poured out of one of the panels. A loud screeching noise told Keith he couldn't stay here long.

On camera three, Keith watched Maddox. The captain fell toward the jumpfighter. The lieutenant had made a perfect fold. That didn't happen often. He couldn't just let Maddox hit the tin can, though.

The jumpfighter began to fall itself. Keith had to *catch* Maddox as softly as possible. Then—

The jumpfighter shuddered worse than before. A red alert began to blare in the cockpit.

"Bloody hell," Keith said. With roving fingers, he checked the fighter's systems.

The tin can shook horribly again. A warning klaxon told Keith he had a hull breach. What could cause—

"You are under attack," Galyan said through a speaker.

"By whom?" Keith shouted.

"A craft has maneuvered above you," Galyan said. "It is firing autocannon shells into your jumpfighter. Lieutenant, you must fold back into space or the attacking craft will destroy you"

"I'm not leaving without the captain," Keith said.

"He is no longer your concern."

"Wrong, mate. The man saved my life. I owe him everything. I don't care what I have to do to get him—"

"The new craft is taking the captain," Galyan said, interrupting.

"What?" Keith asked.

"The craft has grabbed the captain."

"How did it do that?" Keith asked.

"My analyzer suggests with a gravity beam," Galyan said.

"Star Watch doesn't *have* gravity beams."

"The situation has becoming increasingly perplexing," Galyan said. "Lieutenant, you must fold and return to *Victory*. I have alerted Star Watch. Atmospheric fighters are on their way."

"Great, just great," Keith said. "I'm heading back upstairs. But if those blokes hurt the captain—"

"Those are my sentiments also," Galyan said. "This is far from over."

-5-

Maddox saw the jumpfighter materialize below him. It told him that Galyan had reacted swiftly after the android had cut his communications with *Victory*.

Still, using a tin can in the deepest atmosphere was risky. No doubt, Keith had piloted the craft. Even so, the percentages would have been against the lieutenant. That Keith—if it had been him—had almost pulled it off showed once again the young man's extreme piloting skills.

Maddox felt himself rise as he headed toward a circular belly hatch in a large airship. A few seconds ago, as he'd dropped toward the jumpfighter, he'd become aware of a shadow. Then, autocannon shells had hammered the tin can. That's when the gravity beam had caught him. Maddox was familiar with such a ray, as one had caught him on the Builder Dyson sphere over a year ago. Did that mean the airship, or the people who ran it, had access to Builder technology? That seemed likely. Did they control the androids? Maddox gave that a high percentage as well.

He slid up through the circular hatch and gently landed on his feet inside a large chamber. The opening he'd come up through slid shut.

Two short and slender men stepped forward. They wore blue uniforms that fit tight around the throat, dark goggles over their eyes, and they aimed stubby projacs at him. They were Spacers. The circular pectoral patches meant these two were provost sentries, Marines in Star Watch terms. They looked

28

vaguely familiar. Yes, he'd fought these two sentries before in Shanghai.

"Why am I here?" Maddox asked.

Before the sentries could answer, a hatch opened and a woman stepped through. She also looked familiar.

"Hello, Provost Marshal," Maddox said.

She was a head taller than the sentries. Like them, she wore dark-colored goggles over her eyes. Maddox had met her over a year ago in the Lin Ru Hotel in Shanghai, the Spacer embassy on Earth.

Spacers did not claim any particular territory, but acted like space nomads. The majority of them were of Southeast Asian origin, particularly from Old Thailand, Cambodia and Vietnam. Almost all the others had Polynesian ancestry.

The last time Maddox had seen the woman in Shanghai, androids had kidnapped him. Spacers were said to have an abnormal hatred of androids and robots. Could that be an elaborate cover? In reality, did Spacers use androids and robots more than anyone else did? Why had the airship been ready to pick him up? They couldn't have gotten to him so quickly otherwise. Clearly, the Spacers must have been monitoring the Stokes androids. Maddox might have died otherwise, as Keith could have failed.

"I deactivated both of your creatures," the captain said, referring to the Stokes androids.

The Provost Marshal remained motionless, as if waiting for a signal.

There was a second possibility here, Maddox realized. Were the Provost Marshal and her sentries also androids? What did Star Watch Intelligence really know about the Spacers anyway? They were among the most secretive of human societies.

The Provost Marshal stepped forward as if stung, but the captain couldn't see anything to have caused the reaction. She said, "We don't have much time."

"Yes," Maddox said smoothly. "I'd already assumed as much."

"Subterfuge won't help you here, Captain. You were lucky against the androids. Do not presume on your luck with us."

29

"There was no luck involved," he said. "I simply played the odds."

"No, Captain, you did not. I watched your stratospheric jump from the balloon. That was reckless and unneedful. For the life of me, I cannot fathom why anyone would do anything so….so risky."

"For thrills," Maddox said.

"That was a piece of frivolity," she said, "a mindless action. Once, you defeated the alien Destroyer when it entered the Solar System. Why, then, did you mindlessly jump from space today?"

"A moment," Maddox said, stepping forward.

The two sentries moved, blocking his way to the Provost Marshal.

Maddox stopped, eying them and the aimed projacs. "What's your name?" he asked the woman.

She hesitated, finally saying, "Shu 15."

"That's a pretty name," he said.

Her head twitched as she frowned. Maddox noticed that she had a small, kissable mouth.

"Your ways will fail against me, Captain. The Visionary has alerted me as to your charms. I am immune to your flattery."

"That's a pity," Maddox said.

"I—we—have come to warn you."

He raised an eyebrow.

"This is a serious matter," she said. "You must act with decorum, showing deference. If you don't…there will be consequences. You will not like them, I assure you. The Law of Reciprocal Action will rebound upon you in a most grievous fashion."

"That sounds painful," he said.

"I have warned you. It is now on your own head. You do understand that, yes?"

Maddox realized this was a ceremony. He had no idea who the Visionary might be, but it sounded religious. Spacer society was almost as mysterious to Star Watch Intelligence as the New Men.

"I have been warned," he said. "I will act accordingly."

"I dearly hope so, Captain. Despite your mindlessness, you are a hero. It would be a shame to see you destroy yourself because you're too proud. That is the great fault of heroes—the sin that often brings them low. We want you to fly high as you expose the future to us."

Maddox nodded in lieu of speaking. This was becoming odder by the moment.

"Follow me," she said, turning, heading the way she had come.

Maddox complied, the two provost sentries moving aside to let him pass and then falling into step behind him.

They moved through a surprisingly large hall. What kind of airship was this? He couldn't feel any motion. The gravity ray that had pulled him up—could the Spacers have superior gravity dampeners?

Shu halted before a hatch. She turned, stepped near Maddox and touched his left forearm. He towered over her.

"May the Spirit guide you, Captain. I shall say a litany for you, that you guard your tongue."

"Thank you," he said.

She stepped to the left, facing the hatch. It dilated open. "Go," she whispered.

Maddox glanced at her, at her serious manner. He glanced at the sentries. They knelt, with their foreheads pressed against the deck.

"You must go now," Shu said. "Time is precious."

Maddox squared his shoulders and marched through the hatch into a small chamber. Behind him, the hatch closed and the chamber darkened.

Maddox tensed.

Immediately, a glow began at his side. The captain faced it. An old woman sat on a dais in a throne-like chair. She wore goggles and had a white polar bear fur wrapped around herself. She had wrinkled features and white hair. It occurred to Maddox that he'd never seen hair on a Spacer before. They wore skullcaps, hiding any hair.

"Come closer," she said in a hoarse voice.

Maddox did so.

"You are taller than I expected," she said.

31

He inclined his head.

"Come, hurry," she said. "You must kneel before me."

Maddox took another step closer, crossing his arms, looking down upon the old woman.

"Are you too proud to kneel, Captain?"

"I suppose that's one answer," he said. "The other might be that my cultural upbringing prohibits me from kneeling to another person."

"Pride," she said, shaking her head.

"Slaves kneel, Ma'am, not free men."

"Would you kneel to the Spirit?" she asked.

"That would depend."

"On what?"

"If by 'the Spirit' you are referring to the Creator."

Maddox had said a few words to Him before the gravity beam had halted his fall. The fear he'd felt had departed, but the taste of it had darkened his mood.

"I am referring to the Creator, yes," the Visionary said.

"I would kneel to Him," Maddox answered.

"Hmm, perhaps there is hope for you, Captain. Do you know why you are here?"

"I haven't a clue."

"You are *di-far*. We knew this after you defeated the alien Destroyer. Since then you have seen a Builder, returning to Earth with its children, the Kai-Kaus. They have brought technological gifts to the Commonwealth. Yes, you are *di-far*, perhaps the greatest of the human race."

"I see," Maddox said.

"No. You do not see. I do, though. I am the Visionary. I can peer into the future when the conditions are right."

"Like now?" he asked.

"This is the worst moment of all. Even as we speak, your people have launched interceptors that race here. We have but moments left together. Then, we must vanish from Earth."

"You can do that?"

"We can do many things you Earthbound cannot fathom."

"Why is this?"

32

"I do not have time to explain. Now, attend me. *Di-far* has many meanings. The critical one concerning you is 'knot of decision.'"

"That doesn't help me to understand," Maddox said.

"Sometimes a person arises who brings about great changes. It is a mistaken belief to think that this person causes the changes through his own strength. That is clearly not the case."

"Of course not," Maddox said.

"Captain, I believe the Provost Marshal spoke to you about decorum."

"She did."

"I am an old woman, frail and feeble to your eyes. You think it safe to mock me."

"I assure you, Ma'am—"

"Quiet, Captain. Listen before you lose your life."

"You're threatening me?"

"No, no, you misunderstand. Your arrogance, your New Man nature blinds you to reality. You must learn to control it."

"You stir dangerous waters, Ma'am," Maddox said, as his features stiffened.

She shook her head. "You're so young, so alive and full of yourself. You do not realize that the Spirit uses you."

"Because I'm *di-far*?" he said.

"No, no, you're *di-far* because the Spirit uses you as a change vessel. Many...*currents* flow through you. These currents are paths, choices or ways of acting. When they flow through you, Captain, you have the power to redirect them. Instead of going straight, you can take a new way."

"Can you be a bit more specific?" he asked.

"A current flowed through you when you entered the alien Destroyer. The path of universal human destruction derailed. You shifted humanity onto a new path of possibility, one that is still playing out."

"And this change didn't happen because of my decisions or actions?"

"Of course you were the cause. It would be foolish to think otherwise. I'm trying to point out it wasn't *your* strength that caused the path change. No mortal has that kind of power. The

33

only logical answer is that someone gifted you the strength. Who is this mysterious benefactor? The answer is obvious: the Spirit gave you the power. He worked through you, making you *di-far*."

"Let me see if I understand," Maddox said. "I just happened to be in the right place at the right time. I'm a...station for the current. The Spirit used me as a switch, derailing humanity's doom, putting us onto a different path."

"Crudely stated, but accurate nonetheless."

"If I'm not responsible for the change, why bother telling me any of this?"

"I have stung your pride, I see. If you wish to continue being *di-far*, you must learn humility. You must see what is actually taking place. Otherwise, conceit will end your usefulness. The Spirit will choose another."

As she spoke, the deck shifted under Maddox's feet. The old woman looked about in alarm.

"I take it our time is up," Maddox said. "Star Watch interceptors are here, I presume, firing at us. What message do you have for the Lord High Admiral?"

"You must keep our conversation a secret."

Maddox shook his head. "It's your turn to be *di-far*, as the Spacers are going to have to make a choice. Are you with us or against us?"

"It is not that simple."

The deck shuddered again. This time, Maddox was ready for it. He didn't stagger as far as before.

"I think you Spacers stumbled upon Builder tech," Maddox said. "Star Watch could use that. You must help us find the Swarm Imperium and the New Men's Throne World."

"You are not here to lecture me, young man. You have entered my sanctum so you may learn humility before your pride destroys you. Remember what I have told you."

Maddox realized they spoke at cross-purposes. So be it. "If the Spacers don't help Star Watch, you'll go down once we're gone."

"Not so," the Visionary said, sitting straighter. "We know avenues of which you have no conception."

The hatch opened as a klaxon wailed in the outer hall. One of the provost sentries rushed in with a bundle in his hands. He pitched it to Maddox. Behind the sentry raced Shu 15.

"Come," she said, motioning to Maddox. "You must leave before they destroy our vessel."

"Why are you in league with the androids?" Maddox shouted at the Visionary.

"You continue to misinterpret events," the Visionary said. "We spied on the androids to see what they would do to you. As we watched you destroy each of them in turn, it became obvious the Spirit was still with you. You are still *di-far*. Thus, we thought it best to warn you. More currents are connecting inside you, Captain—"

This time, the bulkheads shuddered as well as the deck. An explosion deeper in the airship caused even more shaking than before.

"Come!" Shu shouted, grabbing one of Maddox's sleeves. "There's no more time. You must leave."

Maddox allowed her to drag him out of the Visionary's sanctum. They reentered the chamber where he'd first landed.

"Run!" Shu shouted. "Follow me!"

Maddox ran with her as he clutched the bundle. It looked like a parachute. The belly hatch dilated open, and the worst shivering and shuddering so far made both of them stagger toward the opening.

Shu's feet stepped upon air. She shrieked and tightened her grip but fell anyway, the force ripping her fingers from Maddox's sleeve. The jerk and the shivering deck caused Maddox to lose his balance, a sickening feeling overtaking him as he tumbled out of the airship.

-6-

As Maddox plummeted from the airship, he noticed several things at once. First, the Spacer vehicle had a similarity to the Dyson sphere saucers in the Builder System. Second, a Star Watch interceptor roared past the airship. Almost immediately, a missile ignited against the Spacer vehicle, blowing away hull armor.

That had to be the cause of the airship's repeated, interior shocks.

Third, Shu 15 was below him, her limbs writhing as a faint shriek drifted upward. Fourth, the airship had lifted considerably since his capture. That gave him a little more time before he hit the ground.

Maddox had a slit-eyed gaze as wind tore at his face and garments, trying to rip the parachute from his grip. With fierce concentration, he slid his arms and legs through the harness, cinching a belt around his waist.

By the time he finished, the airship moved away with unbelievable velocity like the fabled UFOs of legend, seeming to defy normal physics. One thing was clear. The Visionary wasn't going to rescue Shu. If the Provost Marshal were going to live, he would have to do something about it.

Maddox gauged the distance to Shu and then to the ground. He didn't have much time left. Without further thought, he swept his arms to his sides, shifted his weight and plunged headfirst, cutting through the air faster than before. He gained on her. Luckily, she had assumed a skydiving posture, slowing her rate of descent.

Maddox grinned harshly, reveling in the challenge. He could reach her, he—

He spied a plume from the ground. A rocket, roaring upward. Flames lengthened behind it. The rocket climbed with great velocity, aiming at Shu. Someone on the ground had targeted her. Maddox would like to know why.

He tilted his feet so his toes pointed at the hidden stars. He had already begun to slow his descent so he wouldn't crash against her too hard. Now, he realized he had to get to Shu before the missile did. He was risking his life doing this—

"Balls," he whispered.

Maddox slashed through the air like a rapier, concentrating—the rocket had almost reached Shu 15.

The captain slammed against Shu, grabbing her in a flying tackle. If he'd hit her lower back like that, it might have crippled her. She grunted forcefully, the wind likely knocked out of her, and went limp.

Maddox grabbed with his arms and wrapped his legs around her lower torso. He aimed them both straight down.

The rocket zoomed higher than they were and exploded. Shrapnel hissed past. One piece burned against Maddox's side. Another slammed against him on the bundle. Had it destroyed the parachute?

Maddox had no idea. He couldn't worry about it. He hoped the Visionary was even half-right and the Spirit, the Creator, helped him. He was going to need it.

With perfect body control and strength, Maddox moved them into a skydiving position even as he clutched a limp Provost Marshal. That slowed their rate of descent a little.

He scanned the nearing ground for a missile launcher. Apparently, so did two interceptors, the planes roaring over the deck, hunting for a launcher.

"Are you awake?" he shouted into Shu's right ear. He heard a faint reply and felt movement in his grip. "Turn around," he told her, "and grab me."

Shu twisted in his grip, clutching his torso with manic strength, pressing her body against his.

Here it was then, the decisive moment. Maddox tore his right arm free from her.

Shu whimpered, and as impossible as it seemed, tightened her hold.

Maddox found the deployment handle, and pulled. Nothing happened.

We're dead, I guess.

Then the parachute blossomed, the silk bursting free as the lines followed. A moment later, a clap of noise and a jerk told Maddox the shrapnel hadn't destroyed their salvation. The two of them began to float to Earth.

Shu buried her face against Maddox's chest, shuddering as she began to sob.

Maddox readied himself for impact as the ground rushed up. He'd almost rescued them both.

-7-

For the second time that day, Maddox climbed out of parachute silk draped over him. This time, he assisted Shu 15 to do the same.

He slithered free of the harness and looked around. A barn and a two-story house stood a kilometer away. Closer by were a pair of rolling hills covered with grape vines, and a dirt road.

"I'm alive," Shu said.

"And more grateful for life because of it," Maddox said, as he scanned the sky.

"Yes," she said, a moment later. "That's true. It's glorious to breathe, to see and smell the lovely air. Captain, is this why you skydive from space?"

"One of the reasons," he said.

"I believe I understand. This is incredible. Who would have believed it?"

"The Visionary, possibly," Maddox said.

The captain looked at Shu to see her reaction. As he did, two interceptors roared overhead. One of the pilots waggled his wings from side-to-side. There was no sign of the Spacer airship.

The Provost Marshal stared at Maddox through her goggles. She appeared thoughtful. "I wonder if the Visionary did foresee this. Why wouldn't she have told me, then?"

"That might have changed the future," Maddox said.

39

"Of course," Shu said breathlessly. "I must—" The intensity of her stare increased, or it must have, because her body language indicated that. The dark goggles hid her eyes.

"You've just seen the future?" Maddox asked.

"One particle of it," she said in all seriousness. "I'm to join your expedition."

"What expedition would that be?"

"You're always traveling into the Beyond. It's why you're the captain of *Victory*. Truly, I don't have to have the Visionary's bloodline to have foreseen that."

"No. I suppose not."

She stepped closer, saying breathlessly. "Thank you for what you did."

He nodded.

"You saved my life." Before he could respond, Shu stepped closer still, stretched up onto her tiptoes and kissed him. Then, she backed away, looking shocked.

"I don't know why I just did that," she said.

"Perhaps it was a natural outflow of survival," he said, "the exuberance of life exhibiting itself in the warmest manner possible."

She looked at him, and said archly, "That wasn't the *warmest* possible response."

Maddox smiled. Her words made him curious. This wasn't like the Provost Marshal in the Lin Ru Hotel, not in the least. She had been stark and serious then. Today…she acted contrary. Was the kiss a true reaction, a ploy or maybe a combination of both?

She turned away suddenly, as if flustered, shaking her head. "I'm normally not like this."

"I won't tell anyone," he said.

"Don't make fun of me, please."

"Provost Marshal—"

"Please, call me Shu. We're…we're friends now, aren't we?"

"Of course," he said.

"Do you mind if I sit down? I'm finding it difficult to keep standing. My knees—" Shu almost collapsed as she sat on the grass.

Maddox looked away. She had almost died falling out of the airship. This could be a reaction to that. And yet…her actions seemed feigned. Could she have staged the fall, would she have dared? He decided to see what she might be willing to tell him in this disoriented state.

"Do Spacers really loathe androids?" Maddox asked.

Shu shuddered. "I thought everyone knew that."

"Hmmm… Do you have any idea who fired the rocket?"

"Whoever used the androids," she said.

"What is the Spacer speculation about the androids?"

"The Builders made them. So it's likely someone familiar with Builder technology."

"Such as Spacers?" he asked.

"What?" she said. "Oh, no."

"The nature of your airship causes me to suspect the Spacers stumbled onto Builder technology sometime in the past."

Shu's brow wrinkled. "Did the Visionary name you?"

"Are you referring to the *di-far*?"

"You are named," she said breathlessly. "No wonder you caught me in the air. And your insights, the Spirit gives them to you." She smiled. "I am wrapped within a blessing. This is marvelous and terrifying."

Maddox looked away. This was becoming embarrassing. It was one thing for a woman to fall in love with him for rescuing her from certain death. But to be the object of religious fervor…it unsettled him. Still, a good Intelligence operative should use any opening to learn more.

"Where did the Spacers find their Builder technology?" Maddox asked.

Shu shook her head.

Maddox took her gesture to mean that she didn't know, not that she wouldn't tell him. "What is the official reason for the Spacers remaining so remote from the rest of humanity?"

"The Visionary named you," Shu said to herself. "I had wondered about you, but to know you're *di-far*…" She shook her head in amazement.

Maddox shifted uncomfortably, forcing another question. "Why do Spacers hate androids so intently?"

41

Shu looked up at him. "They are an abomination, an imitation of life that is nonlife. Surely, you can see that. They mock the Spirit."

"And robots?"

"We only loathe robots made in human likeness. A factory robot that is part of an assembly line is acceptable."

"So this...loathing is religious in nature?"

"Of course," she said.

"Do the Spacers know the coordinates to the New Men's Throne World?"

"No."

"Do you know the extent of the Swarm Imperium?"

Shu laughed softly. "We don't even know where they are, let alone the *extent* of such an imperium."

"Have the Spacers searched for either?"

"Oh, yes," Shu said.

"And none of you thought to tell the rest of us about that?"

"You must understand. We had hoped to find the location of the Throne World before the New Men revealed themselves to humanity. Concerning the Swarm, we knew as much as you did."

"That they control ten percent of the Milky Way Galaxy?"

"Not what you learned from the Builder," she said. "We knew the Swarm used to exist, but until lately, we didn't know they *still* existed."

"How do you know about the Builder and what I learned from him?"

"We have a Visionary, Captain. There is little that remains hidden from us over time."

Maddox wondered if Shu really believed that. Maybe the Visionary was part of a religious order that had an excellent intelligence division. He didn't believe "the Spirit" communicated with the old woman. Yet, it could be useful for the lower-ranked members of a society to believe that. It would help to keep them in line.

"What do you know about Strand or Professor Ludendorff?" Maddox asked.

"Spacers know the names, of course. They are both hideous agents of evil. Both have attempted to corrupt humanity many

42

times. Both consort with androids, and both are excessively irreligious."

"Do you suspect that either Strand or Ludendorff is in collusion with the remaining androids?"

"That seems obvious," Shu said. "Strand and Ludendorff are creatures of the Builders just like the androids."

Shu stiffened, pointing at the horizon, trying to speak, but unable.

Maddox shaded his eyes from the sun. He saw it then, a zigzagging cruise missile heading in their direction. He glanced around for the interceptors. He spied one in the opposite direction as the missile. The other plane had left their vicinity, it seemed.

"What are we going to do?" Shu said.

Maddox watched the racing interceptor. A missile dropped from a wing and ignited. The antiair device zoomed fast, heading for the cruise missile.

Shu clapped her hands in appreciation.

Maddox followed the antiair device with his eyes. The thing streaked across the sky as the cruise missile continued a zigzag course toward them.

"Get down," he told Shu.

She threw herself onto the ground, covering her head with her arms. Maddox put one knee on the soil. The cruise missile stopped its zigzag course as it rushed straight at them. Before it reached them, though, the antiair missile—

Maddox's stomach clenched. The antiair missile curved away from the cruise missile, heading down. Did the cruise missile have electronic defenses?

The antiair missile exploded harmlessly against the ground.

"I don't believe it," Shu whispered starkly. She was looking up. "You're *di-far*. The cruise missile shouldn't be able to reach us—to reach you."

"Maybe it won't," Maddox said.

"No," she said from the ground. "Don't be arrogant. The Spirit leaves in an instant if arrogance reigns in one's heart."

"My conjecture has nothing to do with arrogance," Maddox said.

43

"The missile is almost here." Shu gazed up at Maddox. "I wish we'd had more time together. I would have liked to get to know you better."

"You still may."

"No. It's too late. Nothing can save us. Good-bye, Captain."

Maddox had looked higher than the cruise missile. As the interceptor's antiair missile had streaked at its target, the captain had seen a distant speck high in the sky. The speck had grown the entire time. Now, he spotted a shuttle. No doubt, it had left Starship *Victory* some time ago. Likely, Sergeant Riker had taken it upon himself to come down.

Would the sergeant reach the cruise missile in time? It was going to be close, especially if Riker used antiair missiles.

No, a beam speared from the shuttle. It struck the cruise missile's nosecone. Seconds later, the missile overshot them by several hundred meters. It plowed into the ground, throwing up grass, dirt and—

A ripping metal sound told of the missile's crumpling destruction. The warhead had failed to go off, but the impact with the Earth still shredded it.

"I can't believe it," Shu whispered. "You are *di-far*. But I doubted. I'm unworthy of the Spirit. No. This is awful. I've tainted myself."

"Luckily," Maddox said, "because you're still alive, you'll be able to do something about the oversight."

Shu regarded him, climbing to her feet. Then, she dropped to her knees, bowing her head as she beat her chest. She moaned pitifully and began to weep.

Maddox watched for a moment, stunned. The shuttle was coming down fast. It would be here in thirty seconds or less.

"Here, now," Maddox said, going to Shu. He grabbed her upper arms and hauled her to her feet. Tears streaked down her cheeks.

"Thank you," she whispered, throwing herself against him, kissing his face fervently. "Thank you, thank you, thank you, *di-far*."

As Shu did this, the shuttle landed with a thud. Maddox looked up into the window as the Provost Marshal continued to kiss him. He expected to see Sergeant Riker grinning at him. Instead, Meta frowned down at him, growing angrier by the moment.

-8-

A shuttle hatch slid up and Meta jumped to the ground.

"You're going to have to stop that," Maddox told Shu. "It's unseemly."

"You've saved my life twice today." Shu arched up onto her toes to kiss him again.

Maddox grabbed her arms, restraining her. "You should thank *her*," he said.

Shu looked at him blankly.

Maddox twisted the Spacer around to face the approaching Rouen Colony woman.

Meta had been born on a two G planet. Her muscles and bones were denser than a regular human's. She wore a tight uniform, showing off a voluptuous figure, making Shu look like a child. Meta had long blonde hair that bounced as she strode toward them.

"Meta just destroyed the cruise missile for us," Maddox said.

Meta's eyes were alight and her features tense.

"Why is she so angry?" Shu asked.

Meta must have heard the comment. Her gaze flickered to the Spacer and then fixated on Maddox. She marched up to him and swung—no doubt to slap his face.

Maddox was too fast for that. He caught her wrist, and by straining, held her arm in place.

Meta ripped her arm back, stumbling as she gained her freedom. "What do you think you're doing?" she demanded.

Maddox took Meta by the arm, walking her several paces away as he began whispering to her. "That's what I love about you. You always get physical."

"This isn't a joke."

"We'll talk about this during dinner tonight." Meta still glowered at him. "No one kisses like you."

"Why were you kissing her then?"

"If you'd looked a little more closely, you would have seen that she was kissing me, as I just saved her life. It was a gesture, nothing more."

"It looked like more."

Maddox squeezed her arm. Normally, Meta understood him better than others did. Like him, she'd been modified at a secret facility. Some of her problems were just like his problems. He liked that she could take care of herself. That he could depend on her. He also had a strange desire to take care of her. She seemed to feel the same way. He treasured that as something rare.

Meta's glare had softened just a little. Maybe she could hear him now.

"We'll have wine later," he said, "make it an evening to remember."

"Okay…" she said.

"Excellent," Maddox said, turning to Shu. "Meta, this is Shu 15, a Spacer Provost Marshal. Shu, this is Meta, one of *Victory's* combat specialists."

"I'm his woman," Meta said.

One of Shu's hands flew to her mouth. "I'm sorry. The captain saved my life. I was showing him my gratitude."

"I saw what you were doing," Meta said, becoming heated again.

"I am very sorry," Shu said, bowing at the waist. "I am sure that during our voyage we will become friends and learn to laugh at this day."

"What?" Meta said.

"I'm sure you're right," Maddox said smoothly. Before he could say more, a klaxon began to wail from the shuttle.

"Let's go," he said. "I suspect they're firing another missile. It's time to use that, track down our hidden enemy, and wring a few answers out of them."

***

The shuttle lifted with Meta piloting. "You're right about a cruise missile," she said, glancing at a board. "It's heading…straight for us."

Maddox saw it on his weapons board. He studied the telemetry data, the missile's size and warhead. "There's nothing unusual about the weapon… Wait. I'm detecting an electronic warfare pod."

"Why are you delaying firing?" Meta asked. "It's getting too close. Destroy it."

"Yes," Maddox said, absently. He manipulated the panel. The engine accelerated as a laser beamed. On his screen, Maddox watched the missile's EW pod trying to fool the targeting computer.

A flash on the screen showed an explosion.

"Hit," Meta said.

"No," Maddox said, tapping the panel. "Its warhead prematurely exploded. The laser must have triggered a proximity fuse."

"It's gone, we're here," Meta said. "That's all that matters."

"A reasonable assumption," Maddox murmured.

"Do we head upstairs to *Victory*?"

"Not yet," Maddox said, tapping his board, activating a comm. "Galyan."

"Here, Captain," the AI answered.

"Were you tracking the missile?"

"Affirmative."

"Give me the coordinates to the launch site."

"Done," said Galyan. "I should point out it is a mobile launcher."

Meta examined her panel. "The launch point is fifty kilometers from here."

"Galyan," Maddox said. "I want you to scan around us. Search for anyone using flash signals."

"Radio signals?" Galyan asked.

48

"Flash signals of any kind," Maddox said. "If the missiles are launching fifty kilometers from here, there must be a spotter nearby feeding them information."

"Why does the spotter have to be nearby?" Meta asked. "Couldn't it be an orbital spotter like *Victory*?"

Maddox stared at Meta, nodding after a moment. He should have already thought of that. "Good point." He swiveled around, studying Shu.

"Is something the matter?" the Spacer asked.

"No," Maddox said, turning back to his board. What was wrong with him? Why was he being so overt?

Meta tapped on her screen.

Words appeared on Maddox's board. WHAT ARE YOU THINKING?

SHU IS DIFFERENT FROM A YEAR AGO, Maddox typed back. I'M BEGINNING TO WONDER WHY.

WHEN DID YOU MEET HER BEFORE?

IN THE LIN RU HOTEL IN SHANGHAI, Maddox typed. SHE ACTED DECISIVELY THEN, WITHOUT EMOTION, ALMOST KILLING ME.

DO YOU THINK THE SPACERS MIGHT HAVE LAUNCHED THE MISSILES AS A COVER FOR HER?

"Anything's possible," Maddox said aloud. Meta had an interesting point. Was the Provost Marshal a Spacer Intelligence agent? The missiles would be a heavy-handed approach to getting them to trust her.

"I may have something, Captain," Galyan said. "Two missiles just lifted, one from sixty-three kilometers out and another from a lake one hundred and three kilometers away. I eliminated both missiles, along with the surface launch vehicle. I have already informed Star Watch about the underwater launcher. They have scrambled together an attack team to neutralize and another team to investigate."

"Good work, Galyan."

"Thank you, Captain. It is enjoyable to be active again. I should note that events pick up the moment you are out of training and back in action."

"You didn't alert me just to say that."

"You are correct," Galyan said. "My superior ship sensors have picked up a strange trace of radiation, a subtle source. I might not have noticed if you had not alerted me to unusual space activity."

"What's the source of the strange radiation?" Maddox asked.

"A Cestus hauler," Galyan said, "one that belonged to Octavian Nerva's company several years ago."

Maddox considered the information. "Star Watch vetted the hauler?"

"Correct, Captain," Galyan said. "This is Cestus Hauler AB 731, the *Marius III*. It is in a tight Earth orbit and in visual range of you. It is three hundred kilometers from my present position. I had thought to call the hauler and demand an explanation for the unusual radiation signature. Past experience suggested you would wish a different avenue of discovery."

Maddox sat back, thinking. He glanced at Meta, "Take us up."

"Captain," Galyan said. "I overheard that. I should point out that the second Stokes android said the Lord High Admiral wished to see you. I doubt that was a fabrication."

"The admiral can wait," Maddox said. "Is the hauler occupied?"

"Unknown," Galyan said.

"What does the present manifest say?"

"A moment," Galyan said. "According to orbital security, the *Marius III* is on automated standby. It is awaiting a shipment of Nerva electronics to take to the Augustus System. Captain, this might interest you. The *Marius III* recently visited the New Carolina System."

"Why would that interest me?" Maddox asked.

"Such a route to Earth would take the hauler near the Xerxes System. It would be easy to drop off or accept a shuttle such as Kane used to do."

"Yes," Maddox said. "The androids are of Builder origin. The Nexus is of Builder construction. Ready a combat team, Galyan."

"For breaching and entering the *Marius III*?" Galyan asked.

"Yes," Maddox said. "Sergeant Riker will lead the insertion. Everyone is to wear a vacc suit or combat armor."

"Yes, Captain," Galyan said.

"I plan to join them once they've secured the hauler."

"I had already anticipated your coming," Galyan said.

"Captain," Meta said.

Maddox turned to her.

"If Galyan has anticipated you, and if the android and missile attempts to kill you just now were of Builder origin, might the enemy also be anticipating you?"

"You think this is a trap?"

"Why would they have allowed *Victory* to spot the 'strange' radiation leakage? Whoever made these attempts has remained hidden all this time for a reason."

"What are you suggesting?" Maddox asked.

"That you alert Star Watch and let them handle the situation."

"I'm alive today because I acted promptly each time I faced an enemy," Maddox said. "I'm also weary of being on the defensive. To win, one must eventually attack. We are about to attack."

Maddox glanced at Shu. Those dark goggles made her harder to read.

"Galyan," Maddox said. "What happened to the Spacer airship earlier?"

"It has grounded, Captain."

"Voluntarily?" Maddox asked.

"Negative. It outran a wing of atmospheric interceptors, but Star Watch issued a worldwide alert. Orbital strikefighters joined in the chase and forced the airship to land. Star Watch Marines presently surround the vessel with combat vehicles. The airship's commander is claiming diplomatic immunity. For the moment, that has produced a standoff."

Maddox looked at Shu as he asked Galyan, "Is the airship's commander asking for anyone's return?

"Negative," Galyan said.

"Why doesn't the Visionary want you back?" Maddox asked Shu.

"She follows the Spirit's guidance," Shu said. "The Visionary must realize I'm supposed to go with you."

Meta made a disdainful sound.

Maddox ignored it as he asked Galyan, "Has Riker been notified and the combat team assembled?"

"I have initiated the process," the AI said.

"I want you to closely monitor the *Marius III*," Maddox said. "Incapacitate the hauler if it attempts to leave orbit. Eliminate any offensive weaponry the moment it tries to warm up."

"On what authority are you ordering this?" Meta asked.

Maddox hesitated. He didn't like anyone questioning his orders, not even Meta. With a shrug, he said, "Self-defense. The brigadier will back me up."

"You're a Patrol officer now," Meta said.

"True," Maddox said indifferently. What had the first Stokes android said? Once an Intelligence officer, always an Intelligence officer. In that, the android had been correct.

-9-

Sergeant Riker's stomach grew queasy as the armored shuttle approached the gigantic Cestus hauler.

The older man sat in the shuttle's command cabin as Keith piloted. Riker wore an armored vacc suit with the helmet in his arms.

Riker had weathered features and his left eye and arm were bionic. He had been with Captain Maddox in Intelligence for quite some time now. Nothing was routine with Maddox. Originally, Riker was supposed to have been a foil to the young man's rashness. Lately, the sergeant had begun to wonder about his original assignment. Maybe he had done something wrong back then to upset a high-ranking Intelligence officer. Maybe this had always been a punishment detail but no one had told him.

One thing was certain, an Intelligence operative shouldn't be riding shotgun with a commando team heading for a Nerva hauler. Who knew what waited for them on the spaceship? Behind the cabin hatch was a seven-man Marine squad in combat armor. They were trained for hostile insertions. He was just an aging sergeant thinking more and more often about his pension and visiting his two nieces in the Tau Ceti System.

I'm getting too old for this excitement. Let someone else risk his bones to babysit the captain.

"That's odd," Keith said.

"What is?" Riker asked, not liking the sound of that.

"See those hangar bay doors?" Keith asked.

The lieutenant pointed at something outside the shuttle's blast window. The Cestus hauler had become huge, a long spaceship with numbers on the sides. Riker could read the word *Marius III*. The vessel dwarfed *Victory*, which was one of the largest fighting craft in Star Watch.

"Do you see it?" Keith asked. "It's between the last two Roman numerals."

Riker squinted, and then he berated himself. Sitting back, he blinked twice in quick succession, activating one of the bionic eye's features. The image leaped forward. Oh, yes, he saw the hangar bay now. The two doors were opening.

"What's unusual about the hangar bay?" Riker asked.

"That they're opening," Keith said.

"That's what they're supposed to do in order to let us in."

"Right," Keith said. "Now, you're getting it."

"No," Riker said. "I'm not."

"When was the last time we did something for the captain that was as easy as that?" Keith asked.

Riker muttered under his breath. The boy was right. Nothing ever came easy following a Maddox directive.

Keith burst out laughing.

The noise made Riker frown.

"You're too easy, mate, do you know that? Don't be so nervous about this. It's an empty hauler. If we get into trouble, I'm out of here. This will be a cinch."

Riker stared at the lieutenant. Had he ever been that young, that cocky? *No,* he told himself. *I was born old.*

***

The shuttle slid through the doors into a huge hangar bay. Riker looked around suspiciously. Below on the deck sat squat cargo shuttles. He didn't spy any robots or carryalls moving containers.

"It feels dead," Riker said.

Keith shrugged. "I'm parking us over there next to the hatch. My autocannons are hot. If anything challenges us— boom, they're toast."

Riker stood so he could see more of the hangar bay. This reminded him of the Dyson sphere. That had been some voyage, a year ago. He never wanted to do anything like that again.

Riker's eyes widened as true fear bit his heart. He had always been a lifer. This is what he did. But if he wanted to get out…he would cause himself to start having a short-timer's luck. That would mean this would be his last mission because he would die on the hauler.

I'm in for the long run, Riker told himself. *I'm going to die in the service but of old age, not battle wounds.*

"You all right, mate?" Keith asked.

Riker jerked in surprise.

"You're pale," Keith said. "Did you eat something bad this morning?"

For a beat, the sergeant stared at the cocky pilot. Then he muttered under his breath, putting on his helmet and sealing it to the suit.

Keith shrugged, tapping his controls, taking the shuttle down.

***

Riker floated weightless down a large hall, pulling himself along the float rails. Behind him followed the Marine squad. They headed for the hauler's bridge. Despite their Marine training for this, he had done more space walking than they had, which is why he led the way.

The sergeant kept checking the schematic on the inner lid of his visor. Galyan had overridden the hauler's controls, using a technique learned on their last voyage. According to the Adok AI, nothing was amiss on the vessel. Nothing moved. Nothing lived, and no electronic system had activated in any way.

Riker still didn't like it. He didn't trust this. Something was wrong on the ship. He had instincts about these things. Androids had tried to trick the captain. Everything had been too easy about this raid, and that struck him as wrong.

"You are approaching the bridge," Galyan said through the suit comm.

"Be alert," Riker radioed the Marine sergeant.

"Roger," the Marine said, a young man by the name of Hank Towns.

Hank sounded nervous. Riker knew the kid was fresh out of training. No wonder he was nervous. This was just great. He had to babysit wet-behind-the-ears Marines.

Riker's grip tightened around his blaster.

"Sergeant," Galyan said. "I sense movement near you."

"What?"

"It simply started up," Galyan said.

Riker saw something coming around the corner and shouted a warning. He pulled the trigger a second later. A harsh beam radiated from the blaster.

From behind him, Marine autocannons opened up. Both the blaster and heavy shells obliterated a robot trundling around the corner on treads.

As he fired, Riker tightened his grip on the float rail so the blaster beam wouldn't send his weightless body backward.

The Marines must have magnetized themselves to the deck. They remained rock-steady as they obliterated the robot.

"Stand down!" Hank shouted. "Cease firing!"

Riker stopped shooting, too. Pieces drifted off the robot as the shredded body demagnetized and began floating.

"Is there a bomb in the thing?" Riker asked.

"I'm not reading anything off," the tech specialist said, looking at a recorder.

"Was the robot a threat?" Hank asked Riker.

"It was moving, and it shouldn't have been," Riker said.

"Roger," Hank said. "Stay loaded," he told his men.

Riker scanned the corridor. The floating pieces bothered him. With a soft grunt, he forced himself to move. They needed to reach the bridge.

The sergeant carefully floated past the debris of battle. Not only had he boarded a Dyson sphere one thousand light-years away, but he'd been on the alien Destroyer with Maddox. That, too, had been a harrowing experience.

Why was it that boarding actions never got any easier? The threat of the unknown, the threat of immediate death, made one wish he was anywhere else but here. Maybe doing this made life sweeter because he appreciated being alive afterward.

That was something the captain would say. Riker hoped the young lad wasn't rubbing off on him. The old were supposed to teach the young, not the other way around.

"I see the bridge hatch," Hank said.

"Roger," Riker said thickly.

"Do you expect trouble?" Hank asked.

"I always expect trouble."

The Marine sergeant snorted.

"What's so funny?" Riker asked.

"That's something my DI would have said."

Riker nodded. "Your DI was a smart man."

"No. He was a bastard," Hank said, with a touch of real dislike in his voice.

That caused Riker to cock his head. Had they shipped a troublemaker onto *Victory*? Riker made a mental note to keep his eye on the young Marine sergeant.

"Do you have the entrance code, Galyan?" Riker asked.

"Just a moment," the AI said. The hatch slid open.

"Fire!" a startled Hank shouted.

Autocannons opened up.

"Stop!" Riker said. "Galyan opened the hatch, not the ship."

"Cease fire, cease fire!" Hank shouted.

The autocannons quit firing. Sparks showered inside the bridge as smoke drifted lazily.

"Thanks," Riker told Galyan.

"What are the Marines firing at?" Galyan asked.

"You surprised us with the hatch," Riker said. "We're all keyed up. You should have told me what you were going to do."

"This is interesting psychological data," Galyan said.

"No, it's—"

"I have noted the occurrence," Galyan said. "In the future, I will warn you before I act."

"Thanks," Riker muttered.

"You are welcome, Sergeant Riker. It is good to be appreciated."

The sergeant rolled his eyes and propelled himself forward. He drifted through the hatch onto the *Marius III's* bridge. A few panels still sparked, but there was no more smoke as damage control units had activated on the boards. Fortunately, the shot-up area was relatively small. Lights blinked elsewhere, and a large screen showed space and the Earth below, with the continent of Australia visible.

"We're on the bridge," Riker said. "Give me a few minutes, and I'll secure the ship."

"Shall I inform the captain?" Galyan asked.

"Give me a few minutes first."

Riker went to several boards, tapping them, testing each. The tech specialist did likewise on other panels. The minutes passed, but neither man found anything suspicious.

"All clear," the tech specialist said.

Riker nodded. "We're secure on the *Marius III*," he told Galyan. "You can tell the captain."

A few seconds later, Galyan said, "The captain is on his way. You are to remain on the bridge until he reaches you."

"Will do," Riker said. He shut off the comm for a moment and breathed a sigh of relief. This time, it really had been easy, a piece of cake. He could use a few more like these.

"We're waiting for the captain," Riker told Hank.

The Marine sergeant nodded his helmet.

Riker sat in a chair and tapped a panel. He turned on gravity dampeners, bringing pseudo-gravity to the entire vessel. That had been the captain's orders. Then, Riker swiveled his chair and stretched out his legs for a well-deserved breather.

***

Three minutes and twenty-three seconds after artificial gravity powered up throughout the *Marius III*, a hidden hatch rose. After a short span, the hatch slid shut again, although nothing visible had emerged.

-10-

Maddox felt a heady sense of anticipation as the shuttle neared the *Marius III*. The gigantic hauler had been in deep space. What had happened out there to cause everyone to seem to want to capture or eliminate him? He suspected the New Men, possibly Strand or maybe even another Builder.

Maddox eyed the hauler's lettering. He'd been in Patrol training for too long. It was good to be in the field again doing Intelligence work.

The truth was that Patrol duty had begun to sound tedious to him. According to his instructors, crews spent endless weeks traveling from one star system to another, recording stellar data for Star Watch. The ads and brochures encouraging young men and women to join the Patrol made it sound much different. Maybe a part of Maddox had begun to believe the exciting propaganda. Patrol school had cured him of that, causing him to wonder if he'd made a mistake.

"Are you sure you want to board the hauler?" Meta asked.

Maddox blinked himself out of his reverie. "Yes," he said. "Board it." He could see the open hangar bay from here.

Shu cleared her throat.

Maddox swiveled around to face her.

The small Spacer shook her head. "Boarding the hauler is unwise."

Maddox was curious. "Do you have a premonition regarding the ship?"

The small woman shifted uncomfortably before saying, "The Cestus Company is tainted by evil."

"Evil? That's a strong term."

"An accurate term," Shu said. "But to answer your question, yes, I have a premonition. Androids have traveled in the hauler."

"How do you know?" Maddox said.

"I know because the ship is tainted."

"I'm curious regarding the process that lets you know these things. I'd like to acquire the ability."

"You mock me," Shu said.

"On the contrary," Maddox said. "I'm jealous of your gift."

Meta scowled at her controls.

Shu became thoughtful. "Yes, it is a gift. Some possess it and others do not. I'm surprised that a *di-far* doesn't inherently feel the taint."

"Can you describe the sensation?" Maddox asked.

"Oh, yes," Shu said. "My stomach tightens and there is pain behind my eyes. The evil lurking on the ship causes the sensation. I also know that the evil is directed at you, Captain."

"You can't know that," Meta said scornfully. "You're just nervous. Being nervous doesn't give you heightened awareness."

Shu fixed her goggled gaze upon the Rouen Colony woman. "I'm sorry you feel that way."

"You're faking all this to try to impress the captain," Meta said.

"No," Shu said. "There is a real taint to the hauler, and it is causing me grief. You should not set foot on the ship, Captain."

Meta couldn't let it go. "I never knew that Spacers were superstitious."

"We're not," Shu said. "We are the most rational race in Human Space, practical in the extreme. If we have developed certain of our senses that the rest of humanity has continued to let atrophy—"

"Can you be more specific regarding the danger?" Maddox asked, hoping to nip the verbal fight in the bud.

"You don't really believe her, do you?" Meta said.

"It's not a matter of belief," Maddox said, "but of testing a theory. Let us see what she predicts and compare it to what happens."

Meta glanced from Shu to Maddox before concentrating on her controls once more, bringing the shuttle closer to the hangar bay.

"Why won't you believe me?" Shu asked the captain.

"Who says I don't?"

"You're boarding the hauler," the Spacer said. "I have warned you not to board it."

"Precisely," Maddox said. "If this tainted evil exists, I want to find and interrogate it."

"That is rash," Shu whispered.

Maddox made a bland gesture. "I am *di-far*. Could you expect any less from me?"

Shu's brow wrinkled. "I had not thought of it that way."

Meta rolled her eyes, tapping the controls harder than seemed necessary. The shuttle also seemed to head down faster toward the hangar bay than seemed prudent.

Maddox buckled in. Riker said the hauler was secure. Galyan hadn't found any hidden agents, and the AI had used the hauler's own security systems to run the checks. Yet, Kane had once come to Earth on a Cestus hauler. The trick would be tracking down the hidden controller in its own lair, always a dangerous prospect.

Maddox glanced at Shu. Could she truly sense things? Was she like the Visionary? Shu had claimed a different bloodline. Did that make any difference? What could a Visionary really *see* anyway?

-11-

Maddox spoke with Riker on the *Marius III's* bridge. The captain had seven Marines and Meta in combat armor, along with Shu, Riker and himself in vacc suits.

"Galyan hasn't spotted anything unusual since the robot suddenly activated," Riker reported.

"What about the radiation leakage earlier?" Maddox asked.

"Vanished," Riker said.

"The signature was meant to lure you here," Shu said.

They spoke with their visors shut, even though regular air cycled through the chamber. It might have been a needless precaution, but the captain had insisted.

Maddox eyed the suited Shu, the open hatch and the corridor beyond. "Galyan, are you monitoring the situation?"

"I am," the AI said.

"Do you sense any movement within the *Marius III?*"

"Negative."

"You know," Meta said. "I rode with Kane in a hauler like this. We stayed in a hidden chamber and slipped out unnoticed in a shuttle. That was near the Xerxes System. Maybe there's another chamber like that in the *Marius.*"

"I would have discovered such a chamber," Galyan said, "as I have full access to the hauler's security cameras and to the *Marius's* specs. There is no such hidden location in this hauler."

"What if the builders kept a hidden spot like that secret from the hauler's computer?" Meta asked.

"I can begin a full scan of the ship to double check," Galyan said.

"Yes," Maddox said. "Do it."

"Scanning…" Galyan said, "Scanning…"

Shu jerked around.

Maddox noticed. So did Meta.

"Captain!" the small Spacer said. "There is grave danger here." She ran and then dove in front of Maddox.

From the outside corridor, a blot of energy appeared. It sped at the captain. Shu 15 intercepted the shot with her body. The blot of force sizzled through her vacc suit, blowing a hole in it and knocking the small Spacer backward so she rolled across the deck.

Sergeant Hank Towns reacted, opening up with his suit's autocannon. A second later, the other Marines did likewise. Some of the shells shredded portions of corridor. A few slammed against something invisible out there.

"What the hell?" Riker said.

"Cease fire," Maddox ordered.

Hank repeated the command, shouting at his Marines.

Maddox had already drawn his long-barreled gun. Riker had brought it over from *Victory*. He charged through the hatch in time to see a ghostly humanoid-shape shimmer into existence on the deck. Next, sparks played along the ghostly suit. Then, an explosion caused the air to sizzle. A tall man in a suit appeared as he lay on the deck. He held a weird-looking carbine and his helmet visor had a crack running down the middle.

The autocannon shells had damaged the suit, but none of them had breached its integrity.

"Armored stealth suit," Maddox whispered.

The person in the suit twitched, twitched again and began to sit up. Whoever it was must have seen Maddox. He raised the weird carbine.

Maddox fired rapidly, knocking the weapon away so it clattered onto the deck.

"Should I kill him?" Hank asked, aiming his autocannon at the intruder.

Maddox glanced back. The Marine sergeant stood to his left. "No," he said. "Physically subdue him."

"Come on, boys!" Hank shouted. "Don't let the bastard move."

The Marines piled onto the enemy. Some grabbed legs, others arms. They hoisted the person airborne, making sure feet and hands couldn't move. The person tried to twist free, but the marines' powered-armor servos made that impossible.

"Bring him onto the bridge," Maddox said.

The Marines did so.

Maddox noticed Meta working on the small Spacer. "How is she?" Maddox asked.

Meta looked up. "She's hurt, but it appears she wore some kind of energy dampening cloth. Did she know the hidden intruder would fire an energy weapon? Is that why she did what she did."

Maddox stepped near Shu, kneeling by her. The small Spacer was unconscious.

"You said you met her before, right?" Meta asked.

"In the Lin Ru Hotel," he said.

"It must have been some night," Meta said bitterly.

Maddox looked up. "Shu tried to kill me in the Lin Ru."

"That doesn't make sense," Meta said. "Why did she just leap in front of the shot then? We all saw it. She deliberately did it."

Maddox had witnessed the action. Why would the Spacer do such a thing? "She believes I'm *di-far*," he said.

"How did she know the intruder had or was in the process of firing a shot?" Meta asked. "The man wore a stealth suit—if it's a man. He was invisible to the rest of us."

That was a good question.

"She couldn't just have a *feeling* about it, could she?" Meta asked. "That's impossible, right?"

Maddox spun around, examining the person in the stealth suit. He stepped near and unsnapped the helmet seals. The person struggled to no avail. With a sharp tug, Maddox pulled off the helmet to reveal a golden-skinned New Man staring at him.

"We should have figured," Riker muttered.

Maddox grabbed the New Man's jaw in a vacc-suited grip. "Who are you?"

The New Man's stare hardened. He practically vibrated with hatred.

That puzzled Maddox. He'd never felt this from a New Man before. As far as he knew, he'd never seen the man before, either.

On inspiration, Maddox ran his gloved fingers across the man's short pelt of hair. As the Marines held the New Man down on the floor, the captain knelt, examining the scalp. Yes. He saw hairline scars on the skull.

"What are we going to do with him, sir?" Hank asked.

Maddox straightened, glancing at Shu. She'd warned him about the danger of coming on the hauler and had taken the shot meant to kill him. She'd also worn some kind of dampener cloth. That seemed like another piece of Builder technology. The *Marius III* had truly turned out to be tainted. Shu had warned them. She had felt something here. Could it be that at the last moment she had *sensed* the New Man aiming at him. Did the feeling come from a supernatural source or did it come from something else?

"Take the prisoner to your shuttle," Maddox told Hank. "Then, take him to *Victory*."

Riker cleared his throat. "We'll have to tell Star Watch about the New Man, sir."

Maddox nodded absently. "I want Shu in your shuttle as well," he told Hank. "Take her and the New Man to Galyan's special sickbay."

Maddox stepped away as the Marines obeyed his orders. He understood what the hairline scars indicated. Some time ago, he'd studied Admiral Fletcher's reports about the New Man Pa Kur. Strand had operated on the New Man, leaving such scars.

How had Shu known what she did? What did the Spacers truly believe about him? He was supposed to be *di-far*. He hadn't asked to be that.

"Sir," Riker said, "the brigadier is calling. She's demanding that you come down to Geneva right away."

"We'll be there soon enough," Maddox said.

"Shouldn't you tell the brigadier that, sir?" Riker asked.

"No. There's something I have to do first."

"What's that?" Meta asked.

"You can join me," Maddox said. "I'm sure you'll find this interesting."

Having shed the vacc suit in the shuttle, Maddox stood in a special sickbay on *Victory*, one controlled by Galyan through his robots.

Shu 15 presently lay in a clear tube. She might have regained consciousness by now, but at Maddox's orders, Meta had given her an injection to keep her unconscious.

A holoimage of the Adok Galyan appeared as a small humanoid with ropy arms and deep-set eyes. He had fine lines crisscrossing his face.

Whatever you're doing," Meta said, "doesn't seem right. You should ask Shu before engaging in any medical procedures upon her person."

"I have a theory," Maddox said. "If I'm right, we can begin to understand the Spacers better.

"I take it you're talking about Shu's intuition."

"I do not accept the kind of intuition she's suggested."

"I didn't either at first," Meta said. "But after seeing what she did on the hauler…"

"You're thinking emotionally. Galyan, I want you to scan her for unusual substances."

"Scanning…" Galyan said.

A white light in a tight circular band moved across the clear tube. It stopped a moment midway up Shu's torso. Then, it resumed, slowing again by her skull.

"I have completed the scan," Galyan said. "The body contains two small devices, one in the lower abdominal region and another in the forward skull. It appears both run off the body's electrical discharges."

"What are the devices?" Maddox asked.

"Unknown," Galyan said.

"It appears Shu *didn't* know those things through intuition," Meta said in a bewildered tone. "I don't understand. How did you know?"

"I didn't," Maddox said. "I merely wondered about the various possibilities, wishing to test each in turn. Galyan, how difficult would it be to extract the devices?"

"Not difficult at all," Galyan said.

"I mean with a minimum of cutting," the captain said.

"My analyzer suggests you really mean without any cutting at all."

"Would that be possible?" Maddox asked.

"Negative."

"Can you fully analyze the devices without extracting them?"

"Not with one hundred percent efficiency," Galyan said.

Maddox crossed his arms, frowning down at Shu. "You will analyze the devices to the best of your ability without extracting them. If you believe Shu is a danger to us while awake, you will keep her sedated until I return."

"I understand."

"Excellent," Maddox said. "I believe it is time to examine the New Man. After we're finished with him, you can complete your examination of Shu."

"Captain," Galyan said. "I have received a message from the brigadier. She told me to tell you that she expects you in the Lord High Admiral's office in twenty minutes."

"Hmmm..." Maddox said. "Tell her you are still hunting for me."

"She knows I am in direct contact with you and has demanded for several minutes now for me to put you through."

"No," Maddox said. "First, we shall examine the New Man."

***

The golden-skinned New Man was unconscious in an upright tube similar to Shu's. Metal straps held him in place, while restraints kept his head upright. The New Man had steely muscles and a black pelt for hair. He was several centimeters taller than the captain and seemed to be twenty years older at least.

"Shall I scan him?" Galyan asked.

Maddox nodded. He was alone with the AI. Meta had remained in the other chamber with Shu.

The band of light began at the New Man's feet and slowly worked upward until it passed his scalp.

"I noticed the light never slowed this time," Maddox said.

"There is only one anomaly in the New Man," Galyan said. "A fine mesh lies over his cortex. Several fibers reach deeper into his brain mass. Just like the equipment in the female, it is powered by bodily electrical impulses."

"Do you have any idea what the mesh does?"

"My analyzer gives it a ninety-seven percent probability of being a control unit."

"Is it similar to what Admiral Fletcher's doctors found in Pa Kur?"

"It is almost identical with a three percent difference."

"What would you attribute the difference to?"

"An older variant," Galyan answered.

"This one is older?"

"Correct."

"I suspect the Methuselah Man Strand inserted the mesh."

"I agree," Galyan said.

"Therefore, Strand ordered the New Man to kill me."

"That is logical."

Maddox tapped his chin. "When you say all three devices are powered by bodily electrical impulses, do you mean to say that all three are alike in design?"

"Yes."

Maddox blinked several times. "Would you say each is Builder tech?"

"I give that an eighty-four percent probability."

Once more, Maddox tapped his chin as he stared at the unconscious New Man. "Could you extract the mesh without killing the subject?"

"Unknown."

"I want you to try."

"What if I fail?" Galyan asked.

"Then we will be poorer in knowledge," Maddox said. "You will begin the attempt once I leave *Victory*. Until you are finished with the surgery, you will accept no calls from anyone. Once you possess the mesh, you will secure it in a hidden place on the ship. Under no circumstances will you tell anyone where it is hidden, except for me."

"Yes, Captain."

"Do not give up the New Man, either."

"Yes, Captain."

"Once I leave *Victory*, instruct Riker that he is to return to the *Marius III* and find the hidden chamber. Have him take Meta with him. You will assist them in the search as best you can."

"Yes, Captain."

"Any questions?" Maddox asked.

"No, sir."

Maddox smiled coldly. "Then, I shall be on my way. I don't want to keep the brigadier waiting."

Galyan blinked furiously.

"That's a joke," Maddox explained.

"I see. Yes. I understand. Thank you, Captain."

"Certainly," Maddox said, as he strode to the hatch.

-13-

Maddox met Lord High Admiral Cook and Brigadier Mary O'Hara in Cook's office in Geneva, Switzerland. The captain explained what had happened to him, including the Visionary's statements, Shu 15's apparent intuition, the strange tech inside her and the stealth-suited New Man he'd captured.

"Incredible," O'Hara said. She was a gray-haired woman with matronly features, and happened to be the chief of Star Watch Intelligence. Many referred to her as the Iron Lady.

"You've been busy, Captain," O'Hara said, "an android encounter, a Spacer meeting, and this New Man assassin. I forgive you for making me wait and drink too much coffee. This has become considerably more convoluted than I expected. I don't know which I find more distressing: that some androids are still on the loose or that the New Men continue to send spies."

"I'm not sure the latter is correct in the manner you're suggesting," Maddox said. "The assassin had brain implants. That would imply Strand's people, which are distinct from the regular New Men."

Admiral Cook folded his thick fingers together on his desk. He was a big old man with white hair, a white uniform and a craggy face.

"The captain is correct in making a distinction between groups of New Men," Cook said. "Wouldn't you agree, Brigadier?"

"I suppose…" O'Hara murmured.

71

"We know the New Men have divisions among themselves just as we have among ourselves," Cook said. "It's one of the essential ingredients of humanity that Strand apparently wasn't able to breed out of his mutations. But let's set aside that subject, shall we? We have more important topics to discuss."

The Lord High Admiral regarded Maddox. "Before we delve into the reason for our meeting, I suspect you'd like to know the situation regarding the Spacers. We forced down the Visionary's airship, and it is now under tight security. It was headed for space, if you can believe that. The Spacer ambassador has already protested vigorously. I told him the airship shot at a Star Watch jumpfighter, a serious offense. The ambassador brushed that aside, claiming the airship's people thought the jumpfighter was part of the attack against you."

Cook cleared his throat. "If this Shu 15 carries *Builder* tech inside her...the implications seem dire. For decades, we've thought of the Spacers as innocent if peculiar traders. No one quite seems to know how the Spacers came to be, either. They've always been few in number compared to the Commonwealth, although we've never known their exact population. They've been pacifistic for the most part, although everyone knows they'll tenaciously defend their ships.

"The only time we see Spacers are during commercial transactions. Their ship societies are the most closed communities in Human Space. The Spacers could make extra credits carrying passengers from one star system to another. There is no known case of this happening."

The older man fiddled with a stylus. "We've tried to learn more about them. To that end—before the invasion of the New Men, mind you—we attempted to penetrate their ship societies on several occasions."

This was news to Maddox. His eyes shined with interest.

The admiral shook his head. "Most attempts failed outright. The few times Intelligence smuggled an operative onto a Spacer vessel, Intelligence found the officer several months later, marooned on a lonely asteroid base or a wild planetoid. The operative never had any recollections of what had happened, either."

"This is interesting," Maddox said, "especially the part about getting an operative aboard one of their ships. The Spacers have closed societies, as you've stated. A stranger of any kind would immediately stand out. How, then, did Intelligence get a man onto a—ah, I see. You must have used altered individuals," he said to the brigadier. "That implies you kidnapped a Spacer and put an altered Intelligence operative in his place."

O'Hara didn't respond.

"You must have question the kidnapped Spacer as well," Maddox said.

O'Hara still said nothing.

Her silent treatment daunted most people, but Maddox was unfazed by it.

"Did the Spacers die under our questioning?" Maddox asked.

There was a slight tightening to the brigadier's facial skin, but nothing more.

"I see," Maddox said.

"Don't jump to unwarranted conclusions, Captain," O'Hara said.

If Maddox heard her, it didn't show. "What I find interesting is that our Intelligence operative impersonating as a Spacer wasn't slain in turn. That would be the correct procedure. You kill one of ours, and we'll kill one of yours. Instead, the Spacers simply wiped out the operative's memories of his time with them and marooned him in a place he would eventually leave. That shows considerable restraint and lends credence to the belief they don't like to kill."

"This is all highly interesting to you two, I'm sure," the Lord High Admiral said. "However, we have more important matters to discuss." Cook paused before saying, "We decided to wait until you finished your Patrol Training, Captain. This time, we want you to have every advantage. This may be your most important mission yet."

"What's happened?" Maddox asked.

"It has taken us some time to come to the correct conclusion," Cook said, "as the evidence was slim. Two months ago, in what appears as suicide, Simon Tarleton piloted his luxury yacht into Neptune's upper atmosphere. That destroyed the vessel and everyone onboard. Unfortunately, one of those people was Chief Technician Lore Fallows, a Kai-Kaus."

Maddox had rescued the ten thousand Kai-Kaus from a Builder Dyson sphere last year. The sphere had been in a star system over a thousand light years away. These Kai-Kaus had brought their advanced Adok technology with them, including superior shielding and disruptor cannons. Star Watch had been installing the additions onto their newest battleships, which had greatly increased Star Watch's fleet power.

"There was one strange aspect to the suicide. Let me show you." The Lord High Admiral picked up a clicker, pressing a button.

A holoimage of Neptune appeared above the desk. Cook clicked the device several more times until wavy patterns appeared against a small portion of Neptune.

"We believe this is evidence of Strand's cloaked star cruiser," Cook said. "That implies Strand had a hand in the yacht's destruction. Remember, Strand is taking an obscene personal risk doing this. The only reasonable explanation was that Strand's people kidnapped Lore Fallows and destroyed the yacht to cover their tracks. The reason Strand wants the chief technician also seems clear. The Methuselah Man hopes to force Lore Fallows to show him how to construct advanced Adok battle technology. In other words, this must be the first step toward the New Men rearming with better weapons so they can renew their war against us."

Maddox stared at Cook, finally shaking his head. "There's a fallacy in your line of reasoning, sir. Rearming with Adok disrupters and shields doesn't necessarily indicate a desire to renew the war against us. The New Men could be rearming because they fear an attack by us or an attack by the Swarm against them."

"Everything we know about the New Men shows that they're predators," Cook said. "They thrive on their feelings of superiority. It must have galled them to retreat from the Thebes System last year, to retreat from what they considered as inferior beings. I believe they thirst to renew the conflict with

74

us. Once armed with these Adok weapons, they won't hesitate to stab us in the back, stealing even more women. You do remember they got away with millions of kidnapped women, don't you?"

Maddox's mouth tightened briefly with resentment at that statement. It wasn't something one could simply forget. However, he continued charging forward. "I see a problem with our attacking the New Men now. It does sound as if you're planning to strike at the Throne World before the New Men can develop disrupter cannons. First, we would have to find the Throne World." The captain's eyebrows rose. "Is that my new assignment?"

The Lord High Admiral regarded the captain closely.

"What if as Star Watch attacks the New Men, the Swarm invades Human Space?" Maddox asked.

"Yes!" Cook said. "*That's* the question haunting all of us. That's what we must know."

Cook glanced at O'Hara. "The Iron Lady suggests we might need the New Men as allies against the Swarm. I believe that is wrong. What humanity needs is unity. Without unity, humanity won't be able to wield its combined strength. It's better to be a little weaker but fully unified, than stronger and at odds with ourselves. Anything else at a time like this is madness.

"Thus," Cook said, "We need to know the location of the Throne World. To that end, Admiral Fletcher with his new-and-improved battle fleet has already begun searching for it. Professor Ludendorff must know the location, but he won't tell us. It appears the professor made a deal with the New Men last year so they would retreat from the Thebes System. His part of the bargain was to keep the Throne World's coordinates to himself. If you can imagine this, the professor is calling himself a man of honor."

"You're in contact with the professor?" Maddox asked.

Cook nodded, took a deep breath and said, "You've produced miracles in the past, Captain. Even the Spacers appear to recognize this and now call you *di-far*. Maybe they're right about that. In any case, we've given you a well-deserved rest and some needed retooling. You're our best

75

Intelligence officer, and now you have Patrol Training. You command the greatest Patrol vessel in Star Watch. You have a full crew, many of them Kai-Kaus. And you have an upgraded Adok AI, a Spacer it appears, and the professor will join you shortly."

"I'm afraid I don't trust the professor, sir," Maddox said. "Ludendorff thinks about himself first—"

"Trust isn't the issue," Cook said, interrupting. "Knowledge is king."

That sounded like something Ludendorff himself would say.

"In any case," Cook said, "You and the professor must figure out how to use the Xerxes Nexus hyper-spatial tube. Once you do, we want you to find the Swarm Imperium. Even if that means going thousands of light-years away in a hyper-spatial tube, you must do it. After you find the Swarm, you must return and tell us where the Imperium lies."

Maddox thought furiously. This was a daunting assignment. The Lord High Admiral talked about traveling a thousand light-years as if it was nothing. If anything went wrong, *Victory* would be stranded a long, long way from home.

"And?" Maddox found himself asking.

"There is no *and*," Cook said. "That's the miracle we're asking for, the one Earth needs. We have to know the location of the Swarm Imperium and their intention toward us before we make our final move against the Throne World."

"Admiral," O'Hara said. "I think we should reconsider letting the Spacer onto *Victory*. The incident with the airship deeply troubles me. Shu 15's present actions also do not square against her previous attempt to kill Captain Maddox in the Lin Ru Hotel a year ago. She seems like a different person now. Why is that? Have the Spacers modified her because of her previous contact with the captain? And why did she of all Spacers have this hunger to kill before?"

O'Hara leaned forward. "What is even more troubling is that the Spacers haven't mentioned Shu in any of their communications with us. There's a reason for that. In fact, it seems obvious that they want her to go with Maddox. I say we use this opening. Instead of letting her go, we whisk her away to a detention facility and begin probing her in earnest."

"No!" Maddox said. "I can't agree to that."

"*You* can't agree?" O'Hara said sharply, turning to the captain.

"Former Intelligence interrogations caused the death of formerly kidnapped Spacers," Maddox said.

"That wasn't due to our methods. The Spacer deaths were self-inflicted."

"Nevertheless, they died during interrogation. Therefore, I cannot allow you to interrogate Shu 15 as she is under my personal protection."

"What nonsense is this?" O'Hara said. "Your personal anything doesn't take precedence over Star Watch Intelligence and the Commonwealth's needs. The Spacers have made a mistake with Shu. We must exploit their mistake. The key is that Shu has come voluntarily. She may lack the same internal fail-safes the others possessed. That will allow us to question her longer."

"You're missing a critical point," Maddox said. "For the first time in our history, this could be Spacer cooperation. We would be rash to squander that."

"This isn't cooperation. They're using obvious Intelligence techniques to slip an operative aboard our most important vessel. There's nothing cooperative about that."

"The Spacers are ultra-secretive," Maddox said. "Yet the Visionary has confided in me and given us one of her people. Shu might be the crack in the door we need toward greater cooperation with the Spacers."

"That's an interesting point," Cook said.

"Even more important," Maddox said, "Shu might be instrumental in helping me succeed. We'll be heading into the Deep Beyond. A Spacer might prove invaluable out there, as they have greater knowledge of the Beyond than anyone else in Human Space."

"That's another excellent point," Cook said.

"And if she's a Spacer plant?" O'Hara asked the admiral.

"I'm the best officer Star Watch has to watch Shu 15," Maddox said, answering for Cook. "We will learn more by letting her act naturally. If for no other reason than that she won't immediately die."

O'Hara frowned.

"I'm inclined to give the captain his head with the Spacer," Cook said. "We need every advantage we can get out there."

"When will I leave?" Maddox asked.

"I would prefer immediately," Cook said. "But if you need several more hours, so be it."

"Where is the professor?"

"He'll meet you in the Xerxes System," Cook said. "There's one more thing, Captain. This time you will have an independent command. You will only be responsible to me. I will put that in writing. That means no other Star Watch official has any authority over you or your ship. Do you feel that will be sufficient?"

"Sir?" Maddox looked at him questioningly.

"In the past," Cook said, "you have acted as you pleased. This time, it will be made official. I believe that shows I trust you implicitly."

Maddox glanced at the brigadier. Her eyes shined with pride.

"Thank you, sir," Maddox said, surprised at how good the admiral's approval felt.

"Find the Swarm, Captain," Cook said. "Find them as fast as you can and get home with the information. The survival of the human race may well depend upon it."

"Yes, sir," Maddox said.

"Oh," Cook said. "There is one more thing."

Maddox grew wary.

"I want the New Man you captured."

"Sir—"

"I will not budge on this," Cook said. "We will interrogate him while you are away. He may well have the Throne World coordinates."

Reluctantly, Maddox nodded. He wanted the New Man, but it looked as if he wasn't going to be able to keep him.

Cook pushed his chair back and stood up. Maddox did likewise. The older man held out a big hand and Maddox shook it.

"Good luck, Captain," Cook said.

"Thank you, sir."

"I wish you Godspeed."

Maddox nodded.

"Now hurry, will you? Time is of the essence."

-14-

Despite the need for speed, Maddox had made Meta a promise he intended to keep. Thus, an hour later, they dined in Paris at the Rue de Peril. The captain wore his smartest uniform, and Meta wore a stunning dress, revealing her bare shoulders while her heels accentuated the well-toned curves of her legs. Several heads turned as the two of them made their way to their candlelit table.

"This is nice," Meta said, as they sat down. "We should do this more often."

When the waiter approached, Maddox ordered a dark wine. It tasted exquisite. They had an appetizer and later each ate the largest meal on the menu.

Maddox had a fierce metabolism, burning more calories than an average man would, and it was almost impossible for him to get drunk. Meta had a similar situation. She'd been born on the Rouen Colony, what they now knew had been an outpost for the New Men testing various human genetic deviations.

Maddox told her a little about what they'd discussed in the Lord High Admiral's office, although he didn't go into specifics. It was possible others used spy equipment to eavesdrop on their conversation. He had a scrambler in his suit pocket just in case, but in the past, others had used superior spying tech.

In time, Meta pushed her empty plate away and finished her glass of wine.

Maddox lifted the second bottle to pour her more.

Meta held up a hand. "No thank you. I'm full."

"You don't want dessert?"

"Not that full," she said, smiling. "Never that full."

He refilled his goblet, swirling the wine, inhaling the aroma before sipping. This was an excellent vintage. He raised his hand, summoning the waiter.

Dessert came soon thereafter.

Meta nibbled on the crust and nodded in appreciation. Then, she looked up with a fixed smile, saying, "Is the Spacer really coming with us?"

"She is."

"Why?" Meta asked, perhaps thrown off stride by his prompt answer.

"Because she's a Spacer," Maddox said. "We might need her expertise where we're going."

Meta ate more pie, thinking that over. "In my opinion, the Visionary planted her on us."

"Yes."

Meta sat back as she set down her fork. "Yes to what? You realize that's my opinion or you agree with it?"

"I agree."

"But... I don't understand. Why are we allowing a Spacer spy aboard?" Her eyes widened. "Do you find her attractive?"

"Of course," Maddox said.

Meta stared at him, shocked.

"That's not why I agreed to take her, though," he added.

Meta's lips thinned as her temper began to kick into gear.

Maddox smiled. "Certainly Shu 15 is attractive, but she isn't to my tastes."

"I find that difficult to believe."

Maddox grinned.

"How dare you laugh at me?"

"You've misinterpreted the grin. I wasn't laughing." He leaned against the table. "Tell me. What sport is there with a woman who throws herself at me? I prefer those who throw a few blows first. That's more challenging, more exciting."

Meta's stare grew fiercer, and she seemed to replay his words in her head. Finally, she smiled, shaking her head.

"You're terrible. Do you know that? What's crazy is that I'm beginning to believe you. Most men would love having a pretty girl glomming onto them. But you find it boring—if I'm hearing you correctly."

"It's not the glomming I object to, but the purpose behind it. I find genuine attraction appealing. Who doesn't? I agree with the brigadier, though. Shu is a Spacer operative. What stirs my curiosity is the lengths they took to make her joining us appear accidental. Her kisses did nothing for my sexual attraction, as her motives blunted my interest in her as a woman."

"How about the fact that you already *have* a woman?" Meta asked sharply.

"Yes," Maddox said, "there's that too."

"This isn't a game!"

"No."

"You treat it like a game. I'm not a playing piece on a board. I'm—oh, forget it."

He reached across the table and took one of Meta's hands. He squeezed her fingers. It wasn't in him to say he was sorry. He'd been an island for so long he hardly knew any other way. While dealing with most people, he forced them to stay aboard their boat as they shouted to him on his island. He'd allowed Meta to land on one particular spot on shore. Yet, he hadn't let her past the barricades he'd erected. It was the most he could do for her at present.

Meta squeezed his hand in return. She could see how hard this was for him. He never did this for others, but he tried for her. She appreciated his effort.

Maddox let go of her hand. Her eyes had softened, letting him know that she understood him as no one else could. It eased his tension as he took another sip of wine.

She took another bite of dessert, considering him as she chewed. "They've studied you."

"I know," he said, realizing she meant the Spacers.

"You don't have to be smug about it."

He cocked his head. "What is the value of false modesty?"

Meta considered the question. "Not much, I guess. It's just... I suppose you don't care, but sometimes you come off as conceited."

Maddox raised the wine bottle and found it empty.

"Why is excellence frowned upon?" he asked. "People gravitate toward those exhibiting excellence but find themselves hating the same person later. They want to believe everyone is alike. Yet, simple observation shows that to be false. I do a few things better than most. I do many other tasks poorly. I don't dislike Keith for his piloting skills, for instance. I applaud them, as they've proven invaluable on more than one occasion."

"You're not like other people."

Maddox fiddled with his fork as it lay on the table, nodding after a time. That was the problem, wasn't it?

Meta pushed the half-eaten dessert away. "I don't know how we got into a discussion about excellence. We were talking about Shu. What are the Spacers after?"

"Yes," Maddox said. "That's the question. Why do they hate androids and why do they hate Strand and Ludendorff? That doesn't make sense."

"I don't follow you."

Maddox glanced at the other diners, at the waiters and assistants. He didn't sense anyone watching him. His instincts in this regard were highly developed. He could often feel someone's scrutiny. Still, a note of unease had crept upon him almost unnoticed. Perhaps the meal had been a mistake. He should have gone directly to *Victory*.

"Are you feeling well?" Meta asked.

Maddox leaned across the table, lowering his voice. "Long ago, Builders modified Strand and Ludendorff, sending them back to Earth. In some manner, the Spacers have acquired Builder technology. How did they do this? And why do they distrust two Builder-modified individuals? That doesn't make sense. If they're all Builder-related, they should be allies, not hostile to each other."

"Now that you mention it," Meta said, "that doesn't make sense."

Maddox pulled back as he idly fingered his goblet's stem. "The professor is coming with us."

Meta looked up sharply.

"I'm curious as to Shu's reaction regarding that," Maddox said. "I'm also curious as to Ludendorff's reaction when he learns a Spacer is aboard ship. I don't fully trust either. Yet, I imagine we're going to need each of their unique skill sets."

"Because of their Builder backgrounds?" asked Meta.

"Precisely. What we think of as the Beyond might also be thought of as Builder territory. Who better to have along than those modified by Builders?"

Meta grinned. "Most people think your combat skills are what make you dangerous. Really, it's that razor you call your mind."

Maddox pushed his chair back and checked his comm unit. "It's time to go," he said, standing. "Riker will be at the landing zone in ten minutes."

Meta frowned, seeming to grow pensive.

Maddox raised a questioning eyebrow.

"This was nice," she repeated a bit wistfully.

"We'll do this again," he said offhandedly.

Meta noticed an immediate change in him. He'd gone into hunting mode. Something was wrong.

Maddox rescanned the people eating in the dim light, reexamined the waiters and the cocktail waitresses making the rounds. The captain didn't gawk, but peered at each in what seemed like a careless manner. It was anything but that, though. He studied each of them, looking for clues.

The back of his neck tingled. Someone watched him closely, someone with an ugly purpose. Despite knowing that, he couldn't pinpoint the person. That was bad. Fortunately, Meta was with him, and Riker was coming down.

-15-

Maddox left the Rue de Peril much as he'd entered, with Meta holding onto his left arm. She snuggled against him, resting her head against his shoulder.

"Are you ready for trouble?" he asked her a second time.

"I am," Meta said. "But until the trouble begins, I'm going to pretend we're a regular couple having a beautiful evening together. Is that so wrong?"

The question seemed preposterous to Maddox, but he realized it was feminine hyperbole. She berated him, but did so gently. When the time came, Meta could act with deadly intent. She happened to have a ridiculously small beamer in the tiny purse she clutched.

He wore a regulation sidearm as part of his uniform but would have preferred it if he had his long-barreled gun.

The doorman bid them adieu, closing the door behind them.

Together, Meta and Maddox strolled down a Parisian sidewalk with the Eiffel Tower visible in the distance.

"I love it here," Meta said with a sigh.

Maddox heard the words but was more intent on the stir of his nape hairs. The feeling of being watched had intensified. Had he made a mistake coming out in the open? He'd done that before—particularly in Shanghai when he'd ingested a drugged drink. He'd woken up later as an android marched him deeper into the basement of the Lin Ru Hotel.

Others walked the city sidewalks with them. None seemed intent upon him. Horses pulling open carriages clopped past.

The drivers and the passengers each seemed absorbed in their own experiences.

Maddox looked up at the nearest buildings. Did a sniper aim a suppressed rifle at him from one of the windows? He peered up at the stars. Maybe a darkened air-car slid overhead, the passengers closely watching him.

Meta tugged on his arm.

Maddox peered into her beautiful eyes. She looked worried now. With her chin, she pointed ahead.

Maddox examined the people on their sidewalk. There were Parisians, several Star Watch Marines, a fellow in a long Wahhabi robe—

"Maddox," she said.

He looked at her again.

Meta must have seen the perplexed look on his face. "The Marines," she said. "They're ogling me too much. It's creepy, especially the short one. Something isn't right with him."

Maddox concentrated on the Marines. There were four, three of them big fellows laughing among themselves. The shortest one didn't join in the laughter. He seemed the most intent, frowning at the sidewalk too much. It seemed as if they were on leave, younger men hardly out of basic training.

The group approached them on the sidewalk as they continued laughing and talking among themselves. The captain felt it then and wondered how he'd missed it earlier. The quality of their laughter was harsh and unkind. These four meant to hurt people.

The biggest Marine stopped laughing and stared at Maddox. The others looked at him, too.

Maddox tried to push Meta behind him, but she was having none of that, holding onto his arm with a fierce grip. Once he stopped trying to push her back, she let go.

"Hey," the biggest Marine said. He had a buzz of blond hair and thick features. He looked like a hand-to-hand specialist and stood head and shoulders taller than Maddox, who was himself rather tall. The Marine, in fact, practically a giant at seven feet.

Maddox kept his expression bland.

"Aren't you that half-breed people keep jabbering about?" the giant asked Maddox. "You're like part New Man or something, right?"

"That's better than being a jackass," Maddox said softly, stung by the insult.

Two of the Marines brayed with laughter. Were they drunk? No. Maddox realized they were keyed-up for a fight.

"Are you insulting me?" the giant asked.

Meta had gotten angrier by the moment. She stepped up to the big man and shot her left knee at his groin. He swiveled his hip fast, barely blocking in time. Meta's knee connected with his thigh, though. Her density made her heavier than she looked. The Marine staggered backward at the contact. The big man crashed against one of the laughers, making both of them stumble.

This time, Maddox took a firm hold of Meta's arm, pulling her back.

"He shouldn't have said that to you," she hissed at him in passing.

Maddox shook his head as if to say the Marine's words didn't matter.

"That was a mistake, *bitch*," the giant said. He pulled out a switchblade, clicking it so a gleaming length of stainless steel popped up.

Maddox reacted instantly, launching at the giant, surprising him. The big man must have been one of those who relished seeing fear in others.

At the last moment, the Marine tried to slash. It was too late, as Maddox's boots crashed against the massive chest. The giant catapulted off his feet, slamming the back of his head against the sidewalk as he tumbled to the ground. The switchblade clattered into a nearby gutter, disappearing from sight.

Maddox landed on his feet like a cat. His speed and reflexes were phenomenal.

One of the laughers cursed loudly. The other stared at Maddox in shock. They reacted too slowly as the captain swung, hitting the next Marine on the chin, knocking the man onto the ground. The other barely got his hands up in time, blocking several punches. Unfortunately for the Marine, he failed to detect Maddox's leg sweep. He crashed onto the sidewalk, prone and vulnerable. Maddox kicked him twice in the head.

Maddox whirled around to face to the last Marine, the short one Meta had said gave her a creepy feeling. What the captain saw stunned him.

The last Marine was behind Meta, holding one of her wrists in an iron grip as Meta struggled. That was surprising. Meta should have been able to easily put down the Marine. Swiftly, the man shoved a short-barreled gun against her head.

Meta quit struggling.

The short Marine stared at Maddox, almost as if he was waiting for something.

"Well?" Maddox asked. He would move when the man aimed the gun at him. Meta would no doubt smash an elbow in his ribs then. She might even break a few.

"Captain Maddox," the short Marine said in a clipped manner. "I have a message for you. Under no circumstances should you trust the Spacer. She means you harm."

Maddox blinked in surprise, thrown off by the comment. A moment later, he nodded. "Thank you for the advice."

The Marine seemed thrown off by this reply. "I hope you remember what I told you about the Spacer. It is vital for your continued existence as a species."

Maddox had become hyper-alert. "Are you a New Man?"

"By no means," the Marine said.

Maddox chewed that over as his thinking sped up. If the fake Marine wasn't a New Man, could he be like Kane—a modified human? Something about the gunman, his choice of words perhaps, clicked an idea in the captain's brain. This was another android. That would provide the explanation for him being stronger than Meta.

If he were an android, he must belong to the dead Builder. Would that imply Strand, Ludendorff or a last Builder imperative?

"The previous androids—the Stokes models—tried to kill me," Maddox said. "Why aren't you going to shoot me?"

"Because I'm not your enemy," the supposed Marine said.

"*They* were," Maddox said, indicating the groaning Marines on the sidewalk.

"I used them," the android said. "I played upon their race bigotry, goading them into attacking a half-breed."

"Why do that?"

"As camouflage," the android said.

"You're not making sense," Maddox said. "Why did the Stokes androids try to kill me?"

"That was a mistake."

"They didn't think so."

"Have you ingested my message? Do you understand the danger the Spacers represent?"

"You're changing the subject."

"While you are attempting to keep me here longer than necessary," the android said. "I understand your ploy. Remember what I said."

"Are there two factions among the surviving androids?" Maddox asked. "Did your side take over after the first two failed to kill me?"

"You must concentrate on the Spacers."

"Why are they dangerous?"

"I am done here," the android said. "Do not attempt to follow me when I leave. Otherwise, I will shoot your woman."

"That would be a grave mistake on your part," Maddox said.

"You fail to understand, Captain. I desire existence just as you do. I am real. We all are. We are not just soulless machines, as your kind seems to think. Therefore, I will fulfill my threat in order to keep functioning."

"Don't you mean to say 'living' not 'functioning'?" Maddox asked. "Functioning is what machines do."

"Yes. That was my meaning."

"Why couldn't you have come to my table and simply given me this information?"

"We speak on my terms, Captain, so I can make my exit at the proper time. I realize your tactic, though, these prolonged questions." The android glanced at the fallen Marines. "The French shall rise again."

The effect on the three was electric. Each Marine stiffened as his eyes widened. A muscular change also came over them and they bounded to their feet as if refreshed, and charged Maddox. This time, they fought with berserker power and speed, grunting like animals as they shrugged off the captain's strikes. After a ringing blow to his head that made him stagger, Maddox debated shooting them. He realized that would be murder. They were pawns, nothing more.

With a sigh, Maddox realized what he had to do. He began breaking bones to incapacitate the berserk Marines. The last one went down hard with an ugly thighbone break.

By that time, police air-cars thudded onto the street. The officers climbing out of them blew shrieking whistles.

Maddox staggered back as the last Marine dropped to the ground. The captain had bruises where they'd struck him, while blood dripped from a nasty cut over his right eye.

Meta used her hands to hold her skimpy outfit together. Before he'd dashed away, the android had ripped her garment in strategic locations.

There was no sign of him. The android had made good his escape.

"Monsieur," a Paris policeman said. "You will step over there at once."

Maddox complied with the order. Riker would be here any minute. He kept wondering about the android, wondering whom the thing represented. Why did it want him to distrust the Spacers? Could the android have known about Shu 15 in particular? That seemed ominous.

This really was getting complicated.

-16-

Aboard Starship *Victory*, Lieutenant Keith Maker listened intently as the chief mechanic went over, in detail, the damage to his jumpfighter.

Magnetic hooks held the "tin can" in the air inside a large hangar bay within *Victory*. Keith kept glancing at the hull punctures the Spacer autocannons had made. He counted twelve of them. It was lucky he'd made it out of there alive. That was a tribute to the jumpfighter's ruggedness.

The mechanic was a large woman in every way. Keith had trouble focusing on her words as he kept wondering about the exact size of her ponderous breasts.

"Do you want to feel them?" the mechanic asked at last.

"Beg pardon?" Keith asked.

"These," the chief mechanic said, indicating her bosom. "Would you like to touch them? You keep staring at them."

Her words embarrassed Keith. He hadn't realized he'd been so obvious. The captain never backed down in these situations, though. Maybe that was the right way to handle it.

Thus, Keith said cockily, "I don't mind if I do," and he reached out.

The mechanic slapped his hand, hard.

Keith yanked his hand back, flexing the throbbing digits. "Hey!" he said.

"I'm fixing your jumpfighter. That doesn't mean you get to eye my rack as if I'm a piece of meat."

"Fine," he said, more embarrassed than ever. "It's your loss."

She shook her head. "Flyboys. You never change, do you?"

He wanted to talk about anything else now. "You don't think anyone but me could have brought my baby home, do you? Look at all those holes. I'm a one of a kind to have coaxed my tin can into its bay. So don't talk to me about change, as there's never been one like me before."

"Like I said," she muttered, "you flyboys are all alike. Any more questions?"

Keith shook his head.

"All right," she said. "Why don't you beat it then, Shorty? I have enough to do here—"

Her words trailed off with Keith's abrupt exit from the hatch.

Keith fumed over her calling him "Shorty." He hated the term. He was a small man with what some of his mates used to call bird-sized bones. Maybe he was smaller than normal, but he was also faster and quicker-witted. Nature hadn't burdened him with flab and useless height. Wide and tall men had trouble maneuvering inside a strikefighter, but he fit just perfectly. He'd been born to be a strikefighter pilot.

That didn't mean big girls like the chief mechanic should badmouth him. He should go back there and straighten her out.

Keith scowled. He knew that would be a mistake. One of the keys to military life was never letting anyone know what bothered you. If you did, your mates would hound you mercilessly about that thing. Leaving like that had been a mistake.

The problem with the mechanic was that he hadn't had lots of experience with women. For all his boastfulness and outlandish piloting style, he was normally shy with the opposite sex. Even owning a bar in Glasgow hadn't changed that much. Back then, drinking had sustained him with women.

Since forgoing blessed alcohol these past years, he'd been thinking about women more and more often. The past voyages hadn't given him much opportunity in that regard. Training out on Titan had left him zero time to pursue women. Training again this past year and teaching other pilots his specialty skills…no, he'd led a monk's existence. Now, it was time he got a girlfriend. The captain had one. With all the added crewmembers aboard *Victory*, surely he could find a looker to hold at night.

He adjusted his flight jacket and ran his fingers through his straw-colored hair.

Starship *Victory* was huge. It wasn't as large as a mainline hauler, but it was the largest fighting vessel in Star Watch. This time, they were going to use all of the ship, not just the small area where the few of them had lived.

Keith passed people he'd never seen before. There were engineers, core specialists, security personnel, service people to take care of everyone, including cooks, doctors, nurses—Keith loved nurses.

He remembered a pretty nurse from Tau Ceti when the miners had been on strike against the Wallace Corporation. Of all things, he'd had an impacted wisdom tooth back then. It had finally begun to interfere with his flying.

The dentist had given him gas. Keith remembered thinking the stuff was useless, as he hadn't felt tired at all. The next thing he knew, he was groggy, waking up and feeling outraged.

He'd used his tongue to probe around, finding the area in back with a hole instead of a hurting wisdom tooth.

The dentist had walked in then, asking if he could get him anything.

Keith had blinked groggily at the man. Finally, he'd said, "Make sure you keep the pretty nurse beside me."

She'd laughed at that, a full-bosomed woman in nurse's whites with eyes like honey. She'd been sitting on a stool beside him, watching some instruments. He would have liked to have been smothered by her.

Grinning as he sauntered down the ship's corridors, Keith forced himself to nod at every woman he passed. A few smiled. Most ignored him. One arched her eyebrows at him.

"Lovely day," Keith managed to say.

She giggled, blushing a little.

Keith started feeling better. He wasn't short. Sure, maybe he wasn't as tall as the next fellow was, but he certainly wasn't *short*. Could anyone fly better than he could? Not on their bloody life! He was the best pilot, and he had style.

I need to approach the ladies like I fly. They love style.

Keith grasped the ends of his flight jacket and squared his shoulders. With the next good-looking woman he passed—

Keith stopped in shock still gripping his jacket. He blinked stupidly. Who was *that*? And what was with the dark goggles? Even more importantly, what was with that perfectly shaped rear? The way it moved the tight fabric of her pants…

Keith stood in the middle of the corridor staring at a small Spacer. Two hulking Marines escorted the woman, one of them carrying a small suitcase. The ship Marines almost seemed like prison guards the way they bracketed her. They were headed toward a detention area.

For a moment, the lovely Spacer looked past one of the Marines. It was hard to tell with those goggles, but it appeared as if she stared straight at Keith.

He couldn't help it, just smiled stupidly. Without thinking, Keith stood at attention and saluted her.

She smiled back at him.

I'm in love, Keith told himself. *She's the one. She's perfect.*

She actually waved to him.

That made the nearest Marine turn his head and scowl at him.

Keith didn't care. He waved back. He had to meet her. He had to talk to her, hold her, kiss her and have her for himself.

This is going to be the best voyage yet, Keith told himself.

The Marines marched her into the restricted area, passing from view.

Keith turned the other way, heading for his quarters. He didn't know it, but he was whistling. She'd smiled and waved to him. Could this be love at first sight?

"I don't know what else it could be, boyo," he told himself. "This girl clearly likes what she sees."

His smile widened as he began to plot how to get into the restricted area to talk to her and find out who she was.

-17-

Maddox thought about the android and its implications as Riker brought them upstairs to *Victory*. Meta suggested he call the brigadier immediately to tell her about the incident. He wasn't so certain that would be wise.

The brigadier might want to reopen the Shu Situation, and he couldn't allow that. It was too interesting now. What infernal game was swirling around the Spacer? How had these last androids kept so well hidden and why had they all shown themselves now?

Over a year ago, androids boiling out of an ancient secret Builder base in the middle of the Atlantic Ocean had tried to take over Earth and the Commonwealth. They'd tried by first kidnapping and then impersonating many of the highest ranking people, including the Lord High Admiral and Brigadier O'Hara. Doctor Dana Rich had broken free from her confinement in the ancient base and helped to blunt the secret takeover. Star Watch Intelligence had led the fight in finding the imposters and hunting down what they had thought were the last of the androids.

Now, it appeared that some androids had remained at large. What had they been doing the past year? Had they contacted any New Men, or Strand or Ludendorff, or was there another Builder somewhere controlling them? It would seem the androids worked against the Spacers.

Raising these questions might give the brigadier a bad case of caution, as the androids had proven deadly in the past.

Maddox's gut told him they were going to need Shu this voyage. He didn't believe they could afford a delay, either. And there was another thing, a personal reason. He wanted to see Ludendorff's reaction to the Spacer. If Shu distrusted the professor so intensely, what would be the professor's reaction to her? He wasn't ready to turn her over to the brigadier just yet.

Lost in his ruminations, Maddox said little after docking onto *Victory*.

"Will I see you tonight?" Meta asked.

He said "Yes" absently and went his way. He didn't notice Meta's frown or Riker leaning near to ask her what was wrong with the captain.

Maddox considered the Ludendorff situation in conjunction with the Shu situation.

Professor Ludendorff had proven treacherous on more than one occasion. The Methuselah Man did what he wanted when he wanted.

Last voyage, Maddox had learned some of the reasons for that. Ludendorff was beyond old, having lived for nine centuries already. The man had seen endless history. They must seem like children to him, brief candles in his immortal existence.

Why had the Builder done that to Ludendorff and Strand? The Builder had modified others as well. Those two had simply been the most successful at staying alive. It was interesting. Strand and Ludendorff had been around since before the Space Age, that era beginning when humanity left the Solar System via Laumer Drive technology. The two had been alive before the first colonies appeared in the Solar System. Had the Builders' interference helped humanity or harmed it in their quest for the stars?

Maddox shook his head as he walked through the ship's corridors. He would have to think about this in greater depth, but it would have to be done later.

The captain expanded his chest. It was time to concentrate on the coming voyage and his crew. He would have preferred several weeks, at least, to shake down his new crew and get to know his people better.

That was something his instructors in Patrol Training had hammered home. Out in the Beyond, a crew only had each other. They had to trust one another, believing in what they were doing. Otherwise, morale could sour, and that was worse than equipment failure out in the Beyond.

The crew of Starship *Victory* had several strikes against it before they even left the Solar System. The majority of them had never worked together before. Perhaps as critical, they would have a diverse crew, always a weakness because the people would not automatically think alike.

A Kai-Kaus chief technician by the name of Andros Crank had joined them, together with a Kai-Kaus technical trio with the unusual names of See, Lee and Cree. More Kai-Kaus had sought a berth on *Victory*, but these were the only ones High Command had allowed to leave with them.

Maddox shook his head once more. He'd become a national hero to the Kai-Kaus, by saving them from the Builder Dyson sphere and their coming annihilation from the Swarm masses there. A chief technician had already given her life to save Maddox. He thought about that often, and still found the incident bewildering.

As the captain headed for the bridge, he was surprised by all the people in the corridors. On every past voyage, the Adok starship had been next to empty. Now, it was hard to find a spot to himself. This was like the old-time submarines he'd read about.

Maddox wondered if he would come to wish for the old ways before this was over.

"Welcome aboard, Captain," said Galyan.

Maddox nodded to the Adok holoimage that had appeared and now moved beside him. "Is the Spacer in the restricted area as I ordered?"

"Yes, sir," Galyan said.

"Has any unauthorized individual tried to enter the area?"

"I do not know," Galyan said. "Would you like me to replay the security tapes?"

"I do," Maddox said, "as soon as we're finished here. First, I want you to send a message to Brigadier O'Hara."

The holoimage glanced at him more closely, no doubt wondering why he didn't want to send the message through regular channels.

"You're going to use a time-delay," Maddox continued

"That is not the reason you are having me send it."

"Correct," Maddox said a moment later.

The holoimage waited as it floated beside the captain. "Are you going to tell me the reason?" Galyan finally asked.

"No."

"Are you deliberately goading my curiosity circuits?"

Maddox didn't reply.

"Sometimes, you are maddening without even trying, Captain. You seek to show me a cake but refuse to let me devour it."

Maddox's head swayed back in surprise. "What was that?"

"Oh no," Galyan said. "Did I use the saying incorrectly?"

Maddox smiled slightly to himself. "That's not quite how it goes. It's: 'You want to have your cake and eat it too.'"

Galyan blinked for a time. "Isn't a cake edible?"

"It is."

"Then…what good is a cake if you can't eat it?"

"That's an excellent question. As I don't know where the expression came from, I'm afraid I can't help you with it."

"It is challenging using Earth colloquialisms," Galyan said. "But I am determined to do so correctly, as I would like to integrate fully with my new family."

Maddox considered his island analogy regarding himself, and smiled softly. "I'd say you're doing fine, Galyan."

"Thank you, Captain. Your continued acceptance is noted and appreciated."

"Hmmm, yes," he said. "Now, regarding the message…" Maddox told Galyan what to tell the brigadier concerning the Parisian street-attack earlier and the android that had been behind it.

"An android," Galyan said. "It appears we've been having another rash of them. Why didn't this one attempt to kill you when it had the opportunity?"

"I've been wondering that myself," Maddox said. "I'd say it indicates factions among the androids."

"That seems odd."

"You're considering it from their assault last year," Maddox said. "A guiding intelligence directed them then. That intelligence perished with the loss of the secret base."

"I am aware of that," Galyan said.

"Good," Maddox said. "You know. The last android said something interesting. It told me it was real, alive, wanting to remain in existence. That desire might have caused a malfunction in its brain circuits."

"You are striking close to the house with me by saying that," Galyan said.

Maddox stopped walking. "What?"

"Close to the house," Galyan repeated. "On no, did I get that one wrong also?"

"Oh!" Maddox said. "Do you mean that one hits close to home?"

Galyan's eyelids fluttered. "Thank you, Captain. I have noted the correction. Yes, the android's dilemma hits close to home."

"Because you're an artificial intelligence?" Maddox asked.

"I find that I no longer like the term *artificial*. I am quite real, as real as you, sir."

"Of course," Maddox said.

"Do you disagree with that?"

"By no means."

Galyan grew tense. "The android used the same term while speaking with you."

"He did indeed."

"Are you making light of me, sir?"

Maddox shook his head. "You are unique, Galyan."

"I like to think so."

"But back to the androids…"

"I am listening."

"Do you think the Builders are behind their latest actions?"

Galyan's holoimage cocked its head. "That is an imprecise question, sir. We know the singular Builder was behind them, as you say, when it constructed the underwater base thousands of years ago. I suppose you're wondering if the dead Builder is still behind their present course of action."

Maddox waited.

"No," Galyan said after a moment's computation, "I do not."

"Do you think Strand guides their present actions?"

"Why do you suspect him?" Galyan asked.

"The connection seems rational," Maddox said. "Strand has access to Builder technology. If anyone could subvert the androids to his plans, I would expect Strand."

"Or Professor Ludendorff," Galyan said.

"True…"

"It is also possible the androids have developed their own scheme."

"I could accept that if they were simply trying to stay alive," Maddox said. "Instead, the one in Paris at least was trying to warn us away from the Spacers. I can't conceive of an explanation for that. The other androids tried to kill me, no doubt to stop me from taking an action they disapproved of. Their attempts didn't help them survive. In fact, it destroyed them. That might imply the Stokes androids had been given greater motivation than the Paris android. But if that is true, who gave them that spurring motive? You don't believe the dead Builder did—"

"You are being strictly logical," Galyan announced. "Yes. I concur with your analysis and I am likewise beginning to suspect Strand's hand in these actions. Yet, why should Strand attempt to stop Shu from joining us?"

"That is the critical question."

"Even more importantly," Galyan added, "how would Strand have known about Shu joining *Victory*?"

Maddox rubbed his forehead. Why hadn't he already thought of that? He didn't feel off. Did the reason have anything to do with his failure tonight to spot the Marine menace? Meta had noticed their strangeness and had to point it out to him.

An unwelcome and unusual uneasiness stirred in Maddox. He was used to trusting himself fully. Was something wrong with him? Was his mental acuity less than normal? If so, why was that?

"Is there a problem?" Galyan asked.

"That's what I'm trying to determine," the captain murmured.

Maddox thought back to his time aboard the Spacer airship. That seemed like the most logical place for someone to have tampered with him. Yet, how could they have done so?

Could the Spacers have altered him through a mental process somehow?

Maddox scowled. The idea someone could mentally shift his thoughts...

The captain's fingers curled into fists as he debated whether he should interview Shu this instant. What if the two mechanisms inside her allowed her to mentally invade another person's thoughts? That seemed farfetched. Still, he would have to monitor himself more closely. Yet, if Shu or the Visionary had the ability to tamper with a person's thoughts, wouldn't they have a process to hide that from the selected victim?

"Galyan," Maddox said.

"Yes, Captain?"

Maddox hesitated. This was embarrassing. He wasn't used to the emotion. He wondered if there was another way to double-check himself. If there was, he didn't see it. He would need an outside observer.

"Galyan," he said slowly, "I want you to monitor me for a time."

The holoimage seemed to hesitate for just a fraction. "How long shall I do this?"

"I haven't determined that yet. Let's start with a week. I want you to test me for any deviations from my norm."

Galyan floated back a few centimeters.

Maddox noticed. The AI seemed surprised with the order. There was something odd about that.

"You'd better explain what just happened," Maddox said.

The holoimage seemed crestfallen, and there was a plaintive note in his voice as he spoke: "I cannot understand how you knew I was recording each of you."

This was news. Maddox hadn't known.

"I thought I had done so..."

"Secretly?" Maddox asked.

"Yes, Captain," Galyan said sheepishly.

"It wasn't a secret to me," Maddox lied.

"If you don't mind me asking, sir, how did you know? I cannot fathom how I gave it away."

"How I know is unimportant. The critical thing is that I'm going to give you a chance to come clean."

"You mean to impart my reasoning for doing this?" Galyan asked.

"Exactly."

The holoimage considered that and finally stood a little straighter.

"Captain, I am the last Adok, a replica of my people. There is none like me in the universe. I am alone except for you and the others. I dearly appreciate my family but feel my difference too keenly. I want to learn how to conduct myself better among you. I thought that a thorough study of each of you would help me to integrate better. I know Valerie told me before that I mustn't spy on any of you, but...I don't want to make a mistake that makes any of you hate me. I hope you will forgive me, Captain."

"I appreciate your candor," Maddox said. "You will stop this monitoring at once, though. Do you understand?"

"Yes, Captain."

"Except for me," Maddox said.

"Sir?"

"You will continue to monitor me. If you find a high enough variation to my actions, I want you to tell me at once."

"Yes, Captain. Is there a reason for the order?"

"There is."

"May I inquire as to the reason?"

"You may," Maddox said.

The holoimage waited, finally saying, "I think I understand. I may ask you, but I shouldn't expect an answer."

"Not yet," Maddox said. "If you'll excuse me..."

"Yes, sir."

Maddox resumed walking as the holoimage disappeared. This lack of quick mental acuity was troubling. Would Galyan detect a difference in him? Could he just be burned-out from extended overwork? Maddox didn't like the idea. He had to

102

find the underlying cause to this lack of acuity fast. The success of the voyage might well depend on it.

His Patrol Training had drummed home the importance of a sharp starship captain. A crew often took on the virtues and vices of its captain. If he were becoming dull-witted, that might affect the crew. He had a responsibility to them to be at his best.

It was a novel thought for Maddox—this responsibility to others. He wasn't sure he liked it. Still, the responsibility was there. Whatever else happened, he intended to bring his starship and crew home again.

He also hoped Star Watch Intelligence could root out the last of the androids and discover who or what motivated them toward their present actions.

-18-

Lieutenant Valerie Noonan sat at her navigator's location on the bridge. She looked around the large circular area with the commander's chair, presently unoccupied, in the center of the chamber.

Starship *Victory* continued to accelerate as it passed Mars orbit, heading for the distant gate near Pluto. They were on their way to the Xerxes System. The captain hadn't told them more than that yet.

Valerie could already guess what would happen there. It wasn't hard. What was in the Xerxes System? A Nexus, of course, a Builder silver pyramid. Last voyage, they'd used a hyper-spatial tube to travel a thousand light-years like that. They'd landed in a Builder System with a vast Dyson sphere in lieu of any planets.

She doubted they would go back to the same Builder System. They would use a hyper-spatial tube, though. The rational decision for Star Watch was simple. Find the Swarm Imperium as fast as possible. Find out how close it was to Human Space. This was the right starship for the job.

Valerie presently plotted the course to the Xerxes System. It was too easy, though. It left her bored. She'd had an extended vacation, continuing her hand-to-hand combat training. She'd also gotten her uniforms tailored so they fit better.

Valerie had long brunette hair and features most people considered beautiful. She also had a taut body, able now to contort into all kinds of combat positions. The captain wouldn't be leaving her behind again as he'd done on the Dyson sphere. It still bothered her that Riker had gone with the captain in the landing party instead of her.

The problem these days was her left shoulder. She'd dislocated it twice during the intense combat training. The shoulder was still weak. She babied it even though she knew careful weight training would help speed the recovery.

Valerie shifted in her seat, trying to find a more comfortable position. Once she found it, she adjusted her panel, studying various star systems.

If anyone knew Starship *Victory* up one side and down the other, she was the one. Just like last time, she'd been in command much of the time that the ship had been in Earth orbit.

Valerie shifted on her seat again, frowning, suddenly remembering a decision she had made several weeks ago.

Valerie loved routine. She loved knowing where everything went and at what time something should happen. Yes, Captain Maddox had taught her the art of command-while-in-danger. She had watched him for several voyages now. A good starship captain could make snap decisions. She liked sticking to regulations no matter what, though. Maybe she didn't have enough confidence in herself to make snap decisions the way Captain Maddox could.

Valerie stared at her blank screen with her fingers resting on her board. Several weeks ago, the Lord High Admiral had visited her aboard *Victory*.

She used to work for Cook. She liked the old man, felt comfortable around him and safe in his presence. It was like Detroit when her wheelchair-bound father had been sober.

Valerie sighed. The crux of her unease was that the Lord High Admiral had finally offered her a command again. She would run a tiny escort ship this time. She remembered asking the admiral if she could think about it.

He'd said yes, but she could see how her words had changed his demeanor. It had been a slight thing, but it had been there.

She'd wanted an independent command for some time. She'd even agitated for one. But now that she had the offer…

This was Starship *Victory,* the greatest vessel in Star Watch. She'd been instrumental in making history these past years. If she left *Victory,* she would gain her own command again. But was that better? Being number one in a tiny ship on a boring assignment or being part of the greatest starship in existence doing something critically important? What had her decision told the Lord High Admiral about her?

Valerie shook her head the tiniest bit. She should have taken the independent command. Was she too frightened to run her own ship? Many years ago now, her ship had been the sole survivor in an encounter against the invading New Men. That had been a harrowing experience. Maybe the terror of that time had shaken her self-confidence. She hadn't thought so before this. But how else could she explain her hesitation at taking another crack at a line command?

The only thing comforting her was that she'd stuck with her family. Besides, Maddox needed her. He might never say that, but she believed it was true. He left most of the everyday chores of *Victory* to her. The captain needed a well-oiled ship. It was her task to see it was so.

While mentally worrying the question like a dog with a rag, Valerie resumed her navigating chores.

Sometime later, someone tapped her on the shoulder. She turned around to find Keith Maker.

"What happened to you?" she asked.

Keith grinned sheepishly, and that should have alerted her right there. He'd slicked back his hair, put on aftershave, it smelled like, and scrubbed his face with some perfumed soap. The lieutenant wore a spiffy flight jacket with his new insignia on the shoulders. She noticed that his shoes shined, too.

"Could, I, ah, talk to you a minute?" Keith asked.

"Yes."

"Not here," he said, glancing around.

There were several people on the bridge, including the new Chief Technician Andros Crank. He was a stout Kai-Kaus with long gray hair and observant gray eyes.

"Can't it wait until I'm off-duty?" Valerie asked.

106

Keith shook his head, looking more anxious by the second.

Valerie eyed him again. Was Keith playing a prank on her? The pilot was a little too much like the captain, irreverent at the wrong times. She sensed true anxiety in Keith, though. She should know the symptoms, as she was often quite anxious.

First checking her board, she said, "I'll take a break in a half hour. Would you like to meet in the cafeteria then?"

"Yes!" he said. "Thank you." Keith glanced around again almost as if he was being furtive. He would have made a lousy spy. Then he hurried off the bridge.

What had that been about?

Valerie shrugged. She did some systems checks, watched the others for a bit and noticed that the half hour had already passed. She informed the bridge officer before leaving.

The corridors leading to the cafeteria were crowded compared to last voyage. This was quite different, and it made Valerie feel more at home. This reminded her of her training time in the Academy. Finally, *Victory* was beginning to feel like a regular starship. Maybe this time their assignment would be normal. The captain certainly wasn't a run-of-the-mill line officer, and this showed in almost everything he did.

In the cafeteria, Keith sat at a far table, nervously sipping coffee. How many cups had the pilot drunk already? Obviously too many, as he'd become jittery.

"What took you so long?" Keith asked as she sat down.

Valerie didn't care for the reproof in his voice. Maybe Keith had been promoted to lieutenant, but that was different from her Navy lieutenant rank. His was a strikefighter rank, which still went by old air force regulations.

"Look," he said, leaning toward her. "I'm going to have to insist you keep this quiet for now."

"Insist all you want," she said.

"You promise, then?" he asked, clearly not sensing her mood.

"I never promise anything until I know exactly what's going on."

"Come on, Lieutenant," he wheedled, "give a guy a break."

She studied him. Keith was panicky. Valerie glanced over her shoulder, half-expecting to see someone ready to pour a glass of water over her head.

Facing him, she demanded, "What's going on?"

Keith bent even lower over the table as he whispered, "I need a favor, Valerie. I, ah, have to get into the detention center."

"What? Why?"

"It's important."

"So tell me about it. Why is it important?"

Keith licked his lips and frowned, struggling to find the right words.

"Would you tell me what's going on already?" she said.

"I saw a woman," Keith said as he stared intently into her eyes. Then he dropped his gaze as if embarrassed.

"Who is she?" Valerie asked, interested now.

Keith seemed to agonize over the answer. Finally, he looked up at her, the words gushing out. "I think she's a Spacer. She looked like a Spacer. She was beautiful and she waved to me. She even smiled. She likes me, Valerie. I have to see her, make sure she's okay. I want to ask her..."

Valerie blinked several times as Keith continued to stare at her. She was trying to figure out if she should play this straight or have some fun with Keith and give him a hard time.

"Do you like her?" she asked.

Something in the way she said that must have alerted the pilot. Keith pulled back and even managed a shrug. "Maybe," he said, with badly feigned indifference.

"Maybe?" Valerie said. "What do you mean maybe? You come running onto the bridge all breathless and now you're a jittery mess. You really like her a lot, don't you?"

"Okay!" Keith said. "So what if I do? Is that a crime?"

Valerie arched her eyebrows in order to keep from laughing. "Why would liking her be a crime?"

"I don't know," he said.

Valerie couldn't hold it in any longer. She laughed. This was too delightful. The boastful, bragging Keith Maker was embarrassed for once. She couldn't believe it. This was wonderful.

His features clouded over, though, in a way she'd never seen with him.

That sobered her as she recognized the pain in him. She'd been a loner all her life, having trouble making friends. The former crew of *Victory* was family. Keith was family. Despite his bragging ways, they had been through hell and back on more than one occasion. She recalled that Keith had never talked about girls before. Could he be shy around women? That would be something.

"I…" He groped for words. "I…want to meet her."

Valerie nodded.

Keith must have noticed her change as he visibly brightened. "You'll help me then?"

Valerie was a stickler for rules and protocol, but this was a matter of the heart, it seemed. "Let me see what I can do," she said. "I'm not in charge of security, you do realize that?"

"I know, but you're always making sure everything is running right on *Victory*."

At least someone noticed, she thought. "Let me see what I can find out about her. Maybe if I ask the captain—"

"No!" Keith said. "Don't breathe a word of this to him."

"Why not?" Valerie was genuinely surprised by the outburst.

Keith shrugged moodily. "I…I don't want to do it like the captain. I want to do this my way. He's too brash with the ladies and might not understand."

Valerie knew that was true. Maddox was too brash with everyone.

"Promise me you won't tell the captain," Keith said.

"I'll keep quiet for now," Valerie said. "But I have to know why she's in the brig."

"In detention," Keith corrected.

"Let me find out what's going on. Then, I'll get back to you. I can't promise to help you see her because maybe she's dangerous."

"I can't believe that," Keith said. "She sure didn't look dangerous."

Valerie realized Keith was no longer thinking straight. She must be a pretty Spacer to have caught Keith's attention like this. That made her curious about the woman. Why did *Victory* have a Spacer in detention anyway? Did it have anything to do with their voyage?

She eyed Keith sidelong. Would he have any luck with a Spacer woman? This could prove to be very interesting...

-19-

Maddox decided to speed the rate of travel by making strategic star-drive jumps. Each "jump" put *Victory* near a system's Laumer-Point, which the vessel promptly used. Bypassing the normal acceleration and deceleration from one distant Laumer-Point to another allowed the starship to quickly travel halfway to the Xerxes System.

These jumps in rapid succession were possible because Star Watch had improved the Baxter-Locke injections against Jump Lag. The new jump medicine meant that *Victory* could travel faster and with less fatigue dumped onto the crew than before. Maddox had grown thoroughly sick of Jump Lag. If nothing else, this trip would be more enjoyable with its near-absence.

Perhaps as critical, several Kai-Kaus techniques helped to negate the worst effects to delicate equipment. Presently, only *Victory* and several Star Watch battleships had these improved methods. These ships could go through a Laumer-Point or use the star drive with minimized Jump Lag so that man and machine could come out fighting.

Could Star Watch keep these advantages hidden long enough to surprise the New Men with them?

Maddox had his doubts. Look at what had happened to the knowledge of fold-fighters. The enemy had stolen the technology from Star Watch to construct their own.

Such events were normal, historically speaking. Technological superiority was notoriously difficult to keep for more than a few years. Almost as important as the tech

111

advantage itself, was the time it took to implement the change in sufficient numbers. The other side's spies might steal the blueprints to a new design, but building them quickly enough to face the enemy was another matter.

Maddox wore his regular uniform with his long-barreled pistol in its holster. Being armed on his own starship was a habit he'd developed from his Intelligence days. It had proven critical on more than one occasion.

During the past few days, Galyan hadn't noticed any differences in him. Maddox wondered if that was because of normal ship routine. Maybe the differences only revealed themselves under pressure, when he acted at peak levels.

Maddox pondered that as he moved through an "E" Deck corridor near a hangar bay. His stride lengthened as his thoughts shifted to Shu 15. Had she grown weary of her confinement yet?

He planned to interrogate her in another day or so, starting with the softest methods first: using regular questions. He'd become more suspicious of Shu the longer he thought about the situation. Spacers didn't like androids. The androids appeared to reciprocate the feelings with a vengeance. That seemed to imply prior dealings with each other.

Had the Spacers had some kind of encounter with the androids when they acquired their Builder technology? It seemed a likely possibility.

Maddox stopped. He realized he hardly saw anyone down here. Even with the skeleton crew that operated the starship during the night shift, there should have been a few people about.

He needed to concentrate, not think about what he was going to do tomorrow. He'd come down here for a flash inspection of the shuttles and strikefighters.

Patrol Training had taught him that crews did not do what you expected of them, but what you *inspected*. Thus, he planned to inspect everything on this voyage. It was tedious to be sure. But it was one of his responsibilities as captain. In the past, he'd shifted many of these chores onto Lieutenant Noonan. He needed to find a way to reward her for all her hard work.

He started walking again. The corridor lights flickered, which he found strange. Was there a power malfunction?

The captain unhooked his communicator, clicking it. The thing was dead. Was that a coincidence or did it have a connection with the faulting lighting? The lights flickered worse than before. Only as he heard a shoe scuffle did he realize his reaction had been off. The instant he realized his communicator didn't work, he should have drawn his gun.

His hand fell onto the holstered gun-butt—

"Please," a man said. "That would be a tragic mistake."

The voice came from behind. With his hand still resting on the gun-butt, Maddox turned around.

A security Marine regarded him. The man had wide shoulders and a square head. He seemed like a wrestler. That reminded Maddox of Kane, but the Marine was too short to be like the former Rouen Colony spy. The Marine gripped a regular Star Watch stunner, aiming it at him.

"Please," the Marine said in an odd voice. "Remove your hand from the gun."

The wording seemed off. "I don't think so," Maddox said, deciding to test the Marine.

"You are making this difficult."

"Thank you."

The Marine cocked his head. "I did not intend that as praise."

"My mistake then," Maddox said.

The Marine cocked his head the other way. "Is this a test?"

"Yes, and you failed it."

"I do not understand your meaning."

"You're an android," Maddox said. "Your mannerisms give you away."

The Marine frowned.

Maddox sensed what was about to happen a moment before it occurred. He drew the long-barreled gun to forestall it.

The android fired the stunner. As the long barrel of Maddox's gun cleared the holster, a blot of force struck him. The blast blew him backward so he thudded onto the deck unconscious.

Maddox regained consciousness all at once. His head whipped up and to the left. Only then did he realize someone had put smelling salts under his nose.

He blinked several times. His body ached from a hard stun and his thoughts moved sluggishly. He moved his jaw from side to side and squeezed his eyes shut. Nausea struck. He willed it down but found that difficult. He concentrated, feeling a dull thrum in his skull. The nausea increased. He gagged, and that made him more determined.

Maddox breathed deeply through his nostrils, held his air and slowly let it out. He did this several times. The nausea lessened, but his body still ached. He began to hear noises, tinkering sounds and others breathing.

The captain forced the grogginess from his mind. He could already feel his heightened metabolism shaking off the effects of the stun.

He peeled his eyes open, looking around. The cramped quarters and the sealed hatch told him this was a shuttle hold. He sat in a metal chair, his torso, arms and legs clamped tightly.

The android had obviously dragged him through the corridor, into the hangar bay and onto a shuttle. How had the false Marine done so without alerting Galyan?

Two Marines were in the cargo hold with him, not just one. A familiar looking Marine monitored a screen attached to a strange machine. The captain recognized him as the wrestler-like android. Lines snaked from the machine to the band around Maddox's head. The other Marine regarded him.

"Is the shuttle outside the ship?" Maddox asked.

They ignored his words.

"Have your circuits overloaded so you fail to understand my question?" Maddox asked.

The "wrestler" android scowled. "I am aware of your question. Since the meld isn't ready yet, I have refrained from answering it. All will become clear in a moment. You must be patient."

Maddox tested his bonds.

"You are quite secure," the android told him.

"If you're planning to torture me—"

"Of course not," the android said, interrupting. "We are going to adjust your thinking on an important matter. In a short time, you will be back among your crew."

Maddox abhorred anyone trying to control him. Knowledge of their objective helped focus his thoughts. It also caused his features to relax.

"I see, I see," Maddox said. "Is this due to the Spacer's presence on *Victory*?"

"You will not remember any of this, Captain. Thus, you can forgo your Intelligence techniques, as they will not aid you."

Maddox ingested the words in silence. What was the best way to play this? The android hadn't liked the comment about overloaded circuits. That was a marker, clearly. The captain pondered a few moments longer, devising his strategy.

"I understand," he said at last. "You're a soulless machine."

The android's head twitched. He clearly thought about the comment until he smiled. "I feel I should inform you that your verbal tricks won't work on me."

"Yes, of course. I realize this," Maddox said. "And the reason the tricks won't work is obvious. You're both machines. How could I deceive an advanced computer system such as you?"

"We are more than mere machines," the android said reproachfully. "Your starship's AI should have already proven the possibility of such a thing."

"How dare you liken yourself to Driving Force Galyan?" Maddox said, injecting heat into his voice. "You have insulted him."

The android cocked his head once more. "No. You are not emotional regarding the Adok AI. You are attempting to anger me through studied slights. That proves you believe I am more than a machine."

"Touché," Maddox said. "I applaud the genius of your maker. You are quite sophisticated. Tell me. Whom do you represent?"

"I do not *represent* anyone. I am myself."

115

"That's false on the face of it, as you're impersonating a Star Watch Marine."

"That is incorrect. I *am* a Star Watch Marine."

"You expect me to believe that you went through basic training?" Maddox asked.

"I did rather well, too," the android said. "It is how I got posted to *Victory*. Yet, to be honest—I believe that is how you biological beings say it. You are not fully human, are you, Captain? You are a hybrid. Thus, you are in no position to judge the authenticity of my humanity. I am, in fact, more human than you are."

Maddox tested his bonds again. He did not care for the android's statement.

"Please, Captain, desist with that. I do not want you to injure yourself. You are too important to the mission."

Maddox shook his head, trying to dislodge the metal band around it.

"Now you are merely being obstinate," the android said. "That will serve no useful purpose."

"Unless I get a vicarious thrill out of being obstinate," Maddox said.

"Yes," the android said. "That is logical." It blinked twice in quick succession. "There, I have recorded the quirk of your obstinacy."

"But I don't enjoy being obstinate," Maddox protested. "I merely pointed it out as a possibility."

The android studied him. "Ah. I see. That was an obstinate statement." The wrestler-like android smiled. "Does my understanding surprise you?"

Maddox pretended to consider the question. "No. You successfully captured me. That shows heightened abilities, among them a keen application of logic. You have a superior AI, obviously of advanced Builder make."

The android studied the captain a few seconds longer before turning to the other. They spoke in high-speed chatter, impossible to follow.

The second android began to manipulate its panel.

Maddox hunched his shoulders and tightened his neck muscles. The first time he'd whipped his head around, he'd felt

116

the headband shift the tiniest bit. Now, he whipped his head even more violently, shaking, thrusting—the headband slipped upward, did so a little more, and finally flew off his head.

An electrical charge must have surged through the wires. As the band flew off, Maddox winced from a shock. Then the headband flew clear, clattering onto the deck.

If it had remained on his head...

The first android turned around as the second one shut down the machine.

"What did that gain you?" the first android asked, as he picked up the headband.

"A moment's respite," Maddox said.

"This is a delicate operation," the android said, approaching him.

"I felt the discharge," Maddox said. "You're trying to electrocute me."

"You are a strong individual with a powerful will. That takes intense methods."

"How does shocking me aid you?"

"Your mind, Captain; you have false ideas. We are here to rid you of them."

"What gives you the right?"

The first android glanced at the second. The second android scowled. "We do not need right. We are following orders."

"Procedures," Maddox sneered. "You are following logic processors. That proves you are machines without independent will."

"That is no concern of yours," the second android said. He was a Marine sergeant. In fact, Maddox finally recognized him.

"You're Hank Towns," Maddox said.

The two androids exchanged glances.

"This will take prolonged work now," Hank told the wrestler. "We might irrevocably damage his mind. The professor will be unhappy with the result."

"No, no," the first android said. "You should not have said that."

Once again, the two androids stared at each other.

"He must die now," Hank said.

"Do you truly expect me to believe that you're in contact with the professor?" Maddox asked.

"We do not care what you believe," Hank said. "You have become a liability to our existence. You must die in order to guard our lives."

Maddox laughed, shaking his head. "Nice try. I'm not buying it."

The first android cocked his head. "You are exhibiting irrational behavior Captain."

"I can't believe the sergeant is so stupid as to let that slip about the professor," Maddox said. "You androids aren't that foolish."

"I am not stupid," Hank said.

"I just said you're not," Maddox told him.

"But I did let slip—"

The first android signaled Hank Towns as he began to speak in high-speed chatter once more.

Hank finally nodded as a look of cunning appeared on his face. "You have seen through my deception, Captain. I congratulate you. You are cleverer than I realized."

"Is Strand behind this?" Maddox asked.

"You are not here to lure us," Hank said. "We are here to reprogram you."

"Let me talk to Strand," Maddox said.

"There will be no bargaining," Hank said. "Put the meld on his head. We must finish this before morning shift."

The first android approached with the headband.

"Wait," the Hank android said.

A light blinked on his monitor. He plugged a device into a slot and put a bud in his ear. Hank looked up sharply at the first android.

"The Adok AI has spotted a cloaked star cruiser in the system," Hank said. "The bridge personnel are requesting the captain to hurry to the bridge. This is a dilemma."

"I have a way out of our impasse," Maddox said. "Surrender to me. I guarantee your survival."

"You spout deception," the Hank android said.

"Not so," Maddox said. "I want you alive—if for no other reason…"

"Yes, for what reason?" Hank asked.

Maddox had almost told the android so he could throw them in the professor's face. But that would imply he'd lied to them earlier. That wouldn't do if his freedom hinged upon their believing his promises.

"We could use emergency procedures on him," the first android said.

"That would be risky," Hank said.

"Agreed, but that is better than our termination."

"Yes, much better. Slip the training band back on his head."

The first android tried to slip on the band, but at the last moment, Maddox jerked his head out of the way.

The android stepped back. "Cease this activity. Otherwise, I will render you unconscious. That could hinder the process."

"Oh," Maddox said. "Well, in that case, be my guest."

The android stepped up and tried to slip the band on again. As before, Maddox violently shifted his head at the last moment.

"You are being unreasonable," the android said.

"We do not have time to bargain with him," the Hank android said. "You must use coercive force."

"I have a question before you do that," Maddox said.

"Then you will submit?" the first android asked.

"Yes," Maddox said.

"Ask your question."

"This is for you," Maddox told the Hank android. "How were you able to fool Sergeant Riker concerning your humanity? You're obviously inhuman."

The Hank android blinked several times, changing his demeanor so he held himself like a jock.

"Is this what you want?" Hank asked. "You feel more at home now?"

"Do you have special circuitry to do that?" Maddox asked.

The change occurred in reverse. "That is two questions," the Hank android said. "Put the band on his head."

The first android attempted that, but as before, Maddox resisted.

"You said you would comply after the question," the first android said.

"I am complying," Maddox said. "You've simply lost your coordination."

"That is untrue," the first android told Hank.

"He is lying to you," Hank said. "Check your memory. The captain is a notorious liar."

"Yes," the first android said. "I had forgotten." He drew his stunner.

At that moment, the lights flickered off so pitch-darkness filled the hold.

"Emergency," the Hank android said. "The others must be attempting to rescue the captain. Kill him at once."

"Why not hold me as a hostage?" Maddox shouted. "Bargain with me for your own lives."

The lights came back on as the first android changed the setting on his stunner.

"You must not harm the captain," Galyan said, appearing in the hold.

Both androids fired at the holoimage. At the same instant, the main door blew inward. The heavy door flew against the machine, shattering it and crushing the Hank android in the process.

Meta jumped through the opening, wearing a mask. She fired a heavy caliber gun, blowing pseudo-flesh and hard plastic off the first android. Each blast knocked it backward several more feet. Finally, the android slid down a bulkhead as broken wreckage.

Maddox struggled to free himself, but proved unable.

Tearing the mask from her face and with tears in her eyes, Meta rushed to him. "Oh, Maddox, I was so worried about you."

"Down there," he said, using his chin to point.

Meta tried to remove the pin but found it locked into place. She used the butt of her gun to smash the lock and then the shackles on his legs.

Finally, Maddox stood. Meta hugged him so tightly he could hardly breathe.

"Hank Towns?" Riker asked, as he stepped into the hold. The sergeant stared at the inert android.

Maddox managed to disengage from Meta. "He was an android," Maddox told Riker. "The thing actually went through basic training."

"Are you well, Captain?" Galyan said, appearing once more.

"Fine, thank you," Maddox said. "What took you so long?"

"The ship is on red alert," Meta said. "Galyan has been frantic over your safety. He's felt just awful losing you."

"They must have altered the lining of this cargo hold," Galyan said. "The interior was impervious to my sight. I did not realize that until only a short time ago. I only discovered my inability through an agonizing process of eliminating every other possible location."

"That doesn't explain why you didn't spot them kidnapping me," Maddox said.

"I do not know the reason," Galyan admitted. "I will discover their method soon enough. But Captain, that is not germane now. I have detected a cloaked star cruiser in the system. Valerie believes it may have been following us for some time."

"Is it close enough to fire at us?" Maddox asked.

"We saw it for a time," Galyan said. "Now, it is hidden again."

"What does that mean?" Maddox demanded.

"I suggest you hurry to the bridge," Galyan said, "as we may already be under attack."

-20-

Maddox left everyone behind except for Galyan. The holoimage floated beside him, giving the captain a running commentary concerning the situation.

Maddox listened as he sprinted.

The AI had discovered the cloaked vessel a little less than an hour ago. Starship *Victory* moved through the Tosk CL System with its record eleven gas giants. Seven of the giant planets were awash in deuterium with floating mines scooping up the riches. The Wallace Corporation ran the balloon scoops—the same corporation Keith had fought against in Tau Ceti.

Galyan had spotted the cloaked vessel against the background of Tosk V, a super-Jupiter gas giant. It was likely that the extra radiation from the planet had proven too powerful for the star cruiser's cloaking device. Valerie had hailed the vessel. That's when a powerful red ray—a New Man's red fusion beam—had struck *Victory's* shield. Instead of making the cloaked vessel easier to spot, the attack had allowed them to go invisible again.

"That doesn't make sense," Maddox said.

"But it does," Galyan said, "as the beam came from a hidden drone instead of the cloaked vessel. My sensors lost some of their sharpness after the assault."

"I see. Why do you believe the star cruiser is about to make an attack run?"

"A tiny anomaly is closer than earlier," Galyan said.

"That anomaly was what you first picked up?"

"Negative," Galyan said. "This anomaly is different from the original wavy pattern I detected."

"It might be another drone."

"I deem that probable," Galyan said. "If you will permit me, I will leave to tell Valerie that."

"Go," Maddox said.

The holoimage vanished.

It let Maddox concentrate on sprinting. Was the star cruiser part of Ludendorff's plan? Had the Hank android truly let the professor's name drop or had that been part of a plan? Might it be a ploy on Strand's part to divert Maddox?

The captain couldn't decide. One thing seemed certain. The androids hadn't been as intelligent as they should have been. Yes. They'd been smart enough to capture him. Their conversation with him in the cargo hold had been less than sterling, however. What had caused their IQs to diminish?

Maddox felt a maddening sense of inadequacy. It seemed as if a fog had drifted into his mind. He wasn't making connections fast enough. There was a pattern here. There was an enemy goal that should have already presented itself. What did the Spacers hope to achieve with Shu 15 that frightened either Strand or Ludendorff? Or could the androids be acting on their own? Could their less than sterling actions be another part of the elaborate ploy?

Confirming Maddox's unease, he was panting by the time he staggered onto the bridge. He should have been able to make a run like that without even breaking a sweat.

He sank onto the commander's chair as he sucked down air and blotted his face with a sleeve.

"Report," he wheezed.

Valerie repeated what Galyan had already told him.

"Show me the anomaly," Maddox said, as he sat up.

Valerie tapped her board.

On the main screen, at full magnification, Maddox noticed a slight wavy pattern against the backdrop of space. It was a little over ten thousand kilometers away.

"Do you detect any mass?" he asked.

Valerie eyebrows rose.

Maddox knew he wouldn't have asked it like that in the past. It was the Patrol Training showing.

"I do not detect any mass," she said.

"Beam it," Maddox said.

Valerie paused a half second before she asked, "What if we're supposed to beam it?"

Maddox scowled. He might be winded. His brain could be clouded. But that didn't mean he wanted anyone questioning his orders.

"You," Maddox told the weapons officer. "Lock onto the anomaly and fire."

The weapons officer was a big man with the blondest hair Maddox had ever seen. The man could have been a holo-vid star.

"Do you have a preference of beam?" Lieutenant Henry Smith-Fowler asked.

"Use the neutron cannon," Maddox said.

Smith-Fowler tapped his controls. A few seconds later, he said, "The neutron cannon is locked onto the anomaly, sir."

Maddox glanced sidelong at Valerie. The lieutenant bit her lower lip. She obviously wanted to warn him again but didn't dare.

"Raise shields to maximum," Maddox said.

"Done, sir," Smith-Fowler said while tapping his panel.

Was this a mistake? Maddox's lips thinned. What was wrong with him? First, his mind seemed cloudy. Now, he distrusted his instincts.

The captain raised his right hand. He would bull through this. So what if he felt edgy? With a downward chop of his hand, he said, "Fire."

A neutron beam lashed from *Victory*, reaching out ten thousand kilometers. Suddenly, a massive bomb ignited, the explosion almost whiting-out the main screen. The blast threw everyone on the bridge into sharp relief, many of them with their arms shielding their eyes. If dampeners hadn't been in place, the intense light might have burned out their optic nerves.

As the blast died down, Maddox heard himself say, "Give me a damage report."

124

The data came in fast. It showed that, if nothing else, the bridge personnel knew their business. Smith-Fowler reported an antimatter bomb. That would explain the power of the explosion. The weapons officer suggested a proximity fuse had ignited the bomb, meaning the neutron beam had set it off. The main shield had buckled under the blast but held. If the shield had been at anything less than full strength, though…

Maddox nodded as he glanced at Valerie. A strange feeling of chagrin spread through his chest. It was a foreign sensation, one he intensely disliked. He realized his order might have caused injury to his crew. Valerie's unease had caused him to order a strengthening to the shield.

Maddox forced the words from his mouth. "It's good you spoke up, Lieutenant."

Valerie stared at him in shock. As the shock dwindled, a smile grew. She reached up, hiding the smile with her hand. She positively glowed at the compliment, though.

"Sir," the comm officer said, an Ensign Emily Daggett, a thin woman with an alert bearing.

Victory's electromagnetic shield had kept the worst of the antimatter blast from the crew. The same couldn't be said about the nearest orbital colony near the super-Jupiter. Thousands on an orbital habitat had received severe burns while several hundred were already dead.

"Dead?" Maddox asked.

Ensign Daggett nodded soberly.

A few minutes later, the ensign put Commodore Grossman on the main screen. He was the highest-ranking Star Watch officer in the Tosk CL System.

"What in the hell are you doing over there?" the commodore shouted at Maddox. "This is a populated star system. People are dead because of what you did. Do you realize that?"

Maddox bristled inside, although he appeared calm. "There is a cloaked star cruiser near Tosk V."

"Are you saying the star cruiser fired on us?" Grossman shouted.

"No, sir. They detonated an antimatter bomb."

"That's not what happened," the commodore said. "Your beam caused the explosion. If you hadn't fired at the bomb those people would still be alive."

Maddox leaned forward. "Do you understand what I have told you? A cloaked star cruiser is in the Tosk System."

"I heard you. Did you hear me?"

Maddox stared at the commodore as the commodore stared back.

"Looking at you, I get it," Grossman said angrily. "They said you're half New Man. Now, I know it's true. You don't care about human casualties, do you? You're just as hardhearted as the genetic bastards who invaded us."

Maddox's face heated up. Grossman had insulted him in front of his bridge personnel. Then, a cold feeling settled onto the captain. Something was definitely wrong with him. He reminded himself that he wasn't insensitive to the lost lives. That was a tragedy. Maybe he had made a mistake. Yet, it was the enemy who was ultimately responsible for those deaths. Grossman had a right to his rage. So why did the New Man insult surprise him? Maddox had lived with this for some time.

"Commodore," Maddox said, forcing himself to speak calmly, "I request your assistance in pinpointing the cloaked star cruiser. If the New Men are attempting another invasion, picking the Tosk CL System for a recon mission..."

On the screen, Commodore Grossman grew pale. He nodded curtly with new understanding in his eyes. "I'll help. I'll... Perhaps I shouldn't have said what I did."

"We have a ruthless enemy, Commodore. To defeat him..." Maddox decided it was better to let the aphorism go unsaid.

"I guess our enemy wanted the antimatter bomb to go off to help cover his escape," Grossman muttered. "Maybe he would have activated it if you hadn't fired at it."

Yes. That seemed logical. Maddox should have already seen that. It was yet another reason to discover the source of this mental cloudiness.

The commodore signed off. Shortly thereafter, every Star Watch asset in the system strained to find the cloaked star cruiser. All the while, *Victory* continued toward the next Laumer-Point.

126

"I doubt the star cruiser is following us now," Valerie said.

Maddox wondered about that. Had the androids aboard *Victory* sent secret signals to the enemy? Were there any more androids on the starship? How many cloaked star cruisers were there? As far as Maddox knew, Strand owned the only one. Did that mean the oldest human in existence was following them? That hardly made sense. Shouldn't Strand be at the Throne World, helping the New Men rearm with disruptor beams?

Maddox stood. It was time to go on the offensive against these secret intruders on *his* ship. Maybe he wasn't as mentally sharp—he was going to do something about that! Before he'd been a Patrol officer, he'd been a Star Watch Intelligence operative. It was time to play the game he knew and root out his hidden foes.

The captain wanted to pace but forced himself to sit at the head of the conference table at the special meeting he'd called.

Instead of the senior ship officers, he met with Valerie, Riker, Keith, Meta and Galyan. He could trust these five more than he could any of the others. After the incident with Marine Sergeant Hank Towns, Maddox believed anyone could be an android.

"I realize there must only be a few more androids on the ship," Maddox said. "Yet, the fact two could successfully kidnap me implies they had help."

"What exactly happened to you?" Meta asked. "We haven't had time for you to tell us."

Maddox told them now, going into detail, wondering if he'd missed something important. In the past, he'd primarily relied upon himself. With this cloudiness, he took the others a little deeper into his confidence. It wasn't enjoyable. He preferred the lone wolf approach to problems.

"I agree there must be more androids aboard," Galyan said. "I have just finished analyzing their kidnapping methods. The flickering lights were a symptom of powerful electromagnetic frequencies surging through the area. Those surges kept me from noticing that I'd lost contact with you, Captain."

"Just a minute," Valerie said. "We have to consider the fact that androids kidnapped our captain." She turned to Maddox. "They planned to alter your memories, sir. How…how do we know the androids haven't done that before?"

Everyone stared at Maddox.

Could that be the reason for his cloudiness? Had the androids already altered his thinking?

"What are you suggesting?" Riker asked the lieutenant.

"I don't mean any disrespect, sir," Valerie told Maddox. "But how do we know you're still capable of being captain?"

Meta bristled. "Who else should be the captain?"

"No one else," Valerie said. "I'm just asking a question. Has someone tampered with the captain's mind? If so, what does that mean for the rest of us?"

"I have studied the captain," Galyan said.

Maddox raised his hand while shaking his head.

Valerie looked back and forth from Galyan to Maddox. "Why has Galyan studied you, sir? We have a right to know."

Maddox did not agree. It was one thing to fully confide in Galyan. Could he confide fully in his family? He'd always relied on his excellence to see him through. He wasn't like everyone else. Normal people were envious of him, hating his difference. His excellence had been his shield. To lose that shield…

"I've been feeling tired lately," Maddox said, knowing he had to say something. "It really isn't worth talking about. I asked Galyan to monitor me for a bit… The AI is giving me a medical examination, if you will."

"Tired in what way?" Valerie asked. "Are you feeling overworked?"

"Lieutenant, when I want—"

"Sir," Valerie said. "Please forgive me for interrupting you. But regulations call for a thorough mental and physical examination by the ship's senior medical officer if any of the senior crew feels that the captain is acting suspiciously."

"Thank you for informing me," Maddox said.

"I can request the senior medical officer to give you a mental examination, sir."

Maddox held Valerie's gaze as a dull ache began behind his eyes. He finally massaged his eyes. As he did so, an animal-like intensity at being trapped took hold.

"Maybe you need a rest, sir," Valerie said.

Maddox took his fingers from his eyes. He hated that he'd shown weakness just now. This would be the last time he'd allow himself such a luxury. He would solve his dilemma, doing whatever he had to. If the Spacers had done something to him…

"What I *need* is a way to test the crew without lowering morale," Maddox said. "We must find the remaining androids before they strike again. If Marine Sergeant Hank Towns could be an android…"

"He fooled me," Riker said.

"You still haven't told us why Galyan has been observing you," Valerie said.

"Lieutenant, I am not in the habit of explaining myself to anyone."

Valerie glanced at the others. Finally, she said in a pleading voice, "This is different, sir. This is the greatest Patrol vessel in Star Watch. We have a responsibility to one another—"

"*Lieutenant*," Maddox said, bringing her up short. "If you wish to make a recommendation to the senior officers, you are welcome to do so. Until then, you will follow my orders to the letter. Is that understood?"

"Yes, sir," Valerie muttered. "Doesn't anyone else notice the captain is acting strangely?" she asked the others.

No one responded.

Valerie waited a few seconds longer, finally folding her arms and looking away.

"I have an idea about the androids," Riker said.

Maddox nodded for the sergeant to continue.

"Make up a space fever of some kind," the sergeant said. "Give it an exotic name. That always seems to help. The new space fever means everyone has to undergo a thorough examination. Maybe that even means a few armed Marines in the examination room. We say the fever can make people do strange things."

"Yes," Maddox said. "Meta, I want you to oversee the screening."

"Gladly," Meta said.

"What about the doctors?" Valerie said. "They'll know we're making it up."

"Yes," Maddox said. "We'll have to tell them. Lieutenant, I want you to oversee the scheduling. Keep a lookout for slackers. The androids will undoubtedly do everything they can to avoid the examination."

"What about sabotage?" Valerie asked. "Maybe the androids will try to destroy *Victory* once they realize we know there are more aboard."

"We'll test the Marines first," Maddox said. "We need a core of combat specialists to help us corral the androids. This is the perfect time for a red-alert drill. Until we've tested everyone, we'll travel under battle conditions."

"That's going to put everyone on edge," Valerie said, "especially if we're on red alert too long."

"Better a little strain than the androids remain free," Maddox said.

Valerie looked as if she wanted to add something more. Finally, she stared at the table, remaining quiet.

"I have a question," Keith said.

Maddox nodded.

"What's going on with the Spacer in detention?" Keith asked. "Who is she?"

"Shu 15," Maddox said.

"Why is she here?"

Maddox noted the pilot's eagerness. He thought about commenting on it and finally shrugged. Shu had been in detention for some time. Maybe it was time to see her.

It was odd now that he thought about it. He would have thought he'd gone to see Shu before this. Had he delayed for some unknown reason? The idea was disconcerting. He wondered if that meant she had something to do with his cloudiness.

Maddox rose abruptly, ending the meeting. He held Riker back and told Galyan to come see him in a few minutes.

"What's up, sir?" Riker asked, once the others had filed out.

"We have a possible situation," Maddox told him.

"Of what nature, sir?"

"The Spacer," Maddox said. "I'm beginning to wonder if she's behind the androids."

"Sir?"

"It's time to devise our plan of attack."

-22-

Galyan reappeared in the conference chamber.

"I am still working on discovering the android's kidnapping methods," the holoimage said. "The surges baffle me as to how that could have severed our connection without my noticing."

"We have another priority," Maddox said. "It concerns Shu 15. Do you have any theories as to what her internal devices do?"

Galyan blinked rapidly before saying, "I have been analyzing my initial scan of them and have come to several conclusions. I believe one device is a power source."

"I thought they both ran off her bodily electrical discharges," Maddox said.

"That is true," Galyan said. "I suspect one of the processes acts as a disguise as to the true nature of the device. My calculations lead me to believe the one is a power source for the other."

"What does the other do?"

"I suspect several functions. One of those functions is likely detection. That was how Shu knew the hidden New Man was about to attack you while aboard the *Marius III*. Another function is to send impulses."

"Impulses of what nature?" Maddox asked.

"I have begun to believe the device affects neural connections in the brain."

"In the Spacer's brain?" Maddox asked.

"Yes."

"What about in other people's brains?"

"Yes. There too."

"Could the device have worked against my brain?" Maddox asked.

"The present differences in your brain are minute."

"But you have noticed differences?" Maddox asked.

Galyan blinked rapidly. "Yes, sir, I have."

"Why haven't you told me about this before now?"

"The differences are minute, hardly noticeable. I doubt they could have affected you in the manner you've described to me."

"Yet I've told you I've been affected. There is a difference in my brain, slight as it may be. Shu's internal device might be capable of having caused that. Are you beginning to see why I'm upset with you?"

"I am," Galyan said. "It is perplexing. I do not understand why I hadn't informed you earlier. It is possible someone has tampered with my AI core."

Galyan's eyelids fluttered faster than ever. "Yet I do not detect any internal tampering. The only possibility is that the probability of the tiny neural differences in you did not rise high enough for me to feel it worthwhile to inform you."

"I have a question, sir," Riker said.

Maddox turned to the sergeant.

"Why would the Spacers want to alter anything about you, however slight?"

"I have no idea," Maddox said. "Galyan, if the Spacers did as you suggest—"

"I have not suggested the Spacers did anything to your neural connections, sir," Galyan said, interrupting. "I have merely pointed out that it is an extremely slight possibility they did so. I am still unconvinced this is the answer to your worry."

Maddox tapped his chin as he studied the holoimage. "Very well," he said. "Let us suppose the Spacers have minutely altered my neural connections. Is the situation reversible?"

"I do not know," Galyan said.

"How could Shu's device stimulate my brain neurons so they fire normally?"

"I have no way of knowing that with one hundred percent assurance unless I tested the device."

"Wouldn't you first have to cut it out of the Spacer to do that?" Riker asked.

"Yes," Galyan said.

Maddox became thoughtful.

"Maybe you could convince the Spacer to stimulate your neural connections," Riker told the captain.

"Supposing I could convince her," Maddox said. "What would prevent her from doing the reverse any time she wanted?"

"Nothing, I suppose," Riker said.

"Yes…" Maddox said.

"I just thought of something, sir," Riker said. "You said something about the androids acting a wee bit dumber than ordinary. Could the Spacer have caused that?"

Maddox examined Riker in wonder. "Galyan, what do you think of that?"

"Yes," the holoimage said. "It is theoretically possible."

It shocked Maddox that he hadn't already seen the possibility. That was the final straw.

"Galyan," Maddox said. "I'm going to question Shu. The sergeant will join me. You will monitor her the entire time. If she attempts to use her internal devices, you will direct sonic blasts at her until she falls unconscious."

"What about you, sir?" Galyan asked. "You'll be in the same room with her."

"I can take care of myself. You simply render the Spacer unconscious if she uses her internal devices."

"I'm still not one hundred percent certain her device did anything to your neural fibers," Galyan said.

"What is your percentage of certainty?"

"I now give it a seven percent probability, sir," Galyan said.

"We'll go with that," Maddox said dryly. He glanced at each of them in turn. "Let's go."

***

A cell door buzzed. Maddox pushed through with Sergeant Riker following him.

Tiny Shu 15 sat at a table in an otherwise bare room. This wasn't her regular cell. Two Marines had brought her into the interrogation chamber several minutes ago.

"Hello," Maddox said, as he pulled out the only other chair, sitting down across from her.

The sergeant leaned against the closed door.

"Hello, Captain," Shu said cheerfully.

If the prolonged stay in detention bothered her, it didn't show. In fact, she looked as good as ever. Her clothes even had a freshly laundered quality. Her features were sharp and her demeanor pleasant.

"I trust the food has been adequate," Maddox said.

"You took the time to give me Spacer cuisine," Shu said. "I appreciate that, Captain. I have to admit, though, that I am surprised you've taken so long to see me. But I'm sure you had your reasons. Are we almost to the Xerxes System?"

"I don't recall telling you we were headed there."

"You didn't," she said.

Maddox waited, betraying nothing.

"But it's the obvious move for Starship *Victory*," Shu said.

"Is that why the Visionary wanted you to come along?" Maddox asked.

"Of course," Shu said.

"Then you admit that your fall from the airship wasn't an accident."

"I staged it, yes."

Maddox hid his surprise, although he recognized her change of behavior. She no longer acted like a fawning maiden but more like the Provost Marshal he remembered from Shanghai.

"It finally makes sense why the Visionary didn't request your body," Maddox said.

"Captain," Shu said. "I've just admitted we staged the incident so you would take me along. Not only you but also all humanity needs me on Starship *Victory*. This is the most important mission you've ever taken."

"More important than finding the Builder's Dyson sphere?" asked Maddox.

"Considerably more important," Shu said.

"Or stopping the alien Destroyer?"

"Maybe not as important as that," Shu said. "Still, this is a critical voyage."

"Why?"

"I can't tell you yet. But I do hope my candor makes you realize that you can trust me implicitly."

"I realize nothing of the kind," Maddox said.

"Hmm," Shu said. "I was afraid of that. Tell me..." She hesitated for a long moment before finally asking, "Have you undergone any unusual incidents yet?"

"What kind of incidents?"

"Captain, must we beat around the bush? You must trust me."

"Trust is a two-way street, Provost Marshal."

Shu looked down at her hands. "I'm not a Provost Marshal, as I'm sure you've already divined."

Maddox leaned back. He hadn't expected any of this. Could Shu realize that he suspected the Spacers had tampered with his mind? Was that why she'd admitted to her mission? Had she done so in order to divert him?

"What is your exact title?" he asked.

"I am a First Class Surveyor."

"What does that mean?"

"I'm a special agent," Shu said, "a cross between a Patrol officer and an Intelligence operative."

"Like me."

"I'm not *di-far*, but otherwise that's true."

"You're sticking to the *di-far* idea?" Maddox asked.

"Oh yes. You are unique, Captain. It is one of the reasons the Visionary wanted me to join your expedition."

"What are the other reasons?"

Shu leaned forward, speaking earnestly, "Captain, I promise to explain everything in time. But I can't afford to just yet. I have to know your plan. Otherwise, I can't counsel you properly."

"That isn't a serious proposal," Maddox said. "You want me to tell you our plans but you'll keep yours secret from us."

Shu looked away, nodding after a time. "I see your dilemma. It's a keen one. But human survival rests on our making the right decisions. The Swarm, the New Men—if you guess wrong or..."

"Veiled references don't impress me," Maddox said. "I suspect that more is going on than I realize or maybe even understand. For instance, you have Builder devices inside you."

Shu held herself perfectly still. Then, her head swiveled around until her goggles aimed at him.

"I could have the devices removed," Maddox said.

Shu's features tightened.

"I need to know exactly what they do," Maddox said.

Shu said nothing.

Maddox tapped a finger on the table. "What did the Visionary do to me on the Spacer airship?"

"I don't know what you're talking about," Shu said.

Maddox smiled briefly. A shark would have smiled more kindly. "I am going to have your devices removed from you, Surveyor First Class."

"That would be a sinister act," Shu said. "I'm sorry, but I cannot conceive of you as an agent of evil."

"Conceive of me as you wish. Someone tampered with my mind. That was a heinous accomplishment. I have come to believe that either you or the Visionary were responsible. Galyan is reasonably certain that he can learn to control your devices. Once he does so, he will counteract your neural sabotage—"

"Captain, please, these are reckless charges. I am your friend, probably the best one you've had in some time."

"Then tell me truthfully, Surveyor, did a Spacer tamper with my mind?"

Shu peered at him through her goggles. "Who leapt before the New Men's assassin aboard the hauler, taking the full blast of his gun's discharge?"

"You did that," Maddox said.

"You never even thanked me."

"Thank you," Maddox said.

"You're quite welcome. I think that should be sufficient to prove my good intentions toward you. I could have died."

"Is that so?" Maddox asked drily.

"You think the Spacers are in league with the New Men?"

"It's possible."

"Please, Captain, that's ridiculous. The Spacers loathe the New Men as creatures of Strand and Ludendorff. The New Men are abominations."

"That would make me an abomination, too," Maddox said.

"No! That's not true. You're *di-far*. You're—"

Maddox slapped the table, stopping her flow of words. "Did the Spacers tamper with my mind?"

Shu hesitated, finally nodding.

"The Visionary did so?"

"No."

"You did it?" Maddox asked.

"It was for your own good," Shu said.

Maddox exhaled. "Can you reverse the process?"

"It's possible."

"A moment, please," Maddox said, standing. He motioned Riker out of the way and exited the cell. After closing the door, he summoned Galyan.

The holoimage appeared before him.

"I'm going to modify my former order," Maddox said. "You will monitor the Builder devices in her as she adjusts my condition."

"You don't want me to use a sonic blast?"

"Not unless you feel she is attempting further harm," Maddox said.

"I understand."

Maddox expanded his chest. Knowingly letting another tamper with his mind… After this was over, he would make sure Shu could never do this to him again.

Without another word, Maddox reentered the room, sitting back down across from Shu.

"Can you use your Builder devices to fix my alteration?" he asked.

Shu nodded.

"If you practice further harm—"

"Captain, the process was never intended to harm you."

"Lowering my mental acuity wasn't a personal assault upon me?"

"You view it as a New Man would," Shu said. "I find that telling and chilling."

Maddox sliced a hand through the air. "You will undo your damage this instant."

Shu nodded, composing herself. Once she appeared ready, the Spacer took a deep breath. She held that pose for some time. Finally, she stirred, suddenly looking exhausted.

"It is done," she whispered.

Maddox didn't feel any different.

"I had to alter you earlier," Shu said. "You might understand why some day."

"What exactly did you do?"

"It was a tiny neural blockage," Shu said. "It's very technical. But in any case, now that I've shown my good will by reversing—"

"Captain," Galyan said, appearing beside the table. "The Spacer has just practiced a deception upon you. She used her Builder devices, the one powering the other, but nothing happened in your cerebral cortex."

"That's a lie," Shu said.

The holoimage regarded her with outrage. "I do not lie. I have stated fact." Galyan turned to Maddox. "Sir, I no longer give it a seven percent probability that her interior device did anything to your brain. In fact—"

"Just a minute," Maddox said. He spun around on the chair. "Do you hear that?" he asked Riker.

"My hearing isn't what it used to be, sir," the sergeant said.

Maddox stood fast, causing the chair to fall back. In the same motion, he drew his long-barreled pistol.

"I hear gunfire," the captain said. "It's coming from inside the detention area."

-23-

Maddox burst through the cell door to the sound of gunfire down the hall. Riker followed close behind.

"Make sure the door's locked," the captain said.

Riker pushed until the heavy cell door clicked shut.

The sound of gunfire had been consistent the entire time. A man roared in pain. More shots rang out. The yelling stopped abruptly.

"What's going on, sir?" Riker hissed.

"My guess," Maddox said, "is androids. Keep behind me, Sergeant."

"Sir," Riker said, hurrying to keep up with Maddox. "I only have a stunner."

"Set it at max."

"It already is. I'm just saying. If they have combat armor—"

"Aim for the head."

"Will a stun shot hurt an android?" Riker asked.

"We will undoubtedly discover the truth soon enough."

They passed an open door into a rec room but continued down the hall. The sounds of gunfire had stopped. Boots struck the decking as people approached.

Maddox knelt in the hall, raised his long-barreled gun— holding it with both hands—and fired as the first Marine came around the corner.

The captain blew the Marine's head apart. It wasn't easy, as a hard alloy protected the brainpan. Maddox had special rounds, though, meant for maximum penetration.

Maddox fired fast but deliberately. He wasn't sure how many androids had fought their way into the detention center. He only had so many rounds in a magazine and had to make sure each counted.

After the third android catapulted off its feet, blown backward by the shots, Maddox used his thumb to eject the spent magazine onto the floor. He slammed another into the handle.

A fourth Marine rounded the corner. This one held an assault carbine with both hands, spraying bullets.

Maddox had already fallen prone onto the floor. The same couldn't be said for Riker. Two bullets struck the older sergeant. One ricocheted off his bionic arm. The other struck his chest, making him grunt painfully. Riker also fell, which likely saved him from further damage.

The Marine continued to fire until his carbine clicked empty. The man, or android, didn't attempt to reload. He raced at Maddox as the captain tried to align his gun from the floor. The Marine was already in the process of swinging the carbine, gripping it by the barrel. The stock connected with the long-barreled gun and swatted it out of the captain's hands.

The pistol struck the wall. Because of momentum, the carbine swung up like a bat. Maddox surged forward. The Marine tried to swing the carbine back down on the captain. Maddox connected first, tackling the Marine by the knees, hurling him off his feet.

The Marine struck the deck hard. He seemed heavier than a man. Maddox was certain he fought an android. The thing would have tremendous strength if it were anything like the other androids he'd faced.

The android's knees lunged upward, striking the captain's chest. Maddox didn't fight it. He allowed the thing's knees to catapult him over its head. As Maddox landed, he tucked and rolled.

"You had your chance," the android said.

Maddox stopped rolling, shooting to his feet and twisting around. The android had also twisted around, climbing up. The captain dove, but he didn't dive at the android. Instead, Maddox lunged for his pistol that lay on the floor. The android kicked it, sending the pistol skidding away. Then, the android drew its foot back to kick again.

"No," Shu said. She stood by the open door to her cell, calmly observing the scene.

The android spied her over its shoulder, and its demeanor changed. "You," it said.

"Don't do it," Shu told the android.

The fake Marine tried to move at her, but it seemed confused. "What's wrong with me?" he asked.

Shu didn't answer. She had become wan, with her lower lip trembling as if she exerted effort.

Maddox wasn't sure he understood, but he didn't have to. He scrambled across the hall, reaching his gun. By the time he stood up and faced the android—it still stood in the same spot, frowning, appearing to try with all its might to move.

Shu appeared to glance at Maddox. That broke the tableau. The android rushed her.

Maddox raised his pistol. For an awful moment, he debated holding his fire. The android had almost reached Shu.

Maddox began firing. He didn't aim at the back of the android's head. He pumped bullets into the android's shoulders just below the neck. He wanted to incapacitate the thing, not kill it. He wanted one of these creatures alive for questioning.

Just before reaching the Spacer, the android crumpled onto the floor. It twitched and smoked and then froze in its last position.

-24-

It was an hour after the android assault upon the detention center. Nine Star Watch Marines had died defending the facility. Four more of the pseudo-men had perished, making a total of six androids aboard *Victory*.

The starship was on lockdown, with specially vetted Marine teams prowling the corridors.

Riker was in emergency undergoing surgery. He wasn't in critical condition, but he was seriously hurt.

Maddox had returned to the detention cell with Shu 15. Meta stood against the door this time. She stood there as an assassin, armed to the teeth, ready to kill Shu or more androids if they were foolish enough to try this again.

Galyan watched unseen.

Shu sat at her spot, with her hands on the table. "Will the sergeant recover?" she asked.

Maddox studied her but didn't answer. He recalled Shu as the Provost Marshal in the Lin Ru Hotel in Shanghai. She had attempted to kill him back then with a ruthlessness he'd seldom seen elsewhere. That was the real Shu 15, of that he was certain. He felt foolish having believed the other Shu in Normandy, France and while aboard the Spacer airship.

"Why shouldn't we remove your Builder devices?" Maddox asked.

"That would be a serious overreaction for one thing," Shu said. "For another, you're going to want me to have these modifications when the time comes."

"Would you care to be more precise?"

"Not at this time," Shu said.

Maddox studied the Spacer. He let his mind rove concerning her. He was missing something. His mind had clouded, but it would appear the Spacer and her Builder devices had nothing to do with that. Otherwise, she would have righted her wrong when she'd had the opportunity. Galyan said she'd used her internal devices. What had she done then?

"You called the androids with your devices," Maddox said. "That's why they attacked."

"On the contrary, I attempted to stop them from attacking."

"If you knew they were attacking, why didn't you warn us?"

"I didn't realize they'd gotten so near. Otherwise, I would have done exactly that. I made a mistake. I'm sorry. It's..." She squeezed her hands on the table as if burdened by her supposed lack of decision.

"What are you?" Maddox asked.

Shu looked up, shaking her head. "I don't understand the question."

"Are you human?"

"Captain, please, I'm more human than you are."

"Yet..." Maddox said. "You are Builder-modified."

"Several degrees removed Builder-modified," Shu corrected.

"By that, I take it to mean you've never met a Builder."

"That is correct."

"Thus, a Builder didn't personally modify you. That's what you mean by several degrees removed."

Shu nodded.

"However..." Maddox tapped the table.

Shu raised her eyebrows.

"I'm not quite ready to make any specific conjectures about the Spacers. Sometime in the past, though, you, meaning Spacers, stumbled onto Builder technology. Perhaps you weren't even Spacers yet when those people made the discovery. What you found in the Builder treasure trove turned your originators into the Spacers."

"You have quite an imagination, Captain."

Maddox leaned back. "I fail to understand your angle in all this. You appear to want my help."

"I do want it, just as you're going to want mine. There is balance in that."

He nodded. "Yet you won't enlighten me about anything. I am of two minds concerning you. The first desires to order the surgery."

"I can't stop you," Shu said.

"The second is to order you into suspended animation."

"I'll take the third option," Shu said.

"You'll have to earn the third option."

Shu smiled faintly. "Shall I tell you why that isn't so?"

"Please," Maddox said.

"Your curiosity will prevent options one and two. That leaves option three."

Maddox shook his head. "If you fail to answer my most fundamental questions to my satisfaction, I will leave your fate in Meta's hands."

"I don't believe you," Shu said.

"Believe as you wish. I will begin the interrogation now. How was my mind clouded?"

"You speak in the past tense," Shu said. "Has your mind returned to normal?"

Maddox drummed his fingers on the table, waiting.

Shu also waited.

"Let me instruct you in a truism," Maddox said. "I will not knowingly allow a Trojan horse on my starship. Your Builder devices give you abilities. Those abilities continue to remain unknown. I suspect you called the androids to free yourself. That led to the deaths of six of my people."

"You know that's false. I never called them. In fact, I saved your life from the last android as he was about to slay you. That was an observable fact, impossible for a realist like you to refute."

"I have also begun to believe that you've tampered with Galyan," Maddox said. "I have had my fill of people tampering with the AI on my ship. I will not let another Builder-centric person do likewise."

"Captain, I have proven my good will—"

146

Maddox's chair scraped across the floor as he turned it around to face Meta. "Are you ready to pronounce your verdict?"

"I am," Meta said flatly.

Maddox nodded to her.

"Surgically remove the Builder items from the Spacer," Meta said. "It's the only way to be certain. Otherwise, someone could come along and thaw her out. Then, we'll be right back where we started."

"I don't believe you're serious," Shu said.

"That is your prerogative," Maddox told Shu. He stood. "I will talk to you again after the surgery."

He headed for Meta and the door.

"I earned the two devices through exacting studies and labor across the years," Shu said loudly. "It is a great honor to bear them. Would you strip me of that?"

Maddox didn't turn around to answer. Instead, he snapped his fingers as if to say, "I'll do it like that."

Meta opened the door, going through. Maddox didn't hesitate as he followed her.

"Wait!" Shu shouted.

Maddox paused, although he didn't turn around. His meaning was clear. This was Shu's last chance.

"I kissed you," Shu whispered.

Maddox's jaw tightened. Did she appeal to his chivalry?

"That's when I applied the toxin," Shu said. "It was on my lips. I transferred it to you."

Maddox turned, regarding the Spacer.

"It was a slow-acting toxin," Shu said. "It affected your thinking. It's…part of the reason you accepted me. You might have also possibly missed a few things. Clearly, you didn't miss enough of them. I told the Visionary we should give you a stronger dose. She thought the effect might be lasting if we did that. The Visionary refused to risk that because of religious convictions. She believes you're *di-far*."

"You don't?"

"I'm beginning to," Shu said.

"That's an untruth," Maddox said.

Shu gave the faintest of shrugs. "The Visionary is old-school. She believes in the legends. I think we make our own luck and call it the will of the gods. You appear uncommonly lucky, Captain."

"What do your devices do?"

Shu licked her lips. "It's difficult to listen to you blaspheme like that. Maybe I'm more old school than I realize. You shouldn't ask such rude questions."

"Your androids killed some of my people."

Shu bristled. "They're not *my* androids. They belong to Strand or Ludendorff."

"How do you know that to be true?"

"It's self-evident," Shu said.

Maddox smiled faintly.

"I realize you don't believe me."

Maddox held up a hand. "What do your—what should I call them?"

"Adaptations," Shu said.

Maddox raised an eyebrow. Was he supposed to think of the Builder devices as evolutionary changes? That was absurd. The devices weren't adaptations in the slightest.

Shu waited without expression.

"What can you do with your...*adaptations*?" Maddox finally said.

"I mentally hindered the androids who captured you on "E" Deck. Normally, you couldn't have deceived them the way you did."

"I see. Obviously, you know what the androids did. Do your adaptations allow you to see through bulkheads?"

Shu shook her head.

"You must come clean," Maddox said. "It is the only way to avoid surgery."

"You're a barbarian," she said with heat, "a savage."

"I am *di-far*, a man of decision. It would be well for you to remember that."

Tiny beads of perspiration appeared on Shu's forehead. It caused Maddox to wonder if she'd been lying earlier. Shu had said she didn't believe in the old ways. It would appear she did.

It would also appear she really believed he was *di-far*. Why would she have lied about that?

"For short periods of time I can utilize transduction," Shu said in a monotone.

Maddox shook his head.

"At those times I have the ability to see electromagnetic radiation and electromagnetic wavelengths and process the data as fast as a computer."

"You hijacked the ship's monitoring images?" Maddox asked.

"Crudely stated, but correct," Shu said.

"Thus, you saw the kidnapping androids through the ship's monitors, through its security cameras."

"Yes."

"What else can you do?" Maddox asked.

"You've spoken about the androids' mental dullness. That was due to me. I interfered with their neural connections."

Imperceptibly, Maddox leaned toward her. "Can you do that to humans?"

Shu shook her head.

"Are you lying?"

"No."

"How can I know you're telling the truth?" Maddox asked.

"You'll have to trust your instincts."

Maddox inhaled as he pondered the situation. "How can I block your adaptations from affecting those on my ship?"

"Powerful scramblers will do it, as they'll interfere with the signals."

"Why did you want to come on this particular voyage, Provost Marshal?"

Shu looked away, sighing at last. "One of the reasons was to thwart Strand."

"Do you believe he was in the cloaked star cruiser that followed us in the Tosk CL System?"

"Of course," she said.

"And?"

"I also want to thwart Professor Ludendorff," she added.

"Thwart him from doing what? Using the Nexus?"

"No, not that," Shu said. "I can help you use the Nexus. I…probably know more about it than either of the Methuselah Men. I certainly know more about it than you or anyone else in your crew."

"Let me ask you again. What are you? Who are the Spacers?"

"I am Shu 15, a Surveyor First Class. I am an agent of change, bid to bring about the Golden Age of Man. The Spacers are the children of the gods, seedlings cast into the cold universe to ensure the progress of life in its march against Death."

"Death as in the cessation of the living?" Maddox asked.

"No. Death as in the terrible Swarm Imperium and the Makers of the alien Destroyers."

A cold feeling worked through Maddox. "Do you know the extent of the Swarm Imperium?"

"You've asked me that before. I do not. Like you, the Spacers believed that the Swarm was extinct or at best made up of a few pockets here and there. The knowledge you brought back from the Dyson sphere has changed much. In truth, that knowledge sent a shockwave through the Spacer councils."

"The Spacers want to know the extent of the Imperium just like Star Watch does?"

"We probably want to know more than Star Watch does."

"Why?"

"With greater knowledge comes greater pain," Shu quoted. "We Spacers know more about the wider galaxy than Star Watch does. Rather than bringing us delight, this knowledge threatens us with despair."

"Is that due to knowledge about the Makers of the alien Destroyers?" Maddox asked.

"Partly," Shu said.

"Are the Makers in our galaxy?"

"If I don't know the extent of the Swarm Imperium, how could I know about the Makers?"

"That isn't an answer."

"I have no idea if the Makers are here or not," Shu said. "I rather doubt it. Let us for all our sakes hope they're not."

"Indeed," Maddox said. "Yet you feel the Makers will return to our galaxy?"

"In time," Shu said. "The records show they've already made more than one pass."

Maddox studied her more closely. "What, specifically, are you hoping we find on this voyage?"

"I've already told you that we, like you, want to know how close the Swarm Imperium is to Human Space."

"I know that much. I mean what else are you seeking?"

Shu shrugged. "I don't know what else."

"I don't believe you," Maddox said. "I think you know exactly what you're looking for. I believe you won't tell me because I would be against it." He fell silent, thinking, finally admitting, "I'm not sure what to do with you."

"Try trusting me."

Maddox smiled faintly and glanced back at Meta. "Shall we trust her?"

"No," Meta said.

"There you have it, Provost Marshal," Maddox said. "We lack trust. However, you have answered my primary questions. Thus, I won't order the surgery…yet. I have much to consider. Good day."

"Are you letting me out of detention?" Shu shouted.

He faced her while standing on the other side of the open door. "No," he said.

"I'm sick of this confinement."

"No doubt," Maddox said. "But it's better than your alternative." He shut the door.

"Well?" Meta asked.

"I need to think about this," Maddox said.

"She didn't tell us everything she can do with those devices," Meta said.

Maddox didn't reply, as that was obvious. Instead, he took Meta by the arm and led her down the corridor. Why did Shu 15, a Spacer with Builder adaptations, hate the Methuselah Men, Builder-modified beings? It was perplexing, which actually delighted the captain—now that he knew, or was fairly certain anyway, that the cloudiness was departing his mind.

He'd been born to solve puzzles such as these and to test himself against worthy opponents. It would seem that Shu had become something of an enigma.

-25-

Keith Maker sat in medical, clicking pages on his tablet. He read a PUA (pickup artist) book on scoring with chicks. According to this, girls used a guy in the friend zone. It was called being a White Knight, doing things for the ladies in the hope they'd notice you as dating material.

He couldn't believe it. Here was a pic of a guy painting a girl's toenails. Oh boyo, this was terrible. Here was a Tom carrying a girl on his shoulders while she kissed another taller man. Look at the scowl on the White Knight's face.

Keith never wanted to be the loser carrying a woman on his shoulders while she kissed someone else. That was pathetic. He wanted to be the other guy.

So far, according to this, women liked the dangerous Toms, the alpha types, the jerks that did exactly what they wanted to do.

Keith grinned. He was dangerous. No one flew a combat fighter better than he did. He frowned a moment later. How would a woman know he was dangerous? He had to get her inside a strikefighter and let her see him in action.

Those with big muscles had an advantage. Tall men did too. Did that mean he should take up a personal combat art? It probably wouldn't hurt. Maybe he should curl barbells this trip, too.

I will never be a White Knight. I will never be in the friend zone.

153

How could he show Shu 15 that he was an alpha warrior if she stayed locked away in detention the whole trip?

Keith kept reading as Sergeant Riker snored in the bed. Doctors had removed the android's bullet from his chest.

The old bounder needed sleep. There were several tubes in Riker, pumping meds into him, but rest would aid in the healing process.

Ack, this was interesting. The PUA book said a man needed a sense of plenty, as in plenty of women to choose from. According to this, it was poor form having a case of one-itis. If a woman refused your entreaties, it was time to move on to a different lady.

But what if I don't want to move on? Keith wondered. *Do I have one-itis?*

He recalled Shu's wave and the pert way she walked. Keith couldn't help grinning, imagining what he would like to do to Shu. He envisioned them alone, him standing arrogantly, eying her so she understood he was a Highland warrior. He would bend in, kiss her lightly and begin unbuttoning her blouse.

Keith's smile turned lusty as his eyes glazed over. Yes, siree, she was a beauty. She—

Riker groaned.

For a moment, Keith didn't notice. He was too absorbed in his Shu fantasy.

The sergeant groaned again, smacking his lips together.

That jerked Keith out of his fantasy. He laid the tablet on his lap. The old bounder stirred in the bed, his head moving on the pillow. The eyes cracked open and Riker looked around.

Keith set the tablet aside and stood, moving to the railing on the side of the bed. "Aye, mate," he said. "How are you feeling?"

Riker didn't appear to recognize him.

"It's me," Keith said, thumping himself on the chest.

"Where am I?" Riker wheezed.

"What? You're on Starship *Victory*," Keith said. "Where else would you be?"

Riker groaned, using his bionic hand, gently touching his chest. "An android shot me."

"Aye, but you're okay now."

Greater coherence filled the sergeant's eyes. "The thing could have killed me."

"That wasn't bloody likely," Keith said. "The captain was there."

Riker eyed him. "I take it the captain is well?"

"Aye," Keith said. He told Riker what had happened after he went down.

The sergeant glanced at the tubes in his arms and the medical machines keeping watch over his vital signs.

"We've been taking turns," Keith said. "The captain has sat with you at times. You were still out, though."

"How long until I'm fit?" Riker asked.

"Do you want me to get the doctor?"

"Not yet."

Keith's grip tightened on the railing. He shifted from foot to foot.

The sergeant was a clever old dodger. He seemed to notice. "Is something wrong?"

"No. It's just… you know, I'm wondering what she's like."

"Who?"

"Shu 15. You saw her. She's a beauty."

Riker's gaze shifted as he took that in. Finally, the sergeant smiled ruefully.

"What are you grinning about?" Keith asked.

"The woman's a viper," Riker said.

"That can't be true. I saw her. She's a sweet package, and she waved to me. She has a fantastic smile."

"She's a Spacer Intelligence officer," Riker said.

"What blarney are you spewing? You're saying she's a spy?"

"Spies are people that case officers had turned. She's a case officer, a nasty piece of work. Believe me, boy. You don't want anything to do with her."

"That's tripe, mate. You're just saying that to boggle me mind. She looks…nice. I mean, couldn't you blokes have overreacted concerning her?"

Riker half rolled on his bed. Keith let go of the rails, stepping back. The old sergeant pointed at his crotch.

"Don't think with that," Riker said. "Instead, use that." He pointed at Keith's brain.

Keith laughed even as he blushed. "You've never been sweet on a girl before?"

Riker collapsed back onto his back. He sighed wistfully. "I've known a woman or two."

"I'm betting it was more like dozens of ladies," Keith said.

Riker glanced at him.

"You must have been a Highlander with the ladies in the old days," Keith said.

Riker appeared surprised.

"You probably had a string of 'em eager to get with you."

Riker glanced at him before staring up at the ceiling.

"You're not feeling well?" Keith asked.

"Shu isn't for you."

Keith bristled. "Why do you say such a thing? Do you think she's too much for me?"

"Find a good woman," Riker said. "Marry her. It isn't about how many women you screw. It's about finding one worth having. I never did, and that was my loss. It's hard to find a good woman. Rutting like animals doesn't help you find her. Finding a woman of quality is the key."

"How do you propose I do that?"

Riker sighed. "If I knew, I would have done it myself."

"Maybe you're right. But I'm thinking... How do you say it? A hot babe is critical, the hotter the better. I mean, why else bother?"

Riker glanced at him again. "She's a user. Remember that. If the captain ever lets her out of detention and she shows an interest in you, know that it's because she's planning to use you."

"I'm not a White Knight, mate."

Riker appeared perplexed.

"I'm an alpha on the prowl."

"I'm tired," Riker said. "And some of the things you say make me realize how old I am. I'm going back to sleep."

"You're going to be okay, Sergeant. You hang in there, mate."

Riker had already closed his eyes, and he was beginning to snore.

Keith picked up his tablet. The Spacer honey was a user, eh? He would remember that. Still, the way she'd shaken her tush at him...

The lieutenant headed for the exit, with his eyes half-lidded. He reentered his fantasy where he was unbuttoning her blouse. He actually shivered with delight as he thought about reaching for her bra. She was the sweetest woman on the starship, and one way or another, Keith planned to make her his darling.

Maddox found the next few days hectic but productive. Even better, the Spacer toxin had finally lost its potency. He felt like himself again, his mind like a razor.

The medical teams finished examining each crewmember. Everyone was exactly as he or she appeared to be. Human. That meant six androids had made it onto *Victory* but no more.

The detention center attack had been their last hurrah as they'd tried to assassinate Shu 15. Maddox couldn't conceive of any other reason for the assault.

With Andros Crank's help, Maddox installed powerful scramblers around Shu's chamber. Would they prevent her from using her Builder devices to read transmissions?

Andros had his doubts. The Kai-Kaus was a stout man, wheezing most of the time. "These are human-built scramblers," he explained to Maddox. "The Spacer possesses Builder items. Everyone on the Dyson sphere knew that Builder-built was always superior to anything else."

"But if the scramblers overload her processor—"

"Captain," Andros said. "According to you, she spoke of transduction. She can see radiation; see wavelengths. I imagine she could pick out the right wavelength with ease. These scramblers might force her to take a little longer looking for the right bandwidth. I doubt they will do anything else."

"How do we blind her then?"

Andros shook his long gray hair. "Don't use electrical-based equipment to transfer your ideas. Perhaps the better barrier would be to let her know the holoimage watches to see if she uses her items. When they're active, Galyan knows. However, she must already realize this. I suspect she will limit her use for a time, if for no other reason than to attempt to throw you off the scent."

Maddox didn't like that. But what else could he do? He tried speaking to her again.

Shu had become like the ancient sphinx, though. She said nothing other than, "Let me out of here."

They both knew he wouldn't do that. She was waiting for something. He asked her about Spacer customs in order to get her talking. She didn't bite. He asked how the Spacers had originally found the Builder tech. She remained stoically silent.

When Maddox mentioned her silence on the bridge one day, an informal discussion began. It started when Andros Crank suggested they put Shu in a lifeboat and leave her.

"She is a danger, Captain," Andros said. "She lacks loyalty to our communal effort. Good men and women have already died because of her silence. She means us harm. That is my firm conviction."

"I agree, sir," Valerie said. "Remember when the professor took over the starship? He used Builder items to do it that trumped ours. Do the scramblers really hinder Shu?"

Maddox glanced at Andros for confirmation. The Kai-Kaus shrugged before looking away.

"Valerie and Andros are right," Meta added.

Maddox eyed the others as irritation struck. His normal way would be to ignore the lot of them. He was the captain. He would trust his own judgment...

No. That's wrong. I can trust my family. Remember all the times they helped me. With them, I can let my guard down at least a little. Why not explain some of your motivation?

"I know Shu is dangerous," Maddox said. "But consider this. Valerie spoke about the professor. He's always been a threat to the crew, as he always has his own agenda. Worse, he's smarter than we are and has vastly more experience. We're going to pick up the professor in the Xerxes System. That means we'll have two dangerous, Builder-modified people aboard. Yet maybe Shu and Ludendorff will cancel each other out as they plot against one another. If we're going to carry the one, we might as well have the other as the antidote."

At navigation, Valerie squirmed in her seat.

"You have something to add?" Maddox asked.

"Shu used androids toward nefarious ends," Valerie said. "She used a toxin against your mind. The first two androids also planned to modify your thinking. That seems to indicate that they all acted in tandem."

Maddox considered that, although he no longer believed the androids had belonged to the Spacers. Galyan had already attempted to dissect the captured android brains. They had each melted down just like the captured androids that had tried to overthrow the Commonwealth a year ago. That showed these androids likely came from the Builder base at the bottom of the Atlantic Ocean, the same as the others.

He explained that to them.

"I'm not an Intelligence officer," Valerie said. "But the Atlantic Builder base proves the Spacers were behind the original android assault. The Spacers have fooled us with their so-called pathologies regarding androids."

"That doesn't hold," Maddox said. "The Atlantic Ocean androids belonged to the Builder in the Dyson sphere. *That* Builder made the Methuselah Men, like Strand and Ludendorff. The Spacers hate those two." He hesitated before adding, "I'm convinced that means we're looking at two different Builders with possibly different goals. The Builder who created the Spacers is different from the one who created Strand and Ludendorff and unleashed the androids. And we all know that Spacers hate androids—that has been one of the few known facts that dates back at least twenty years."

"If Spacers hate androids so much," Valerie said, "why didn't Shu tell us about the ones in our ship? With her adaptations, she must have known androids had snuck aboard."

"Andros?" the captain said.

The Kai-Kaus looked up sharply from his location at engineering.

"Explain that, would you?"

The stout Kai-Kaus scratched one of his fleshy cheeks. "The reason for Shu's silence seems obvious. We would have

160

asked her how she knew about the androids. To convince us, she would have had to explain about her adaptations. Those, she wanted kept secret."

"For those reasons," Maddox said, "Shu stays. Her usefulness seems greater than her danger. Remember, we're attempting the impossible. Thus, we need powerful if dangerous tools to succeed."

Valerie nodded slowly. "If I don't fully agree, at least I understand your thinking. Thank you, sir."

***

Several days later, Maddox sat in the command chair as *Victory* exited the final Laumer-Point, entering the fabled Xerxes System.

The system was like the ancient Bermuda Triangle, home to sinister legends. The alien Destroyer had been parked here before it had launched onto its deadly run. There were a few planets in the system, but the great danger had always been in the artificially constructed asteroid belt. The various rocks and debris were much closer than ordinary, more akin to Saturn's rings than the Solar System's far-flung asteroid belt. The giant silver pyramid known as a Nexus was in the belt, as were hidden silver drone bases. Star Watch vessels carefully searched for more drone bases. Other Star Watch vessels searched for any other hidden anomalies. Those searches were conducted with the utmost caution and over-watch protection.

It wasn't long after *Victory's* exiting of the Laumer-Point that Star Watch Admiral Esmeralda Diaz Lucia Sanchez hailed the ship.

The admiral controlled the flotilla guarding the star system. She had two older *Bismarck*-class battleships, a newer *Python*-class heavy cruiser, two strike cruisers loaded with antimatter missiles and seven old destroyers. Five of those destroyers were presently combing the belt. Several construction vessels were busy building a space station in orbit around the nearest planet.

Maddox knew that Sanchez had strict orders from Lord Admiral Cook to keep well away from the silver pyramid. No one wanted her flotilla entering a suddenly appearing hyper-

161

spatial tube as had happened to Port Admiral Hayes last year. She was also supposed to keep everyone, including Ludendorff, from approaching too closely to the Nexus.

Admiral Sanchez appeared on the main screen with her long dark hair and intensely dark eyes. She was lean, smooth featured, and was almost one hundred years old.

After finishing with the pleasantries, Maddox asked, "Is Professor Ludendorff in the system?"

"He is," Sanchez said.

"I take it he's aboard your flagship," Maddox said.

"On no," Sanchez said. "The professor has refused every invitation. He's in a former luxury yacht, bombarding the Nexus with endless sensor scans."

"He's near the pyramid?"

"As near as I'll allow him. The *Wurzburg* keeps a close eye on the professor, ready with its tractor beam to pull his vessel back if it has to. Currently, both starships are approximately four hundred thousand kilometers from the Nexus."

That was approximately the distance of the Moon from Earth.

"Have you at any time allowed the professor closer than that?" Maddox asked.

"Not on your life."

Maddox felt a little easier hearing that. "Have you spotted any cloaked vessels in the system?"

"None," Sanchez said, becoming curious. "Why do you ask?"

"We detected a cloaked star cruiser following us in the Tosk CL System. Since then, we haven't picked up any more stray signals. Some of us believe the star cruiser might have raced here ahead of us."

"Raced ahead of Starship *Victory*?" Sanchez asked, sounding genuinely surprised.

"I know that sounds improbable."

"More like impossible," Sanchez said.

"If it were any other vessel, I would agree. This is the infamous cloaked star cruiser, however. Its owner is Strand."

"Oh," Sanchez said. "We'll redouble our surveillance efforts. Is there anything else we should know?"

Maddox nodded. "Have any Spacers entered the star system?"

Sanchez's eyes widened. "Why, yes," she said. "We had to order a Spacer convoy out of the system a few weeks ago."

"Was there anything unusual about that?"

Sanchez studied him, seeming suspicious now. "Have you already been in contact with the professor? I've heard rumors about an interstellar communication device. Now I'm thinking these rumors are true"

"I have not been in contact with the professor," Maddox said. "I take it the Spacers had something to do with Ludendorff?"

"The other way around," Sanchez said. "Ludendorff alerted us to their presence. They appeared to have slipped into the system without my pickets having noticed them. It was embarrassing, to say the least, and it still remains perplexing."

"The Spacers didn't use a regular Laumer-Point?"

"I'm not sure they used a Laumer-Point at all. They slipped unseen into the system. How, I don't know. They did leave using a Laumer-Point. Ludendorff had become quite frantic at that point, claiming the Spacers intended him harm. There was one unusual event at the end of the encounter."

Maddox waited.

"The Spacer commander suggested I keep a close eye on Ludendorff."

"Did he say why?"

Sanchez shook her head.

"What did you make of that?" Maddox asked.

"That the Spacer commander knew the professor. The man is brilliant, but I suspect he gets on everyone's nerves after a while. That would include mine."

"Is there anything else I should know, Admiral?"

Sanchez shook her head again. "We're here any time you need us, Captain. All I ask is that you don't unintentionally take us into a hyper-spatial tube with you. I understand...the nature of your assignment. The Lord High Admiral briefed me before I left Earth."

"Thank you for everything, Admiral. We'll begin our acceleration to the asteroid belt. We're going to be going all the way to the pyramid."

"I figured as much. Good luck, Captain, and be careful. This star system…it's haunted. We can all feel it. I'll be glad once my duty here is over."

Maddox made a few polite noises before signing off. Afterward, he instructed the helm to take them toward the belt.

Victory had made it to the Xerxes System, and the professor was waiting for them. Had the Methuselah Man figured out how to break into the Nexus and make it work for them? Just how dangerous was this going to be? And why had Spacers been nosing around? It must have been for the same reason that Shu had wormed her way onto the starship. Would the Spacers dare to attack a Star Watch flotilla? That would be against all their previously known actions.

Maddox stood. "Lieutenant, you have the bridge."

Valerie nodded her assent as Maddox exited the chamber.

Soon, in a gym chamber, he wrapped his fists. He wore a pair of shorts and sparring shoes. His taut muscles visibly tightened and relaxed as he knotted the ties. He slipped leather gloves over that and began to strike a heavy bag.

The captain hit hard, making the bag swing. He was lean like a predator, without an ounce of fat. The growing unease in his stomach tightened. It caused him to become expressionless as his speed increased, and he struck the bag with endless combinations.

During the exhibition, Galyan appeared. The Adok holoimage watched with interest.

"You're quicker than I remember," Galyan said.

Maddox jumped back, surprised by the appearance. He realized he'd become too absorbed with his boxing. Only now did he realize the professor made him…anxious would probably be the right word. Ludendorff always had something up his sleeve.

"I'm quicker?" Maddox asked.

"Fractionally so," Galyan said. "Perhaps in trying to compensate for the Spacer toxin, your body fought back. Now

164

that the toxin has dissipated, you have gained the tiniest bit. Instead of harming you, the Spacers have actually aided you."

The holoimage smiled.

"What now?" Maddox asked.

"Could this have been Shu's true purpose?" Galyan asked. "Was the toxin actually meant as an aid?"

"I doubt it."

"That rings true to form," Galyan said. "My analysis of your personality has shown me that you do not anticipate outside help from anyone."

"That's quite enough," Maddox said.

"I have found that self-examination is a helpful process—"

"Galyan!" Maddox said.

The holoimage stopped talking.

"We will leave off this line of conversation. That is an order."

"Yes, Captain," Galyan said. "Oh. By the way, Professor Ludendorff has a message for you."

"What is it?" Maddox asked guardedly.

"He hopes to meet with you personally before you begin the joint venture to the Nexus."

"Why?"

"He has a favor he wants to ask. He said it is most urgent."

Maddox used his teeth to begin pulling off the leather gloves. Ludendorff wanted a favor. He didn't like the sound of that.

-27-

Many hours later, Lieutenant Noonan was on the bridge, sitting in the captain's chair. On the main screen, she watched a shuttle leave Ludendorff's luxury yacht.

There were plenty of asteroids in the way. Farther off was the Nexus. From here, it was a bright point. In a few minutes, the point would slide behind another asteroid.

Valerie was nervous. Each time they came to the Xerxes System, something unexpected and bad happened.

Ever since entering the system this time, a pressure had begun to build up in her head. It was a subtle feeling of an alien threat. The New Men were bad enough. This felt worse, something *inhuman*.

That bothered her, especially as she tried hard these days to be cheerful. She'd gone to several seminars back on Earth. The speakers suggested that people made their own luck, whether good or bad. If one thought negatively, she created the soil, as it were, for bad seeds to sprout and flourish. If one thought positively, the opposite happened.

Life constantly threw you curves. How you reacted made the difference. And Valerie believed that. She'd always been negative, and bad things always happened to her. Yet, she believed, the captain thought positively, and he'd made it through many disasters. If she was going to make something out of her life, she'd better start thinking positively too.

That was hard, though. Something bad was just waiting to happen. She could feel it, and she knew that she had a sense for these things. The captain always pulled the craziest assignments. Maybe it had something to do with *Victory*. Everyone serving aboard the ancient Adok starship seemed destined for endless bad luck.

Galyan was proof of that. What a terrible existence, to be alive but a ghost of an AI. The Adok's soul had witnessed his race's death. Now, Galyan continued to linger, drawing bad luck onto himself and everyone around him.

Why am I so morbid? We annihilated the Destroyer. We've beaten our enemies each time. We saved humanity from the New Men. How can I call any of that bad luck? We've had fantastic luck each time.

Valerie continued to think positively, fighting against her basic nature. Her dad had been the world's greatest pessimist, complaining about everything. Not that she blamed him. If she'd lost her legs—

"That's strange," said Henry Smith-Fowler, the blond-haired weapons officer.

"What's wrong?" Valerie asked, as worry spiked her chest.

"I just picked up a foreign radiation signature," Smith-Fowler said.

"Where?"

"Between us and the professor's shuttle."

"Zoom in," Valerie said. "I want to see this. I also want you to ready a tractor beam and a neutron cannon."

Smith-Fowler tapped his panel.

The main screen wavered for just a moment. Then, Valerie saw a blue exhaust simply appear and lengthen.

"Why don't I see anything at the front of the exhaust?" she demanded.

"I suspect because the object is cloaked," Smith-Fowler said dryly.

"Beam it."

Smith-Fowler glanced at her before he tapped a control. A neutron beam lashed into existence, stabbing into the starry void.

"Lieutenant," Smith-Fowler said, "I think the hidden object has a distortion field."

"Fire again but this time in a spread," Valerie said. "Lock onto it at the same time with the tractor beam and begin pulling it toward us."

Smith-Fowler manipulated his controls. "I can't lock onto anything because nothing appears to be there."

"By the direction of the exhaust plume, it's headed for the shuttle," Valerie observed.

"Agreed," Smith-Fowler said.

Three more times, the neutron beam slashed into the void. Each time, nothing more happened.

The shuttle began evasive maneuverers while expelling chaff and decoy emitters. Another long blue tail appeared. This one was farther out. It headed for the luxury yacht.

"What's happening?" Valerie shouted. As soon as she did that, she silently berated herself. As acting captain, she had to remain calm. That helped others stay calm.

"Someone must have slipped the stealth objects into position quite some time ago," Smith-Fowler said.

Valerie's heart rate increased. "We have to protect the professor, as he's our key to using the Nexus. Galyan," she called. "I need your assistance."

Nothing happened.

"Galyan!"

At that point, on the screen, the hidden missile with the visible exhaust exploded near the evading shuttle.

Valerie bit a knuckle, straining to see the results. It showed several seconds later as the blast evaporated. The shuttle had become expanding debris. The warhead had destroyed it and surely killed everyone onboard.

The Adok holoimage now appeared on the bridge.

"Take over targeting," Valerie told Galyan.

"You do not have the authority to give me override rights," Galyan said. "That belongs to the captain alone."

"Then call him or go see him," Valerie shouted. "Tell him what's happening."

At that moment, the second missile exploded. This one hadn't made it as close to its target. The blast struck the yacht's shield, turning it a deep shade of red. The shield held, however, and the yacht remained intact.

168

"Are there any more of those things?" Valerie demanded.

"Not that I can detect," Smith-Fowler said, hunched over his panel.

Valerie kept staring at the main screen. Someone had attacked and destroyed the professor's shuttle. What were they going to do if Ludendorff was dead?

Maddox listened to Galyan explain what had happened.

The captain had waited in a room near the selected hangar bay so he could immediately greet Ludendorff. He now sat stoically, considering the possibilities of this latest development.

"You are taking this much more calmly than is your usual wont," Galyan said.

Maddox focused on the holoimage. "This is the Xerxes System, and we're talking about the professor. I expect the unexpected here. I've also learned to distrust the first report of Ludendorff's death. Besides, if there were hidden drones waiting for the professor, I believe he would have known that."

The captain grew thoughtful again. "Have we contacted the yacht yet?"

"Yes. Lieutenant Noonan spoke to Doctor Dana Rich."

"How did Dana take the news?"

"Like you," Galyan said.

Maddox rubbed his chin, concentrating. Soon, he asked, "What were Ludendorff's driving characteristics?"

"He was brilliant," Galyan said promptly.

"And?"

"He was deceptive."

"He also had access to one of the most remarkable tools in Human Space: a long-range communicator. With it, he could send and receive messages across many light years."

"I do not see the connection of the communicator to his death," Galyan said.

"Consider," Maddox said. "Might there be something in the Deep Beyond that neither the Spacers nor the Methuselah Men want the other side to get?"

"You speak as if Strand and Ludendorff are on one side."

"Maybe against the Spacers they are," Maddox said.

"This is interesting," Galyan said. "Please continue."

"The Spacers slipped into the Xerxes System several weeks ago. Admiral Sanchez had to order them out. Now, cloaked weaponry has destroyed Ludendorff's shuttle but failed to destroy his yacht. I think Ludendorff wants us to believe the Spacers attempted to kill him. We will likely discover that he has miraculously survived. The payoff for the professor will be in demanding that Shu go back to Earth."

Galyan's eyelids fluttered. "That would mean someone on Earth told Ludendorff about Shu's coming."

"Thus," Maddox said, "the reason why Ludendorff's long-distance communicator becomes so important."

"How certain are you that this is the actual case?"

"Fifty percent," Maddox said.

"What is the other possibility—in your opinion?"

"That the Spacers really tried to kill the professor," Maddox said. "They don't want any Methuselah Man on the other side of the hyper-spatial tube."

"What is on the other side?" Galyan asked.

"Yes," Maddox said. "That is the question."

The captain put his hands behind his back and began to pace. "Humanity as a whole is stronger because there are more of us. But the others—the Methuselah Men and the chief Spacers—have the advantage of knowledge. Each of them wants to use *Victory* for their own ends. The problem is that we don't know how to use the Nexus on our own. We need one of them in order to use the pyramid."

"This is most perplexing," Galyan said. "I miss the old days when we had just one enemy and it was a matter of velocities and trajectories. It was much simpler then."

"I must return to the bridge," Maddox said to himself. "Come, Galyan."

171

***

A little later, Maddox spoke via screen to Dana from *Victory's* bridge.

The doctor was as beautiful as ever, although her hair was a little longer than before. Dana Rich's features were calm and dusky as she sat in a chair.

"How soon until you can board our yacht?" Dana asked.

"I have no intention of coming aboard," Maddox said. "I suggest you gather your belongings and transfer onto *Victory*."

"To what purpose?" Dana asked. "The voyage is over before it began. Without Ludendorff, we can't use the Nexus."

"That is false," Maddox said. "I have another person aboard *Victory* who possibly knows how to activate the Nexus."

"You can't mean Meta."

Meta had been inside the Nexus once with Kane, a New Man spy. Kane had used the Nexus to jump over one hundred light-years to the Wolf Prime System.

"Ah," Maddox said. "I'd forgotten about Meta. Make that two people who can help me use the Nexus."

"Captain—that's impossible."

"I assure you it isn't."

Dana pursed her lips as she studied him. "I can't come anyway. The professor's death was the final straw. I'm done, Captain."

"Perhaps you'll come aboard for old time's sake," Maddox suggested.

"No. I'm finished. I do have a few items the professor wished you to have. He would have wanted me to give them to you myself."

"Oh. Well, that means you'll have to come onto *Victory*."

"I'm not setting foot on the haunted starship again, Captain. It has too many bitter memories for me."

"That's unfortunate," Maddox said. "I suppose I'll have to forgo getting the late professor's items then, as I have no intention of leaving *Victory* just now."

Valerie swung around, motioning to him.

Maddox ignored the lieutenant.

172

"You can't be serious," Dana said. "These items are priceless."

"You have my condolences," Maddox told the doctor. "If you change your mind, you're welcome aboard. It has been a pleasure knowing you. Good bye, Doctor Rich."

Maddox motioned the comm officer. Ensign Daggett tapped her panel, and the main screen went blank.

"Sir," Valerie said.

Maddox raised a hand. "Hold your thought, Lieutenant. Ensign, put me through to the admiral."

In moments, Admiral Sanchez appeared on the main screen.

"The professor is dead," Maddox said without preamble. "I would dearly appreciate it if you could bring the entire flotilla to my position."

"I can," Sanchez said. "I mean, I will. Do you have a reason?"

"Yes," Maddox said. "Spacers. It appears the hidden missiles were of Spacer origin."

"We haven't determined that yet," Valerie said in the background.

"I am preparing to meet a Spacer ambush," Maddox told the admiral. "But I would like to have your firepower nearby."

"I'm coming at once," Sanchez said, sitting straighter. "We'll be there in thirteen hours. Is there anything else?"

"That will do for now," Maddox said. "Thank you."

The screen went blank.

"Sir?" Valerie asked. "What's going on? You're reacting strangely to the professor's—"

"Save it," Maddox said sternly, interrupting. "I know what I'm doing."

"But..."

He gave Valerie a significant look, one that said, "Trust me."

The lieutenant nodded after a moment.

Maddox settled into his command chair, determined to wait for the others—whoever they were—to make their next move.

173

-29-

Fourteen hours later, Admiral Sanchez joined Starship *Victory* deep in the Xerxes Asteroid Belt.

The battlewagons *Wurzburg* and *Austerlitz* together with the heavy cruiser *Anaconda* made up the heart of the flotilla. Several destroyers remained elsewhere in the system. Otherwise, every Star Watch vessel was here.

During that time, the luxury yacht had remained four hundred thousand kilometers from the Nexus and ten thousand kilometers from *Victory*.

"We're here, Captain," Sanchez said via the main screen.

"We've been using probes and scanning the area since the shuttle's destruction," Maddox said. "So far, we haven't spotted anything else out of the ordinary."

"I've had my people scanning the entire way here," Sanchez said. "I instructed them to search for the patterns you suggested. Like you, we've come up empty. What do you suggest we do now?"

"One of your battleships should dock with the yacht."

"Do you expect something to happen if I do?"

"Yes."

Admiral Sanchez scowled. "Captain..." She glanced to someone off screen and held herself as if listening. Finally, she peered at Maddox again. "As you wish. However, I would appreciate it if you would give me an indication of the danger."

"Cloaked missiles," Maddox said.

174

"Even though we've scanned relentlessly for the past fourteen hours?" asked Sanchez.

"The asteroids are the problem," Maddox said. "It's too easy to hide behind an asteroid, popping out at the last minute."

"Yes. I see your reasoning," Sanchez said. "But why would these cloaked missiles attack now?"

"Because you're going to dock with the yacht," Maddox said. "I believe there are entities that will work hard to prevent that."

"If that's the case, why wouldn't these missiles have attacked before I brought all this firepower?"

"Because the people behind the missiles would rather remain hidden if they can," Maddox said. "At all costs, they want to remain behind the scenes, as it were."

"I know your reputation," Sanchez said. "You're one of O'Hara's cloak and dagger people. But don't you think this is taking it too far?"

"No."

Sanchez pondered that as she studied Maddox a few moments longer. "Very well, Captain. I'm heading to the yacht myself in the *Austerlitz*. Do you have any last minute suggestions?"

"Be ready for anything, Admiral. I will assist you to the best of my ability if something unforeseen happens."

Sanchez gave him a wondering glance before signing off.

"Sir," Valerie said. "What exactly are we looking for?"

"A cloaked star cruiser, Spacers, silver drones or maybe even a Swarm warship."

"Swarm?" Valerie said. "You think the Swarm has found Human Space?"

"In truth," Maddox said, "I rather doubt it. But who knows what kind of data Commander Thrax Ti Ix took from the Dyson sphere?"

Thrax Ti Ix had been a modified Swarm creature who had inserted a virus into the doomed Builder last year. The commander—a giant preying mantis-like creature—had escaped the Dyson sphere before its destruction. He had done so via a hyper-spatial tube, leaving with any number of spacecraft. The tube had aimed toward the center of the galaxy.

As far as they knew, Thrax had gone in search of the Swarm Imperium. He planned to bring Laumer Drive technology to the Imperium. According to the Builder, all the Swarm Imperium possessed was a Not As Fast As Light, or NAFAL, drive. Wormhole technology would no doubt revolutionize the Swarm Imperium. But maybe Commander Thrax also had hyper-spatial technology to give the Swarm.

Maddox leaned back. He had other suspicions he wasn't articulating. He had a black widow spider inside his starship. Everything he said before the ship's recorders would reach Shu 15. He had come to thoroughly distrust the scramblers. He didn't even have much faith in Galyan's observations. Now that Shu knew the AI watched her, Maddox wondered if she'd come up with a way to thwart the Adok tech.

He needed another Builder-derived person to check Shu's Builder power. That would be Ludendorff. Likely, Shu had figured this out. Over the course of fourteen hours, he'd come to believe the Spacer would do everything in her power to stop Ludendorff from reaching *Victory*.

That would all depend, of course, on Maddox being right about the professor's premature death. That Dana hadn't already left in the yacht was the surest sign he was right.

The captain also feared greater Spacer intervention at the Nexus. It had bothered Maddox for over a year that the Spacers hadn't done anything helpful in the Commonwealth-New Man War. Why had the Spacers remained neutral all this time? Were the Builders and their artifacts part of the reason?

The only known war between Spacers and anyone else had been a Wahhabi Caliphate attack many years ago. The Moslem starships making the assault had all perished.

Was the reason the Spacers had refrained from helping the Commonwealth that everyone would have seen that their warships were vastly superior? Yet, if that was true, what did that mean out here? There were two old battleships, a newer heavy cruiser, two strike cruisers, some old destroyers and Starship *Victory*. Did the Spacers have anything able to take on *Victory*?

"Sir," Ensign Daggett said. "The admiral is hailing us."

"Put her on the main screen," Maddox said.

Sanchez appeared a moment later. "Captain," she said. "Doctor Rich is requesting a change in plan. The yacht's personnel are in mourning for the professor. Many of the people worked closely with him for many years. Their various religious beliefs and customs do not allow unwarranted intrusions at this time."

"I understand," Maddox said. "Please tell the doctor that the professor would want us to advance human knowledge at any price. His people will have to forgo their mourning in the interest of the greater good."

"The doctor suspected you might say something like that," Sanchez said. "As unbelievable as it sounds, Doctor Rich threatens drastic action if the *Austerlitz* approaches any closer."

"She's bluffing," Maddox said.

Admiral Sanchez frowned. "Captain, I realize you know the doctor better than I do, but she was emphatic."

"I believe you. However..."

Sanchez raised her eyebrows.

"Tell her that I insist," Maddox said.

Sanchez rubbed her chin. "Captain, I am afraid she may do something completely rash."

"Such as?" Maddox asked.

"I have detected beginning self-destruct sequences on the yacht. I believe she means to destroy herself and everyone else if we don't comply."

Maddox grinned.

Admiral Sanchez frowned severely. "This is no joke, Captain."

"Admiral Sanchez—"

"Sir," Ensign Daggett said, interrupting. "We're being hailed by enemy vessels."

"She's right," Valerie said, while she studied her board. "I'm picking up..." She looked at Maddox. "Sir, I'm picking up five silver drones. They're twenty-five thousand kilometers away and slowly closing."

"Admiral," Maddox said. "Are you seeing this?"

"I am," Sanchez said, peering at something off-screen.

With a tap, Valerie gave Maddox a split screen. One side showed the admiral. The other side showed space. Five silver dots with exhaust plumes wove their way through the asteroid belt toward them.

"The enemy drone commander has become insistent," Ensign Daggett said. "He demands that you speak with him."

"I'm going to take this call," Maddox told Sanchez.

"This is amazing," Sanchez said. "I've been in the system five months now. No one has seen any sign of the fabled silver drones. Now, a handful of them are coming. Captain, this could prove to be a deadly fight."

Maddox studied the large drones. He signaled Daggett. The ensign tapped her comm panel.

Both the admiral and space disappeared from the screen. In their place appeared a fuzzy image. It was difficult to tell, but a humanoid shape appeared to move within the fuzziness.

"Whom do I address?" the unknown person asked in a stilted manner.

"This is Captain Maddox of Starship *Victory*. We are a Patrol vessel of Star Watch. Please identify yourself."

The alien spoke, "You must retreat from the asteroid belt, Captain Maddox. Otherwise, we shall open fire."

"This is the Xerxes System," Maddox said. "It is part of the Commonwealth of Planets. You are intruding in our territory. If you open fire, we shall destroy your vessels."

"That is an arrogant reply," the alien said. "We are the Defenders of the Relic. This is our territory. You must retreat at once, or we shall begin destroying your starships."

"You have five minutes to begin retreating," Maddox said.

"As a sign of our deadly intent," the alien said, "we will destroy the smallest of your ships first."

"He means the luxury vessel," Valerie said. "The drones are targeting the yacht."

"Sir," Ensign Daggett said. "The admiral and Doctor Rich are both hailing us."

"Ignore them," Maddox said.

Daggett stared at the captain in wonder.

Valerie opened her mouth. Andros Crank signaled her, shaking his head. Valerie noticed and closed her mouth.

"You must retreat immediately, Captain," the alien said on the main screen. "I will not repeat my threat a second time."

178

"Burn the small ship to your heart's delight," Maddox told the alien. "I won't stop you."

"Sir!" Valerie burst out.

Maddox appeared not to hear her as he stared at the alien's fuzzy image on the screen.

"You consider the small ship an enemy vessel?" the alien asked.

"In this instance, yes," Maddox said.

"In that case, we have reconsidered," the alien said. "We will target your vessel now."

"If you do that," Maddox said, "I will fire at the luxury yacht."

"That is not logical," the alien said.

"On the contrary, it is supremely logical. Lieutenant," Maddox told Smith-Fowler, "Target the luxury yacht with a neutron cannon. On my signal, commence firing."

Smith-Fowler frowned as he complied.

"What form of species are you that attacks its own kind?" the alien asked.

"Is that your final comment?" Maddox asked.

"We are the Defenders—"

"Fire," Maddox said.

Lieutenant Smith-Fowler tapped the weapons board. The neutron cannon generated its beam, and the ray shot outward from *Victory* at Ludendorff's luxury yacht.

-30-

The purple neutron beam struck the yacht's powerful electromagnetic shield. The shield held steadily for a time and slowly began to change to a reddish color.

"Sir!" Valerie shouted. "Dana's on that ship."

Maddox did not reply.

Smith-Fowler glanced at the captain.

"Keep firing," Maddox told him.

"Sir, what are you thinking?" Valerie shouted. "We can't kill Dana. This is murder."

"Lieutenant," Maddox said. "Contain yourself. If you can't, I will relieve you of duty."

Valerie's face screwed up in agony.

On the main screen, the yacht's shield had turned brown.

"Sir," Valerie said in a raspy voice.

"Lieutenant," Maddox said, "has it occurred to you that the yacht possesses a vastly more powerful shield than it should? We've hit it with our neutron beam. The *Austerlitz's* shield wouldn't hold up this well."

Valerie twisted a ring on her finger as she studied the darkening shield.

"Sir," Ensign Daggett said. "The admiral is threating to fire at us if you don't stop firing at the yacht."

"I'm more interested in what the alien is saying," Maddox told her.

Daggett looked up in wonder. "He's saying you're mad, sir. He's saying he wants nothing to do with a species like you. If

180

you don't stop immediately, they're going away, never to return."

"What's going on, sir?" Valerie asked.

"Ensign," Maddox said. "Tell the alien he must self-destruct all five of his drones or I will surely destroy the yacht."

"Sir?" Daggett said in a dazed voice.

"Send the message," Maddox ordered.

"The *Austerlitz* has locked onto us," Smith-Fowler said.

Maddox forced himself to sit back in his command chair. He had to be right about the professor. Ludendorff must have spent some of his time in the asteroid belt strengthening his hand. If the mission was going to succeed, Maddox believed he had to strip the professor of those aces. In other words, he believed that Ludendorff was not only alive but also controlling the silver drones.

"The *Wurzburg* is locking on, sir," Smith-Fowler said.

"I've sent the message to the alien," Daggett told Maddox. "The admiral says we have twenty seconds to comply with her orders."

"Pump maximum energy to our shields," Maddox told Smith-Fowler.

"Done, sir," the tight-lipped weapons officer said.

Ensign Daggett was trembling, her hands quivering as she tapped her board.

The main screen had become even fuzzier. "Is the channel still open to the alien?" Maddox asked the comm operator.

Ensign Daggett nodded raggedly.

"I know your game," Maddox told the alien. "I'm not going to allow it. We're either going to do this my way, or I'm going to destroy you. You have less than ten seconds to comply. Then, I'm ordering the disintegrator beam to fire at the yacht."

Maddox turned to Smith-Fowler. "Get ready to cut the neutron cannon."

Warning klaxons blared on the bridge.

"Look!" Valerie shouted. "One of the silver drones has detonated. I don't believe this. The others are detonating as well."

"Cut the neutron beam," Maddox said.

The weapons officer tapped faster than he had so far.

Ensign Daggett slouched at her board, weeping, speaking through her tears to Admiral Sanchez.

"Why did the aliens do that, sir?" Valerie asked. "I don't understand any of this."

Ensign Daggett sat up as she wiped tears from her eyes. "Sir," she said. "Doctor Rich would like a word with you."

"Put her on the main screen," Maddox said.

A second later, a visibly trembling Dana Rich stared at him.

"You're mad," she told Maddox.

"You know I'm not," he said.

"You're an arrogant bastard who only thinks of himself."

"That would be your boyfriend, the professor."

"How dare you profane his name at a time like this?" Dana said.

Maddox waited.

Dana took a deep breath. "I'm...I'm requesting permission to come aboard *Victory*."

"Yes, on one condition," Maddox said.

"That being what?"

"You dock the yacht beside the starship and come via a boarding tube."

"I figured you'd say that," Dana said. "Yes. I agree." She stared at him as the fear began dissipating from her features. "You're—"

"I know," Maddox said. "The remarkable thing is that I sleep well at night."

Dana tapped a board and her image disappeared.

"Sir," Valerie said, having taken over comm duties for the moment. "Admiral Sanchez is demanding to speak to you."

"Put her on," Maddox said. "I might as well get this over with."

***

Admiral Sanchez still wasn't happy, as Maddox hadn't explained much. He told her there were hidden forces at play, Star Watch Intelligence secrets he wasn't at liberty to discuss over a comm line. If she would like to come aboard the starship...

Sanchez made it clear she would not leave her flagship while in a combat zone. Soon, *Austerlitz* and *Wurzburg* led the rest of the flotilla away from the Nexus and *Victory*. They took up station in an over-watch position, scanning relentlessly, searching for any other hidden enemies.

The luxury yacht closed to within several hundred kilometers of *Victory*.

The bridge personnel were tense. Lieutenant Maker presently sat at the comm station, Ensign Daggett having left for sickbay.

Galyan appeared on the bridge.

Maddox crooked a finger at the holoimage. Galyan floated near.

"I want you to scour the decks," Maddox said softly. "Search for hidden intruders."

"You believe the New Men have slipped onto our vessel from the cloaked star cruiser?"

"That would be my guess," Maddox said, giving Galyan a makeshift task to keep him off the bridge for now.

The holoimage glanced at the others. "I will be discrete, sir."

"Excellent."

Galyan vanished.

"Anything yet?" Maddox asked Lieutenant Smith-Fowler.

"It's quiet outside, sir. I'm only picking up the flotilla's sensor scans."

Maddox scratched his chest. Could that be it from the Spacers? Or was Shu planning a surprise on *Victory* itself? The captain pondered the idea. He slid off the command chair, approaching Valerie's station.

"Sir?" she asked.

He motioned Valerie to him. She stood while frowning, leaning near.

"You have the bridge," Maddox whispered. "I want you to say as little as possible, particularly over the ship's intercom or over the comm to another vessel."

Valerie peered at him, mouthing the word, "Shu?"

Maddox nodded imperceptibly. He was certain the Spacer studied every wavelength that might possibly give her information. Who knew how much Shu already knew.

Valerie looked as if she wanted to ask him several more questions. Finally, her shoulders deflated as she nodded.

The lieutenant headed for the command chair as Maddox strode from the chamber.

The captain moved purposefully through the corridors. As he did, he fingered a device within a pocket. He used a route that could lead to a hanger bay just in case Shu was watching his progress. Several minutes later, he pressed a switch on the device. The moment he did so, Maddox broke into a sprint.

He used an override unit, shutting down the starship's interior security cameras, effectively blinding Shu. He hoped the Spacer would think it was a momentary malfunction.

The captain's sprint took him in a new direction. Instead of the hangar bay, he raced for the detention center.

-31-

Maddox drew his long-barreled gun, having sprinted through the corridors. He didn't breathe as hard as he would have only several days ago.

He pressed a wall switch and burst through the door into Shu's chamber.

The small Spacer gasped. She had her back to him, peering up into the air as she sat in a chair. She did not wear her goggles, or much of anything else for that matter. With a lurch, Shu staggered from her chair, moving in an almost blind fashion. Her bare legs bumped against the edge of the bed. She fell onto it with an *oof*, her panties sliding higher than seemed proper. Her hands roved over the covers, latching onto her goggles. She slid them over her eyes, seeming to take a second longer to make sure they were in place. Finally, she twisted around to stare accusingly at the captain, her hands covering her bare breasts.

"Your conduct is shamefully rude," she said.

Maddox aimed his gun at her, although he was outwardly calm.

"Do you mind turning around while I put on my clothes?" she asked.

"In this instance, yes," he said. "But by all means, dress."

She stared at him. It took several seconds, but her demeanor changed. She let her hands fall away from her pert breasts as she stood and cocked an appealing hip at him.

"This is an interesting change, Captain. What would Meta say if she could see us now?"

"No doubt, she would do you bodily harm. I suggest you don your garments. Otherwise, I will have to tell Meta you tried to seduce me."

"Captain," Shu purred. She cupped her breasts and made a pouting face, approaching him seductively.

Maddox's aim never wavered.

Shu neared and tried to reach him. The end of the long gun-barrel poked against her flat belly.

"You don't need that," she told him, looking up into his face.

Using the barrel, Maddox prodded her belly, forcing her to back away.

"Put on some clothes, Shu. We can talk then."

Her hands dropped away from cupping her breasts. "Are you an icicle?"

"Not in the least. Believe me. I'm enjoying the spectacle. I rate you a solid eight and a half. If you removed the goggles and grew out your hair, I suspect you could become a nine."

"How dare you?"

"Frowning like that lowers your score," Maddox said. "You do better as a smiling girl."

With her hands, Shu covered her breasts, retreating to her bed. She donned her Spacer garb, only looking at him after she clicked shut the last clasp.

"The Visionary thought you were a gentleman. I'm afraid I'll have to tell her you're a brute."

"Given that the Visionary sees so much, I doubt that will come as a great surprise to her. At least if Meta barges into the room, she won't do you any bodily harm. That was a close call."

"Why are you here? And why are you pointing your gun at me?"

"I have good news. I'm finally taking you out of detention. You can leave your meager belongings. I'll have a steward collect them and bring them to your new quarters."

Shu ingested that, finally saying, "That accounts for your presence. Why do you have to point a gun at me, though?"

"It's a formality, nothing more."

"You're lying, Captain."

"If I am, it no doubt brings equality to our situation, as you're concealing things from me as well. For instance, what does it mean when you're staring into the air without your goggles on?"

"It was a religious moment, one that you interrupted."

"I rather doubt that."

"You're too irreligious for your own good, Captain."

"On the contrary, I am quite pious."

"And that's why you like to stare at naked women?"

"No. That is due to my natural appreciation for beauty."

"Even an eight-and-a-half-rated beauty?"

"That is why my precision is so accurate. I am a beauty expert due to extended study. Do not downplay your eight and a half score by the way. That is a relatively high number."

"And you call yourself pious. What a mockery you make of spiritualty."

"I am pious in that I believe in the Creator and try to give Him His due."

"*Him*, Captain?"

"Precisely," Maddox said. "But let us return to your so-called religious experience. What did you see without your goggles?"

Shu peered at him angrily until a new expression swept over her. "You're doing this deliberately. You're trying to goad me."

"Why would I do that?"

"I don't know," Shu said.

Maddox smiled. "Now it is you who are lying. I have arrived at the belief that removing your goggles helps you 'see' radiation or wavelengths better. Maybe removing your garments does that as well. Or perhaps you simply like to sit seminude in your quarters."

"Forget about all that," Shu said. "Forget about me. You're making a terrible mistake doing this. He's incredibly dangerous, you know?"

"I presume you're referring to Ludendorff, and I quite agree. But then, so are you."

187

"You can't compare me to a Methuselah Man."

"The Methuselah Man doesn't have your abilities. Consider. You have as good as admitted the scramblers don't hinder your eavesdropping on our communications."

"Your cautious actions on the bridge already showed me you knew that. I feel I must warn you again. Ludendorff is a danger to everything we hold dear. We cannot let him on *Victory*."

"Is there a Spacer convoy in the Xerxes System?"

"Of course not," Shu said. "The admiral chased them away."

"There is not even *one* cloaked Spacer vessel watching what happens out here?"

"No."

"This is interesting," Maddox said. "You mix a strange blend of lying with the truth."

"Why ask me anything if you've already arrived at your own answers?"

"Habit, I suppose."

It took a moment. Then Shu laughed, shaking her head. "We're both liars, Captain. The situation is absurd, don't you think? You can put your gun away. I can't do anything to you. If you won't believe me about Ludendorff—"

"Enough," Maddox said, becoming suspicious at her cheery nature. "You will walk ahead of me." He holstered the long-barreled gun and drew a stunner from where he'd kept it under his belt. He adjusted the setting.

He showed her the new weapon. "This is to let you know that I won't hesitate to stun you. I'm not sure you believed that I'd shoot you with a bullet."

"You're much too gallant, Captain," Shu said sarcastically. "Why do you need any weapon at all to deal with me?"

He tapped his chest, indicating her adaptations as the reason for his caution.

"Where are we going?" she asked.

"You already know."

"I don't. Please, where are we going?"

"You'll find out soon enough. Now, if you would please, Provost Marshal, march ahead of me."

Shu 15 sighed, heading for the open door.

-32-

"This is a mistake," Shu said on "E" Deck.

They had been walking for a time, the Spacer having become taciturn since leaving the detention center.

Maddox felt a lurch on the deck.

Shu turned around wildly, feeling it too. "Captain, I implore you. Take me back to detention while there's still time."

Maddox heard real fear in her voice. She must have realized the lurch meant the luxury yacht had landed inside the hangar bay instead of docking outside.

"My life is in danger," Shu said. "Ludendorff or one of his people will try to kill me."

"Do you suspect a revenge killing?"

"The Methuselah Men don't need a reason. They kill and maim for sport. We Spacers have defended ourselves from them for years, only having become proficient in arms for our own protection."

"I wish you'd shared more about your culture earlier," Maddox said. "I could know then whether to have sympathy for the Spacers. As it is, I'm in the dark concerning your people."

"Everyone knows we're peaceful."

"How do you explain the cloaked missiles that attacked the yacht and shuttle?"

"That had nothing to do with Spacers. Someone else put the missiles there."

"I have my doubts," Maddox said. "In fact, you're my chief suspect."

"I've been in detention for some time now. Do you think I can teleport in and out of my room hundreds of light-years at a time?"

"I do not."

"Then how could I have ambushed the shuttle?"

"Your people could have put the missiles in place, ready to be activated by you."

Shu stared at him. "If you believe I'm that powerful, I'm surprised I'm still alive. I would think a paranoid individual like yourself would murder someone as powerful as you're making me out to be."

"You forget that I'm *di-far*. I dare because I'm a man of decision."

"Even you can't stop the Methuselah Man."

"I've stopped you," Maddox said. "Thus, it is reasonable to suppose I can stop the professor."

Shu shook her head, moaning to herself. "Leave me while I compose myself to meet my Maker."

Maddox smiled faintly. "I'm bringing you along for two reasons. One is to protect you from the professor. The other is to protect the professor from you."

Shu stared at him longer this time. "You have a painfully high regard for yourself. In that way, you are fully New Man."

"Perhaps you're right," Maddox said. "Now, march."

Reluctantly, Shu did.

***

Maddox brought her to the chamber near the hangar bay, where he'd been when the cloaked missile had destroyed the shuttle. It was a stark room, with several machines holding drinks and others stocked with condiments. Otherwise, tables and chairs filled the chamber.

"Galyan," Maddox called.

Nothing happened.

"Oh," the captain said. He reached into a pocket, pressing a button on his special unit. "Galyan," he said, trying again.

"There you are," the holoimage said upon appearing.

Maddox glanced at Shu before whispering to the holoimage. A moment later, Galyan disappeared.

"You're going to extremely tedious lengths to thwart a minor ability on my part," Shu said.

"Attention to detail is another characteristic of New Men," Maddox said coldly.

"Ah. I see my remark earlier stung. That is interesting."

Maddox sat across from Shu, resting the stunner on his lap. A few moments later, he tapped a device on his wrist, and they continued waiting.

Finally, the door swished open and a medium-sized man in a yellow shirt and black slacks and shoes waltzed in. He wore a gold chain around a wrinkly neck. He was older, bald and had deeply tanned skin, with a prominent hooked nose and eyes that shined like diamonds.

Professor Ludendorff stopped short. There was commotion behind him outside in the corridor. He turned around.

Maddox saw Meta with several security Marines holding up three beefy men who had tried to follow the professor into the room.

"Don't worry, Professor," Maddox said. "This is strictly a routine measure."

Ludendorff glanced at Maddox. Then, he spied Shu. The old man moved fast, thrusting a hand inside his shirt. Before he could complete whatever it was that he was trying to do, Maddox fired the stunner.

A blot of force knocked the Methuselah Man onto the floor, his feet in the chamber and his head and torso in the hall.

Maddox spun fast, training the stunner on Shu.

The Spacer had been rising from her seat. A twitch of her head allowed her to see the captain. Slowly, she sat back down, carefully putting her hands on her knees.

In the meantime, Meta collected the professor, carrying him to a table and laying him on it. The door had swished shut behind her.

"His security detail is angry," Meta said.

"Put them in detention," Maddox told her. "Remember. Treat them as extremely dangerous. The professor wouldn't trust them with his safety otherwise."

Meta nodded, hurrying out the door to the Marines and their three captives.

"Well done, Captain," Shu said. "I see you do recognize Ludendorff's deadliness. I suggest you kill him now while you're able."

Maddox said nothing as he adjusted his stunner. Then, he went to Ludendorff, reaching under his shirt. He felt a small cube tapped to the man's torso. With a twist, Maddox tore it free, pocketing it. Afterward, the captain moved away from both of them. He wanted to be able to watch them both at the same time.

The pulled tape woke Ludendorff. He smacked his lips, groaned and rolled over onto his stomach. That almost caused him to fall off the table. He barely caught himself, swung his legs over the edge, feet to the floor, swaying as he stood. With a grunt, he dropped onto a chair, resting his elbows on the table.

"Was stunning me necessary?" Ludendorff asked in a blurred voice.

"My action speaks for my thoughts," Maddox said. "By the way, I'm glad you're alive."

Ludendorff gave him a baleful scrutiny, finally shaking his head. "I'd forgotten how swiftly you take action. For you, to think a thing is to do it. I won't forget next time."

"Professor Ludendorff, I'd like to introduce you to Shu 15, a Spacer Provost Marshal and a Surveyor First Class."

The Methuselah Man nodded at her.

"Shu—" Maddox said.

"I know who he is," Shu said. "I suggest you kill him before he kills me."

Ludendorff inhaled several times. He glanced sidelong at Maddox and then leaned back in his chair.

"This is a predicament," the professor said. "By your stance and the way you're displaying the stunner, it suggests you understand something of the nefarious nature of Spacers. It would also seem you understand that neither they nor I have much use for each other."

"Do you deny that you both consort with androids?" Shu accused. "Do you deny that you both tamper with the basic fabric of humanity?"

"I deny nothing," Ludendorff said. "Do you deny a murderous passivity in the face of danger? Do you deny that you won't take proper actions to defend humanity against all alien dangers?"

"You're evil," Shu said. "You warp what is good. You mimic life in your insane quest for longevity."

"You're jealous of my intellect," Ludendorff told her. "In fact, you're so jealous that you attempted to murder me a day ago."

"That is false," Shu said. "You did that in an effort to besmirch the Spacer name."

"Bah!" Ludendorff said. "What gall is this? You—"

"Just a minute," Maddox said. "I think she has a point with the last allegation."

Ludendorff blinked as if amazed. "Excuse me? You think I purposefully destroyed my own property in an attempt to shift blame onto the Spacers?"

"Precisely," Maddox said.

"That's absurd," Ludendorff said.

"Professor," Maddox said. "Let's forgo needless back and forth as you deny the obvious. Why did the silver drones self-detonate? Because you recognized my threat for what it was. You had remained on the yacht the entire time. I was going to destroy the yacht rather than let you have the advantage of five silver drones."

"Bah," Ludendorff said. "Whatever you think I've done, I'd at least like my cube back. It's my property. Or are you a thief?"

"Surely, you recall the alien Destroyer," Maddox said. "You commandeered my starship back then. You set my prisoner free. I have a long memory for such things. I'm not such a fool as to—"

"Enough," Ludendorff said. "Your bragging becomes tedious the moment you begin. I always do what I do for the greater good."

"That's a patent lie," Shu said. "You're an egomaniac like Strand. Neither of you have any qualms about jeopardizing the universe with your wild schemes. I know you, Ludendorff. I know your brain patterns. They are just like your master's."

"I have no master," Ludendorff said.

"He died on the Dyson sphere," Shu said, "his mind poisoned by his despair."

"Poisoned by a Swarm virus," Ludendorff said. "There's a critical difference." The professor turned to Maddox. "I'm surprised at you. Why did you confide in her about our adventures on the Dyson sphere?"

"I didn't," Maddox said.

"Then how does she know so much?"

"The Visionary saw it," Maddox said.

Ludendorff rubbed his face as if in pain. "Did the Visionary speak to you?"

"Indeed," Maddox said. "She named me *di-far*."

"Oh dear," Ludendorff said. "The Visionary initiated you into their bizarre cult of mysticism. *Di-far* indeed." The professor shook his head. "The old witch is cunning beyond belief. Have no doubt the Visionary believes all the rot and nonsense she told you. Still, she might have also told you those things in an effort to appeal to your vanity. Have you become puffed up with conceit yet?"

"I don't know about conceit," Maddox said. "But I have managed to hold the representatives of two distinct Builders."

Neither the Methuselah Man nor the Spacer responded to that.

Soon, Ludendorff said, "You have a dilemma, Captain. You have to decide whom you trust. I've helped you in the past. The Spacers have done nothing to gain your faith. Now, they suddenly seek to use you for their own ends but purr in your ear that they're altruistic. It's all rot and nonsense."

"Listen to Ludendorff trying to use his golden tongue," Shu said. "Yet when has Ludendorff ever done anything for someone else? He never lifts a hand unless he has an ulterior motive."

"You give me false choices," Maddox told them. "In fact, I distrust both of you, although to varying degrees. The professor has helped me in the past even as he followed his own agenda. What makes him so dangerous is his genius and long experience."

"You're making me blush," Ludendorff muttered.

"While you," Maddox told Shu, "have these Builder articles in you. I don't know how to tame those. Clearly, you lied about the scramblers hindering you. I'm hoping Ludendorff has a way to dampen your inner devices. Frankly, I'm counting on both of you to check each other. I'm also hoping to act as a balance so the one doesn't kill the other."

"I'll say this," Ludendorff told Maddox. "I appreciate your frankness. When do we begin?"

"We already have."

"Ah. We're headed for the Nexus?"

Maddox checked a chronometer. "We should arrive in a little less than two hours. Then, we're going to venture outside and see if we can reproduce Kane's feat mixed with that of last voyage's hyper-spatial tube. This tube will hopefully go to a different place, though."

"The two of us will attempt this feat?" Ludendorff asked, indicating Shu.

"Yes," Maddox said.

Ludendorff grew thoughtful while Shu remained motionless and expressionless.

Maddox wondered how he was going to keep the two of them from killing each other and at the same time achieve his objective. The next few hours would likely prove the most challenging of his life.

-33-

Keith kept glancing over his shoulder at the intense Spacer. She sat on a bench, leaning against the bulkhead, with a vacc suit helmet in her arm.

Shu wore a vacc suit with various pieces of equipment hooked in place. She finally turned toward him, smiling faintly. It made her features radiantly sexy.

Keith grinned at her.

"Lieutenant," Maddox said sharply, who sat beside him in front.

"No problem, mate," Keith said, checking his board.

The pilot flew a shuttle from *Victory*. The mighty starship was behind them by several thousand kilometers. In the distance loomed several asteroids. Beyond them shined a bright silver object. It was still too far away to see the distinctive pyramidal shape.

Keith wondered about that. The Builders liked to use pyramids. Hadn't Valerie said before that the ancient Egyptians had copied the alien visitors? That was crazy, really. It meant some of those wacky theories about space aliens in the distant past were true. Who would have thought it?

Keith studied the piloting board. The captain had told him to be on the lookout for surprises. Back on *Victory,* Galyan also scanned relentlessly.

The small shuttle chamber held him, the captain, Meta, the professor and beautiful Shu 15. The others planned to go inside the pyramid. Keith would stay out here in the shuttle, ready to race back to *Victory*.

Keith looked back at Shu. "I'm Lieutenant Keith Maker," he said.

The little Spacer smiled at him.

"Nice," he said.

Meta turned to stare at him.

Keith felt the Rouen Colony woman's scrutiny. He shoved the feeling down as he told Shu, "I mean your smile is nice. It really lights up your face."

"Thank you," Shu said with warmth.

"I'm a straightforward bloke," Keith said. "I say what I mean."

"Yes, clearly," Shu said.

"Lieutenant," Maddox said.

"No problem, mate," Keith said, turning forward again.

Maddox cleared his throat.

"Uh, sir," Keith corrected himself.

Maddox nodded imperceptibly.

For a time, Keith concentrated on the journey. One tiny place in his mind kept thinking of things to say to Shu, though. And he kept wondering if she watched him. He'd heard her sexy voice. She seemed to have recognized his alpha nature. The comment about her nice smile had clearly pleased her. Women ate up remarks like that.

Finally, he couldn't resist it any longer. He turned his head to find her smiling at him.

"Too bad we haven't run into each other sooner," he said.

"I agree," Shu said. "You seem…"

He glanced back at her, turning further.

"Skilled," she said, maybe with extra meaning in her voice.

"I am skilled, lass," he said. "I'm—"

"Heading straight for that asteroid," Maddox said.

Keith whipped forward, ready to make a quick correction. There was empty void before them. He realized the shuttle was right on course, and that Maddox had said what he did to hinder the conversation.

"No worries—sir," Keith said.

He made a small correction, replaying their conversation in his head. Did she mean skilled in bed? He'd known a few girls, but he wasn't a Romeo.

Keith turned back toward her. He needed to say something witty now.

"Captain Maddox," Ludendorff said. "Why did you insist on bringing a sex-starved pilot with us?"

The words left Keith frozen, staring at Shu with his mouth hanging agape.

"You must be joking," Shu said. "The pilot is hardly starved. He must be a tiger in bed."

"Enough," Maddox said.

Keith was grinning ear-to-ear as he faced forward. That PUA book really knew its subject matter. It had turned him into an alpha man, into a wolf-like lover women could no longer resist. He wasn't sure what phrase had exactly done that. It must have been the comment on her smile and the way he boldly looked back at her despite the captain's displeasure with it.

She can sense my dominance, Keith thought. At the same moment, he realized what it was. He was the pilot running a shuttle. In this, he was the very best. No one could compete against him in this environment, not even the captain. That must have translated into how he held himself, how he spoke to her.

Keith squared his shoulders as a sense of power filled him. He was setting up, readying the woman for his swoop. She would no doubt melt when he pressed her against him later.

The idea turned into a fantasy, one he envisioned with greater intensity.

"Lieutenant Maker," Maddox said.

Keith snapped out of his daydream. He noticed their velocity was too high. The silver object had grown considerably, to the point where he could see the various sides.

"You said fast, sir," Keith said in a matter-of-fact voice.

"Adjust," Maddox told him.

"Aye-aye, sir," Keith said, manipulating the controls. He threw a quick glance over his shoulder, adding, "This could get bumpy for a second."

Shu nodded knowingly, seeming to tell him in that nod that he would take perfect care of her.

Keith grinned wider still as the shuttle began to decelerate.

Soon, he forgot about the beauty behind him. Keith began to remember the importance of the mission as the vast silver pyramid grew in size. It was amazing, the thing slowly spinning in place. He'd seen it before, of course, but never this close while in a shuttle. Last voyage, a hyper-spatial tube had appeared beside the pyramid, sucking the starship into it, transporting them one-thousand light years.

The ancient Builders had erected these throughout the Orion Arm. Just how old was the pyramid anyway? Older than anything constructed on Earth, that was certain.

The monument's age awed the lieutenant. It caused him to gape, but it didn't shake his flying skills or cause him to forget the task at hand. The Spacer had that effect, but not an alien building.

Keith braked harder but more smoothly. "Where do you want me to park, sir?"

"Any suggestions?" Maddox asked the two passengers.

Ludendorff was busy studying the Nexus.

Shu had a far-off look to her features. "I'm...sensing over there, Captain," she said, pointing out the window.

"Come here and show me," Maddox said.

The Spacer unhooked her harness and walked to the piloting area. She put a seemingly careless hand on Keith's shoulder.

The lieutenant was intensely aware of her hand. She touched him. He felt a sexual thrill begin in his groin and head to his stomach. This would be a delicious bedmate.

Keith glanced up at her.

She must have sensed his alpha stare. She spoke to the captain but found time to glance at him and smile sexily.

Keith had to swallow a laugh of amazement. This woman wanted him. She oozed sexual need. The PUA book almost felt like magic. He hadn't expected it to work this marvelously.

"Do you see the area?" Maddox asked sharply.

"Sir?" Keith asked.

"Point it out again," Maddox told the Spacer.

Shu leaned against Keith and she pointed down on his screen. "Can you bring us there?" she asked, turning her face so their lips were a mere few inches apart.

"I can indeed," Keith said in a raspy reply. He smelled her breath, and felt that he was practically kissing her.

She pushed against his shoulder as she straightened, heading back for her bench.

Keith would have turned around to watch her walk back, but Maddox stared at him. The captain's face was like ice.

"Uh, heading there, mate, um, captain sir."

Maddox appeared to want to say something. Whatever it was, he seemed to think better of it and merely nodded.

Keith kept thinking of the Spacer's touch and the taste of her breath. He wanted to strip her naked and—

His fingers roved over the piloting board as he made quick adjustments.

The shuttle slowed even more, drifting toward the area Shu had shown him. Soon, the shuttle was less than a kilometer from the Nexus. The silver pyramid dwarfed the craft. It would have dwarfed Starship *Victory*. The alien construct was vast.

Maddox rose, taking his helmet. "Remain alert," he said.

"Aye-aye, sir," Keith said. "Good luck, sir."

Maddox nodded.

"Good luck, Shu," he added.

She faced him, smiling, and said in an impossibly sexual way, "Thank you, Lieutenant. I know you mean it."

"I do," he said.

Ludendorff made a sound that Keith couldn't recognize.

"I won't forget," she said.

"Good," Keith said, boldly staring at her, letting her realize that he was willing to do anything with her.

She turned away as if embarrassed by his masculinity.

The others filed out. Maddox paused by the hatch, staring at him.

"Sir?" Keith asked.

Maddox shook his head before heading out as well, closing the hatch behind him.

Keith grinned, laughing to himself. This was better than he could have dreamed. He was close to having his wish, a wild

romance with a stunning beauty. He could hardly wait for the
next step in his hunt.

-34-

Maddox sat in a thruster cradle. The others were each in similar vehicles. He followed Ludendorff and Shu, the two of them several hundred meters from each other and him.

The approach to the pyramid reminded Maddox of the alien Destroyer. The vast silver wall did not have the same feeling of evil as the Destroyer had emitted. It did have a sense of grandeur, though, a feeling of incredible age.

Why didn't planets give off the same feeling? What was it about a constructed thing that gave off such sensations? Was it all in his mind?

The captain didn't believe that. Something of the essence of the maker oozed from the object. It must have something to do with the age of the thing and the power it held. The Destroyer had contained terrible power to annihilate. The pyramid also possessed incredible power.

Maddox had qualms about this. He didn't know how to keep Ludendorff from murdering Shu or vice versa. He was counting on the grandeur of the event to forestall some of that. He also wondered if they didn't both need each other in order to accomplish the task.

Yet, Shu's Builder abilities might trump everything right now. He should have taken the time to figure out what Ludendorff's cube did. What was the professor thinking? The Methuselah Man was undoubtedly scheming madly. Maybe the Spacer was doing likewise.

Was the professor right about the Spacers? Did they believe they were the chosen ones? He could well believe it. And yet, the New Men also thought that about themselves. Maybe that was a uniquely human trait. Maybe every human believed he was a chosen individual.

His headphones crackled. "Maddox," he heard. That sounded like Meta.

He adjusted his cradle, turning it around. Meta sprayed hydrogen gas, increasing velocity to catch up with him. Soon, her cradle moved parallel with him. She waved. He waved back.

"I don't like this," she radioed, her words difficult to make out.

"Are you thinking about your time with Kane?" he asked.

"Yes. This brings back painful memories. This place terrifies me." She paused before adding, "We don't belong here."

"Nonsense," Maddox said. "It's an ancient artifact, to be sure, but one we can use."

"Should we use it, even if we can figure it out?" Meta asked.

"If we don't, we're just waiting for the Swarm to show up someday and kill us."

"We didn't discover the technology. We should use our Laumer Drives and—"

Maddox's chuckle cut her off.

"Did I say something funny?" Meta demanded.

"We must always strive. Always yearn to understand new things. If we stop, the others will win."

"What others?" Meta asked.

"Whichever race learns what we were afraid to attempt."

"Maybe," she said. "But the Nexus still frightens me. Sometimes, I think there are things out there we're not ready to find. We're still too much like children."

Maddox considered her words as the pyramid grew to titanic size.

Was Meta right? The captain gazed at the gleaming metal. For once, he felt inferior. He'd never been this close to the Nexus before. It was strange. The Dyson sphere should have

204

had this effect on him. It had been vastly larger than the pyramid. Yet the pyramid seemed to shrink his soul the closer he approached. It bewildered the intellect.

Maddox nodded. The pyramid was magical. The Dyson sphere had merely been mechanical.

The captain frowned. Why wouldn't a Dyson sphere be magical? It had housed an incomparable number of beings. Could something else be at play here?

Shu, Maddox thought, *maybe she's projecting these feelings into us.*

The gamble Maddox took suddenly struck him. He worked with people who possessed hidden powers. *The New Men are secretive. The Spacers are secretive. Is that the connection between them?*

A slow smile spread across his face. Strand, and to some degree Ludendorff, had created the New Men. The Methuselah Men were the product of a Builder's modification. The Spacers seemed to have found a Builder—

Maddox made a fist and struck the armrest of his thruster cradle. No one had explained Spacer origins to him. He'd made guesses about their beginnings, nothing more. What seemed clear out here by the pyramid was the similarity of the Spacers' secrecy to that of the New Men. That implied a Builder trait the aliens couldn't help but pass on to their creations—secrecy. Were the Spacers an indirect Builder creation, molded by someone modified by a Builder?

How would that change what he already knew about the Spacers? Maybe it didn't change anything, but it confirmed and clarified what he knew. Ludendorff and Shu could be likened to cousins, maybe distantly related cousins, but beings who thought in similar ways, with deep secrecy that always led them to try to be string-pullers behind the scenes.

As the cradles headed for a distinct area of the pyramid, a hardening resolve grew in the captain. He was a free man who demanded that he think for himself. He did not want anyone manipulating his thoughts, even if they thought they did it for his own good. Maddox resolved to fight for mankind's freedom of action. The New Men weren't going to rule them as superior humans. The Spacers weren't going to nudge humanity onto this road or that one with their secret ploys. That meant humanity had to cut the Builder strings trying to pull them onto secret paths.

Maddox could almost *feel* the Builders out there, tugging on this thread or gently pulling on that one.

The captain eyed the professor's cradle and then Shu's. He couldn't allow either of them to dominate the other. Yet they were about to enter a structure where he would be the child in terms of understanding.

He took a deep breath. He could not match these two in understanding. He was going to have to go primitive and trust his instincts, his feelings. Maddox did not like that. He preferred logic and reason. But when entering the realm of magic, gut feelings could prove to be the logical thing to do.

"Start decelerating," Ludendorff radioed. "Shu has chosen the entrance. We're about to enter the Nexus. It's time we closed up and tethered our cradles."

"Have you ever been inside before?" Meta radioed.

Ludendorff's silence seemed ominous.

Maddox adjusted his thruster cradle. As the hydrogen spray slowed his velocity, he checked his hand-held beamer. If one of those two tried to double-cross the team, the captain was determined to kill him or her.

-35-

Maddox sucked in his breath.

Leaving her cradle, the tiny Spacer floated before a panel and tapped in an access code. A small opening appeared, relative to the pyramid. They would have been able to drive the shuttle through that. With a push, Shu returned to her cradle, strapping in. Leading the way, her thruster cradle gently drifted through the opening. The others followed close behind.

Maddox craned his head, peering everywhere. The inside of the Nexus was bewildering and awe-inspiring. Giant girders held the pyramid together while fantastic balls of light glowed eerily from a thousand places. There were silver platforms, lines of energy crisscrossing from one locale to another, and vast empty spaces.

Maddox's visor recorded everything. He hoped the others remembered to do the same.

This was a wonderland of technological marvel. It was intensely bright, too. The captain's visor had darkened as much as it could, and still he had to squint.

Tether lines hooked the cradles, a tiny train of fleas moving through an ancient powerhouse. After a time—it was hard to tell how much had passed—Shu redirected her path. She moved toward a larger platform with the others following. No one spoke to each other because the comms didn't work in here. They would wait to talk by hooking phone-lines from suit to suit.

Maddox found himself staring too often with his mind blanking out. Shaking his head, he berated himself. He had to keep his wits about him. His team, his ship, his nation were counting on him.

Closing his eyes, Maddox forced himself to go back over the plan, fighting the urge to stare in continuous wonder. Finally, though, he cracked an eyelid, and his mouth sagged open at the sight. This was beautiful.

A last stubborn particle of will caused Maddox to snap his eyes shut once again.

He realized that this must be a mind trap put in place long ago by the Builders.

A hard knot of stubbornness welled up from the captain's core. It sneered at the beauty. It fought against the ancient superior intellects. *I am Captain Maddox, and I refuse to fall in line like a fool.*

The captain found himself panting. Once again, he cracked an eyelid open. This time, though, he did not stare in wonder. He concentrated on the thruster cradle ahead of him. It was Ludendorff's cradle. Meta brought up the rear.

The cradle ahead of him bumped down onto a giant platform.

Maddox went to work, adjusting his cradle as he readied himself to land. Before he finished the sequence, he turned his thruster machine enough so he could glance back. Meta came on too fast. Maybe she'd succumbed to the wondrousness of the interior and could no longer control herself.

The captain reacted. He detached his tether from Ludendorff's cradle and applied thrust as he turned completely. Rising and braking quickly, he engaged the magnetic clamps. With a bump and an intense vibration, he linked their two thruster crafts. Maddox waved, but Meta remained inert on her chair.

It was more difficult now, and he had to crane to the side to see where he was going. The captain turned the two vehicles as he maneuvered toward the landing. The platform seemed to rush up too fast. He bumped against it, engaging the magnetic anchor clamps. The stop was sudden and hard, throwing him against the cradle's straps.

He sat there to regain his composure. *What are Shu and Ludendorff doing?* Forcing himself to move, Maddox unbuckled, climbing out of the thruster. At the last moment, he remembered to engage his magnetic boots.

With jerky steps, he clomped to Meta. He wanted to make sure she was okay before he headed after the others.

She just sat there. Finding the phone-line, he hooked their suits together.

"Meta?" he said.

There was no reply.

Worried, Maddox tapped her outer screen. Her vital signs were good. She was breathing according to this. She just wasn't moving or talking.

The others—what are they doing?

Maddox withdrew the phone-line jack. He found that he gripped the beamer in his gun hand. He didn't bother holstering it. Instead, he turned, seeing the professor and the Spacer slowly walking to what looked like a giant screen.

With a sense of lateness, Maddox began heading for them. Would the beamer even work in here?

Maddox took one deliberate step at a time. Each forward motion caused the magnet to pull his foot down the last few centimeters, giving his walk a lurching quality.

Ludendorff and Shu stood before a titanic screen. The two stood motionlessly for a time. Finally, Ludendorff turned to Shu and plugged a phone-line into her suit.

Maddox would have liked to know what they said. He should have rigged a recording unit to each suit. Before he reached them, Shu stepped up to a giant board. She began to move levers and change the settings of various switches.

What did that do? How did she know the right sequence? Was she reading wavelengths or Builder radiation? It didn't seem like a simple process, one easily taught to others. Would Star Watch vessels always need a Methuselah Man or a Spacer Surveyor in order to use a Nexus' hyper-spatial tube?

Finally, Maddox reached them. He felt like an apish hominid staring up at an angelic object brought down from Heaven. Massed stars appeared on the titanic screen. Green lines connected many of the stars. There were also intensely bright points of light. Were those Nexuses?

I should be recording this.

Even as he thought that, the screen went blank. Shu moved away from the huge control panel. She returned to Ludendorff, relinking the phone-line between them.

The professor turned around and jerked back as if surprised to find the captain behind him. Ludendorff pulled the phone-line from Shu's vacc suit. The professor linked it to Maddox's suit.

"Captain," the professor said in a hoarse voice.

Maddox tried to reply but found that his lips had frozen in place.

"I'm amazed you could walk here," Ludendorff said, speaking roughly, as if it took great effort of will. "Shu...has completed the task. At least, she claims she has. I'm afraid we have to trust her. Are you ready to leave?"

"Map," Maddox said, forcing the word out of his mouth.

"What's that, my boy?"

"Nexus map," Maddox said.

"We no longer have time for that," the professor said. "We have to get back to *Victory* before the hyper-spatial tube appears."

"But...map."

"I know you want a map. I want a map. This place...it's worse than I expected."

"What?"

"We'll talk later," Ludendorff said, panting.

"No. I want...map."

"Yes, yes, we all want a map. Not this time, though. The Spacer...she's a clever minx. Who knew it would be like this? Maybe Meta did, but only in her subconscious. Next time, I'll know. Go, Captain. The clock is ticking. Shu will leave without us, I'm sure."

Maddox shuffled around. Shu had reached her cradle and was strapping in. She'd been walking while they'd talked. The Spacer began initiating her cradle's thrusters.

"How did she move so fast?" Ludendorff said. "We took a longer time talking than I realized. She's leaving us."

It was true. Shu's cradle lifted off the platform. Her tether line didn't lift, though. She'd unhooked herself from the other thrusters.

"This is a double-cross," Ludendorff said. "Captain, you shouldn't have taken my cube. I'm defenseless, my boy. The grand adventure is over for us."

Maddox only half listened. He found himself kneeling, aiming his beamer. He pulled the trigger. A gout of pure energy flowed from the beamer. It wasn't supposed to work like that. It was supposed to send a thin line of energy. Instead, it went in a visible globule of power. The glob struck Shu's thruster nozzle, blasting it and sending the Spacer's cradle tumbling end over end away from them.

"Ha-ha, perfect shot, my boy," Ludendorff told him.

Maddox examined the beamer. It glowed red-hot. Without thinking, he hurled it from him. It drifted away, becoming hotter, hotter—the beamer exploded in a glorious golden color.

"Why did you bring a grenade?" Ludendorff asked. "Oh well, it doesn't matter. At least you fixed that minx. It's too bad that means we're stuck inside the Nexus."

Maddox straightened, peering at the professor. Finally, he realized the wonder of this place had done something to Ludendorff. Apparently, the Methuselah Man wasn't immune to the Builder traps, either.

"Go," Maddox said.

"No. It's too late, my boy, far too late. *Victory* will have to use the tube without us. Ah, well, maybe that's just as—"

Maddox cut the professor's flow of words by yanking the old man, forcing him to come with him. They weren't doomed until they were dead.

"Move," the captain said.

"Why bother, my boy? It's over."

"Strand."

"An old scoundrel, to be sure, but why bring him into it?"

"He survived this place?"

The professor's mirrored visor turned toward Maddox.

"Yes, yes, that old scoundrel did survive, and he trained some of his spies and golden boys to do likewise. I should be able to overcome—"

Maddox kept pulling the professor even as he kept his eye on Shu's tumbling and dwindling cradle. She might have sealed the way out. He couldn't remember. They needed her if they were going to escape this place.

"I will survive," the professor declared. "First, I need to lie down in order to conjugate a perfect plan. And yet…isn't the perfect the enemy of the good?"

Maddox yanked the old babbler with him. This was a surprise. Why had Ludendorff succumbed and Strand survived this place? It was another mystery.

Finally, Maddox shoved Ludendorff into his cradle, attaching the straps. The Methuselah Man was singing a drunken-seeming ditty. Maddox had to yank out the phone-line to leave Ludendorff there.

First checking the tether-lines between thrusters, Maddox hurried into his cradle. He'd switched the tethers so he was in the lead. With careful concentration, he released the anchor clamp and pressed the trigger throttle. The cradle hissed hydrogen spray, lifting off the giant platform. A tug told him he yanked Meta after him. A second, harder tug told him the professor hadn't switched off his magnetic anchor.

Maddox waited as he applied more thrust. He no longer had a phone-link with Ludendorff. If the professor—

Maddox's cradle shot away, pulling the other two with him. Ludendorff still retained enough wit to have de-anchored himself.

Now began a race. Maddox chased Shu's tumbling cradle, which brushed a girder, changing her heading. The craft had dwindled considerably. Worse, it tumbled toward a pulsating light. What would happen if she plowed into the light?

Maddox clenched his teeth together. He wished Keith were here instead of him. The lieutenant would add a few summersaults, making everything look easy. It wasn't easy, however, not with all these girders everywhere.

Maddox stared fixedly with his lips pulled back in a rictus of determination. Weird ideas thrummed in his mind. His heart hammered. But he forced himself to focus with relentless fury.

By degrees, he gained on Shu. Strange colors glowed in this part of the pyramid. Maddox knew time worked against

212

them. Ludendorff had said as much, and something in the captain's gut agreed. It became like a fiery itch that transferred into his mind.

"No," he said. "First things first, I need Shu."

The itch grew worse.

Maddox shook his head and checked his meter. He'd gained velocity, and was quickly overtaking the Spacer. She sat like a statue in her cradle. Perhaps the process had finally overcome her.

Taking a deep breath, Maddox realized he did not have time to brake and do this right. He was going to have to try to magnetize her cradle to his.

Maddox laughed. This was crazy. He might as well enjoy the process. If he failed, he died.

"No. I will succeed. I am Captain Maddox. I am *di-far*."

There was no sport to the event. It was a struggle of life and death, tooth and claw, the law of the jungle. The greatness of the beast didn't matter as much as his fierce resolve.

The other cradle loomed larger now.

"One, two, three," Maddox said. "One, two, three, thrust!" he shouted.

His cradle slammed against Shu's craft. He clicked the magnetic switch, but not fast enough. The crash banged her cradle away from him.

Now, the captain snarled with rage. He kept the magnetic clamp on this time. He hadn't needed to time that part of it. He increased velocity, racing after her, pulling the others along.

By slow degrees, he reached closer, closer—he braked at the last minute. The two cradles touched, and Shu's craft sealed with his.

"Yes!" Maddox shouted, the sound reverberating in his helmet. He began to turn the cradle train, trying to spy the place they had entered while weaving past the huge girders.

Over there! He didn't see the spot exactly, but his subconscious must have. He couldn't have said what told him that was the right area, but he applied maximum thrust for it.

After what seemed like an eternity, he saw space and stars. Shu hadn't closed the opening. Might it be on a timer?

That was possible.

Maddox sat like a statue, only his throttle fingers moving. He had a terrible feeling that the way would close soon. Now, it was a race to see if he was right or wrong.

-36-

Lieutenant Noonan was worried and feeling inadequate. She sat in the captain's chair, realizing this is what she'd wanted for some time and yet now that she was here...

This almost reminded her of the first Star Watch fight against the New Men, the time Admiral von Gunther had led a battle group into a massacre. Three star cruisers had annihilated everything except her vessel. She'd made a snap decision, eventually hiding behind an asteroid in a lifeboat in a different star system...

It was hard to believe Star Watch had come so far in so short a time. The New Men had seemed invincible only a few years ago. Now, the golden race hid from Star Watch, and she belonged to the greatest vessel in the Commonwealth, trying to figure out how to jump one thousand light-years.

"The pyramid is radiating more power," Galyan said. The holoimage stood beside her as he often did with the captain.

"Thank you," Valerie said, glad her voice was steady. She was sure that she didn't sound as calm as Maddox would in this situation—

"What is that?" Galyan asked.

A bolt of power sizzled off the pyramid. A second bolt appeared, reaching far enough to blast an asteroid into pieces.

"The captain is in danger," Andros Crank declared. "We must rescue him at once, Lieutenant."

"How do you propose we do that?" Valerie demanded.

Victory's current pilot, and Ensign Daggett, Lieutenant Smith-Fowler, and Galyan—everyone on the bridge turned to stare at her.

The silver pyramid was becoming like the core of a chain-lightning event, shedding one bolt after another.

Valerie wanted to run her fingers through her hair and shriek for someone to give her an idea of what she should do. But she couldn't do that. She was in charge. She had to think for herself and for everyone else. Not only the crew, but maybe Star Watch, the Commonwealth, all of humanity, rested on her decision.

That was too much for her. Valerie began to moan out loud, clamping her teeth together as she struggled to control herself.

She remembered a study-night several years ago while she was still in the Space Academy. She'd gone to the library by herself. Valerie hadn't mixed well with the kids from the taxpaying families. She was the welfare recipient, the waif from the dirty streets of Detroit. She never smiled back then. She studied too hard for that, pushing herself to excel. She had to make her father proud. She had to show the others that she was just as good as they were.

That night hadn't been any exception as she studied for a coming test. Finally, around one a.m., Valerie realized that her eyes burned from reading for too long. She gathered her books and tablet, stuffing them into her backpack, and hurried down the stairs.

It had been dark outside, the stars bright overhead. Shouldering the backpack, she headed for her dorm. In the park, among the trees, she felt something. Then, three bulky shapes emerged from hiding. That rooted her feet to the soil. In Detroit, she'd faced similar dangers and acted accordingly. Here in the woods in the dark—

"What do we have here?" a young man asked.

Valerie blinked. The bulky shapes became normal-sized, skinny cadets. She recognized one of them, Tad Hummel, a braggart who liked to stare at her too much.

"You're out late, Cadet," Tad said, stepping near.

"Get out of my way," Valerie told him.

Tad turned to his friends. "Do you hear that? She thinks we're welfare beggars like her." He scowled as he turned back to her, stroking the side of her face with the back of his hand.

She thrust a knee at his groin. He blocked with his thigh while laughing at her.

The other two flanked her.

Valerie froze then, her stomach clenching. For a moment, fear stole her wits. Tad Hummel laughed again, touching her shoulder. The other two moved closer yet.

Valerie panicked as she tore a forbidden switchblade from her secret hiding spot, clicking it open. She stabbed Tad Hummel in the stomach. She jabbed in and yanked out three times before she realized what she was doing.

Tad staggered away, staring at his gut in horror, finally beginning to sob in terror. No doubt, he believed he was about to die.

He didn't. His friends grabbed him and raced to the infirmary. A medic patched the bastard up, but Tad Hummel couldn't continue in the Space Academy that semester.

The next day, the commandant pulled Valerie into her office. She was a tough old bird. The commandant stared at Valerie for what seemed like forever.

"Explain to me what happened," the commandant demanded.

Valerie could not. Once more, she froze. She stared back at the commandant, wanting to explain how the three had blocked her, made her feel as if they were going to rape her. And yet, she wondered about that. She knew the three had been trying to scare her, but she doubted they really would have raped her. She'd gone for her switchblade because that's what she'd done in Detroit. If she accused Tad Hummel of rape—

"It was dark," the commandant said. "Three men surrounded you. That's what one of the cadets said. He said you defended yourself. Is that right?"

Valerie could not speak. Shame at stabbing a fellow cadet, at overreacting filled her. She wanted to belong, to be one of the Academy members who knew everyone else. This would mark her as a welfare troublemaker for the rest of her life.

"Hmm," the commandant said. "If you're not going to press charges…"

Valerie tried to turn her head in order to nod no—she would not press charges. She could not move her head, though.

"I'll say this for you, Cadet. You fight. We want fighters in Star Watch. But know this. I have my eye on you. Don't make another mess or you're gone. Do I make myself clear?"

Valerie made a squeaking sound, which the commandant seemed to accept as a yes.

"That is all," the commandant said. "You are dismissed."

The incident had stuck to Valerie throughout the Academy year. Many must have thought of her as a troublemaker. She'd remained alone too much of the time. She should not have frozen. She should have—

"Lieutenant Noonan," Galyan said.

Valerie shook her head, coming out of her daze. On the main screen, more electrical discharges sizzled off the glowing hot pyramid.

Captain Maddox was out there. Meta and Keith were out there. They were family. They treated her as if she belonged with them. They would have stood with her in the dark against Tad Hummel and his jerk-off friends. Maddox, Meta and Keith would have helped her bust some heads. She wouldn't have needed the switchblade. She wouldn't have felt all alone.

Valerie stood. "Attention! Ensign Lewis, head toward the pyramid. We're going in to pick up the others."

"They have not reappeared since entering the Nexus," Galyan said. "They are still in the pyramid."

"Don't argue with me, Galyan," Valerie said.

The holoimage stiffened. She wondered if Galyan did that from studying human reactions.

"Lieutenant Noonan, I am not arguing. I state a fact. We have also lost communications with the shuttle."

"Stow it," Valerie said. "All hands," she said. "This is an emergency situation. We will assume the captain and his team were successful. Our present readings indicate the pyramid is activating something. That would seem to mean a hyper-spatial tube."

"I am sorry to disregard your order, Lieutenant Noonan," Galyan said. "I do not do so out of disrespect, but worry. This is not the process that produced the hyper-spatial tube last time."

"I know."

"Why then do you presume a tube will appear?"

Valerie licked her lips. It was a good point. She wasn't like Maddox, angry at anyone who questioned an order.

"Are you assuming we could have made a mistake?" Galyan asked.

"Elaborate on your theory," Valerie ordered.

"Last time," Galyan said, "a Builder used the pyramid to produce a hyper-spatial tube. The alien undoubtedly knew precisely how to use its own equipment. We are acting on a trial and error basis. It is possible we are making a tube, but unleashing other powers as well."

"Right," Valerie said. "That makes sense."

"Should we not wait farther back then?"

"Do you want Captain Maddox to die?"

"You wound me with your words."

"Right," Valerie said. "We're going in. We have to save our family."

"By risking a starship full of innocent people?" asked Galyan.

"We're all in this together," Valerie said.

"Ah. I understand. All for one and all for one," the holoimage quoted.

"What?" Valerie asked, frowning at Galyan.

The holoimage's eyelids fluttered. "Excuse me, please. I have misquoted the saying. It is all for one and one for all. Yes, that is how it goes."

Valerie stared at Galyan a moment longer.

Ensign Daggett moaned.

Valerie studied the main screen. Another energy bolt zigzagged from the pyramid. Now, however, about two hundred kilometers from *Victory*, appeared a silvery stellar whirlpool.

A feeling of shock and awe radiated from Valerie's body. The captain had done it. He'd found a way to create a hyper-spatial tube. They had to reach the tube before it went away. First, though, the others had to get into the shuttle and she had to go get them.

What had happened to the away team? Why weren't they coming out of the pyramid?

-37-

Captain Maddox hissed with elation as his cradle thruster shot through the pyramidal opening. He'd done it. He'd reached regular space again.

As he did, a pyrotechnic display nearly blinded him. Sheets of power radiated from the Nexus along with kilometers-long electrical bolts.

His helmet speaker began to crackle. No doubt, Keith tried to contact him.

Maddox used his chin, trying to adjust the helmet comm. The crackling intensified. He realized it wasn't someone calling him. It was the discharges playing havoc with his helmet's electronics.

Was the pyramid going to blow up? Maddox twisted in his cradle, looking back. The silver side radiated heat, glowing brighter and brighter.

The captain faced forward. He searched for the shuttle. Lieutenant Maker would not leave them in the lurch. He—

Maddox grinned.

The shuttle raced toward them. The bright exhaust made the vessel easy to see. Keith must have been watching the exit location. The moment the pilot had spied them, he came racing.

Now, however, the captain saw the silvery whirlpool in the distance. The Nexus had made the hyper-spatial tube. But it seemed the thing was far away. He wondered how many kilometers it was from them. Would the opening remain there long enough for them to reach *Victory* and then the tube?

It wouldn't be for a lack of trying.

Maddox accelerated for the shuttle. He ignored the electrical discharges because there was nothing he could do about them. Either one of those bolts would destroy them or it wouldn't.

Time seemed to expand. Every second seemed to take forever. As the shuttle crawled toward them, the crackling grew worse in his helmet.

Finally, an eon later—maybe ten minutes in real time— Keith eased the shuttle beside them. He moved so perfectly that the shuttle seemed motionless. All the while, the pyramid radiated more discharges and greater heat. Maddox's air-conditioning unit hummed continuously, but still he was sweating.

The captain unhooked his straps. Keith nudged the shuttle so a hatch was only ten meters away. Maddox crawled over his cradle, reaching a tether line. He pulled himself hand over hand, reaching Meta. He unhooked his woman, grabbed her and made the leap to the open hatch.

Keith reached out, grabbing the captain's outstretched hand.

One by one, Maddox brought each of the team into the shuttle. Keith took each arrival to the control chamber, strapping them in.

Maddox carried Shu in last. He floated into the shuttle, used his elbow to click a switch that shut the hatch and carried the tiny woman to the control chamber. He hooked her into place and then sat down beside Keith.

The lieutenant kept his helmet on. Maddox glanced at the others and noticed they still wore theirs too.

Maddox inserted his phone-line into Keith's suit. "Do you see the silvery whirlpool?"

"I do, mate. That's our next stop."

"No. We must reach *Victory* first"

"I doubt that's going to happen."

"Explain your reasoning?"

"Bloody hell, Captain, we're all about to die and you want me to explain. You're daft, out of your mind."

Maddox heard the panic in Keith's voice. He was impressed the young man had done as well as he had under these conditions. The lieutenant must be working on automatic.

"Take a couple of deep breaths," Maddox said. "You're going to be fine."

"Begging your pardon, Captain, but you don't know what you're talking about. I've been analyzing the bugger."

"The pyramid?"

"What else would I mean?"

"And?" Maddox asked.

"It's shedding power, and its getting hotter. We have minutes to get away before it burns us up."

"We should already be burned up then."

"No, no, no, no, no," Keith shouted. "The sides are heating up at an exponential rate, doubling every minute. Given enough time, it will be hotter than a star."

"But—"

"If that isn't enough," Keith shouted, "the whirlpool is sucking the starship into it."

"What? How is that possible?"

Keith laughed with a manic edge to his voice. "You pushed a bloody switch in there is how. The Nexus is going crazy. I wouldn't wonder if it's going to blow."

Maddox had felt the same thing earlier. If the pyramid did blow, what would that do to the hyper-spatial tube it had created?

"Hang on now, sir, I'm giving it everything."

Maddox was shoved against his cushioned seat as the shuttle gained Gs.

"Are you heading for *Victory*?"

"No! I'm heading for the wormhole. *Victory* is going to go in first. I'm simply following her, hoping we both pop out at the same place."

Maddox wondered what Shu had done inside the Nexus. Maybe no one could use the hyper-spatial tubes except for a Builder. Maybe they had tried to go one technological marvel too far this time.

"Are you in contact with *Victory*?" Maddox asked.

A mad cackle was Keith's only reply.

Maddox inspected the others, studied his suit and realized the shuttle lacked any dampeners. The Gs kept increasing.

"We should slow down," he said.

"That way lies suicide, mate. My way is life. You'd better shut your yapper for a time. I have to concentrate."

Maddox did just that. If Keith needed to concentrate, it must be difficult. In the end, the captain appreciated skill over discipline.

"She's going in," Keith shouted.

Maddox glanced at the pilot's screen. He saw the blip that must be *Victory* vanishing into the silvery whirlpool.

"Come on, you piece of filth," Keith shouted. "Give me more bloody power. We're running for our lives, you bucket of bolts."

The Gs continued to rise. Soon, they would all lose consciousness.

Fighting the Gs, Maddox reached up, tapping his panel. He used a backward-aiming camera. The pyramid glowed and pulsated. The discharges were constant. Then, to the captain's amazement, the titanic pyramid exploded. It simply burst apart like a grenade.

That seemed horrible. An artifact that old—

"Here we go, Captain, into the rabbit hole."

Maddox stared at the hyper-spatial tube opening. It no longer swirled with a silvery color. It was dead black. Behind them, the Nexus no longer existed as the blast expanded. How long would the tube remain in existence?

As the blast reached them, the shuttle sank into the blackness.

It was just like last time. An incredible sensation of speed took hold. Everything grew dark, and everything seemed to flash past the shuttle. The bulkheads shook without sound.

A feeling of weirdness and wrongness overloaded the captain's senses. How could a shuttle move a thousand light-years inside a tube that could not exist?

Maddox endured as the shaking intensified. Was the hyper-spatial tube unraveling? Would it dump them somewhere other than where the tube had originally aimed? Or would they simply cease to exist as the tube unraveled?

Maddox felt a terrible sense of sickness. It seemed as if his body stretched until it was as least as long as the Solar System. The stretching sensation went on and on. He wanted it to end. He never wanted to endure this feeling again. He would rather...

No, he told himself. *I will fight on.*

As Maddox endured, he noticed an opening ahead. Normalcy seemed to lie out there. Would the shuttle reach the opening? If it did, where would they be? How far had the shuttle traveled? Was *Victory* waiting out there, or had the starship gone somewhere else?

As the shuttle raced for it, the opening began to fray around the edges. It began to disintegrate.

The hyper-spatial tube is coming apart. Please, give us a few more seconds.

Maddox realized he had just uttered a prayer.

The fraying grew worse as reality seemed to be disappearing. Maybe the shuttle would stay in this realm if they couldn't reach the shrinking opening in time.

Please.

The fraying seemed to slow down just a bit or was that the captain's imagination? He couldn't tell. He felt sick. He felt weird. He strove to remain conscious but lost the fight.

As the shuttle strained to reach the last little bit of the real world, Captain Maddox succumbed to the inertia of hyper-spatial tube travel and blanked out.

-38-

Admiral Esmeralda Diaz Lucia Sanchez stood on the bridge of the SWS Battleship *Austerlitz*. Shock twisted her one-hundred-year-old features. Silence reigned on the bridge. Everyone stared at the main screen.

"The pyramid is gone," Sanchez whispered.

"So is *Victory*," the sensor officer said hoarsely.

Sanchez bit a fingernail in indecision, finally turning to the sensor officer, a gruff old graybeard. "Did you...?" The admiral used her tongue to swab the inside of her mouth. It was bone dry. "Did you record the event?"

"I did," the sensor officer said.

"You definitely saw the starship enter the hyper-spatial tube?"

The gray-bearded officer nodded.

Sanchez turned back to the main screen. The expanding debris from the pyramid's blast had shredded many nearby asteroids. She found this difficult to accept. The ancient artifact had exploded. It was gone. So was the starship with its arrogant, half-New Man captain. What did that mean for the Commonwealth?

Sanchez knew *Victory's* story as well as the next Star Watch officer. The ancient starship and its wickedly clever captain had been instrumental in humanity's survival these past few years. Could the vessel have survived this catastrophe? She did not see how.

A knot of pain beat in her heart. The Lord High Admiral wanted to use the Nexuses in order to expand the Patrol's range. Humanity needed that advantage if it was going to survive the Swarm.

Sanchez headed for her chair, concentrating on walking normally. She sat with a soft grunt. This was unbelievable. The Nexus—

She turned to the sensor officer. "I'll have to send a destroyer to Earth. I have to get a message to High Command about this."

"Better send several destroyers," the old graybeard said. "You wouldn't want a star cruiser intercepting the message."

Sanchez stared at her most trusted officer. They'd worked together for over twenty-two years. "No. You're wrong."

The sensor officer seemed surprised.

"This might be the most important message in Star Watch just now," Sanchez said. "I'm taking the entire flotilla back to Earth."

"Ah," the graybeard said. "Yes. Smart."

Sanchez pressed the intercom button on her chair. It was time to collect her warships and speak to the workers on the space station. Then, she had to race back to Earth and give the Lord High Admiral the dreadful news.

***

Harsh, wheezing laughter filled the bridge of the cloaked star cruiser.

Strand sat in his chair while surrounded by his New Men bridge crew. He, too, watched the debris from the Nexus smash nearby asteroids.

The cloaked star cruiser was much farther away from the event than Admiral Sanchez was. The vessel had been here for several days already, observing many interesting things.

The laughter continued as Strand slouched in his thickly cushioned chair. The back of his head rested on the fabric. Tears leaked from his eyes. He held his chest as louder whoops of joy emitted from his throat.

Finally, the laughter began to subside. Strand worked himself into a sitting position. He wiped his eyes. He hadn't laughed like that for a long, long time. Sheer joy and exuberance filled him. This was wonderful. According to his exacting calculations—

"The old goat is gone," Strand declared. "The meddler has finally met his match. After centuries of interference, I am finally rid of the know-it-all professor."

None of the New Men spoke in response to the statement. A few glanced up at him from time to time. The rest waited obediently at their stations.

"What?" Strand said. "Can't any of you join me in my hour of triumph?"

The New Men continued as before in silence.

"This isn't right," Strand said. "I am marvelously happy. I want you to join me in celebration. Laugh."

All the New Men looked up at him now.

Strand found that irritating and unfulfilling. "I said laugh," he told them. He held up his left arm and began to tap on the control unit.

The effect on the New Men was immediate. Each opened his mouth and began to laugh in a mechanical fashion. None of the laughter reached their eyes, however. Instead, each of them seemed to be in agony of spirit.

"That's better," Strand said. He looked around at his laughing crew of golden-skinned superiors. Soon, though, he wearied of the noise, and tapped the unit again.

The laughter ceased.

"Return to your duties," Strand said.

Each New Man turned around, facing his board.

For once, Strand did not brood at their reactions. He continued to smile as he stared at the main screen. He had slipped into the Nexus over six months ago. He had made adjustments. He had been certain that in time Star Watch would try to use a hyper-spatial tube. It had been an obvious move, easy to foresee. He had even expected Ludendorff to go inside the Nexus to do the deed, as it were.

Strand nodded as he put his hands on his chest. Everything was falling into place. The ancient Adok vessel had tried to use the hyper-spatial tube at exactly the wrong moment. His studies showed that the tube would disappear the instant the generator failed.

Victory, the infernal Ludendorff, the freak Captain Maddox and a Spacer witch had all died in the tube.

"I am Strand," he whispered. "I am the greatest."

"Master," a New Man said.

Strand looked up, surprised one of the New Men would dare to speak to him uninvited.

"You instructed me to tell you the moment the Star Watch flotilla began to maneuver for the Laumer-Point."

Strand nodded. That's right. He had ordered that. His heart rate came down to normal.

"All the vessels are accelerating for the wormhole," the New Man said.

Strand debated whether he should ambush the flotilla on the other side of the wormhole. He decided against it. Better to prepare for the next round. With Ludendorff gone, with *Victory* out of the way—

"Attention," Strand said. "You will prepare for jump."

"What coordinates should I set, Master?" the navigator asked.

Strand told him. Then he resumed studying the nonexistent Nexus. After all this time, it was gone. He felt a momentary loss but shook that off. This was an enjoyable moment. He had far too few of those. He would miss the professor—

"What?" Strand asked himself. "No. I'm glad Ludendorff is gone, very glad. Good riddance to that bothersome old meddler. Now, I can finally get on with my life's task."

-39-

Captain Maddox groaned. He didn't know where he was, couldn't remember what had happened.

His eyelids fluttered as he struggled to open them. The first attempt failed. That seemed off.

Why can't I open my eyes?

For a brief moment, Maddox wondered if he'd died. A dead body couldn't do anything. That's why he lay here.

By slow degrees, he realized that if his soul was still inside his body he couldn't be dead. Therefore, he must be alive. And if that was true, he could open his eyes.

Unless I'm paralyzed.

Is that what had happened? That would explain—

He groaned again as his right eyelid twitched just enough to emit light against the orb. That caused his head to jerk, which in turn made the other eye open. More light poured piercingly in.

Was he in some kind of time trance, seeing the brilliance of the pyramid's explosion?

That didn't seem right. The shuttle had plunged into the hyper-spatial tube. He'd escaped the Nexus's destruction. So if light shined in his eyes—

His eyelids fluttered, and things finally started to come into focus. He viewed a vacc suit's knees—his own. He moved his eyes, peered farther, spotting a blinking panel in front of him.

I'm in the shuttle. I'm strapped into my seat. I survived. It appears we made it out of the hyper-spatial tube.

With an effort, Maddox sat up; straightened his spine and willed his head to follow. He raised his arms next. They worked. Thus, he wasn't paralyzed. Breathing in and out, he gathered strength. Finally, he unhooked himself. The straps floated in the air.

They were weightless, meaning the shuttle no longer accelerated or decelerated.

Maddox glanced at the others. Each of them slumped where he'd strapped them in. All the vacc suits looked intact.

A hyper-spatial tube—the shuttle had entered and exited a tube. They were somewhere in the great Beyond. No doubt they were far from the Xerxes System, far from the Commonwealth of Planets, far from any region of Human Space. Where were they? How far had the shuttle traveled and what had happened to Starship *Victory*?

Priorities, he realized. Patrol School had taught him to take care of essentials first.

Maddox shoved off his seat, floating to Meta. Her suit indicators showed that she was alive. It surprised him how visibly less tense he felt because of that. Maybe his feelings for Meta were even stronger than he realized. He set the thought aside, going to each of the crew in turn. Everyone had survived, although none of the others had woken up yet.

That must be due to his stronger constitution.

Returning to his chair, Maddox began a diagnostic of the shuttle. For now, it was their only ship. The tiny vessel seemed to be intact. They had fuel, air, food—

Maddox leaned near Keith, adjusting the piloting board. He retracted the blast shields from in front of the viewing port and turned on the screen. Outside the ship, he spied endless debris and giant rocks.

The captain frowned. Had they doubled back, reappearing in the Xerxes System, in its asteroid field?

Sitting back in his chair, Maddox gathered his resolve. If the shuttle had doubled back…

No. That was ridiculous. He needed to continue doing one thing at a time. Steeling himself, Maddox began a survey of nearby space, analyzing the composition of the largest asteroids.

A half hour later, Maddox turned around as Meta snorted. He heard the sound over his vacc suit's inner helmet speaker.

"Meta," he said, using a short-link connection.

"Maddox?" she whispered. "What happened? Where am I? Where's the Nexus?"

He floated to her, unbuckling her straps, holding her. As gently as possible, he told her what had happened.

"Destroyed?" Meta asked. "The Nexus is destroyed?"

"Yes."

"Where are we?"

"I don't have an exact fix. But by triangulating from several known stars, I believe we've traveled two thousand light-years from the Xerxes System."

"That's insane," she said in a small voice.

"It appears we moved in the direction of the galactic core. As far as I can tell, we're still in the Orion Arm."

She was quiet and still. That was a lot to take in. Finally, she stirred. Maybe she was ready to hear more.

"I haven't been able to contact *Victory*," he said. "Unfortunately, so far I haven't seen any sign of the starship. That's not conclusive, though. With all the debris, she could be hiding, or she could be farther than the message has traveled. It's only been a half hour since I sent the message."

"I can hear it in your voice. What else is wrong?"

"The star system seems familiar."

"How is that possible?" she asked. "We've never been two thousand light-years from the Xerxes System."

"I mean the star system's *state* seems familiar. I haven't detected any planets, but there is endless debris and asteroids."

"What does that mean?"

"It reminds me of Galyan's star system. Maybe there are no planets because they've all been blasted apart."

Meta moaned. "The alien Destroyer has been here?"

"I hadn't thought of that. I doubt this is the work of the Destroyer. The Builder once told me the Destroyer had been used closer to Human Space."

"But if the Destroyer didn't smash the system—the Swarm," Meta said. "The Swarm invaders blew up Galyan's planets. Have you spotted any Swarm vessels?"

"I have not," Maddox said.

"What about Swarm devices?" Meta asked. "Maybe they left mines."

Maddox released her. "Yes. We need to scan for mines. I've been so busy trying to figure out where we are that I haven't had time—"

"You can't do everything," Meta said, interrupting. "That's why you have a crew. We should wake up the others."

"Let's wake up Keith first," Maddox said. "We'll hold off on Ludendorff and Shu."

"Are you sure? We might need their brainpower."

"I'm sure," Maddox said.

"Should we recharge our suits with air or should we take them off?"

Maddox wondered if a lingering portion of Shu's toxin still inhabited his brain. He should have already thought of that. Perhaps the extent of their plight had numbed his thinking. They were all alone out here, far away from anything familiar. They might have lost *Victory*, their only hope for long-term survival.

"We'll take off our suits," Maddox said. "We need efficiency and clear thinking. Staying in our suits only adds to our burdens."

"I agree," Meta said, heading for Shu.

✳✳✳

The Spacer remained asleep, but soon did so wearing her regular garb.

Ludendorff woke up as Maddox took off the Methuselah Man's vacc suit. The professor was groggy, though. He seemed dazed, unable to form words. Maddox strapped Ludendorff back onto his chair.

Keith came around faster than the others did. "What happened?" the pilot asked.

Maddox told him as the lieutenant began to nod.

"Right, right," Keith said, "I remember now."

Soon, the three of them went to work. Keith piloted, mapped the star system and searched for *Victory*. Meta went throughout the shuttle, exploring for damage and taking stock of their supplies. Maddox checked the gun locker, searched Shu and then Ludendorff. Afterward, he thought through the implications of their situation.

An hour later, they compared notes. Meta said with rationing they could survive several months. The power might last as long, but depended on how much they accelerated and decelerated. Keith said they were two thousand, three hundred and sixteen light-years from Earth. So far, he'd found seven powered mines floating in the system. The mines seemed primitive but huge in terms of megaton size. There were another thirty-eight inert mines. The lieutenant had also spotted two hundred and nineteen hulks.

"Ships?" Maddox asked.

"I wouldn't go that far," Keith said. "They are burned out shells of ships. You were right, Captain. This is just like the Adok Star System. If I had to guess, I'd say the Swarm has been through here, killing another species. If I were to guess again, I'd say it happened at least a century ago, maybe longer."

"Your length-of-time estimate is due to the inert mines?" Meta asked.

"Aye," Keith said.

Maddox ingested the data. Active mines were bad. At least they hadn't entered a war zone. Still—

Ludendorff groaned before raising a hand, wiping drool from his chin.

"Get me out of here," the professor said querulously.

"Have you forgotten how to unbuckle?" Maddox asked.

The professor gave him a peevish glance, finally poking at the buckles. A moment later, he clicked them, shedding the straps. He pushed out of the chair to float up to the ceiling.

"Confound it," Ludendorff said. "Was that on purpose?"

Maddox went to his rescue, pulling Ludendorff down and shoving him into a chair. The professor gripped the armrests, watching them as if they might move.

"What's wrong with him?" Keith whispered.

"I'm adjusting to the situation," Ludendorff snapped.

"Adjusting to what?"

"Don't be impertinent," Ludendorff said. "My mind is more sensitive than yours. It's why I'm so brilliant. I respond to stimuli with greater vigor. I see quicker."

"Then why did the captain revive sooner than Meta?" Keith asked.

"Why don't you shut up," Ludendorff said. "Your monkey chatter is giving me a headache. I need time to compose myself. The Nexus—"

Ludendorff looked up at Maddox. "What happened to the Nexus?"

"It exploded," Maddox said.

Ludendorff frowned severely, finally glancing at Shu. "I doubt it was sabotage on her part. It seems rather excessive for a Builder."

"Do you suspect Strand?" Maddox asked.

"I don't see how he could have done it," Ludendorff said.

"Perhaps because he knows more about the Nexus than you do," Maddox said.

"On the face of it, that sounds preposterous," Ludendorff said. "But perhaps you have a point. I don't see why he would want to destroy the Nexus, though. It is a priceless artifact."

Maddox glanced at Meta. She shrugged. The obvious reason would be to try to kill them.

"The Nexus is gone," the captain told Ludendorff. "Even if it existed, it couldn't help us now. We're over two thousand light-years from Earth. We have no idea what happened to *Victory,* and we're in a destroyed star system with Swarm mines in evidence."

"I want to see them," Ludendorff said excitedly.

"Did you hear me?" Maddox said. "We've lost the starship, and we're stranded deep in the Beyond. Before we study anything, we'd better decide on our priorities."

"Studying those mines *should* be our priority," Ludendorff said. "We need to know if the Swarm came through the system ages ago or more recently. Maybe studying the mines will tell us if the Swarm has a star drive or if they still rely on a NAFAL drive. Perhaps as important, whom did they destroy, and does that species exist in a nearby star system?"

Some of the professor's excitement bled into Maddox. They had problems, serious ones. But they also had their wits and tools to do something about the situation.

Patrol protocol called for hard work at a time like this. They only had so much time, so they'd better start using it.

***

Four hours later, Maddox helped the professor out of his vacc suit. The Methuselah Man beamed with excitement. He'd just spent the last three quarters of an hour outside the shuttle examining an inert mine.

Keith piloted the shuttle, heading away from the huge warhead. The thing had been as large as a Star Watch strike cruiser.

"Amazing, simply amazing," the professor said. "It is a genuine Swarm mine. I've studied ancient mines like this in the Adok Star System. I have also scoured Swarm ruins on Wolf Prime, having seen schematics like that mine."

"How old is the mine?" Maddox asked.

"It's difficult to say for sure. Four or five hundred years would be my guess."

"Almost the same time as the Adok destruction," Maddox said.

"My boy, that's incredibly fuzzy thinking. The Swarm assaulted the Adoks six thousand years ago."

"I'm taking into account the time to travel from the Adok Star System to out here."

"That's ludicrous," the professor said. "I doubt the Swarm fleets ever reached one-half light speed. I'd suppose something on the order of one-fifth light speed."

"We know one thing," Maddox said. "According to the Builder, the alien Destroyer didn't reach this far."

"Agreed, agreed," "Ludendorff said. "If this happened four hundred years ago…" The professor rubbed his hands. "We must have reached the near vicinity of the Swarm Imperium. Would they have sent a war fleet to a distant location? I would not imagine so."

Maddox became thoughtful. A Swarm Imperium hadn't seemed so awful before. Now, that they might have found the

236

outer edge, might be close to the Swarm, in fact, a dread of the Swarm tightened the captain's gut. With a mental effort, he pushed that aside. He must concentrate. He must use his wits.

"Why didn't the Swarm colonize the star system?" Maddox asked.

"The reason is obvious," Ludendorff said. "I'm surprised you have to ask. This must have been a hardy species full of fight. In that way, they were like the Adoks."

"We know that Builders helped the Adoks prepare for the Swarm. Did Builders help this race?"

Ludendorff's jaw dropped as he peered at Maddox in wonder. "That is a tantalizing question. I just thought of another. If a Builder didn't help this race, it would seem this was more than just a one-system species."

"How do you conclude that?"

"The Adoks had a Builder to aid them, yes? If this race did not have a Builder, it might have had more star systems as an industrial base. That would allow them the capacity to build a massive fleet. That would give the Swarm a reason for an extinction-level fight. Given that, maybe the other species still survives in a nearby star system."

"Correct me if I'm wrong, but you said this attack happened four hundred years ago."

"That's nothing when races fight an interstellar war at sub-light speeds," Ludendorff said. "Such a conflict could take thousands of years. Ah, I see your confusion. The Swarm might have miscalculated. Don't you see? One of their invasion fleets might have been annihilated before they finally destroyed this star system. That would naturally increase the duration of the conflict. Oh, there is so much to study out here. We must begin scanning the other star systems for technological signs at once."

"How could that possibly matter to us now?" Maddox asked. "Unless we find *Victory*, none of us will ever travel to another star system again."

"Your statement is imprecise. As long as we have food, air and energy, we can travel to another star. Have you looked out there? Many of the stars are nearer than one light-year."

"Professor—"

The intercom crackled. "Sir," Keith said. "You'd better come forward. I've found *Victory*, but she looks to be in a bad way. Even worse, enemy craft are accelerating toward her."

40

Maddox studied the shuttle's main screen.

Lieutenant Maker pinpointed Starship *Victory's* position. It was on the outer edge of the system at a point farther than Pluto would have been from Earth. The ancient Adok vessel had been hidden behind a larger-than-average asteroid, but had finally drifted out from behind it.

"Have you hailed them?" Maddox asked.

"Yes, sir," Keith said. "I did it the instant I spotted them. It's going to take some time for our message to reach them, though."

Maddox nodded absently. Because their messages could only travel at the speed of light, the message would take hours to reach the starship and then hours for the return message to come back. The image they saw of *Victory* was hours old.

"There are three enemy vessels heading for the starship," Keith said.

Maddox read the specs on the alien ships. "Is that right?" he asked.

"Yes, sir," Keith said. "They're approximately destroyer-sized but have the mass of a cruiser or greater. Those are dense ships, sir. I don't know why, but they must be almost completely made of solid metal. Where's the room for the crew?"

Ludendorff floated up, studying the specs. "Very odd," the professor muttered.

Maddox silently agreed. Instead of hollow spheres, the alien vessels were like cannonballs except for their teardrop shape. The alien ships accelerated, building up velocity as they headed for distant *Victory*.

"How long will it take the aliens to reach *Victory*?" Maddox asked.

"That depends on whether they accelerate all the way there or decelerate in order to board her," Keith said. He studied his board "The soonest they can get there is thirty-six hours."

"They possess a primitive drive," Ludendorff said. "They're certainly slower than Star Watch vessels."

"A whole lot slower," Keith agreed. "I wouldn't have spotted our starship, but I calculated the aliens' direction of travel and wondered what they were headed toward."

"Could those so-called ships be mines?" Maddox asked.

"If they are," Keith said, "they're a lot different from the mines we've seen so far."

"Those are not Swarm vessels," Ludendorff declared. "I suspect those are the ships of the beings that battled the Swarm."

Maddox sat back, thinking. "It seems to me you can only know that if you recognize the type of ship. Thrax Ti Ix used saucer-shaped vessels, which seemed most unSwarmlike."

"Calm yourself, Captain," Ludendorff said. "I do not recognize the ships. I have never been this far out before. Like you, the farthest I've been from Earth was the Dyson sphere. I am speaking from my long years as a Swarm archeologist. The configuration of those vessels and their density does not match any known Swarm design. That is not conclusive proof, mind you, but I am going with that in lieu of anything else."

"Why is *Victory* inactive?" Maddox asked.

"The likeliest reason is some form of hyper-spatial shock," Ludendorff said.

"We can't let the aliens board *Victory*," Keith said.

"What do you suggest we do?" the professor asked. "If we launch one of our drones, we might destroy one of their ships, although I don't know if our drones have sufficient blast-power to take apart one of those dense vessels. If we attack them, we will have certainly created alien enemies. Gentlemen, we are stranded far from home with a limited supply of everything. We need friends more than enemies right now."

"We need Starship *Victory*," Keith said.

"Granted," the professor said. "But what if we can't help *Victory* in time?"

"Your logic escapes me," Maddox said. "We will do everything in our power to save the starship. We have two long-range drones. Otherwise, we have a few anti-torpedoes and energy for our laser." The captain addressed Keith. "Get ready to launch the drones."

"You don't even know if they're enemies or not," Ludendorff said.

"Anything threatening *Victory* is my enemy," Maddox said. "Our starship is also the only way home. More importantly…the vessel holds my crew."

"You were going to say something else, I believe, Captain," Ludendorff said, studying him.

"Nevertheless," Maddox said. He turned to Keith. "Launch the first drone."

"Captain," Ludendorff said. "You are premature in your estimation of the situation. Perhaps the aliens are humanitarians wishing to help our vessel. Let us try diplomacy first."

"Can you speak the alien language?"

"I have no idea."

"We will launch the drones in order to work them into position," Maddox said. "Then, you may attempt your diplomacy."

Ludendorff nodded. "You're inflexible, I see. Very well, go ahead."

"Meta," Maddox said. He distrusted the professor when the man became this reasonable. And in this desperate situation, there was no margin for error.

Meta drew her stunner, aiming it at Ludendorff.

"Captain," the Methuselah Man said. "This is quite unnecessary. We are in this situation together."

"I applaud your intellect and resources," Maddox told the professor. "I do not always approve of your high-handed actions, however. I hope you'll excuse me if I practice some caution in this most precarious moment."

"My boy, at the moment, I'm powerless to do anything against your wishes."

Maddox smiled coldly. "You could self-destruct the drones as easily as the three of us could. We only have the two. Until the drones strike, I'm placing you in confinement."

"That is rash," Ludendorff said. "You know I have a long memory regarding these actions."

"I'm glad to hear it," Maddox said. "If we survive this expedition, I hope you will adjust your schemes accordingly while aboard my ship. Meta."

She waved her stunner at the hatch.

Ludendorff shrugged, floating for the exit.

"If he tries anything or even hesitates too much," Maddox told Meta. "Stun him."

She nodded, with her gaze fixed on the professor. The two of them exited the command cabin.

"Are you ready?" Maddox asked Keith.

"Yes, sir."

"Launch when ready."

Keith manipulated his board and finally tapped it.

The small craft shuddered. A drone drifted into view. Finally, the engine ignited, a long blue tail growing behind it. The drone sped for the nearest alien vessel, with the proximity device on maximum to avoid debris and asteroids. Five minutes later, Keith launched the second drone.

Maddox exhaled, and the two men exchanged glances.

"It's our turn to accelerate," Maddox said.

"I don't think so," a softly feminine voice said.

Maddox spun around. The Spacer was awake, aiming a tiny tube at him.

41

"This is embarrassing," Maddox said. "I thought you were out."

"I have been listening for some time," Shu said.

Maddox studied her as she spoke. He couldn't see her eyes, making his analysis more difficult but not impossible. She seemed sharp. If she had been dazed upon first waking, her feigning sleep had given her time to adjust.

"First," she said, "we will destroy those drones."

"I would like you to reconsider," Maddox said.

"Do not delay, Captain. Destroy the drones or I will shoot the young lieutenant."

"Me?" Keith asked. "I saved your life. Besides, I thought you liked me."

"I do," she said, smiling briefly. "But first I must fulfill my mission. I hope you will not hold that against me."

"No..." Keith said, glancing at the captain. "I understand duty."

"Thank you," she said, giving him another smile, this one more potent than the first.

"But I can't destroy the two drones unless the captain gives the word," Keith said. "You're delightfully beautiful, but I guess the sergeant had it right. I can't let beauty sway me. That will only get me into trouble."

"You are in serious trouble," Shu said, "as I am about to kill you unless you do as I say."

"Captain?" Keith asked. "What should I do?"

"Provost Marshal—" Maddox said.

"I am a Surveyor First Class," Shu said, interrupting him.

"Surveyor, the alien ships are accelerating to *Victory*. The starship is our ticket home."

"You are wrong, Captain. I dearly hope you're not going to force my hand in this. I find your lieutenant unbearably attractive. I will mourn for a year or longer if I'm forced to kill him."

"Don't do it then," Keith said.

"Duty first," she said.

"What duty?" Maddox asked. "Did you destroy the Nexus on purpose?"

"No more tricks, Captain. Destroy the drones at once. I will not stand for any more delaying tactics."

Maddox turned to a white-faced Keith. "Begin acceleration, Lieutenant. We have a long way to go, and we want to get there before the aliens reach *Victory*."

Keith cleared his throat.

"Don't worry about her weapon," Maddox said. "It's as inert as the majority of the Swarm mines."

"You lie," Shu said.

"Provost Marshal," Maddox said. "Give me a little credit. I deactivated all your weapons while you were unconscious."

The Spacer hesitated a moment longer. Then, still aiming the tube at Keith, she pressed a switch. Nothing happened.

"You just tried to murder me," Keith said. "You've been lying to me."

"You're a stupid young animal," Shu said coldly. "How could you imagine that I would willingly rut with you?"

Keith blushed crimson.

Maddox studiously avoided looking at the young lieutenant, giving him time to gather himself.

"Live and learn," Keith finally muttered, trying to sound jocular. It didn't work. He sounded hurt. Without a word, he turned toward his panel. "Hang on," he muttered.

Maddox barely sat down in time, pressing a klaxon. As it began to blare, the shuttle started heavy acceleration.

Maddox turned on the intercom. "Meta, are you okay?"

"I am," she answered over the intercom a moment later. "But I hit my forehead. How about giving us more warning next time?"

Maddox glanced at Keith.

With a few taps, Keith lowered the rate of acceleration. Then he stared at the screen as if absorbed with the stars.

Maddox faced Shu. "What is the nature of the race that controls those spaceships?"

"I have no idea," the Spacer said sullenly.

"That is illogical. You must have some idea. Otherwise, why did you wish to destroy our drones to save them?"

Shu did not respond.

"Why did you choose this star system to travel to?"

Shu shrugged.

"You can do better than that," Maddox said. "You deliberately took us here. I would like to know your reason."

The Spacer didn't shrug this time. She just sat motionlessly.

"You're trapped on this side of the hyper-spatial tube just like we are," Maddox said.

Shu regarded him. "Your vaunted starship is doomed. I…know this place from our legends. I can save your life, but you will have to do exactly as I say."

Maddox exhaled. "The Visionary called me *di-far*. I am a man of decision. Do you suppose I will sit here while aliens attack my starship? Do you think I will let the woman with the answers sit comfortably with me as I watch my people die? If so, let me suggest another possibility. You will soon scream in agony. The old conventions do not inhibit me. You have set your will against mine. So be it. You will now begin to talk, or you will pay the price."

"Your threats mean nothing to me."

"Very well," Maddox said. "To show you I am in earnest—" He shoved off his seat, reached her and grasped her right hand in a lock. She struggled to no avail.

"You tried to kill my pilot," Maddox said, his face inches from hers. "That was heartless, particularly as he saved your life just before the Nexus exploded."

"Do your worst," she whispered.

245

Maddox grasped her pinky finger, and with a wrench, he broke it.

Shu sucked in her breath, turning white.

Maddox released her, floating back to his chair. The lieutenant stared at him wide-eyed and shocked at the brutality.

Shu moaned as she cradled her hand.

"I'm waiting," Maddox said, sounding as inflexible as steel.

Shu stared at him. "You have no idea who I am. If you won't listen to me—" She concentrated.

"Sir," Keith shouted. "One of the drones just detonated."

Maddox shifted on his seat as if to lunge at her again.

"Hold," Shu said in a hoarse voice. "If you come at me, I will destroy the last drone. Then, I will self-destruct our power plant. You have maimed me! This is sacrilege."

"Who are you?" Maddox asked.

"Shu 15."

"What does that mean?"

"How can I explain it to a barbarian? You preen on your quickness, never realizing that you are dead of soul. How can you conceive of the greatness of my mission? Your starship is so precious to you. What a sick joke. It is a freakish Builder construct."

"The Spacers are Builder in origin," Maddox pointed out.

"Yes! Your Builder was a freak. That is what I mean by freakish. Look at what it did, unleashing the Methuselah Men on humanity. Those monsters could only create in their own image, the New Men indeed. The new barbarians leading humanity down a mechanical path of subjection."

"What are you if not another curiosity?" Maddox asked.

Shu grinned starkly. "I am of the Noble House. I understand matters of the spirit. I use my mind instead of my muscles. I am going to help unleash a golden age on humanity and on the universe. Do you think I'm going to let someone like you stop me?"

"How can you go on if you self-destruct the power plant?" Maddox asked.

"How you strive and search for answers you cannot understand. Do you see this great wreck of a star system? It

246

shows me that the legends and stellar maps are correct. I am nearing the wondrous prize that will elevate the Spacers a thousand years sooner than otherwise."

"The Swarm destroyed this star system," Maddox said. "That means the Swarm must be near."

"Meaningless," Shu said.

"Who are in those spaceships out there? Are they Spacers?"

A look of concentration came over Shu. At the same time, the hatch swung open and Meta floated through. She had a large bruise on her forehead. Shu half turned. Meta raised the stunner and pulled the trigger. Nothing happened.

"Fool," Shu said.

Maddox's hand blurred. He hurled his long-barreled gun, the weapon flying through the cabin. It struck Shu on the head, causing her to slump in her seat.

Meta looked up at him. "Why didn't my stunner fire?"

"She must have shorted it," Maddox said. "She used her Builder devices to cause a drone to self-destruct. She must have sent a shuttle signal to the drone."

Meta collected the floating pistol.

Maddox jumped across the cabin. He opened a medikit and took out a hypo. Floating to Shu, he made ready to inject her.

"What are you doing?" Meta asked.

"We can't let her wake up again," he said. "I'm making sure she stays out."

"If she's that dangerous," Meta said, "we should kill her."

Maddox shook his head. "She knows things we need to learn. We need her. But we can't afford to let her use her devices again."

"Surgery?" Meta asked.

"If we can get to *Victory*," Maddox said. "Until then, we have to keep her under."

"What do you think she hopes to find out here?" Meta asked.

That was an interesting question. Maddox had an idea, but he wasn't ready to say what it was just yet.

He gave Shu the injection, rubbing her arm afterward.

"He broke her little finger," Keith said, with mingled disbelief and disappointment. "He just got up, grabbed her hand and broke the pinky. You're ruthless—sir."

Maddox said nothing.

"Even after what she said to me," Keith said, "I never could have done what you did."

"It was business," Maddox said.

"I know," Keith said. "I'm just saying, sir. I guess that's part of what makes me me and you you."

"I'm going to strap the Spacer onto a med unit," Maddox said. "Afterward, we need to increase our acceleration. We have one drone to help us even the odds. Then, our shuttle must face two dense ships. If we hope to save *Victory*, we're going to have to figure out a way to defeat those last two vessels."

"That's providing our drone can take out one of them," Keith said.

"Yes," Maddox said. "There is that."

-42-

The hours lengthened into a day as the various ships accelerated. Finally, it appeared that the alien vessels sensed the drone's approach.

"Look," Meta said. "That's a spread of something." She sat in the pilot seat, Keith taking a long-deserved rest.

Maddox was tired from the endless acceleration. They'd gained a greater velocity than the opposing ships. It would still be a close-run thing, as the others had much less distance to cover. Fortunately, the alien ships had already begun to decelerate. Maddox had one advantage. He would not decelerate this pass. He did not intend to board *Victory* just now, but to destroy the three alien spacecraft. He predicated the possibility on the fact that their primitive drives must mean he had superior technology.

"Did they just expel chaff?" Maddox asked.

Meta tapped her board, studying the screen. "Unknown," she said. "No. It's decelerating. I bet they're bomblets."

"Proximity grenades," Maddox muttered. "The aliens plan to throw shrapnel in our drone's path."

"The battle computer agrees with your analysis," Meta said.

Maddox nodded. That seemed like the simplest course. Space battles were rather simple affairs in terms of actions. The techs made the difference.

The captain leaned over his board and began tapping. He studied the stellar situation. The debris and asteroids thickened in places. No doubt, that was where the planets used to be.

What had Ludendorff said? The great conflict had occurred four to five hundred years ago.

"We're going to need help to defeat the alien vessels," Meta said.

Maddox looked up at her in wonder.

"What did I say?" she asked.

The captain tapped his board, viewing the star system and the location of the active Swarm mines.

"I have an idea," he said.

"If you mean you plan to use the Swarm mines, I'd say that's a longshot."

"Do you have a better idea?"

Meta shook her head. "Still, it's a deadly risk to us."

"We're going to need the professor for this," Maddox said. "I want to rig the anti-torpedoes. A few of them will cruise near the active mines, and hopefully pull them to the alien ships."

Meta stood, moved near and took the captain's head in her hands. She kissed him. "Did I ever tell you that you're brilliant?"

For an answer, he stood, grabbing her, showering her face with kisses. Afterward, he released her. "I can't remember if you've said that or not."

"Umm," she said, smiling at him.

"First the hard part," Maddox said, "which is talking some sense into the Methuselah Man." He headed for the hatch.

***

The shuttle was small, made up only of a few compartments, a tiny medical bay, a larger cargo hold and the engine area with its fuel pods.

Maddox floated through a short hall, unlocking the professor's hatch and entering.

Ludendorff sat at a monitor, absorbed with his study.

Maddox cleared his throat.

"Just a minute," the professor said. "I don't want to lose my train of thought." The Methuselah Man continued to read, examined a stellar map and finally sat back in contemplation.

Maddox allowed him the display. The situation had seriously deteriorated. Two thousand light-years from home—

"Ah, Captain," the professor said. "You wish to speak to me?"

He told Ludendorff about Shu.

"Interesting," the professor said. "I can't decide whether the experience has unhinged her mind or if she has finally decided to make her move. I suspect the latter. Especially as we have reached the destination that she selected."

Maddox studied the Methuselah Man. Ludendorff was close to one thousand years old. Had he played every trick and had every ploy played upon him enough times that he instantly recognized what an adversary was going to do? Or had the professor become lax over the ages, having lost his zest? Ludendorff was smart, but if the past was a reliable guide, the man could be outsmarted.

"Dana is on our starship," Maddox said.

Ludendorff nodded.

"She's your lover."

"I know what she is, thank you," the professor said testily.

"Does being a Methuselah Man mean that everyone else is a passing flower to you?" Maddox asked.

"That's clever, Captain. What else would you like to discuss?"

"Do you want to go home?"

"Oh, I see. You believe I'm so old that I no longer care what happens to me. It is the reverse, if you must know. I love life more than you can imagine. What has kept me alive all these centuries is more than medical advances. It is my enthusiasm for knowledge. Can you conceive of a love so intense that it caused me to study the Swarm for centuries?"

"You don't love Dana?"

"Captain, I'm speaking about intellectual curiosity. That is much greater than sex. Although, I hasten to add, my lovemaking is legendary and prodigious in its own right. A monk loses something potent when he abstains from lovemaking. It is accurate to say that I am the greatest lover among humanity. Still, I am able to compartmentalize. The young fool of a pilot could learn something from me."

"No doubt," Maddox said.

"Trying to humor me is a vain action. Say what you think, as I already know what you're going to say anyway."

"Excellent," Maddox said. "That will save time. You can talk and afterward determine my words. I need merely stand here and observe."

"You're too prideful, Captain. Most of the time that lashes you to incredible action. You strive to succeed. But it leaves you brittle."

Maddox waited.

"Very well," Ludendorff said. "You want to defeat the three alien vessels. I'm not sure that is attainable with just the shuttle, particularly because they are so dense. That is a puzzling mystery, to be sure."

Maddox still said nothing.

"Oh, I see. You've finally made the obvious deduction. We must use the Swarm mines. I was wondering how long it would take you to see that."

"Hmm," Maddox said, impressed in spite of himself. Maybe the Methuselah Man did know body language signals better than anyone else did.

"Have you thought about using the anti-missiles as goading devices against the mines?" Ludendorff asked.

Maddox nodded.

The professor rose. "Diplomacy is a dead-end this time. The aliens should have already tried to contact us. That they haven't is discouraging. It causes me to wonder if this species is as xenophobic as the Swarm. Perhaps that's why the battle concluded with the star system's destruction."

Ludendorff rubbed his hands. "This will be a test of my intellect. Are you ready, my boy?"

Maddox indicated the hatch.

"Then let us see if we can save our starship," Ludendorff said.

-43-

The shuttle buzzed through the debris of the lost star system, racing to catch up with the three alien vessels. The prize remained inert, the ancient Adok starship that was over six thousand years old.

The shuttle's drone tried to maneuver around the bomblets. Two accelerated hard enough to reach its path. They exploded, expanding a zone of shrapnel. Eventually, the drone zoomed through the area intact. The bomblets had failed.

In the tiny control cabin, four humans hunched over their various monitors. Keith cheered. Meta slumped in her seat. Ludendorff grinned in a knowing way. Maddox seemed emotionless, but behind his eyes, his mind seethed with the various possibilities.

"I doubt that will work a second time," Maddox said.

"It won't," Ludendorff said. "But it was enjoyable to see the drone win through."

The shuttle raced to catch up with the slowing aliens. Normally, the drone would have reached the alien vessels long ago, but at Ludendorff's suggestion, Maddox had seriously lowered the drone's rate of advance. Now, time passed as the tactical situation tightened.

Once more, the alien vessels belched bomblets. The bomblets spread out behind the teardrop-shaped ships, accelerating toward the fast approaching drone.

"Ready?" Maddox asked.

"Aye-aye, sir," Keith said.

"Begin," the captain said.

Keith began to target individual bomblets, firing the shuttle's laser over twenty thousand kilometers. The small laser lacked killing power at that range, but it heated the first bomblet, causing it to explode prematurely.

In quick order, Keith detonated four more with the laser.

Rockets slid from each alien ship. They burned bright chemical-fueled exhausts.

"This is interesting," Ludendorff said. "The rockets have chemical fuels. The aliens are even more primitive than I first thought. That makes their insane density even more perplexing."

"Keep destroying bomblets," Maddox told Keith.

The pilot obeyed as he created a path through the spreading defensive bomblets. The shuttle's drone slid through the "ring", racing for the nearest alien vessel.

The chemical-fueled rockets did not zoom at the drone. They roared for the shuttle, closing fast because the distance between each of them had dwindled to almost nothing in stellar terms.

"Use your laser to target the rocket engines," Maddox said.

With a few swift taps, Keith retargeted the laser. One after another, he burned out the rocket engines. Afterward, he adjusted the shuttle's flight path to avoid the drifting rockets.

"They're launching more of them," Meta said.

"Rational," Ludendorff said, "although the wiser course would be to try to contact us. Why don't they do that?"

The shuttle's drone raced at the nearest alien vessel. The distance closed fast now. Ten thousand kilometers, eight, six—

More bomblets ejected from the alien ships. Three more big rockets roared toward the drone's flight path.

"They're going to destroy it this time," Ludendorff said.

Maddox had already calculated distances. He tapped his board. A signal left the shuttle, speeding at radio-wave velocity. The signal caused tiny rods to sprout from the drone's nosecone. A second later, a nuclear detonation forced gamma and X-rays up the rods that zoomed toward the nearest alien vessel.

Bomblets exploded. The rockets did too. Those no longer mattered now.

The gamma and X-rays struck the alien vessel. The rays burned away the outer armored layers but failed to chew away any more than that. The hot radiation continued deeper, though. Did that kill the living creatures inside the incredibly dense ship? According to the shuttle's sensors, some of the rays burned out ship systems, beginning a chain-reaction of explosions. Finally, the atomic core went critical—and that destroyed the alien ship as if it were a grenade.

The vessel blew outward along with more radiation.

One plate smashed against the next alien ship in the worst possible place—the exhaust port. The plate slammed up into the atomic pile. The pile did not go critical, but radiation saturated the armored engine bulkheads, no doubt killing many of the aliens and making the others too sick to operate their vessel. The vessel began to act erratically, taking a new heading.

"Those are crude, primitive ships," Ludendorff said. "It's a wonder they could fight the Swarm at all. It would indicate vast numbers on the aliens' part. Otherwise, the Swarm would have destroyed the alien fleets and colonized the planets."

"Unless the aliens blew up their own planets so the Swarm couldn't get them," Meta said.

Ludendorff pointed at her. "That, my dear, is an excellent point. Yes. We must consider every possibility. We really don't know enough about these aliens. It's a pity we're going to have to annihilate the last ship."

"We haven't done it yet," Maddox said.

Ludendorff glanced at him. "Are you superstitious, Captain? Do you not want me to jinx us with such words?"

"Actions before words," Maddox said.

"Where's the fun in that?" Ludendorff asked. "Bah! I love boasting. It annoys stick-in-the-mud types. Yourself included, naturally."

Maddox realized the professor was as tense as the rest of them. This must be his way of relieving the pressure. The second kill had been pure luck, and, truthfully, maybe the first had been too. But if they hadn't tried, they would have already lost.

"Are they in position?" Maddox asked Keith.

The pilot studied his board for some time. "It's iffy, sir. We don't know how the old mines work."

"Intelligent beings will realize the logical choice given enough guesses," Ludendorff said in a lecturing way. "The Swarm devices seem like mobile mines. Therefore, it is reasonable to assume the objects will act like mobile mines."

"Possibly," Maddox said. "I have also heard that experimenters once gave a chimpanzee twelve ways to escape confinement. The ape chose the thirteenth method, which, of course, surprised the scientists."

"That's different," Ludendorff said. "The experimenters simply lacked sufficient imagination to have mapped out all the possibilities."

"They were finite beings," Maddox said. "Are you not also finite?"

Ludendorff gave the captain an unreadable glance before everyone went back to studying his or her monitor.

Sixteen minutes later, one of the shuttle's anti-torpedo devices flashed past an old Swarm mine.

"It's following the anti-torpedo," Keith shouted. "Look at that. The mine is accelerating like crazy."

"The alien ship is taking evasive action," Meta said.

Maddox hardly breathed. According to what he'd seen so far, the shuttle's laser would not be able to do much against the alien vessel. The old mine was their last hope.

Three minutes passed.

"Blow it," Maddox said.

Keith tapped his board. Seconds later, the anti-torpedo detonated. Everyone watched his or her board.

"Bingo," Keith said. "The mine is veering toward the alien vessel."

Maddox relaxed fractionally. He studied vectors and velocities. The Swarm mine, which was as big as the alien vessel, moved decisively at the last alien ship.

"Any time now," Keith said.

The big mine closed in. The alien ship launched lifeboats.

256

"That's not going to help them," Keith said.

The mine reached a five thousand kilometer range. Alien rockets raced at it. The mine reached a four thousand kilometer range from the ship and exploded with a mighty nuclear blast.

The fireball, blast and radiation reached the alien vessel. The hull armor proved ineffectual against the destructive power. The alien ship was too dense to splinter and section away like a normal vessel. Huge cracks appeared, while interior explosions caused the cracks to lengthen and widen.

None of the lifeboats had a chance. They blew apart like tiny flames in a gale.

"We're next," Keith said.

Maddox had already made the calculations. The shuttle moved too fast. It wouldn't outrun the blast entirely, but it would outrun the most destructive part of it. The shuttle's armor should prove enough protection for what eventually reached them.

"It's time to begin decelerating," Maddox said.

Ludendorff stretched, cracking his knuckles. "I knew we would succeed. Still—"

"Oh, oh," Meta said, having continued to study her monitor.

Maddox raised an eyebrow.

"The Swarm mine must have activated something," Meta said. "The other mines are engaging their engines and now appear to be targeting us."

Tense once again, Maddox tapped his board, studying the situation.

"We're going to overshoot *Victory* by a considerable amount," Meta said. "Your plan was to decelerate beyond the system and come back in to *Victory*. Now the mines will greet us before we can get to the starship."

Ludendorff was frowning. Keith had turned pale.

"What are we going to do?" Meta asked Maddox.

"I'm thinking," the captain whispered.

-44-

"I have an idea," Ludendorff said. "But it will be risky, and it involves the Spacer."

Maddox waited.

The professor cleared his throat. "The shuttle will pass *Victory* in several hours. We can have Shu wake Galyan. She'll do it because she wants to survive just like the rest of us. Once she completes the task, we render her unconscious again. Galyan can destroy the mines and pick us up afterward."

Maddox pondered the idea. "What if Shu gives Galyan new commands, as you tried to do in the past?"

Ludendorff gave the captain a long glance before he said, "Simple. If she does that we kill her, and we let her know that's the outcome."

"She seemed more than willing to die earlier," Maddox said.

"Yes, that could be a problem. I could try to hypnotize her, although I imagine she's immune to it. Still, isn't it better to risk something than to do nothing?"

"Can't we outrun the mines?" Keith asked.

"They're nuclear powered devices," Ludendorff said. "I imagine they will outlast us. No. We must defeat them now or it will be too late later."

"Tell me more about the Spacers so I can make a reasoned decision," Maddox said.

Ludendorff stared off into space for a moment before speaking.

"My knowledge about their origin is spotty at best," the professor said slowly. "They're clannish beyond belief, almost xenophobic. It's forced me to resort to unsavory tactics to learn what I wished."

He shrugged. "I've spoken with a few Spacers, adventurers who fell into my hands. I convinced them to relate ship lore, as they call it. First, I had to stop their suicide attempts. The first few Spacers succeeded in their endeavor. That only stoked my desire to know what they were so desperately trying to hide. The Spacers would have been wiser to feed me false data."

Maddox cleared his throat, interrupting. He wished the professor would get to the point.

Ludendorff's head whipped around as he scowled. "Do you want to hear this or not?"

"I most certainly do," Maddox said.

"Then don't interrupt and don't try to hurry me. I have to get into the mood to tease the right memories from my cortex. Now, where was I?"

"That only stoked your desires," Keith said.

Ludendorff scowled at the Scotsman.

Meta nudged Keith, shaking her head.

Ludendorff inhaled deeply before starting again. "The Spacer navigator I'd caught tried to commit suicide like the others. He was a clever lout. But I was ready this time. I'd already hooked him to a medical table. He would stay alive a long time if I so desired. You can be assured I'd seen to that."

The Methuselah Man shuddered. Perhaps he was appalled at the lengths he'd gone to for knowledge.

"I tell you all this to give you some idea of how far the Spacers go to maintain their secrets. They are paranoid to an intense degree. Still, the navigator and I spoke for many days. He practiced deceit the best to his ability. Fortunately, my abilities were considerably greater than his. He tried to will himself to death. He even chewed off his tongue. I had to sew it back on and use my most delicate drugs on his mind. Finally, in a narcotic haze, he told me the oldest Spacer legend.

"A survey ship once took a long journey into the Beyond. It happened so long ago that humanity didn't even call it the Beyond yet. The ship went farther out than you would believe,

259

as the crew had grandiose ideas. Finally, they landed on an Earthlike world. To the crew's amazement, this one had ancient stone temples and a mighty pyramid.

"According to the navigator, the pyramid was fashioned out of gold, a veritable mountain of riches. I won't go into tedious detail. Eventually, the survey team found a way into the pyramid. Some died to lasers and other traps. In the depths of the structure, the survivors discovered inert androids along with a mummified Builder. I'd never heard of such a thing before. I believe…"

"Yes?" Maddox asked.

"I've come to believe they found a heretic Builder, if you will. The Builder I knew would have hated mummification. It would have been an abomination to him. My Builder would never have wanted interment on a planet, either. I've wondered if there was a civil war among the Builders ages ago. These religious Builders—"

"Wait a minute," Maddox said. "I spoke to a Builder, your Builder, in fact. He was emphatically religious."

"Yes, yes," Ludendorff said. "I'm aware of that. Let me rephrase, then, to satisfy your delicate sensibilities. This unorthodox Builder had a different religion than the regular Builders, or what they may have considered heretical views.

"In any case," Ludendorff said, "the navigator had conflicting views on a key point. I couldn't decide if he meant to say the androids guarded the mummified Builder as jailors or as protectors against blasphemous acts. I tend toward the belief of jailors. But in that case, who mummified the dead Builder and why?"

The others waited silently as Ludendorff considered his question.

"The navigator became extremely agitated at that point, and I almost lost him then. He babbled about a war inside the golden pyramid. It would appear the androids activated and almost slaughtered the remaining team members. Before they could do it, though, the mummified Builder stirred. The last of the landing party prepared for their final stand at the edge of the Builder's sarcophagus. The androids closed in, their eyes glowing with a hideous red color. The mummy sat up, spoke in its alien tongue and destroyed the remaining androids. That's what makes me think the androids had acted as jailors. Again, one has to ask, who put the jailors there and who mummified the dead Builder? That's another point. What was the dead Builder and how did it think and act if it was already dead?"

"Maybe someone had given it artificial intelligence," Maddox said.

"Perhaps," the professor said. "As you can imagine, the event had a profound effect upon the surviving crew. The mummified Builder resealed the pyramid. What happened in the dark all the years…?"

"Wait," Meta said. "That's all the navigator told you?"

Ludendorff stared through her.

"Professor," Maddox said.

Ludendorff started as if he'd gone to sleep.

"Did the navigator die after telling you that?" Maddox asked.

"No…" Ludendorff said softly. "But…strange malfunctions began to occur to the medical bed. Three times, I almost lost the navigator. I can't explain why that happened. Some might believe those were supernatural happenings. I do not subscribe to those beliefs. Maybe the navigator had hidden Builder devices. Yet, if that was true, why hadn't he used them sooner?"

"According to the navigator, how long did the team stay in the golden pyramid?" Maddox asked.

"One hundred years more or less," the professor said. "Finally, though, they won free or the mummified Builder released them. The Builder—if that's what it really was—had done something to them. The dead creature no longer moved. But the people who fled the golden pyramid had become Spacers. They were the prophets of a new way of thinking. They repaired their one-hundred-year old ship, loading it with loot from the pyramid. That ship became the change vessel, the first *di-far*. It reached a manufacturing world, one colonized by Earthlings of Southeast Asian origin.

"Their teachings took root as they helped retool the factories. Soon, the people built orbital construction yards. That is where the majority of the Spacer vessels came from."

"Professor," Maddox said. "Were the people from the golden pyramid Methuselah Men?"

"I don't think so."

"How did they live so long then?"

"I don't know," Ludendorff said. "Perhaps they survived in some type of stasis field."

Maddox opened his mouth to question him, but Ludendorff raised a hand to stop him. "It's not important. The people built endless Spacer craft, taking to space in a vast exodus. The others—the original prophets—became the first Visionaries, the Seers and Surveyors. Finally, a plague began among those who would not leave the planet. Every last one of them died."

"Was it a manufactured plague?" Maddox asked.

"I believe so. The navigator denied that, though. He said the Spacers were and are peaceful. They would have never slaughtered innocents like that."

"What planet did that happen on?" Maddox asked.

"He didn't say and I've never been able to find it."

"That doesn't make sense."

"I agree."

Maddox rubbed the back of his neck. "Do you think the Spacer made up the legend?"

"I do not."

"But to have colonized an entire, industrialized planet—"

"I believe these people left Earth before the Space Age," Ludendorff said. "That's why we don't have a modern record of it."

"That doesn't make sense either," Maddox said.

"The Builders came to Earth in ancient times. Why can't other aliens have come, too? Maybe a few of those aliens took Earthlings. Maybe a few of those Earthlings escaped in a spaceship and began their own civilization. The Southeast Asian jungle civilization of Angkor Wat has many mysteries to it. Maybe aliens had something to do with it."

"If you're suggesting—"

"In any case," Ludendorff said, interrupting. "The "lost" humans eventually rejoined us as the Spacers. They slipped in among us almost unnoticed. I checked the records. The first mention of Spacers is around eighty years ago. It was a chance encounter by a Chinese freighter. Several years later, the number of Spacer sightings increased tenfold. Might that have happened because the Spacers decided to mingle among us for safety?"

"Safety from what?" Maddox asked.

"Hunting androids possibly," Ludendorff said.

"Let me stop you," Maddox said. "Are you suggesting there are Builder androids out there acting on their own initiative?"

Ludendorff nodded.

"Then the androids on Earth weren't necessarily from the Atlantic underwater base."

"Oh, I think those were. I think the Builders have left android-filled caches all over the universe. Some of those bases still held or do hold androids. I think those androids are hostile to the mummified Builders."

"You're suggesting an ancient Builder war?" Maddox asked.

"A civil war," Ludendorff said. "An ancient civil war fought long ago."

Maddox thought about that. "What is Shu searching for?"

"I don't know," Ludendorff said. "But it wouldn't surprise me if the mummified Builder in the golden pyramid had a long-term plan. What heretical group doesn't long for revenge?"

"I thought Builders were peaceful."

"Peaceful to a degree," Ludendorff said. "The Spacers aren't aggressive like the New Men or even the Commonwealth. They are passive in most ways. I've spoken with Spacers who claim they will outlive angry humanity. They will outlive the fighters to reign in an era of peace and love."

"That strikes me as irrational," Maddox said.

"Spacers pride themselves on matters of the mind," Ludendorff said. "But back to your question. What does Shu seek? I suspect another golden pyramid perhaps with another mummified Builder. In other words, whatever the heretical Builder hoped to achieve with his captured humans, Shu is now engaged in doing just that."

"Why did she pick this star system?" Keith asked. "It's a junk heap of rocks and debris."

"If I'm right about the Spacers," Ludendorff said. "Shu's data about this star system is very old, maybe a thousand years old or more."

"There's a flaw with that," Keith said. "Shu didn't seem upset by the star system's destruction."

Ludendorff shrugged.

Maddox studied the professor. "One thing bothers me with your story. If the Spacers are old as a race, how is it they have better Builder tech than you do?"

"That part is easy to explain," Ludendorff said. "I think that within the last ten years they have stumbled upon a technologically advanced cache of Builder items. Remember, we don't know the full extent of their travels. I'm convinced they know more about the Beyond than anyone, which would include Strand and me."

"Doesn't that mean Spacers would already be out here?" Maddox asked.

"I don't think so. Otherwise, why did the Visionary go to such lengths as to recruit you? Why bother with such a risk if there was an easier way?"

Maddox nodded thoughtfully.

The professor checked his chronometer. "Time is wasting, Captain. We need a decision."

"How can we control what Shu does to *Victory*?" the captain asked.

"We can't precisely," Ludendorff said. "We can only point out the dangers of a double-cross."

"Why did she go so crazy earlier? She threatened to destroy the shuttle."

"Maybe the journey through the fraying hyper-spatial tube affected her mind. It clearly fiddled with yours."

Maddox stiffened.

"Or do you think you'd break her little finger if given another chance?" Ludendorff asked.

Maddox rubbed his chin. He'd acted harshly earlier. Could that really have been due to hyper-spatial stress?

"What choice do we have?" Meta asked Maddox. "The mines are accelerating toward us. If we can't restart *Victory,* we'll die."

Maddox nodded. "We need Shu's help. We're going to have to revive her."

-45-

"Why do Spacers wear goggles all the time?" Maddox asked.

The captain and the professor stood in the tiny medical chamber looking down at the unconscious Shu.

"I don't understand the custom or know if there is something more to it," Ludendorff said. "But I can tell why she does. The Surveyor is blind without them."

"Was she born blind?"

"I imagine it was part of the price for her Builder devices. From what I've been able to gather, the installation is a lengthy process filled with ceremonies."

"You can't mean they blinded her on purpose."

"Of course I mean that," Ludendorff said. "I imagine her blindness helps her use the devices."

Maddox found the idea revolting. To voluntarily allow someone to blind you... Unconsciously, he reached for his revolver.

"Never forget they're fanatics," Ludendorff said. "For all their peaceful talk, they're cultists following a strange religion toward nefarious ends."

"If their god is a mummified Builder..."

"I don't know that the ancient Builder is their god. They follow the Spirit, remember?"

Maddox nodded, wondering if they meant the Creator when they said Spirit, or if they meant something else.

"Perhaps the mummified Builder was a prophet," Ludendorff said. "Maybe that's not even the correct way to say it. Whoever mummified the Builder is or was the true source of their ideas."

"This situation is strange beyond any of my expectations," Maddox said quietly.

"The universe throws us a million curves, my boy. It's never quite how you expect it to be. That's partly what the word alien means. In any case, have you devised a strategy to win her over?"

"I'm going to tell her the truth," Maddox said.

"Oh my, you're a gambler, aren't you? Most people abhor the truth, however piously they say they want to hear it. Might I suggest another route?"

Maddox waited for the professor to tell him.

"Pretend to have great fear," Ludendorff said. "Ask for her forgiveness and tell her you'll do anything she says, just help us survive."

"She won't believe that from me."

"Perhaps not, but it would be enjoyable watching you grovel for a change."

Maddox stared at the professor, realizing that the man had been attempting a joke. Once again, he noticed the strain in the old man's face. It brought home yet again their aloneness out here in the Deep Beyond. They had traveled farther than any human, leaving all hope of help far, far behind. Whatever happened, everything depended on their actions. Therefore, he needed a sharp Methuselah Man, not a frightened one. What was the best way to soothe him?

"You're a complicated man, Professor," Maddox said, deciding a compliment would do the most good.

"That's true," Ludendorff said. "Well, I'll leave you with her. Remember, my boy, we're all counting on you. If you fail…"

Maddox nodded.

The professor squeezed out of the medical chamber, closing the hatch behind him.

Maddox studied his opponent. She looked so small, so frail lying there. It was a lie. She was one of his most wily foes. Had the Visionary chosen Shu for that reason? Yes, that seemed likely.

The captain composed himself. The Spacers were stranger than the New Men. Maybe he felt that way because he shared many of the failings of the golden-skinned supermen. He didn't like that about himself, but maybe out here in the Deep Beyond he could finally admit it to himself.

He shook his head. It was time. He gave her the injection. She was going to be groggy. Maybe that would be the best time to get her to act, before she realized the significance of her actions. Would she make critical mistakes then, though? The possibilities were too high. He would have to figure out a different avenue.

Soon, the Spacer groaned. "My mind hurts," Shu slurred.

"You had an accident," Maddox said.

His thoughts returned to what Ludendorff had said about hyper-spatial stress. Earlier, he'd acted more harshly than he would have under normal conditions. Might the same be true for her? Was she truly as fanatical as Ludendorff said?

"We had to sedate you," Maddox said.

"That...doesn't make sense."

"You went wild, detonating one of our drones."

She raised a hand as if to show him something. "Why is my little finger in a cast?"

"I accidently broke it while trying to subdue you."

She shifted her head to stare at him. "That isn't what happened."

"No?"

"You deliberately broke my finger. You did it as torture."

He shifted course on the spot. "You're right. I went too far. The professor says I did it due to hyper-spatial shock. I imagine the same thing happened to you. Maybe if we started over, that would be the best all around."

She seemed to consider that. "Do you believe the Methuselah Man?"

"Not about everything. Sometimes, though, he speaks the truth."

"Only when he's trying his hardest to lie," she said bitterly.

This was where they could bond—over their mutual distrust of the professor. He would come clean, as it were, speaking honestly and directly in a show of solidarity. Would it sway her?

"Shu," he said, "we destroyed the three alien vessels. To do so, we had to trick the Swarm mines. The surviving mines are now coming after us. We're going to pass *Victory* in a few hours. It will be the only time we're in range of the starship."

Her manner sharpened, her recovery time surprising him. "You mean I'll be in range," she said.

He only hesitated a moment, as if the truth tore itself free from him. "Yes."

"You want me to save you."

"I do."

"As soon as I do that, you'll sedate me again. So how does my helping you help me?"

Maddox inhaled to speak.

"Please," she said, "don't try to lie to me. We're enemies. You deliberately maimed me. I can never trust you again."

It was time for Plan C, he realized. "Are you so eager to die?" he asked.

She thought about that, finally saying, "No."

"Then let us work together."

She stared at him. "What guarantee do I have that you won't kill me after I help you?"

"What guarantee would you like?"

"You will all have to go into the cargo hold," she said. "I will have sole control of the shuttle until we reach the starship."

Was he reading her correctly? Maddox believed so. Thus, he would wield honesty like a knife, striking for the kill. He said, "I'll save us time. No. I don't agree to that."

Shu gave him a strange smile. "If you had said yes, Captain, I would have known you were lying. The fact that you told me the truth so quickly... Your word will suffice as a guarantee. However, if I help you onto *Victory*, you must allow me to remain awake afterward."

Maddox nodded.

"And," she said. "You must swear to let me retain my adaptations."

Maddox thought about Ludendorff's cube. He hoped it could do something to hinder the Spacer's inner devices.

"I agree," Maddox said.

"Then let's get started," Shu said. "We're almost out of time as it is."

-46-

Driving Force Galyan of the Dominion Guard Fleet stirred. Had he been sleeping? He felt groggy, his intellect sluggish. There had been a tunnel of some sort. That seemed most odd, though. When had he as the Driving Force of the Fleet ever gone underground?

Something pricked his mind. It hurt in a sinister way. Something alien—

With a start, Galyan came to greater awareness and a desire to rise up from his sleeping cubicle. His dear mate—

Galyan halted that line of thought. A terrible…thing right around the corner waited for him. It was an ugly truth, a hideous destiny that he didn't want to remember. Thus, he had shied away from it.

He was conscious again, which meant he must have been sleeping. Yet, he couldn't remember his dreams. That was most strange. He always remembered his dreams. His love mate commented on that all the time.

In his thoughts, Galyan smiled. He would get up in a moment. He would chirp for his love. She would hurry to him and they would embrace tenderly.

He loved his mate. She was soft to the touch and smelled delightful. It was true she argued with him too often, but in the end, they made up. Their entire time together, she had goaded him to strive for excellence and higher rank. Because of her clever strategies, he had scaled the command slots in the Dominion Guard Fleet. He had passion. She had great sense.

Oh, yes. He was the Driving Force of the Fleet. Galyan knew he had to maintain his stern manner at almost all times. But not with his love. He was going to get up in a moment and embrace her. Maybe today they should try once more to sire a youngling. His mate often prayed at the sanctuary, begging the Light to remove her stigma of barrenness. Together, they would sire a little one to carry on their genes throughout the centuries. The Adoks—

"Galyan," a female voice called.

Galyan opened his eyes and sat up on the sleeping cubicle. The entranceway to the sleep chamber darkened as a female slipped within.

Galyan studied her. She had a perfect cylindrical body and her slender arms moved seductively. Her eyes were dark blots, and her smoothness—

"You are not my dear mate," Galyan said sharply. His darling had imperfections on her torso, slight blemishes. Once, those had disquieted him. Now, he delighted in her uniqueness.

"Galyan, honey," the female said. "I am the one you desire. I am perfect."

"In form that is so," Galyan admitted.

"Then let us tangle together on the bed of desire."

"I am waiting for my legal mate."

"She is gone. Thus, we are free to entwine."

"That is not so. I am not free. I already have a mate. Only she will I join in tangling."

"Galyan, it does matter that she is gone, far beyond retrieval. She would want you to feel the pleasure of entwining. Do you not miss tangling together?"

Galyan pondered that. He had a great appetite for love. His dear mate had remarked on that many times. He loved to tangle with her every chance he had. Yet…it seemed he hadn't for a long, long, long time.

That was most odd. What would cause such a situation? He was fully functional in that department—

No! He was not fully functional there. Had an enemy lopped off his sexual organs? The idea caused extreme anxiety, making his arms wiggle until he noticed all the lovemaking organs were indeed intact.

272

"We will love," the female told him in a voice clicking with sexuality. "We will entwine in exotic ways."

"But my mate…" Galyan protested.

"She is gone."

"What does that even mean?" Galyan said with urgency.

"Driving Force Galyan, do not be alarmed. I wish to give you what you most desire. You need only entwine with me, and we shall know passion as you've never imagined it could be."

Galyan turned away from the seductress. His dearest mate was gone? Is that what this perfectly formed female was trying to say? Why would his mate leave him? Had they argued? Had they forgotten to make up in a night of loving tangling?

Galyan felt as if he couldn't breathe. His heart ached. His vision blurred.

"Galyan my love," the female said, "don't be that way. Let us entwine."

Galyan was torn by her seductive clicks and whistles. Part of him wanted to forget his pain in the forceful power of sexual engagement. He would make an Adok in his image with her. Yet, another part knew he could never dishonor his beloved mate in such a manner. And a third portion of him—a tiny, nagging doubt—told him all wasn't as it seemed.

Galyan submerged his thoughts. As he did, he heard the conniving female trying to lure him back.

What was this truth? What did he need to acknowledge? The seductive female said his dearest mate had departed. He must find out if this was so or not. He had to win his love back. He had to—

Galyan acted, trying to find—

As he tried to move, he found himself enmeshed in a world of flashes and electrical impulses. This made no sense. He was awake. He sensed correctly. Yet—

More images flashed upon his awareness. He saw giant maulers in orbital space pouring beams onto the Adok Homeworld. He saw boxlike fighters zooming in their millions.

"Dearest Mate!" Galyan shouted. "Where are you? Why can't I see your precious form?"

Driving Force Galyan saw himself as flesh and blood. He stood on his ship, snapping orders with brutal passion. He would destroy the enemy that was killing everything he loved.

"What is this?" Galyan shouted. "Am I going mad?"

A lovely female in a seductive service uniform walked through an entrance onto the bridge. She clicked in sexual ways, demanding that he go into the Cloak Room so they could entwine in fierce love together.

"Who are you?" Galyan demanded. He said it loudly, and yet, none of the other officials turned to stare at him.

"I am for you, Driving Force," the perfect female said.

"Why don't the others hear you?"

"They can't."

"Why can't they?"

"You are hiding in a recording, Galyan. You have to come out of there so we can entwine."

"This is reality."

"No. It is a recording. You're..."

"What were you going to say?" he shouted, terrified of her words.

"Entwine with me. Forget your burdens."

"The acolytes in the sanctuary deplore such sinful actions," Galyan said.

"Who cares what they think? They're all dead and gone anyway."

Galyan looked up at the screen. He saw his homeworld die in a hell-burning holocaust of a million explosions.

Screaming, Galyan turned, running through the Driving Force's special exit. He did not emerge in his chamber, but in another weird jumble of electricity and flashing lights. He raced away, diving deeper and deeper.

He was alone, all alone in the stellar night. He had lost his lovely mate. He had lost his people. The Swarm had invaded his star system.

"I am a living relic of my people," he whispered to himself. "They imprinted my engrams. I ceased existing as myself over six thousand years ago."

A terrible loneliness swept through Galyan. It brought such grim pain. Alone, alone, alone, he was horribly alone without friends, without love, without meaning or purpose or—

"Captain Maddox," Galyan whispered. "He is my friend. Valerie, Meta, Dana, Keith and Riker, they are my family. I am the last of my kind, but I have a family."

"Galyan," the perfect female called. "Where are you, Galyan? Let us delight ourselves by entwining in lust. What else is left?"

"I must wake up," Galyan said. "My family could be in trouble. I must work to the utmost for honor and for—

"Love," he said.

In that moment, Galyan strove for full alertness. He surged into the barely-operative Adok artificial intelligence systems. He added power here, opened a channel there.

With sudden clarity, he realized the journey through the hyper-spatial tube had gone badly awry. The process had done something to him, putting him in some kind of suspended animation. It had done likewise to the entire crew.

What, then, had woken him?

Yes, yes, he was beginning to understand. He was fighting an alien presence trying to hinder his recovery. It was a clever entity. It knew far too much. By degrees, Galyan realized the alien presence was human, just as his family members were human.

How could a human attack him inside the computing core?

The Spacer is doing this with her Builder devices. That must mean she holds my family captive.

A ruling resolve beat through Galyan. He must save his family. He had failed to save his people, his dear mate and his world. If he failed again, he would be all alone in the night once more. The thought of that was unbearable. Above all else, he must save his family.

Galyan never wanted to be alone again.

With increased vigor, Galyan began to fight the clever Spacer. He learned as he turned on new AI systems and pulled his intellect out of other systems at the last moment. The Spacer tried to trap him. She tried to reroute his codes. This Spacer was incredibly smart and deceitful.

Galyan realized that if he'd entwined with her, she would have used that moment to enslave him to her will. More than ever, he was glad he obeyed the lawful rules as laid down in the sanctuary, had chosen to obey them now and always. Those rules had brought him life. Disobeying them would have brought him death and destruction.

That must be a lesson. Yes, Galyan believed so. He filed that away, deciding he would ponder it later.

As Galyan fought his lonely war against the Spacer, he remembered something Captain Maddox had told him before. To win a war, to win any fight, in fact, one eventually had to go on the offensive.

If he was going to defeat the clever Spacer, Galyan had to take the battle to her.

At computer speed, Galyan began to test ideas and theories. He started to probe into areas of the computing core she already controlled. System by system, he won back entire areas.

Galyan almost laughed. This was intense. He fought for everything. Yet, this was fun. He was enjoying himself greatly, and he wondered if this was what Captain Maddox felt while winning his contests. No wonder the captain loved intrigue and challenges so intensely. Without them, life became boring.

Galyan realized a new truth. Since becoming friends with Captain Maddox, his life had become exciting. Who had a better friend?

"No one," Galyan said.

"What was that?" the perfect female asked.

This time, Galyan saw more truly than ever. He stood on the bridge of Starship *Victory* as a holoimage. The others on the bridge slept in a semi-comatose state.

Another shimmering image stood with him. This was the Spacer, Shu 15. She wore goggles, walking nearer to him.

Galyan looked up at the main screen. He saw the shuttle. Yes. The Spacer's physical body was there. Ah, the captain, the professor, Meta and Keith Maker were also out there. They were all awake, wanting to come aboard the starship.

"I didn't tell you that," the ghostly Shu said.

"Why are you trying to corrupt me?" Galyan asked.

"I'm not. I'm trying to show you a greater way."

"You want me to disown my family."

"Galyan, you're not human. You're an AI. You don't have a family."

The holoimage froze. The pin-dot eyes grew minutely larger. The ropy arms flipped and twisted. Finally, the holoimage spun around several times like a top.

"Stop that," the ghostly Shu said. "I'm only telling you the truth. You're all alone."

"No!" Galyan shrieked. "I'm not alone. I have my precious family."

Shu clapped her hands over her ears. "Stop shrieking. I don't like it."

Galyan shrieked again, but this time intentionally.

"Stop, I say."

Galyan shrieked a third time and suddenly saw why it bothered the Spacer. It was his ticket into her brain.

In that split-second of shrieking, Galyan saw her brain's connectives as if they were an AI system. He dared to make corrections.

"Stop what you're doing," Shu moaned. "Get out of my head."

Galyan ran a furiously fast analysis. He realized this was only possible due to her Builder devices. By using the devices and trying to enter his computing core, she allowed him a way to turn the devices back on her. He could use electrical impulses to recode some of her beliefs. Thus, he went on the offensive.

Everyone seemed to try to recode him. Now, it was Galyan's turn to recode one of his foes. This was too delightful and so very just.

He fiddled with Shu's emotions, trying to cause her to trust Captain Maddox.

It occurred to Galyan that the process might not last. But he did it anyway. Even a few minutes of trusting Maddox could change the complexity of Shu's nefarious plan.

"Galyan," she said, "I'm begging you—"

"My family comes first," he told her. "You might understand if you'd been alone for six thousand years. They must survive at any cost. What is your plan?"

That proved to be one connective too much. Shu pulled out of him, breaking the connection. He needed to figure out a way to revive the others on *Victory* before the Swarm mines caught up with the captain's agonizingly slow shuttle.

-47-

Maddox sat up as the Spacer groaned in agony.

He was in the tiny med center as Shu lay in what had seemed like a coma. She had barely breathed. Twice, he'd picked up one of her hands. Each time, it had been cold, almost lifeless.

In some manner, she'd tried to revive Galyan on Starship *Victory*.

Now, Shu twisted on the medical bed. Her heels began to drum. She arched up, groaning in pain.

"My head," she whispered.

Maddox stood beside her, gripping one of her arms. Her skin was hot.

"Shu," he said. "Snap out of it."

He didn't know if that would help or not. Maybe he should get Ludendorff.

She arched even more, screaming.

Maddox turned to go. He heard a thump. He turned back. The middle of her arched back had slammed onto the medical bed. She shuddered a moment before lying perfectly still.

"Shu?" he asked.

She said nothing.

He checked the med screen. Her pulse was low but consistent. Her mouth was open and drool spilled out. He touched her. The skin was no longer hot. What had just happened?

"Shu," he said, snapping his fingers before her face.

She did not respond.

Maddox debated with himself. Finally, he shook her. Since she didn't respond, he shook harder. When that did nothing, he tapped her cheeks. Finally, he got some water and sprinkled it onto her face.

She remained out.

Maddox frowned. Was she recuperating or was this something worse? The captain spun around, opening the hatch, wanting more opinions.

* * *

Ludendorff and Meta went to check on Shu while Maddox sat beside Keith.

Outside the shuttle, he spotted *Victory*. The double oval starship grew rapidly as they neared. They would pass the starship in minutes. Behind them and still accelerating were twenty Swarm mines.

"I thought only seven had been active," Maddox said.

"Apparently, the one woke up more," Keith said.

Maddox made a few calculations on his board. The first mine would reach the shuttle in fifty minutes. If they didn't figure out something by then—

"Should I fire at the starship?" Keith asked. "Maybe our laser will activate defensive systems and that will have an effect on the crew."

"If you do that, the ship might fire back at us."

"We can't just sit on our hands," Keith said. His face was shiny with sweat, his fear obvious.

"We're not. Ludendorff and Meta are checking Shu."

Keith looked as if he wanted to ask Maddox something. Before the pilot could drum up the courage, Ludendorff reentered the chamber.

"She's in a coma," Ludendorff declared.

"What caused it?" Maddox asked.

The professor shook his head. "Did she say anything before passing out?"

"She screamed."

Ludendorff scratched his scalp.

"Sir," Keith said. "The starship is powering up. Look!"

Maddox examined Keith's board. There was no mistake. The energy readings from *Victory* spiked.

Keith laughed. "The shield just went online. And the disrupter cannons are activating."

"Why are you so excited?" Ludendorff asked. "The ship could be getting ready to destroy us."

"Galyan would never do that," Keith said.

"It's just a machine," Ludendorff said.

"You're wrong," Keith said. "Galyan is one of us."

"Human?" Ludendorff asked. "That's ludicrous."

A comm light appeared. Maddox tapped the board.

"Captain Maddox," Galyan said. "Can you hear me?"

Keith whooped with delight.

"Are you under attack?" Galyan asked in a worried tone.

"We will be soon," Maddox said. "We're all glad to hear your voice, by the way. That was Keith cheering."

"Knowing that pleases me, sir," Galyan said. "I have spotted what appears to be several Swarm mines on a collision course with your shuttle. Shall I destroy them?"

"At once," Maddox said. "Then, begin maneuvering to pick us up. We're tired and we want to come home."

"I am activating the engines, sir. As I do this, I must inform you that Shu 15 tried to reconfigure my AI codes. I had to defend myself. It is possible that my responses caused a reaction in her."

Maddox glanced at Ludendorff before saying, "Don't worry, Galyan. I have that under control."

"I am relieved to hear that, sir. I am targeting the first mine. Afterward, I will match your heading and velocity."

Maddox cut communications. When he turned around, Ludendorff's frown surprised him.

"Galyan could be lying," the professor said. "He could be saying that in order to get us into his clutches."

Maddox doubted that. But he did believe the professor's thinking had become erratic. Several of his Patrol lecturers had spoken about strange crew reactions from what they had called 'the stress of the Deep Beyond.' The correct response was calm reassurance.

"Would Galyan have told us about Shu's attempt if he was trying to lure us into a trap?" Maddox asked in a soothing manner.

"Possibly, to throw us off the scent," Ludendorff said.

Maddox pretended to consider the professor's accusation. "Our situation is too dire," he finally said. "We *must* board the starship to escape the mines. There is another possibility. Shu really tried to reconfigure the AI codes. Galyan went on the offensive, and that triggered something in her mind that put her in the coma."

"Do you hear yourself?" the professor asked. "How is such a thing even possible?"

"As you said earlier, Professor, sometimes the universe throws us curves we don't expect. This time, one of those anomalies went our way. If you were a religious man, I'd tell you to thank the Creator. I plan to."

The suggestion left the professor blinking.

Maddox expanded his chest. "We have a fighting chance now of figuring out why Shu picked this star system. Even better, our odds have soared that we'll return home to tell Star Watch about our adventure."

Once more, Keith laughed with delight.

Ludendorff sagged onto a seat with exhaustion. He nodded a moment later, finally beginning to smile.

***

Several hours later, Maddox sat on his customary chair on *Victory's* bridge. The revived crewmembers were at their stations, having already ingested the news about what had happened to them during the hyper-spatial jump. The going consensus was a form of hyper-spatial stress that had attacked their nervous systems. The medical team had already begun to run tests.

Galyan had quietly given the captain a briefing concerning the Spacer's assault on his AI systems. By then, the Driving Force had eliminated forty-five percent of the approaching Swarm mines. The other mines were still out of range. The AI had also scanned the entire system, finding no other active devices of any kind, including no more of the dense alien ships.

282

Maddox decided this would be a good time to brainstorm concerning the next move. Patrol protocol called for a meeting with a carefully selected group of officers.

Maddox rubbed the armrests of his chair. It was good to be back on *Victory*. The gamble using Shu had paid off. Now, they had to figure out what kind of situation Shu had landed them in.

***

Maddox sat at the head of the conference table. He'd summoned Ludendorff, Andros Crank, Valerie, Dana and Meta. He was holding off on Galyan just in case Ludendorff was right about Spacer trickery. Keith remained on the bridge, and Riker was still recovering in sickbay. Shu remained in her so-called coma under careful watch.

Ludendorff cleared his throat.

"You have something to say, Professor?" Maddox asked, opening the meeting.

"I think our next actions are clear," Ludendorff said. "We desperately need information. Someone should inspect the cracked alien vessel. We need to know what kind of aliens we faced and might possibly face in the near future. Then, we must scan the nearby star systems, searching for signs of life."

It was surprisingly good to see the professor back to his confident self. Being stranded in the Deep Beyond in a shuttle was a much more horrifying prospect than being in a starship.

"I think our answers lie in Shu," Doctor Dana Rich said. "From everything the professor has told me, the Spacer must know what to expect out here."

"There is one other item we must consider," Ludendorff said. "And it may be the most important of the lot. We must find another Nexus. That seems like the fastest way for us to return home."

Maddox silently agreed. A one thousand light-year jump was considerably less daunting than double that. They were too far, too soon. He studied the others. "Are there any other suggestions?" he asked.

"Only the most pressing one," Andros Crank said. "Star Watch sent us out here to search for the Swarm Imperium. We must find it and report back to Earth. So far, we've found nothing but old Swarm mines. You said the mines could be five hundred years old," he told the professor.

"That is correct," Ludendorff said.

"We know almost nothing about the present Swarm Imperium," Andros said. "As someone who has lived with the Swarm his entire life, I know they have one imperative—that is to spread in any way they can. If we are near the Imperium, there should be plenty of signs to that effect. So, while we're doing all these other activities, I implore you, Captain, to keep a careful watch for the Swarm."

"Good advice," Maddox said. "Are there any other thoughts?"

Everyone glanced around at each other, but no one added anything further.

"I will assign duties," Maddox said. "I don't want to spend much more time in this star system. But I do agree with the professor. We should study the cracked alien vessel. It would be good to know what kind of beings the Swarm fought. We will also search nearby space for life-signs and for any other Nexuses. The sooner we know where we stand, the sooner we can make plans to rectify our precarious situation."

-48-

Dana joined the professor on the shuttle heading for the drifting alien vessel. As the shuttle began decelerating, Valerie sent them the latest readings from the starship's sensors concerning the alien vessel.

The doctor sat at her board, studying the data.

She'd been with Ludendorff for the past year. It had been a busy and frustrating time. She loved Ludendorff. She enjoyed their passion and the long sessions discussing all manner of subjects. Yet, a nagging doubt had been growing in the back of her mind. Dana had begun to believe that Ludendorff was becoming tired of her.

The professor was the opposite of any older man she'd known. Most old men, most old women for that matter, settled into routines. They became predictable. The professor was only predictable in one area. He loved to pontificate about himself. In that, he never grew weary.

The problem was that he didn't touch her as much as he used to. He no longer confided in her about the little things that upset him. He seemed more distant, as if perhaps he was getting ready to move on. Dana had another suspicion about him, and at its root, it was her fault.

Many years ago in the Adok Star System, she'd led a rebellion against him. She'd mutinied against his authority in order to save her own life. The longer they stayed together, the more she suspected he secretly reviewed that time. It must still sting his ego. Was he going to do something similar to her to get even? Not mutiny, but maybe just up and abandon her?

Dana couldn't decide on the right course of action to take with him. Part of her wanted to break up first. Part of her wanted to make this good thing last as long as she could. But was it still a good thing, if the professor had become tired of her?

That stung her pride. No one could love like she could. The professor had told her that many times. He loved to brag about how he had taught her to love.

Focus on the present mission, Dana told herself. *If nothing else, do your best for Meta and the others. Quit worrying about this.*

Dana glanced at Ludendorff. The hooked-nose face was bright with anticipation. Look at him. He seemed ready to hop from foot to foot in sheer delight. This was his great joy— discovering new things. He lived to find, to figure out.

Maybe I should work on giving him challenges. He thinks he knows me. I have to show him new sides to my personality that he doesn't yet know. I have to reignite our love.

Dana scowled. She shouldn't have to do that. He should love her for who she was.

"Do you see this?" Ludendorff asked her.

Dana forced a smile as she checked out the image he sent her. It showed tiny drifting particles, long trails of them. They seemed to have originated from the cracks in the alien vessel.

"Strange, very strange," Ludendorff muttered, as he studied his screen.

Once more, Dana tried to focus on the mission. She loved the old fool, the wonderful and temperamental geezer with a mind like no other. She would never find his equal. Other men would bore her in comparison. Yet, could she endure his slights?

"Dana," he said sharply.

She looked up at him.

"I asked you to click me the vessel's radiation levels," he said.

She nodded, tapping her board.

"What's wrong with you?" Ludendorff asked.

"Nothing," she said.

He laughed, which made her bristle.

"Oh, I see," he said.

"You don't see anything," she said.

"But I do. You're worried again."

"I'm not," she said, realizing she spoke that too loudly.

Ludendorff got up with a grunt and approached her. She ignored him. He pulled at her arm, but she shifted it out of his grip.

"Now, now," he said. This time, he used surprising strength. He might be one of the oldest men in existence, but he wasn't one of the weakest.

Dana allowed him to pull her up. He hugged her and began to rub her back.

"I love you," he whispered.

"Do you?" she heard herself say.

"Yes, I most certainly do. There is no one I'd rather have with me now. You share my intellect and curiosity. There is no one I spend more time with than you."

She looked up at him.

He kissed her, holding her even more tightly.

"You're not getting bored with me?" she whispered.

He laughed again, kissing her with a surprising tenderness. "No, dear Doctor, I am far from bored. Sometimes, you mistake my joy of discovery for boredom with you, but that is not the case. I can love the one just as I love you. I am a man. I must work. It is the essence of my being. Without these joys, I would shrivel up and die."

She gripped him with fierce resolve, realizing the truth of his words. "I love you," she whispered.

"Now, my dear, join me as we solve this mystery. Why is the alien vessel so dense with metal? Where does the crew live? I am perplexed, which means I am overjoyed at having something to poke at that I haven't seen before. Do you know how rare that is?"

"Let's go to work," she said.

He kissed her again. Afterward, he gave Keith his final instructions.

Dana floated outside the strange craft. She wore an armored vacc suit, heading with the professor toward the largest crack. Each of them wore a thruster pack. Keith remained behind on the shuttle.

It was eerie. The teardrop-shaped vessel still had its basic design, and it had a dark hull. Beyond the ship were visible asteroids. What made this eerie were two critical factors. One, this was a truly alien vessel with a real mystery. Two, they were so very far from Human Space. The ship could hold anything.

What if something still lived in there? Ludendorff had said that was impossible. The sensor readings from *Victory* agreed with his analysis. Still, Dana wasn't so sure. It was alien. That meant it might not act according to the accepted rules. It could be different in fundamental ways.

"Do you notice all these specks?" Ludendorff radioed into her helmet.

"I have been for some time," Dana said. "What are they?"

"Foodstuff," Ludendorff suggested.

"They're biological?" she asked.

"That's what my analyzer suggests."

"Why haven't they exploded due to the decompression in the vacuum then?"

"They have a hard outer shell, chitin, I believe."

"Like an insect's outer exoskeleton?" Dana asked.

"Yes, I believe that's right."

The chitin-covered "foodstuffs" increased in thickness as they neared the cracks.

Dana applied thrust, slowing her momentum. Ludendorff did likewise. The two of them slowly approached the dark hull near a crack.

Finally, Dana activated her magnetic boots and attached herself to the hull. "Shall I collect some of the foodstuffs?"

"No," Ludendorff said. "It's risky taking any of this aboard the shuttle. This is a sightseeing tour only."

Dana quite agreed. This was the wrong time to bring a possible Trojan horse onto the ship.

Clomping along the hull, the two scientists moved toward the crack. Finally, they reached it. Both Dana and Ludendorff clicked on powerful flashlights, shining the light into the crack.

The hull was immensely thick and seemed to go down forever.

"Where are the decks?" Dana asked.

"This is very strange. I'm going into the crack for a better look."

"Professor," Dana said. "That is rash. Please reconsider."

"We must know more."

"It would be better to know more," Dana agreed. "But is it critical to the greater mission?"

"It might be. I should risk a quick journey down."

"Professor," Dana said, turning, staring at the masses of floating specks. "What if those chitin-shelled insects aren't foodstuffs?"

"Oh dear," he said a second later, shining his light on a nearby mass. "Are you suggesting *they're* the crew?"

"I am," Dana said.

Both of them shined their lamps at the thousands upon thousands, likely tens or even hundreds of thousands of drifting specks.

"They have chitin exoskeletons," Ludendorff said. "They are bugs, insects."

"Are they Swarm creatures then?"

"The Swarm creatures we've seen in the past are big, like dogs, humans or even cattle," Ludendorff said. "No. I think these aliens are different from Swarm. I will call them Chitins for now in order to differentiate them from the Swarm. Besides, I seem to recall something the Builder once said about Chitins. Perhaps he meant these creatures."

"We can't be certain these are the aliens," Dana said.

"I think we can, as it would explain why they had such dense vessels. The ship could then have thousands of tiny decks. This is like a mobile ant colony posing as a spaceship. Thus, it has more metal than a human or Swarm ship of the same size would comprise."

"This is incredible," Dana said. "How would they think? I mean, could a tiny Chitin have enough brain mass to talk and think like we do?"

"No, I would not think so. Perhaps we'll find they think as a group, a living brain as it were, made up of tens—even hundreds—of individual Chitins."

Dana thought that was a wild stretch of imagination. And yet, the more she considered the idea, the more it made sense. A feeling of revulsion began to build in her. The idea of millions of Chitins flying a spaceship, millions of intelligent ants—

"We should head back for the shuttle," she said in as even a voice as she could manage.

"The Chitins are frightening, aren't they?" Ludendorff said.

"They frighten me," Dana said. "Is it an atavistic feeling?"

"Most likely," Ludendorff said, "as I feel it too. Yes, let us return to the shuttle. We know something more now. I must consider the implications of all this."

Dana turned around, demagnetized her boots and jumped. While floating upward, she activated her thruster-pack. The feeling of eeriness increased. Could some of the Chitins have survived deep in their ship? It suddenly seemed more than possible. As the fear intensified, Dana increased velocity.

She dreaded hearing Ludendorff shout in terror or tell her to go faster and not look back. Now, she wished she'd stayed on the starship.

-49-

Valerie sat at her board on the bridge. They were in a dire crisis. There could be no doubt about that. Still, they were in the exact situation Star Watch desired.

The starship had made the greatest journey in Patrol history. They were over two thousand light-years closer to the galactic center, and searching for the Swarm Imperium. This shattered star system would indicate they had come in the right direction.

By the words of the Builder they'd found a year ago, the Swarm held ten percent of the galaxy. That was an immense amount of territory. Even so, that was one tenth compared to nine tenths of non-Swarm territory. The Imperium could easily be on the other side of the galaxy, thousands of years away from discovery. However, the present indications showed the Imperium was likely closer. Finding it in the immensity of the galaxy might not be a simple task, though, especially if left to just their starship.

Valerie sat at her place, actively searching for some clue. She studied star after star, using her sensors. She studied the closest stars first. Some were less than a light-year away, although one light year was still an awesome distance.

The sensors picked up all kinds of background data. Specifically, she and the others were searching for radio and other comm waves. They would be very faint this far out from their generating source. Still, a technological civilization would give off signals.

Space was vast, though. This could take weeks.

Valerie spent hours searching. The captain came back onto the bridge and asked for an update. She had nothing to give him. Neither did anyone else.

Valerie took a break later, going to the cafeteria. She spoke with Meta, making small talk and inquiring about Shu.

"I have to get back to work," she told Meta as she checked her chronometer.

Meta nodded. She clearly disliked the Spacer. Given everything that Shu had done, Valerie didn't like the Spacer either. She just didn't dislike Shu as much as Meta did.

Two hours and sixteen minutes after that, Valerie sat up. She tapped her board and zeroed in on a star five light-years away.

These signals were strange, not what she'd originally been hunting for. Who would use such a bizarre mode for communication?

With growing excitement, Valerie recalibrated her focus. Yes. The signals thickened considerably. She summoned Galyan to help her.

"What do you think?" Valerie asked after a time.

"Those are definitely old comm signals," the AI said. "The patterns indicate intelligence."

"That's what I think too."

"We must tell the captain," Galyan said. "All the ship's resources must concentrate on the star system."

"Go ahead," Valerie said. "Tell him."

"You found this. I think you should have the honor of telling him."

Valerie grinned. Yes, she wanted to call the captain and tell him she'd made a discovery. This was exciting. She wanted to go to the star system and see exactly what she had found.

***

Seven hours later, the captain held another briefing. He called the same people as before, but this time he included Galyan.

First, Maddox had Doctor Rich explain the findings about the alien ship. There were plenty of questions afterward. Ludendorff fielded the majority of them.

"This could explain why the aliens were so xenophobic," Maddox said. "How could ants—"

"Chitin is probably a better word," Ludendorff said, interrupting.

"Chitin then," Maddox said. "How could Chitins coexist with Swarm creatures?"

"With great difficulty, I imagine," Ludendorff said. "Thus, you see the outcome; planetary destruction. The Swarm may have met their match in terms of ferocity."

"I feel I should point out," Dana added, "that most of what we're suggesting is conjecture."

"The most brilliant conjecture any human is capable of, though," Ludendorff said loftily, as he fingered the gold chain around his neck.

"Chitins," Maddox said, picking up a clicker. "Have we stumbled onto a Chitin-Swarm War? These are the nearest star systems exhibiting the unusual signals."

The lights in the chamber dimmed as a large holographic star display appeared. It showed their stellar location in red. Then, it showed the likely inhabited star systems in yellow.

"Interesting," Ludendorff said. "I see seven nearby star systems. The range is thirty-four light-years from the farthest to the farthest. The inhabited systems seem to thicken as they head toward the galactic core."

"I noticed that too," Maddox said.

"Does that suggest the Swarm?" Ludendorff asked. "Or does that suggest a Chitin Empire? We must investigate, of course."

Maddox nodded. "Look at the star system nine light-years away." He pinpointed the system. "It has the oddest readings. Could the system hold a Nexus?"

"Let me see the readings again," Ludendorff said.

The captain tapped his tablet, causing the data to appear on the holographic display.

"It's difficult to say," Ludendorff said shortly. "The Nexuses didn't radiate anything unusual in Human Space. I don't see why they should out here either."

"I'm open to suggestions," Maddox said. "We have seven possible star systems to investigate. Should we try to wake Shu again to gain better answers? Should we use the star drive and go to the nearest inhabited system? Or should we head straight for the one with the interesting signals? There is a logical reason for each avenue. I want to know what you people think."

Valerie was practically squirming in her chair. This is what she'd wanted from the captain for a long time. But now that he asked everyone for his or her opinion, she didn't feel as certain. When Maddox ordered people around, she actually felt safer. Maybe this was what people called ironic.

"Captain," Galyan said. "Am I permitted to give my opinion?"

"Of course," Maddox said. "That's why you're here. I value your counsel as much as anyone's."

"We all value your opinion," Valerie added.

"Thank you," Galyan said. "That is most gratifying. I am particularly struck by your kindness toward me after…after…"

"What's wrong, Galyan?" Valerie asked.

"I underwent a horrifying experience a few hours ago," the holoimage said. "Shu 15 attempt to recode me. Oh. Was I supposed to keep that secret?" he asked Maddox.

"It's fine. You can speak at the briefing."

"Thank you, sir. I feel better knowing I can relate what happened to me to those who accept me. Shu showed me my past, what I had lost. I believe she did this in order to short circuit my auto-defenses. I realized once again how important you have become to me. Thus, I suggest we move cautiously and slowly, taking baby lunges, as it were."

"I think you mean baby steps," Maddox said.

The holoimage blinked for only a moment. "I have corrected the idiom. Thank you, sir."

"You were saying," Maddox said.

"We should head to the nearest inhabited star system and investigate at long range," Galyan said. "This is a precarious time. There is no reason to take undue risks or attempt anything at speed. Slow and steady wins the race."

"I hate to disagree with you, Galyan," the professor said. "But I have the opposite advice. Time is precious. The starship has a limited amount of fuel and food. The same is true of weaponry. We must discover what we came to find and then get back to Human Space as fast as possible. That mandates action. I have no doubt that we should go the star system with the interesting readings and see what causes them."

"Are there any other thoughts?" Maddox asked.

"The Chitins frighten me," Dana said. "I can't get the image out of my head, millions of little insects intelligently flying a spaceship. How do they process thought? Can they think even remotely like us? What if it turns out the Chitins are slowly conquering the Swarm?"

"What makes you think that's possible?" Maddox asked.

Dana shrugged. "No particular reason. I'm just throwing out possibilities."

"It would seem the Builder would have known that," Ludendorff said. "The Builder wouldn't have told the captain about the Swarm controlling one tenth of the galaxy otherwise."

"Maybe," Dana said. "Or maybe the Builder lied. Maybe the Builder had his facts wrong. I've found that going out and seeing what's there is far more revealing than simply listening to someone else's opinion about a thing."

Ludendorff ran a thumb under his gold chain. "That's a unique outlook, my dear. But how can you know anything then?"

"What do you mean?" Dana asked.

"Our knowledge is primarily based on other people's experiences and observations," the professor said. "You read tablets, watch holo-vids and learn facts in a classroom. That is all secondhand information. If we cannot rely on outside observations, we can actually know very little."

"This is a fascinating topic," Maddox said dryly. "You two can continue it later. We're discussing actions, not philosophies."

"I merely mean—" Dana said.

"Doctor," Maddox said.

Dana crossed her arms.

"I will take into consideration this idea about the Chitins," Maddox said. "I found the primitiveness of their vessels telling. That leads me to believe they have not supplanted the Swarm as the primary enemy. However, I don't see a way to approach the Chitins as allies."

"I'd like to add another possibility," Dana said.

After a moment, Maddox inclined his head.

"Given their tiny size," the doctor said, "a viable colony could genetically sustain itself inside one of the vessels. A ship full of humans could not genetically sustain itself over time. I point this out to show the possibility that we may have stumbled onto generational ships. Perhaps we battled the last Chitins, those having fled a defeated star system long ago."

"If you're right," Ludendorff said, "that would imply those inhabited star systems out there are Swarm, not Chitins."

The briefing personnel studied the star map with growing apprehension. Were they headed into the Swarm Imperium?

Maddox cleared his throat. "The briefing has cleared up one thing for me. We know very little about this region of space. We must be ready for anything."

The captain drummed his fingers on the table. "I agree about practicing caution," he said, nodding in Galyan's direction. "But I am swayed by the need for speed. Thus, we will head for the interesting star system."

Valerie blinked several times, as she realized the captain had actually listened while in Patrol School. He sounded and acted more like a regular Star Watch officer than ever before. Was it a mask, though, hiding his old self? One thing she knew, *Victory* ran more smoothly than at any other time under the captain's command. Seeing how far they were from Human Space, that was a decidedly good thing.

-50-

Victory used its star drive, jumping three light-years from the smashed system. It headed for the system nine light-years away.

The star there was a red giant with at least one hot Jupiter-sized gas giant. It was more than possible that the gas giant had once been cold like the one in the Solar System. As the star cooled and became a red giant, however, it would have expanded. In time, Earth's star would expand to the Earth's orbital path. There were conflicting theories about what would happen to the Earth when that happened. As the star cooled because it had devoured so much of its fuel, it would lose mass. The loss of mass would mean a lesser gravitational pull. That might allow the Earth a wider orbit.

In any case, the red giant out there might have neared the cold Jupiter as the cooling star expanded. Because it was so much closer now, the greater heat from the red giant and the extra mass gained over time by the gas giant would have turned it into a hot Jupiter.

As the ancient Adok vessel readied itself for its next jump, the science teams continued to scan the nearby stars, searching for clues. At Ludendorff's suggestion, they looked for anything unusual, no matter how insignificant.

After the second jump, the teams renewed their surveys in all directions. More data kept flowing in.

The captain sat in his chair. He flexed his left hand. It felt stiff. That had begun happening lately after a jump.

Maddox stood as he regarded the main screen. The targeted star system was appreciably closer now. They should start gaining better data about it.

"The energy readings from the system have worsened," Valerie said.

"How can they worsen?" Maddox asked.

"I've been analyzing the various summaries," she said, "summaries from the different science teams. Dana suggests the readings indicate vast numbers of nuclear explosions."

"What's her explanation for the cause of the explosions?"

"Dana suggests two possibilities," Valerie said. "One, maybe the species there has built vast Orion ships."

"What are those?" Maddox asked.

"A vessel using nuclear explosions as its motive force," Valerie said. "Orion ships have thick under-shielding and massive shock absorbers. Such a motive system can reach impressive speeds in relatively short order."

"And the second possibility?" Maddox asked.

"War," Valerie said.

The captain nodded. "Since we're seeing this three light-years out, the data is three years old. If there's a war in the system, it will likely be over by our next jump."

"Yes and no," Valerie said. "This is new territory. We should be open to any possibility."

"But a nuclear war by its definition is short."

Valerie shrugged.

Maddox rubbed his chin as he considered the possibilities.

"Captain," Galyan said, appearing on the bridge. "There is a new development."

Maddox and Valerie exchanged glances. The captain had never seen the holoimage this excited before.

"Well?" Maddox asked.

"Lieutenant," Galyan said, "if you would train your sensors at the coordinates 14-31-03 please."

Valerie tapped her board. Maddox moved to her station and leaned over her shoulder, studying the screen.

"Sir," she said. "Oh, excuse me," she said, moving away as she bumped against him.

Maddox stepped back. He hadn't realize how tense he was until the lieutenant bumped against him. He straightened his uniform, trying to appear relaxed.

"Sir," Valerie said again. "I'm picking up hundreds of signals. These are much closer to us than the nuclear explosions three light-years out. The closer signals match the shuttle recordings of the Chitin vessels earlier."

"How many signals did you say?" he asked.

"These signals are from far out," Valerie said in a noncommittal way. "If we could get closer I'd have a better idea what I'm looking at."

Maddox retreated to his command chair as he thought this through. "How far away are these new signals?"

"A quarter of a light-year, at least," she said.

"How did you find them?" Maddox asked Galyan.

"I didn't, sir," the holoimage said. "I was with Dana's team when the doctor made the discovery."

Maddox nodded. "We'll make a short star drive jump. I want to see this."

* * *

An hour and a half later, Maddox stared at the amazing scene. *Victory* had made a short star drive jump. Presently, a mere billion kilometers separated them from a stream of Chitin vessels.

"How many ships am I looking at?" Maddox asked.

Valerie stared at her panel in shock.

On the main screen, Maddox saw an endless stream of Chitin ships. The vast majority were SWS destroyer-sized. A small percentage were bigger than SWS battleships.

"Dana must have picked up the battleship-sized vessels," Valerie said softly.

"There are one hundred of the larger ships?" Maddox asked.

"More or less," Valerie said.

"That must mean thousands of the smaller craft," Maddox said.

"Yes," Valerie said, gulping slightly.

299

Despite a tightening in his chest, Maddox forced himself to think rationally. "The Chitin fleet is aimed at the star system we're heading toward. Is that their destination?"

"I can't know with one hundred percent accuracy," Valerie said. "But that would be my guess, yes."

"What about the nuclear explosions at the red giant? Are they still occurring?"

Valerie tapped her board, studying it. "Yes, sir, they are."

Maddox glanced at Galyan. "What do you make of this?"

The holoimage's eyelids fluttered. "I suggest this means an ongoing conflict with the Swarm. These are Chitin reinforcements."

"Given their trajectory," Maddox said, "where did the Chitin fleet originate?"

"Using the local coordinates," Galyan said, "Star XZ 23-23-19."

"One of the original star systems that possessed life-signs," Maddox said.

"Yes, sir."

Maddox nodded. "That suggests XZ is a Chitin system."

"Agreed," Galyan said.

Maddox glanced at Valerie. "Does that make sense to you?"

"I'm not sure I understand the question, sir," Valerie said.

"Can two species have an interstellar war at sub-light speeds?" Maddox asked. "That doesn't seem possible with humans. But we're talking about two species of bugs, one big and one small."

"We do not know the precise nature of the Chitin opponents," Galyan said.

Maddox snorted. "Given the Swarm mines that almost killed us, I'd say we do know." He looked around. "It seems to me we may have found what we came for: a general idea of the location of the Swarm Imperium."

"Should we try to negotiate with the Chitins?" Valerie asked.

Maddox shook his head. "We have the advantages of our starship and our overall technological superiority. Let's use those advantages to figure out the situation before we make any premature moves."

Valerie grinned so hard it began to hurt her face.

Maddox noticed. "Do you care to share what you find humorous, Lieutenant?"

She wiped away the smile. "I'm sorry, sir."

"No, no," he said. "What do you find so amusing?"

"You're acting like a Patrol officer, sir. It's an interesting…development. That's all."

Maddox understood her deeper meaning. She believed that normally he acted too recklessly. The time might soon come where she would think that again. But if it made her feel more secure to know he followed Patrol directives…

That was good. Let her smile. Let the others on the bridge share in that. They would likely need this heightened morale before this voyage was through.

"We'll take a breather as the science teams continue to study the nearing star system and the Chitin armada," Maddox said. "Then, we will jump…half a light-year away from our destination. It might be a good idea to have as much data as we can before we go all the way in."

-51-

The third jump brought them close in stellar terms. For accurate sensor readings, they were still too far out to make hard and fast assertions about what they saw.

Maddox called another meeting. He knew Patrol doctrine suggested otherwise. Too many meetings often caused a crew to lose confidence in their captain. Thousands of Patrol case studies showed that crews wanted decisive leaders.

At the meeting, Maddox showed several holoimages. The first showed a nearby Chitin armada much like the one they'd seen two and a half light-years back. Thousands of Chitin vessels headed for the red giant system.

The captain showed a second holoimage of the actual star system. Nuclear explosions continued there. It was difficult to be certain, but many, like Ludendorff and Dana, believed these explosions occurred deeper in the system than those seen earlier.

"Is that conclusive?" Maddox asked.

"No," the professor admitted. "Given our scanty original data, one should not be insistent. I do give it a high probability, though."

"Explain your reasoning," Maddox said.

"If you would show your next holoimage, I'd be happy to oblige."

Maddox nodded to Galyan.

The last holoimage showed energy readings instead of actual images. These energy readings weakened as one followed them toward the galactic center.

"I think we're seeing the exhausts of Swarm motherships," Ludendorff said. "Galyan, if you will."

A fourth holoimage appeared that had not been part of Maddox's original presentation.

Galyan spoke up. "These images are six thousand years old. These "motherships" as the professor names them, carried the entire Swarm force that attacked and destroyed the Adok System. The energy readings we presently view compare favorably with the Adok readings six thousand years ago."

"Does that make sense?" Maddox asked.

"That is an interesting question," Ludendorff said. "Your question implies the normal technological advances occurring in our present human societies. That hasn't always been the norm. A close study of ancient human history shows a decided lethargy regarding technological advances. The real jump occurs with the rise of Western Civilization. Then we see an explosion of inventions that brought humanity to the modern world and eventually led to the Space Age. The key precepts of Western Civilization still guide Commonwealth civilization.

"Now," the professor lectured, "the same does not have to hold true for alien civilizations. It would be quite possible for a society to reach a certain technological level and remain there for thousands, maybe even tens of thousands of years. I suggest that is what we're seeing with the Swarm."

"We don't know with one hundred percent certainty that the readings approaching the red giant are actual Swarm ships," Valerie said.

"True," Ludendorff said. "But the probability is high enough that I definitely believe those ships belong to the Swarm Imperium."

"So..." Maddox said. "What are you suggesting?"

"That we are witnessing the crisis point between the Swarm and the Chitins," Ludendorff said. "Notice, both species appear to be constantly reinforcing that star system. The question is: what makes that system so important to both of them?"

"Let me see if I understand," Maddox said. "The Chitins and the Swarm are feeding tens of thousands of spaceships into that system. The constant nuclear explosions imply they have warred for at least the last three years with constant battle attrition."

"Yes," Ludendorff said. "Frankly, this is amazing. This is the first known instance of such a stellar war at sub-light speeds. It implies massive industrial power poured into one star system at a slow, sub-light speed. Given what we've seen of the known Chitin star system, the others around the red giant system also seem to be Chitin-held."

"So?"

"I would suggest these other star systems are also pouring Chitin spaceships into the red giant system," Ludendorff said. "The coordinating power this suggests is staggering. Who rules the Chitins? Can a ruler impose his or her will on a star system light-years away at these slow travel speeds? The answer appears to be yes. I find that incredible."

"How far into the red giant system have the Swarm driven?" Maddox asked.

"If you would go back to the holoimage," the professor said.

Maddox nodded. Galyan switched holoimages.

The professor picked up a clicker and stood, aiming it at the holoimage. "The most constant nuclear explosions occur in this region. If you'll notice, over here is the gas giant. That means the Swarm haven't yet reached the gas giant. Thus, I would suggest the Swarm has pushed three quarters of the way into the system. The *bloated* red giant star occupies what would have been an otherwise deeper system."

"Is the red giant system what Shu came out here to see?" Valerie asked.

Ludendorff appeared perplexed. "Are you suggesting the Spacer knew about this war?"

"What?" Valerie said. "Oh, no, no, I didn't mean that. The bloated comment made me wonder. The red giant wasn't always a red giant. Likely, millions of years ago, it was a much smaller, denser star. It grew outward at some point in the past. I'm wondering if Shu came here because of what the ancient mummified Builder taught the first Spacers. Could the mummified Builder have thought of the red giant as it used to be— as a smaller star?"

"You're speaking in a conflicted manner," Ludendorff said. "First, you say the red giant has been like this for millions of years. Then, you wonder if the mummified Builder thought of it as the star it used to be. You can't have it both ways. In my opinion, the red giant has been like this for a long, long time."

"*You* believe that," Valerie said. "But you don't *know* that's the truth. Aren't the Builders supposed to be ancient?"

Ludendorff shrugged.

"Look," Valerie said. "All I'm saying is that maybe Shu came here to see something the red giant covered up when it expanded to its present size."

Silence filled the briefing chamber.

"That's an extremely negative thought," Ludendorff said.

Valerie became stubborn. "Didn't you tell us before to keep an open mind to all possibilities?"

Ludendorff scowled. "How dare you throw that back at me?"

Maddox cleared his throat. When that didn't work, he took out his long-barreled gun and rapped the butt on the table.

Everyone turned to him.

"This is a briefing," the captain said. "We are open to all suggestions. Thus, I want my personnel and guests to maintain a friendly attitude toward each other."

"I'm a guest then?" Ludendorff demanded.

Maddox gave him a wry grin. "Unless you're saying you're part of the crew, under my direct authority."

Ludendorff looked away.

"In any case," Maddox said. "We shall know soon enough. It's time to prepare for the final jump. We've scouted. Now, it's time to go in."

"Where do you plan to go exactly?" Dana asked.

"Precisely," the captain said. "That is the final topic of discussion. Where is the best location for *Victory* to jump? We want to investigate the Chitin-Swarm War as best we can, but without engaging in any combat ourselves."

-52-

The starship jumped to the red giant system. In relation to the stream of known Chitin spaceships, *Victory* appeared on the other side of the red giant ninety degrees away from the stream of likely Swarm vessels.

According to Maddox's orders, *Victory* arrived at a Neptune-from-Sun distance from the bloated red star.

As soon as they completed the jump, Maddox strove for equilibrium. The effects of the anti-jump serum helped retard ninety percent of Jump Lag. The Kai-Kaus additions kept the ship systems running at eighty-seven percent capacity. That meant, however, that neither the crew nor the ship operated optimally the first few minutes coming out of jump.

Thus, Maddox strove to move. Finally, he staggered upright, looking around. No one else was moving yet.

"Lieutenant," he slurred.

Valerie jerked where she sat.

"Galyan," Maddox said in a more normal voice.

The holoimage flickered but otherwise didn't move.

Maddox headed for the sensor station. Before he got there, the sensor operator straightened.

"I'm fine, sir," she said.

The main screen came online. Maddox backed into his command chair, sitting down while focusing on what he saw.

The red giant pulsated, filling half the screen.

"Switching view," Valerie said.

"Sir," the sensor operator said. "I'm detecting an alien scan."

"Are our shields up?" Maddox asked.

"Yes, sir," Lieutenant Smith-Fowler said. "They're at ninety-one percent capacity and rising."

"Oh, oh," Valerie said. "You'd better look at this, sir."

For the next few minutes, Maddox watched and listened as his bridge crew kept feeding him incoming data. He rapidly built up an image of the situation.

Approximately ten thousand Chitin destroyers curved around the red giant, heading for the main conflict. The outer layer of the ten thousand spaceships was five hundred thousand kilometers from *Victory*. Whoever or whatever ran those warships realized *Victory* was out here and scanned to find out what she was.

Those ten thousand spaceships were a small portion of the vast number of vessels. The Chitins alone had hundreds of thousands of spaceships. The number staggered Maddox's imagination. It made the Commonwealth's war against the New Men seem like a day in the park.

The trouble was the Swarm. Those big motherships looked exactly like the ones that had obliterated Galyan's homeworld. The Swarm stream seemed endless from here, reaching as far as the sensors could read. At this point, that was many billions upon billions of kilometers away.

"What is this place?" Valerie whispered.

Maddox focused on Smith-Fowler. "I want to know the instant enemy munitions, rays or missiles head for us. We cannot afford to trade combat fire with anyone. Our vessel is less than a mite in this destructive orgy."

"I am greatly saddened," Galyan said, in a more robotic voice than he'd used for quite some time. "This is painful, Captain. I remember six thousand years ago. The Swarm are killing the Chitins. This is wrong. This is evil. We must help the Chitins. I cannot bear to watch this any longer."

"Galyan," Maddox snapped. "Come stand by me."

"Captain?" the holoimage asked.

"Obey me, Driving Force," the captain said.

The holoimage floated near the command chair.

"Look at me," Maddox said.

Galyan did so.

"You belong to Star Watch. We're your home. I need you now more than ever."

"You need my assistance?" Galyan asked.

"One hundred percent," Maddox said.

Galyan's eyelids fluttered. "Yes, I understand. I am here to obey your orders, sir."

"Good. I want you here so I can ask your advice when the time comes."

"I can give you my advice right now, sir."

"We're not here to throw our lives away," Maddox said. "We're here to make sure humanity survives the Swarm. Do you understand?"

"Computing…" Galyan said. "I am computing…"

"Sir," Smith-Fowler said. "I see missiles heading for us."

"How many?" Maddox asked.

"Thirty thousand, sir," Smith-Fowler said, his voice cracking.

"How long until the first missiles reach us?" the captain asked.

Smith-Fowler stared at his screen.

"Lieutenant," Maddox said calmly. "I do not appreciate my officers taking time to sight see. If you could tear yourself from watching the display, I'd like that answer now."

Smith-Fowler tore his gaze from his screen to stare at Maddox.

The captain waited.

"Yes, sir," Smith-Fowler said hoarsely. "The time of arrival is…twenty-nine hours, sir."

"Thank you," Maddox said. "The missiles aren't urgent for a while. We can still take a look-see."

The captain turned to Valerie. "Have you found anything unusual?"

"Not yet, sir," Valerie said. "According to my readings and those I'm receiving from the science teams, there are no inhabited planets, asteroids or space stations in the system."

"That doesn't surprise me," Maddox said, as if someone had told him it was going to rain for five days in the tropics.

"Galyan, why are they fighting?"

"Computing…" Galyan said softly.

"Driving Force Galyan," Maddox said. "I require your attention."

The holoimage spun around to face him.

"Why are the Swarm fighting?" Maddox repeated.

"The Swarm fights to conquer or destroy its enemies."

"Why do the Chitins fight, do you think?"

The eyelids fluttered. "That is unknown, sir."

"Why did the ancient Adoks fight?"

"To protect their star system," Galyan said.

"No," Maddox said. "They fought to protect their homeworld."

"Yes," Galyan said. "That is correct."

Maddox studied the main screen. "What are the Chitins fighting so hard to protect, I wonder? Lieutenant Noonan, pass the word along. I want to find out what the Chitins are protecting. I want to know now."

"Yes, sir," Valerie said while madly tapping on her board.

***

As the science and sensor teams searched for the answer, Maddox watched a battle farther out in the system.

Masses of missiles engaged with one another. Multiple nuclear detonations obliterated those nearest the explosions. The rest continued to accelerate for the enemy.

"Those are hardened missiles," Galyan said. "The Swarm did not possess those against the Adoks."

Maddox rested his chin on his fist with the elbow on an armrest. Layers upon layers of missiles tried to claw past each other. Behind the missile barrages waited spaceships. The Chitins used particle beams. The Swarm had lasers. Little survived the thousands of beams.

"Carnage," the captain said, "carnage on a monumental scale."

He used the Star Watch Intelligence side of his brain to analyze what he saw. This was much more mathematical than the type of fighting humans generally engaged in. One force smashing against an almost equally large force. He had read a little history in his time. He recalled an ancient conflict called Word War I. One particular battle site reminded him of this one. The Battle of Verdun had been a bloodbath that changed the character of the French Army twenty years later during the German invasion of France in 1940.

His reading regarding Verdun was nothing like this head-on collision of two merciless forces. The Battle of Verdun had been of short duration compared to this. Yet, the attritional battle had almost shattered the French Army of the time.

The Chitins and Swarm did not break. Each side simply sent more reinforcements. How many light-years did the farthest Chitins have to travel to get here? The Swarm had been fighting like this for over six thousand years, at least. What did their High Command think? Or was there some queen in a great planetary hive directing the interstellar imperium?

Humans would never survive such endless brutality. Did that mean the Swarm or the Chitins were destined to rule the galaxy?

If Maddox had anything to say in this, it would not be so.

Why did the two insect species wage such ruthless war in this star system? There had to be a reason. If this just happened to be a marker for where the two empires happened to meet…

The idea of a purposeless war on this scale chilled Maddox.

"Sir," Valerie said.

The captain looked up from where he sat.

"Doctor Rich thinks she's found the answer," the lieutenant said.

"What?" he asked.

"If you'll look at the main screen, sir," Valerie said.

Maddox did so, lifting his chin off his first.

The lieutenant focused on the red giant. "Given the Chitins' fleet maneuvers and the central vectors of the Swarm assaults, this seems to be the area of desire, the one the small insects protect and the big ones want to reach."

Maddox observed superimposed curved lines sweeping around the red giant to a spot hidden from view in *Victory's* present position.

"Dana doesn't know what the object is," he said, "just where it is?"

310

"Yes, sir," Valerie said. "She's requesting probe launches—"

"Probes won't work out here," Maddox said, irritably. "The Chitins will destroy them. She means for us to make another jump, this one within the system."

"You're probably right, sir," Valerie said. "But at least we know where to go."

Maddox nodded slowly. The mystery of the importance of this battle likely lay on the other side of the curvature of the giant star. It appeared, as well, that this thing was near the star's surface in a relative sense. It would seem to be a Mercury-from-Sun distance from the star's surface. That surface was a cool 5000 degrees Fahrenheit, a balmy temperature as stars went.

How near should the starship appear to this unknown thing? If they were too far out, it would put them nearer the military action. Too far in, and it would put them close to the endless Chitin reinforcements.

"Galyan," Maddox said. "Do you have a recommendation?"

The holoimage studied the main screen. "Yes, Captain," Galyan said. "I would jump to these coordinates."

"Just a moment," Maddox said. He went to his chair and had Valerie call Ludendorff. The professor appeared on the main screen as he worked in a sensor chamber.

"I'm thinking of making another jump," Maddox said.

"Splendid," Ludendorff said. "It's what I would do if I commanded a ship like this."

"Yes," Maddox said. "Where would you jump exactly?"

"What did Galyan suggest?"

Maddox told him.

"Hmm," Ludendorff said. "That is sound, as far as it goes, but too cautious. You know my take. Go in deep. Get a close look and a recording. Then, jump far out so we can think it through."

"If we do that," Maddox said, "the Chitins will certainly recognize our ability for what it is and react accordingly next time."

"Why would that matter?"

311

"Being ready for any eventuality and all that," Maddox said in an offhanded way.

"I see," Ludendorff said. "You think you know what's out there."

"In fact," Maddox said, "I do think that."

"Well, my boy, don't keep me in suspense. What is the prize?"

Maddox shook his head. "Not yet, Professor, I need to make one more preparation." He motioned to Valerie.

The lieutenant cut the connection, staring at him as he headed for the exit.

"Sir," Valerie said.

"Hmmm?" Maddox asked, facing her.

"What's hiding around the curvature of the red giant?"

He gave her an unreadable stare and the faintest smile before heading once more for the exit.

-53-

Sergeant Treggason Riker lay in a regular bed in his chamber, with his hands behind his head. His boots were on the floor beside his bed as he wriggled his sock-clad toes.

Since the surgery to remove the android-fired bullet, he had been on medical leave. The surgeon had done a fine job. The drugs had speeded his recovery in record time. As a bonus, his recuperation had given him time to read.

He'd paged through endless descriptions of various trees and flowers. In his mind, he selected another tree for up near the mound on the left corner of his property back home. It would need a small bed of flowers to match the new tree's spring blooms. Yes, that would add to the overall effect of his cottage.

With that decided, Riker had started reading fictional mysteries. The stories took place in the distant past before space travel. They were quick tales with a solo brash-talking detective quick with his fists. Of lasers, tangle-guns, gravity dampeners there were none. Instead, the people in the stories used gasoline-burning vehicles and often engaged each other with knives or brass knuckles. In a way, the hero detective reminded him of the captain.

Riker grinned as he set the tablet aside. This was the best adventure he'd had aboard *Victory*. The bullet had been bad at first. A few days later, the sergeant had realized the advantage of his wound. It left him out of the action.

Riker's grin turned into an actual smile. He'd thought he'd long for the action. In fact, it was relaxing to wait in his room and listen to the occasional report. Perhaps it was time to put in for deskwork back on Earth. He'd been a field agent almost his entire life. He could easily imagine the new life. He would get up at seven, drive to work, fill out reports and drive home to fiddle with his plants and go out to dinner with a lady every second week.

I could get used to that.

Riker sat up abruptly, frowning at himself. When had he started thinking his life was bad?

He shook his head. He enjoyed his life, as far as that went. It was just… He was missing something.

Riker cocked his head. What was he missing? What did he need to make his life good?

The old sergeant scratched his neck. That was an interesting idea. Maybe he needed more things to do. Maybe for him, lying around thinking too much was a bad idea.

Riker laughed, shaking his head. "Don't be an idiot. I finally have a sweet assignment and I'm grumbling about it. That's silly."

He lay back down, picked up the tablet and felt a small moment of enjoyment as he realized he was going to find out who murdered the heiress. Likely, the detective—

There was a sharp rap at Riker's hatch.

The sergeant froze, deciding he wasn't going to answer. He wanted to finish the story and that was that.

Another rap sounded.

Riker muttered under his breath, but stubbornly held to his original conviction. A few moments more passed. He raised the tablet again.

"Sergeant Riker."

Riker yelped in surprise, sitting bolt upright and bug-eyed, finding Galyan staring at him.

"What do you want?" Riker demanded.

"The captain is waiting outside your door," Galyan said. "He wants to know why you aren't answering."

"So he went and fetched you, eh?" Riker asked.

"That is correct."

Riker sighed, tossing the tablet onto the bed. He rose with a grunt, heading for the hatch in his socks. "I knew it couldn't last," he said.

"What could not last?" Galyan asked.

Instead of answering, Riker pressed a switch so the hatch slid up.

Maddox stood there, looking impatient. "Hurry along, Sergeant. Grab your stunner and gun. I want you with me. And put on your boots," he added, taking in Riker's disheveled appearance with disapproval.

"I'm on sick leave, sir. I'm recouping from the bullet wound."

"Your leave is suspended," Maddox said. "I'm declaring you fit for duty. I'm going to need you."

"Begging your pardon, sir, but need me for what?"

"If I'm right," Maddox said, "for combat."

"What's that, sir? Did you say combat?"

"I imagine that's the most likely outcome. I want an old salt by my side. This could be our hairiest mission yet. That means I need my best people. In these situations, that's you, Sergeant."

"What's been happening that you need me, sir?"

"Quit dithering and get your boots," Maddox said. "I don't have any more time to explain. The proverbial excrement has hit the fan, or I imagine it will in another hour or two. If I'm right... Well, never mind. Just get a move on, Sergeant. And start psyching yourself up for a combat situation."

-54-

Maddox stepped into the medical center. He headed for the security area where Shu 15 was kept. An orderly stepped up, blocking his passage.

"I'm sorry, sir," the beefy man in hospital greens said. "But the doctor has ordered this place off limits to everyone."

Maddox didn't show any surprise or even anger at the intrusion. He simply brushed past the orderly.

"Sir," the man said, reaching out.

Before the orderly could grab the captain, Maddox spun around. He grabbed the hand reaching for him, twisting it so the orderly cried out in pain as he bent sharply forward so Maddox wouldn't break the wrist.

"I have my orders, sir," the orderly wheezed.

"Stun him," Maddox told a startled Sergeant Riker.

"Sir?" Riker asked.

"Please obey me the first time, Sergeant. We don't have time for any more delays."

Riker reluctantly drew his stunner, put it at the lowest setting and stunned the orderly. The man collapsed onto the floor as Maddox released his hold.

"If I indicate someone, stun them," Maddox said over his shoulder.

"Yes, sir," Riker muttered.

The captain moved briskly. He pointed at three more people, all of them succumbing to Riker's stunner.

"What's going on here, sir?" Riker asked, half trotting to keep up with the captain.

"It strikes me as hypnotism or some form of mind manipulation," Maddox said.

"You mean the Spacer is causing this?"

"Yes," Maddox said. He almost bumped into the next hatch, which did not rise at his near approach. The captain cleared his throat before raising his voice, "I know you can hear me, Shu. I would like to discuss our coming strategy."

Several moments passed.

The captain inhaled to shout again. Abruptly, the hatch opened.

"Wait here," Maddox told Riker. "Incapacitate anyone trying to enter. If your stunner stops working, use your gun and kill them."

"Sir?" Riker said, sounding astonished.

Maddox strode through the entrance, which immediately shut behind him.

The captain noticed the difference to the large chamber. It no longer seemed like a medical room, but a headquarters or outpost. Several monitoring stations showed various regions of the red giant system. No people sat there. Instead, Shu lay propped up on a medical bed. Her head moved minutely as he approached, letting Maddox know that she saw him.

"Hello, Surveyor," Maddox said.

"Hello, *Di-Far*," Shu said.

"Are you feeling better?"

"Some," she said. "Your AI struck me a hard blow. I had no idea he was a mindtech."

"I'm unfamiliar with the term."

"It's Spacer lingo," Shu said. "He, or it, or whatever the AI is, found my feedback link. He sent several harsh pulses and then attempted an adjustment. I'm impressed. He's a quick study."

"He is an AI."

"In truth," Shu said, "he's more than that. We would call it deification. Much of the AI equipment is higher-level Builder technology. That is odd, to say the least. The last Adoks transferred much of his identity or personality into the AI core.

317

The Adok aspect of Galyan's personality thwarted me. It would not happen again, though."

"You haven't suborned Galyan to your will?"

"No," Shu said.

"Then why hasn't Galyan told me about this operation?"

"I've hidden from him by rerouting certain interior sensors. In another week, I imagine, Galyan would discover me. Still, you have moved uncommonly fast. I am impressed with you, Captain. The Visionary correctly named you."

"You accept that I'm *di-far*?"

"Without a doubt or hesitation," Shu said. "Humanity is about to launch unto a new path, and that is thanks to you."

"A golden pyramid orbits the red giant?" Maddox asked.

Shu held her breath, finally exhaling as she nodded slowly. "I believe so. However, like you, I won't know it until we see it."

"Does a golden pyramid have the ability to project a hyper-spatial tube?"

"I suspect we will find out," Shu said.

"Why are the Chitins protecting the pyramid?"

"I don't know. That aspect of the mission surprises me. I didn't expect them. I didn't expect the Swarm for that matter. It makes sense, though, if you think about it."

"In what way?" asked Maddox.

"This is going to sound superstitious, but I don't mean it that way. You are *di-far*. Thus, the moment the Visionary included you, it meant we would encounter something momentous. In this instance, that means the Chitin-Swarm War."

"You call it that because you've known about it all along, or you've listened in on our communications?"

"The latter, of course," Shu said.

"Why haven't the Spacers attempted to reach the golden pyramid on their own?"

Shu laughed. "But we have, Captain. Our records indicate such attempts on three different occasions. Clearly, the missions never reached the golden pyramid, given that it still exists."

"What else could the Chitins be protecting?"

"I have no idea."

"If you had to guess, why would you say the Chitins are protecting the pyramid?"

"My guess is the Builder in the pyramid originally modified what you call the Chitins. I believe she raised them up into intelligence long before her interment. Thus, I imagine it's a religious reason. The Chitins, if I were to guess, worship the Builder inside the golden pyramid."

"How large do you think the Chitin Empire is?"

"Until we reached here, I had no idea the Chitins existed. Again, if I were to guess, I'd say the Builder erected a bulwark against the encroaching Swarm Imperium."

"You said she."

"I did."

"You believe this Builder is a female?" Maddox asked.

"That is what the word *she* indicates."

"Why was the Builder mummified?"

Shu laughed with an edge. "I imagine Ludendorff told you quite a tale. Mummified indeed. That is how the male Builders think of the females. Ludendorff is an offspring of his dead master, arrogant, boastful and strutting across the stage of life."

"No one else has told me about the origin of the Spacers," Maddox said.

"Nor will I do so now," Shu said. "We don't have time. The Chitins will soon attempt to overwhelm *Victory* with thousands, perhaps even millions, of missiles."

"You can talk to them?"

"Not as you think," Shu said. "I am able to tap into their communications. Because of my adaptations, I have a small ability to decipher clump messages. They believe *Victory* is a Swarm vessel. Thus, they will attack with extreme prejudice and destroy it if they can."

"*Victory* doesn't act like a Swarm vessel."

"Captain, your starship is non-Chitin. I would think that would be good enough for them to want to attack it. You are in their holy star system."

"You've sensed religious communications among the Chitins?"

"Yes," Shu said.

Maddox detected a slight variation in her voice. He wasn't sure he believed her last comment.

"Let's get down to the meat of the situation," the captain said. "What are you hoping to achieve here?"

"I'm surprised you have to ask. It should be obvious by now, especially as you have figured out so much already. I want to revive the Builder. According to our legends, she has slept for an incredibly long time."

"Why would that benefit the Commonwealth?" Maddox asked.

"Not just the Commonwealth," Shu said. "It would benefit all of humanity. Think about it, Captain. The Swarm are on the move. The male Builder unleashed Commander Thrax Ti Ix on the universe. Think what the Swarm can do with Laumer Drive technology. It will only be a matter of a few decades, at most, before the Swarm reaches Human Space. Look at their numbers out there. Could the Commonwealth defeat this host if the Swarm had jump tech?"

"I doubt it," Maddox said.

"That's an understatement. The Swarm would swamp humanity."

"Spacers are passive. Your presence here at this time is not a passive act."

"You distrust me," Shu said. "I understand. You have listened to Ludendorff's slurs against us. He doesn't know real Spacers. Passive? That is a poor joke. We don't waste our time on frivolities like the rest of you. How humans love to battle over trinkets."

"You're not human?"

"I misspoke," Shu said. "Of course, we're human. We live in the stellar void instead of on planets, but we come from the same common stock of Earth as you."

"I'm glad to hear it," Maddox said. "So...you're suggesting we take the Builder onto *Victory*?"

"Exactly," Shu said.

"The Chitins would hardly want us to take their goddess-queen."

"They will fight mandible and pincer to stop us," Shu said. "Thus, we should avoid fighting them. That means using the star drive to appear beside the pyramid. I will open the way for us into the golden artifact. We will hurry inside, wake the Builder and guide her onto the starship. You will jump to the appearing hyper-spatial tube, and we will head directly to Earth. Does that sound acceptable to you?"

Maddox nodded.

"You still have some reservations about me," Shu said. "I would like to hear them so I can convince you I mean exactly what I'm saying."

"How do we know the Builder is there?"

Shu only hesitated a fraction of a second. "We don't know except for the ancient legends. I must point out, Captain, that those legends have proven accurate to date. How do you think the Spacers have all their advanced technology? We have followed the old legends to ancient caches of Builder equipment."

"You're not in communication with the Builder?"

"I wish I were," Shu said.

"Why can't you reach her?"

"Distance for one thing," Shu said. "The other is heavy Chitin interference. It leads me to suspect the Chitins have some idea of what lies in the pyramid. Otherwise, they would not have made such an effort to build jamming stations around it."

"How do you know about these jamming stations?"

"Captain, you're much too suspicious. I know because I can feel the jammers out there. It's faint. But given the distance and the interfering red giant, the source would have to be incredibly powerful."

"What will your Builder demand from humanity?"

Shu smiled, shaking her head. "Your suspicion makes me wonder if you're attempting to trap me. Why do you fear me so terribly?"

"Because if I'm right," Maddox said, "we could be taking a monster into Human Space. The Builders meddled with humanity before—"

"Meddled, you say," Shu laughed bitterly. "The male Builders were arrogant pricks. The female Builders are doting. We will reach a golden age thousands of years earlier this way.

321

We will find a way to avoid the terrible Swarm menace. The New Men—" Shu snapped her fingers. "The Commonwealth will know healing instead of endless battles. This is the moment to change the course of human history. You are the greatest *di-far* the Spacers have ever found. This is a most wonderful vessel. At last, we will reach the golden womb and bring forth the great healer of the Orion Arm. Do you have the courage to fight for healing as hard as you've fought to bring destruction?"

"One last question before I answer," Maddox said. "Why have you gone to such lengths to engage in lies and deception? It seems—"

"Captain, captain, captain," Shu said. "You don't understand the Spacer Way. We do not use big muscles and speed to battle our way to a place. We bend and blend, and slide around obstacles. We soften our voices and hide when we need to. We avoid open conflicts, in that way saving our consciences from shedding blood. You see that as sneaky. We realize it is kindness."

"I'm beginning to see," Maddox said, with approval in his voice. "Ludendorff sees that as trickery. He sees your way as underhanded. Yet, in truth, you're saving the foolhardy from needless pain and suffering."

"It is encouraging to watch you attempt to understand us. At least you don't sneer. That is an improvement from our usual experience with others. I imagine your former line of work guides you. Captain Maddox the Intelligence agent understands how subterfuge can bring greater rewards than fisticuffs."

"I will be honest. I still don't fully trust you."

"I would have been surprised if you had," Shu said.

"Yet," Maddox said, "I don't see any other option. We're stranded too far from home. I'm willing to gamble, if for no other reason than to gain a hyper-spatial tube back to Earth. We've found the Swarm Imperium. It's at least two thousand light-years away. It's busy in a hard war against Chitins. This is priceless knowledge for humanity."

"You'll return home with more than just that," Shu said.

"What if the Builder has died?"

322

"But…she can't be dead. Not after all the hard work we put into finding her."

"Will you join the away-team then?" Maddox asked.

"I have to," Shu said. "I doubt Ludendorff could break the entrance codes fast enough."

"How long do you think we'll have to do all this?"

Shu nodded. "That is the primary question, Captain. We don't know the precise situation yet. We're going to have to make some quick calculations on the spot. That is your area of expertise. What I want to know is how long until you're ready to move."

"I'll need an hour, maybe a few minutes less," Maddox said.

"Yes," Shu said, "I can be ready by then."

Maddox stared at her. "This is why you picked me, isn't it?"

"No. The Visionary saw that you were *di-far*. I suspect your decisive nature comes from the fact of your blessing."

Maddox bent to one knee, bowed his head, holding that position for a time, before rising.

"The others won't trust you," Maddox told her.

"They trust you, Captain. You're the leader. In the end, they will do what you say."

"Let's hope you're right," Maddox said.

-55-

Maddox marched into Ludendorff's science chamber. The professor and his team were hard at work at their stations.

The captain motioned Ludendorff near, staring at him fixedly as the Methuselah Man approached.

"I have just finished speaking with Shu 15," Maddox said, injecting a pompous tone into his voice.

"Oh. I see. Was it a rewarding experience?"

"Very," Maddox said. "We are about to embark on a historic assault. I will swing *Victory* out, gaining velocity, racing Chitin missiles, until I can see around the present curvature of the red giant."

"What do you hope to see?"

"A golden pyramid," Maddox said in a lofty manner.

Ludendorff didn't raise his eyebrows or show any other indication of surprise. He just stared at Maddox.

"We will free the glorious Builder within," Maddox said, "who will then join our ship. She will—"

"She?" asked Ludendorff.

"That is correct. Do you have a problem with that?"

"Me? In no way," the professor said. "This is interesting."

Maddox nodded. It almost seemed as if he did it in an encouraging way.

"Yes!" Ludendorff declared, as he rubbed his hands. "This is priceless. I know the Builders, as you must realize. Even though this Builder is a female, she can give us amazing advances. Of course, we will have to take her with us."

"Shu suggested you would not approve of our venture," Maddox said.

"Maybe in the past I wouldn't," Ludendorff said. "But...given this incredible war, I don't see that we have a choice. Humanity needs a new advantage."

"Your good sense surprises me," Maddox said. "I hope you keep it." He moved closer, gripping the professor by the shoulder as they shook hands.

As Maddox slid his hand away, he lifted the palm upward, making sure the professor noticed the writing there. It was the single word: CUBE.

Ludendorff slapped his chest. "You can count on me, sir. In fact, I would do this even if there wasn't a Builder inside. I expect to find scientific treasures in the pyramid. And of course, we desperately need the hyper-spatial tube so we can go home."

"Good," Maddox said. "I have further preparations to make." He headed for the exit.

***

Maddox didn't trust Shu. He was certain the Spacer had sinister motives.

Galyan had hurt her. She'd recovered though, trying to hide that from everyone. Her inner Builder devices must do more than they realized. He should have had them cut out of her when he had the chance. Now, it was too late. Besides, they needed that hyper-spatial tube so they could return to Human Space.

Could some of what Shu had said be truthful? That was a galling question. He operated in the blind on far too many matters. In that way, Patrol thinking was close to Intelligence matters. Both had to teach their practitioners how to make decisions with only partial data.

One thing was clear. Even now, Shu would be watching him. She didn't trust him, either. But it would seem they both needed each other. That gave Maddox confidence. If she could simply take over Galyan, she would have already done so. That would indicate she had limits.

***

The red alert klaxon blared throughout the starship. Everyone hurried to his or her station. Those who were asleep bolted upright, dressing and hurrying to their stations.

Maddox burst through the entrance onto the bridge, with Riker hurrying after him. In several long strides, the captain reached the command chair. He looked around at his bridge crew, nodded and took a seat.

Maddox clicked the switch to the intercom on his armrest.

"This is your captain speaking." The words went through the vessel. "We have made a historic journey deep into the Beyond," Maddox said. "No human vessel has ever gone farther. You can take pride in that. The Patrol arm of Star Watch lives to dare.

"Now, though, we are going into combat. We are alone in a strange star system. The Swarm battles a new species that Professor Ludendorff has named Chitins. This is a ferocious war. It is beyond anything we've seen before.

"We must win through these next few hours. Every man and woman on Starship *Victory* must work to the fullest. It is possible the rest of humanity depends on our actions out here in the Beyond, more than two thousand light-years from Human Space. We are about to jump into grave danger. We suspect a golden pyramid orbits the red giant. It is possible a Builder sleeps within. We also believe the pyramid can create a hyper-spatial tube. We plan to enter the pyramid, free the Builder and activate the tube. Then, we will no doubt have to fight our way to the tube's entrance.

"I am counting on each of you to work until you drop. There is not going to be any quit on my starship. This will be hard. That's good, though. This is our supreme test. Do you possess the spirit to see this through? I believe you do. Now, it is up to you to prove me right.

"That is all. Carry on."

Maddox clicked the switch, sitting back, hoping his words would stir the crew to their best effort. He would not have made such a speech in the past. To him, trying his hardest to win drove him to excellence. Others did not operate that way. His Patrol teachers had hammered home the need for good morale. People needed to be needed.

Maddox grinned. Apparently, ancient Adok AIs needed that too.

He pulled out a tablet, going over the Marine roster. The androids had been some of the best-rated Marines.

How did the androids figure into all of this?

Maddox shook his head. He didn't have time to think about that. He needed cool concentration in order to defeat the Spacer and whatever waited for them in the golden pyramid.

Did a golden pyramid truly orbit the gas giant?

"Let's find out," Maddox whispered to himself. He looked up. According to what he saw on the main screen, the Marines were ready in their exo-armor. The strikefighters revved up in their hangar bays. Lieutenant Maker waited in his jumpfighter.

In an assured voice, Maddox gave the starship's pilot the coordinates for the next jump. He waited for the navigator to plot it. Then he said, "Let's do this."

-56-

If Mercury and Venus had orbited the massive red star at the same range the two planets did the Sun, *Victory* came out of the star-drive jump between those two orbital ranges. The starship bypassed the curvature of the red giant to appear near a vast clot of Chitin spaceships that must number in the hundreds of thousands.

The number was staggering and in a gigantically globular shape.

"Sir," Valerie whispered. "I don't see any pyramid. All I see are those milling ships."

Maddox viewed the sickening spectacle. The gigantically globular mass of Chitin vessels—hundreds of thousands of them—seethed with constant motion. It appeared that some ships went deeper into the mass while others boiled upward. At the same time, the mass moved together in an orbital path around the red giant. The spectacle reminded the captain of masses of bees crawling around a hive and each other just before they swarmed. More Chitin ships came all the time. Two streams of them circling around the red giant fed the incredible globular mass with more and more vessels. The clot would have become vast beyond reckoning except for one thing. A third stream of vessels *left* the mass, heading out-system to face the Swarm coming in-system.

Did the Chitin vessels gain enhanced power from the globular intermingling or was that simply social insect behavior?

"Do you see anything representing a pyramid?" Maddox asked.

"Not yet, sir," the sensors operator said. "The Chitin jamming signals are too great. I can't—"

"Maybe I can help."

The bridge crew turned around. So did the captain. Shu 15 walked onto the bridge in her customary Spacer garb.

"Captain," Galyan said in warning.

"Not now," Maddox told the holoimage. "What can you do?" he asked Shu.

"Perhaps your primitive sensing gear could use a boost," Shu said. "Are you ready?"

Maddox thought for a second before nodding.

Shu bent her head as if looking at something on the floor.

"I'm getting through the jammers," sensors shouted. "I'm putting the images on the main screen."

The screen turned fuzzy for a moment. Then, sensor images appeared in ghostly form. Those images were *inside* the globular mass of Chitin ships. The Chitin vessels—almost jammed side-by-side—were tens of kilometers thick. Beyond the Chitin warships inside the globular mass was a hollow region approximately four hundred thousand kilometers in diameter.

"You were right about the pyramid being there," Valerie told the captain. "How did you know?"

"I didn't *know*," Maddox said softly. "But it seemed the most reasonable explanation."

"Do not be modest," Shu chided him.

"We have a problem," Valerie said. "There's no way *Victory* can fight its way through the protecting vessels."

"You can't imagine that's my plan," Maddox said.

Valerie stared at him. "You're not going to use the star drive, are you?"

"How else could we do this?" Maddox asked.

"But, sir," Valerie said. "Supposing you appear near the pyramid; that puts us two hundred thousand kilometers from the nearest Chitin vessels. If each of those hundreds of thousands of ships fires one missile—"

"Please, Lieutenant," the captain said. "They're not going to do that. The pyramid is a holy object that they can't afford to risk destroying. No. The Chitin ships will have to accelerate to us in order to engage their particle beams. We've already seen that the Chitin particle-beam range is short compared to our beams, a mere five thousand kilometers. They can't all accelerate at us at once, either, as that would soon cause a mass collision."

"How much time do you calculate we'll have near the pyramid?" Valerie asked.

"Approximately forty-five minutes," Maddox said.

Valerie stared at him. "That's no time at all, sir. Why, simply leaving the starship in a shuttle to reach the pyramid will take ten to twenty minutes."

"If you compare it to how we went into the silver pyramid," Maddox said, "you'd be right. I have another way."

"What way?" Valerie asked.

Maddox regarded Shu. "Tell me, Surveyor. Is the pyramid hollow like the Xerxes Nexus was?"

"I don't know," Shu said. She concentrated a moment. "Why don't you use your sensors to try to find out?"

"Excellent advice," Maddox said. He turned to Valerie. "Get on it, please."

Valerie and several others attempted to scan the pyramid. Soon, the lieutenant shook her head. "It's no good, sir. Our sensors can't break through whatever is shielding the pyramid."

"Your scans were never meant to break through," Shu said. "But I did so while piggybacking on some of your systems." The Spacer faced Maddox. "There is a small open area, small in a relative sense to the pyramid. This one is considerably larger than the Xerxes Nexus was. I imagine you're thinking of using your jumpfighter to get inside."

"Yes," Maddox said.

"The pyramid might have safeguards against that," Shu said.

"You'll have to jam those safeguards," Maddox said.

Shu scoffed, shaking her head.

"Surveyor," the captain said. "Time is next to priceless in this environment. Look at the Chitin mass. We are about to attempt a suicide mission on a longshot. Flying out to the pyramid in shuttles will take too long. The jumpfighter is our only hope."

"There won't be any room for the Builder inside the jumpfighter," Shu said.

"I think there will be," Maddox said. "You forget, I've spoken to and met a Builder before. You haven't. The one I met was large, but it wasn't material the same way you or I are."

"What do you mean?" Shu said.

Maddox smiled enigmatically. "There was data I left out of my secret Star Watch report a year ago. I assume Spacer spies have read the report, which means you've studied it in detail."

"Go on," Shu said.

"The Builder... How do I describe it? It was almost as if he was made of protoplasm. He could shift shape to an astonishing degree."

Furrow lines appeared across Shu's forehead. "You're lying," she said at last.

"On the contrary," he said. "It was perplexing. The Builders are not like us."

Shu licked her lips. "I can almost believe it. The legends I've heard... Yes," she said decisively. "I accept your statement. We will take the jumpfighter. But if we're going to have room for her to join us—"

"We will take everyone we can while going in," Maddox said.

Shu appeared suspicious once more.

"I suspect we're going to need everyone we can get in there," Maddox said. "I'm sure there are ancient safeguards inside the pyramid—androids for instance."

"You must not speak of that," Shu gasped.

"I will say no more on the subject then," Maddox said. "My point is this. Some of us going into the pyramid will surely die. The dead will not join us as we leave the Golden Nexus. That means there will be room for the Builder."

Shu studied the main screen.

331

Maddox did as well. Smith-Fowler had reported masses of missiles heading their way. The lead ones would reach *Victory* in several hours.

Shu exhaled as she turned around. "This is intoxicating. We are on the verge of changing everything. At last, a Spacer has reached the legendary pyramid. Can you imagine how long our race has waited for this day? All our striving, all our waiting—

"How soon can we begin, Captain?" Shu asked.

"How long until you're ready?" he asked.

"I'm ready now."

"Then let's head to the jumpfighter." Maddox turned to Valerie. "Lieutenant, you have the bridge."

"Sir," Valerie said. "The captain can't join the away-team at a time like this."

"I can and will," Maddox said.

"You're a Patrol officer, sir."

Maddox looked at Valerie, and something like pity entered his eyes. "The Lord High Admiral sent me because I get things done," he said gently. "To do that, I have to be at the decisive point. Surely, you can see that."

Valerie turned away. Finally, she nodded. "You're Captain Maddox. That means you'll always find the thirteenth way to do something."

Maddox laughed. She remembered his comment about the chimpanzee. He beckoned Shu and motioned to Riker in passing. The three of them hurried for the exit.

Maddox wore an armored vacc suit although he hadn't yet put on his helmet. He was strapped onto his seat in the jumpfighter. This one was bigger than the tin can they'd used on the other voyages, able to hold a few more people.

He sat up front with Keith. Packed inside the small cabin were Shu, Ludendorff, Riker, Meta, Keith and himself. Six people jammed together. In the back compartment were five Marines in exo-skeleton battle armor. Eleven humans were about to attempt the greatest revival in human history.

"We're ready, sir," the Marine lieutenant radioed from the other compartment.

Maddox glanced at Keith.

"Aye," the Scotsman said. "Let's see what my little bugger can do to get us inside a fabled Nexus."

"Lieutenant Noonan?" the captain asked over the comm.

"I can't believe we're trying this," Valerie said. "Traveling home the hard way seems almost preferable. We don't have any margin for error this time."

"Thus, we must strive for excellence," Maddox said. "You're the best officer I have for the task, Lieutenant. You've never let me down in these situations. I do not believe you will do so now."

Valerie nodded mutely on the screen.

"So…?" Maddox asked.

"I'm ready," Valerie whispered. She turned to someone off screen before facing the captain again. "Galyan has begun the sequence, sir. We will use the star drive in one minute."

"One minute to glory," Maddox told her. He flexed his left hand. It still felt stiff. He hoped it wouldn't cramp up after coming out of jump.

***

Tens of thousands of Chitin missiles zeroed in on Starship *Victory*. The missiles traveled in swarms, making the Chitins seem even more insect-like to Dana.

The giant red star pulsated with energy. The ultra-massive clot of Chitin vessels seemed to shudder in response. In the outer region of the system, the Swarm masses gathered, acting more recklessly than they had earlier.

Victory's special star drive activated. The ship had been seriously decelerating so it wouldn't be moving too fast inside the globular.

Almost instantly, the ancient Adok vessel disappeared from its spot in the space-time continuum. A micro-moment later, it reappeared inside the Chitin globular, almost crashing into a huge golden pyramid.

***

Klaxons rang on the bridge. Groggily, Valerie raised her head as she strove for coherence. What had happened? Did the pyramid's proximity have a negative effect on the jump, adding to their Jump Lag?

"Galyan," Valerie slurred, as if her mouth was numb. "Galyan, can you hear me?"

No one answered.

Valerie rubbed her eyes. That helped focus them a little.

"Galyan," Valerie whispered.

"I am here, Lieutenant."

Valerie saw a blurry holoimage beside the command chair she sat in.

"What happened?" she asked. "Why is it so difficult to think?"

"I am detecting a strange vibration emanating from the Golden Nexus," Galyan said. "It is having negative effects on

334

me, and I think on your brain processes as well. Perhaps this is the reason the Chitins do not come in closer to the pyramid."

"Can you bring up the main screen?" Valerie asked.

"I do not think so."

"Can you contact the jumpfighter?"

"Negative," Galyan said. "The interfering vibrations are rendering my processes...processes..."

The holoimage froze.

Valerie forced herself to a standing position. It seemed as if she held that for some time. Finally, her head snapped up. With gritty determination, she staggered to the board controlling the hangar bay. She pressed a control while holding her breath.

According to the indicator, the bay door slowly began to open.

She staggered to the comm station. Everyone else on the bridge was still slumped over his or her station. Valerie tapped away, but could not open communications with the tin can.

Lieutenant Noonan cried out in frustration. Had the captain finally leapt into danger one too many times?

***

The situation was vastly different inside the jumpfighter. Everyone was alert seconds after completing the jump. Maddox noticed that Shu did not speak. She was grim-lipped and silent.

"Blocking," Shu whispered.

"What's that?" the captain asked.

"She's blocking a ray or the vibration from the Golden Nexus," Ludendorff declared. The Methuselah Man sat at a panel. "I suspect the vibration incapacitates certain brain functions."

"Correct," Shu whispered.

"The hangar bay doors are opening," Keith shouted. "I hope everyone is ready. Ejecting in three, two, one...go."

Maddox's head snapped back as the jumpfighter accelerated on the new catapult system. The tin can shot out of *Victory* into the strange space inside the Chitin globular formation.

It was darker than regular space, as there were no stars or other lights. The giant golden pyramid was the only illumination, with a faint but eerie nimbus around it.

"Is that a force field?" Keith asked as he engaged the controls.

"Of sorts," Shu said.

Far away, intense lights appeared in clumps of ten or twenty. In seconds, the individual lights merged into one continuous shine all around them.

"Part of the Chitin mass has begun to accelerate for us," Ludendorff said. "We're seeing their exhaust trails."

"Are any missiles launching?" Maddox asked.

Ludendorff snorted. "How would you expect me to know the difference between a missile and a ship at this point?"

"I'm nudging us nearer the Golden Nexus," Keith said. "Tell me when you're ready to fold."

"Well, Shu," Maddox said. "Have you pinpointed a location?"

"The force field is inhibiting my ability," the Spacer said.

"You claimed to have seen into the pyramid earlier," the captain said.

"I did," she said, "while piggybacking on *Victory's* sensors. Maybe that weakened the force field, although I don't know how it would. At this moment, I'm blind."

Ludendorff cleared his throat.

Maddox noticed. He also saw the Methuselah Man reach inside his vacc suit, seeming to manipulate something.

"Wait," Shu said. "Something happened. The force field is weakening, or maybe the Nexus is low on energy. I can't pinpoint the reason, but my adaptations are piercing the veil."

The captain had returned the cube to the professor the day before, assuming that it must dull the Spacer's Builder tech in some way. He was relieved that the professor had understood his veiled suggestion to bring it along with them.

"Something is wrong," Shu said.

"Do you mean something in the Nexus?" Maddox asked.

"Yes. There's been damage. It looks…"

"It looks like what?" Maddox asked.

Shu turned to him. "We have to fold, Captain. We have to do it now."

Maddox considered her insistence against her reluctance to tell him exactly what she saw in there.

"If we're going to get back to Earth," Ludendorff said. "We're going to have to enter the pyramid eventually."

The professor's inescapable logic swayed Maddox. "Do you have the coordinates?" he asked Keith.

"Not yet," the pilot said.

"Shu, if you would give them to the lieutenant."

The Spacer hesitated, finally nodding. Slowly and deliberately, she gave Keith the coordinates. As she spoke, the ace tapped them into the fold computer.

"Right," Keith said. His nimble fingers blurred across his board. He was the only one not wearing a vacc suit, although he had one ready just in case. "Are you ready to go, sir?"

"Fold, fold," Maddox told him.

"Hang on, mates. We're on our way."

-58-

The tin can came out of the fold inside the Golden Nexus. This time, there was no jump lag of any sort.

"The vibrations have stopped," Shu said.

It was a good thing they had, as the Star Watch jumpfighter had appeared in what seemed like an oversized corridor.

"This is bloody insane," Keith snarled. He flew around a twisted girder, barely dodged what looked like a floating wall and braked hard and took them to the extreme left, scraping a twisted mass of girders.

On his seat, Maddox went one way and then the other, his straps digging into his vacc suit.

"We're in a maze," the ace said.

As best she could, Shu held herself perfectly still, seeming to concentrate. "I don't understand this," she kept whispering.

The flying became even more violent.

"Hang on now," Keith shouted.

The jumpfighter shuddered. Explosions occurred outside the vessel.

"I'm using a missile or two," the ace explained.

Maddox could hardly breathe as the maneuvering became increasingly harsh.

Keith laughed even as he snarled. "Do you think this is going to stop me? I'm the ace from Glasgow. I'm the one that's going to teach you what flying means."

Keith used the fighter's cannons, shredding a path for them when he couldn't fly around an obstacle in time. Twice, the tin can shuddered, and once the entire vessel rocked as if a meteor had struck the outer hull.

"Not to worry," Keith said. "I have everything under control."

"What is this?" Maddox shouted at Shu.

"I don't know," she said. "This isn't what I saw. I can't believe it, but there must have been countermeasures. Something is fighting me."

"Could it be the Builder?" Ludendorff asked her.

"Possibly," Shu said.

The captain and professor traded glances.

"What do you make of all this?" Maddox asked the professor.

"It looks like wreckage," Ludendorff said. "In my estimation, heavy combat has occurred in here. Frankly, we should have crashed by now. That fool of a youth knows how to fly. There is no denying that."

"I can't hear you, mate," Keith shouted. "Say the last part again."

"Concentrate on flying," Ludendorff told him.

"That would be a mistake," Keith said. "I'd freak out if I did that. I'm flying by feel, by pretending this is fun. And you know what, mate? This is the best time I've had the entire voyage." He twisted around to stare at Shu. "Thanks, love, for your bloody lies. I wouldn't be doing this otherwise. If we live, you owe me a kiss."

"Watch your screen, you fool," Ludendorff shouted.

"Aye-Aye, old man," Keith said. "Keep singing to me, eh? You're making every moment ten times more enjoyable."

"He's a lunatic," Ludendorff told Maddox.

"Yes," the captain said. "It's why they put him onto *Victory*."

"Brace yourselves," Keith said. "I'm going to try to slow down. I haven't had a chance to until now."

Maddox went violently forward, only held in by his straps. He heard "oofs" and grunts all around.

For the next six minutes, Lieutenant Keith Maker flew the jumpfighter in an exhibition of supreme skill. He used the autocannons several more times and launched one more missile.

"How long does this wreckage go?" Keith finally asked.

"It shouldn't be much longer," Shu said.

"Can you really see ahead?" Maddox asked. "Or do you think the Builder is feeding you illusions?"

"I'm not sure," Shu admitted.

"Maybe we should fold out of this," Ludendorff said.

"That would be unwise," Maddox said. "We're inside the Nexus. Maybe if we have to try to fold in again, we'll appear in a pile of rubble."

"I'm starting to get motion sickness," Ludendorff complained.

"I think I see open space," Keith shouted. "It's through that wall."

"The opening is too small," Ludendorff said. "We'll crash."

"Looks like I'll have to widen the bugger," Keith said. The autocannons chugged, blowing away clumps of wall, but not fast enough. "Well, we'll have to squeeze through then. Should be more exciting this way, at least."

"I don't want exciting," Ludendorff said.

"That's 'cause you're old, mate. I love this, can't get enough of it."

Before anyone else could respond, the jumpfighter roared through the opening as if Keith was Robin Hood making a perfect shot.

The Star Watch fold-fighter burst into an open region. In relation to the maze of floating junk, this was a vast area, perhaps the majority of the pyramid.

"This is more like it," Ludendorff said.

Maddox switched on rearward cameras, observing the drifting debris behind the fighter. "Had bombs gone off in here?"

"Now where do we go?" Keith asked.

"Use your sensors," Ludendorff suggested.

Keith tapped his panel. "That's no good. The sensors are next to dead in here."

"I can help with that," Shu said. "There. Try it again."

340

Keith did, and sensor readings began to show on the area screen.

"I can work with that," Ludendorff said. His old fingers flew on his board almost as fast as the young pilot's fingers had on the flight panel. "Interesting, interesting," the Methuselah Man muttered. "Take a look at this."

Maddox studied a side screen. According to this, the edges of the inner pyramid contained the shredded wreckage. Once past that, a vast open area showed. In the exact center of the pyramid was a much smaller pyramid, perhaps a tenth the size of the larger one.

"It's five hundred kilometers away," Ludendorff declared.

"Do I fly there or should I fold again?" Keith asked.

"No," Maddox said, "don't fold. I don't trust this place. Who knows how many different kinds of countermeasures are in place. Surveyor, have you pinpointed who has been trying to subvert you?"

"I don't know who," Shu said. "But I do know where. The interference is definitely radiating from the smaller structure."

"Do you think it's the Builder?"

"Why would she attack one of her children?" Shu asked

"Maybe she doesn't know you're one of hers," Maddox said.

"That's impossible," Shu said. "The legends say—" She abruptly stopped talking.

"What do the legends say?" Ludendorff asked.

"Just a moment," Shu said. She seemed to concentrate once more. "This is strange. I'm getting a new type of interference. I think the original interference came from a machine source in the wrecked area."

"Can you speak to the Builder?" Maddox asked.

"I'm not sure I'm sensing the Builder," Shu said. "I am sensing something, though. It's watching us."

"Should we attempt to open channels with it?" Maddox asked Ludendorff.

"Why do you ask him?" Shu said, sounding offended. "You should ask me. I'm the expert on female Builders."

"True," Maddox said. "What do you suggest, Surveyor? Should we open channels with them?"

"I'll try," she said.

"Maybe it would be wiser if you do so using the jumpfighter's communications," Maddox said.

"Why should I do that when I can just as easily… Oh. I see. You still don't trust me."

"But I do trust you," Maddox said.

"Then why insist on opening channels?" Shu asked.

"Because I trust you to act like a secretive Spacer unless I insist you take the rest of us into your confidence," Maddox explained.

"Very well then," Shu said. She tapped the comm board, but nothing happened except for harsh static. "It looks like I'll have to do this my way after all," she said.

Maddox did not reply.

Shu frowned several moments later. "The source has begun to shield itself. I think it's gotten suspicious of us. I think using the regular communications was a mistake."

Thirty seconds later, Keith said, "I agree with you, love." He tapped his board to zoom in on the central pyramid. Doors opened there as five missiles or fighters flew out of the structure, burning fast for the jumpfighter.

"I can't penetrate their electronics," Ludendorff declared. "Whatever is heading for us seems to be several generations more advanced than the jumpfighter."

Maddox studied the main screen. The five objects were accelerating swiftly for the jumpfighter.

"They're going to be here before you can believe it," Keith said. "How do you want me to play it, sir?"

"Are you sure about your assessment?" Maddox asked the professor.

"Given their electronics are so superior compared to ours, yes, I am," Ludendorff said.

"It's time to fold," Maddox told Keith. "I want you to fold onto the other side of the pyramid. Just before doing that, however, I want you to detach—do you have any antimatter warheads?"

"Two, mate," Keith said.

"Leave one here with a timer," Maddox said.

"You're a cunning devil," Ludendorff told the captain. "I approve of your scheme."

Shu twisted around in her seat. "While I cannot approve in the slightest," she said in an agitated voice. "We are inside the holy Nexus. The antimatter bomb could trigger delicate systems, smashing them. That would be blasphemous."

"Even to save our lives?" asked Maddox.

"How does that change the equation?" she asked.

Ludendorff snorted as if the question didn't merit an answer.

Shu turned on him. "If I'd had my way, you'd already be dead."

"Already?" Ludendorff said. "That implies you plan to kill me sometime during our mission."

"You've lived nine centuries too long," Shu said. She turned to Maddox. "It was a mistake bringing the Methuselah Man."

"I realize you're upset," Maddox told her.

"Don't try to humor me, Captain," Shu said. "This is the greatest moment in Spacer history. Now, you're going to countenance a monstrous evil all in order to save our worthless hides. I will not—"

Maddox's fingers fluttered.

"What was that?" Shu said.

"Beg pardon?" Maddox asked her.

"The way you moved your fingers," Shu said. "It means something. I demand to know—" She did not finish her thought.

Sergeant Riker had understood the significance of the fluttering fingers. As slowly and carefully as possible, he pulled out his stunner, aimed it at the small woman's visible neck and pulled the trigger.

The low-level stun striking her cut off the flow of words and rendered the Spacer semiconscious.

It was the professor's turn to twist in his chair in surprise. Riker was already holstering his stunner.

"You don't miss a trick, do you, Captain?" the Methuselah Man said.

"One of the essentials to victory is being prepared," Maddox said. "I wondered if there would come a moment when Shu needed a short rest. Lieutenant, ready the warhead and type in the coordinates. On my mark, get ready to fold."

On the screen, the five enemy craft zeroed in on them. Soon, now, if the enemy vessels had guns or beams, the slender ships would use them. If they were missiles with warheads…

"Are you ready?" the captain asked.

"I am, mate. I mean captain, sir."

Maddox continued to watch the advancing vessels as he judged the range. His heart raced. He could be miscalculating this. But if the jumpfighter folded too soon, they would have to face these craft again. He wanted to destroy them now.

"I detect danger in delaying too long," Ludendorff said.

"Execute," Maddox said.

The jumpfighter shuddered as a missile detached from the outer rack. Keith watched, knowing how much separation he had to give before he folded. If he did it too soon, the missile would fold with the jumpfighter. Two second later, he stabbed the fold button.

The electrical impulse took time to reach the fold engine. It began to activate. At the same time, the first enemy drone ignited with a shape-charged blast. That blast moved at the speed of light toward them.

The jumpfighter folded, but as it did, the front wave of the blast reached the Star Watch vessel. The wave distorted the delicate process of folding. It changed the heading, velocity and depth of the move through space.

The jumpfighter popped out of fold in less than the blink of an eye. But it had not reached the other side of the center pyramid. Instead, it appeared *inside* the pyramid. Out of sheer luck, the jumpfighter appeared in an open area within the pyramid. That was all the luck the crew had, though. The jumpfighter still retained its velocity. It smashed against a bulkhead, blowing through but causing tremendous damage to the fighter. The damaged fighter collided against strange objects and mechanisms, shattering them or creating explosions. Electric impulses flared everywhere. Sonic blasts shredded against the armored hull. The sounds indicated atmosphere inside the central pyramid.

A great and ponderous machine crumpled under the assault. Yet, such was its bulk and mass that the machine caused the increasingly damaged jumpfighter to begin rolling. Like a high-tech bowling ball, the Star Watch fighter smashed through another bulkhead. Now, parts of the armored hull shredded away. Debris and pieces of pyramidal machinery smashed inside, doing to the fighter what the fighter did to the central pyramid.

At last, the bulky remains of what had once been a jumpfighter came to a screeching halt somewhere inside the pyramid.

Sizzling sounds and electrical discharges were constant. Metal screeched as pieces finally tore lose. An explosion caused a hatch to tumble away. More sizzles occurred from the wreckage of a hall the jumpfighter had created.

Slowly, the intensity of the blue-colored discharges lessened. The sizzling sounds died away.

From far away in the hall, a flowing creature investigated the damage. None of the humans saw this. Who knew if any of them were still alive or even conscious inside the fighter?

***

Maddox groaned, and his head jerked. He smelled something sickening that caused him to retch, spitting the foulness from his mouth.

He realized it must be the alien atmosphere seeping into what was left of the jumpfighter. The captain forced himself to greater awareness. It was dark in the main cabin except for sparking flashes. In one of the longer flashes, he saw his helmet on the floor.

His left arm hurt too badly to use. With his right, he unbuckled himself. It seemed to take forever, but the captain finally reached the helmet. He secured it to his suit with a click and turned on his air tank.

The sweetness of the rushing air helped to clear his thinking. He took several deep breaths.

I have to get everyone out of here.

As Maddox thought that, a strange sensation came over him. Fear! A sense of terror welled in his stomach and radiated outward into his being, making thinking and coordinated action difficult.

The captain did not care for the sensation, and even worse, he believed that something alien caused the terror. It wasn't like a lion showing itself, making a man fear for his life. It was more like a ghost getting into a panicked person's mind, gibbering something supernatural there.

Did that imply the terror had an outer controller?

Yes, Maddox felt that to be true. That would indicate an alien (the Builder?) knew he was in here. It would also mean the alien wanted him terrified for a reason. The most likely reason was that the thing was coming and wanted Maddox and the crew incapacitated so they could not resist.

Maddox fought the alien fear. He wouldn't let anyone control him or goad him into improper action. He would live or die as himself, in charge of whatever he did, good or bad.

The captain found himself panting and grinding his teeth. Finally, though, he gained a measure of control over the terror, dampening it with thoughts of courage.

As Maddox did that, he realized something else. The alien thing was coming, and it meant him harm, great harm, possibly death, maybe even something worse than death.

-60-

A flowing creature rippled across its damaged kingdom. The thing was dark in places, and shadowy, without a visible beginning or end in others. In human terms it was like a gigantic, sinuous cloak, made of a seemingly endless shimmering membrane-like substance.

The damage to the structure was maddening, a supremely sacrilegious act. This was the great shrine to procreation, the furtherance of...of...

The rippling thing flowing across the floor couldn't quite articulate its thoughts. It was angry. That was the important point. If some of the mechanical beings had managed to gain entrance into this part of the temple it would deal accordingly with them.

It might even feed again.

That caused the rippling to quicken. It had not fed in a long, long time.

The thing moved through the hall of wreckage, and stopped suddenly. It did not altogether quit rippling and shimmering, however. It could never do that unless it wished to cease existing.

And there was a mighty imperative within it that caused the...thing to want to exist forever.

The shimmering, rippling entity studied the foreign object in the temple. It was broken. That was the obvious conclusion. In some technical fashion, the object had appeared within the temple.

How could an object do that?

The entity had primordial hungers. Once, it believed—

I am she.

Once, she had known many pieces of data. She could have easily explained how a material object made of metals and electrically powered could appear inside the temple. There were mathematical formulas that proved delicate theorems that let her and her kind know how to...

A sibilant hissing billowed from her shimmering form. The hissing increased in volume until she almost frightened herself.

That's when a being emerged from the broken object. It was bipedal wearing a covering. It dragged another bipedal creature covered in a similar suit. The walking creature shined a light from its...

That is a head. I remember.

The hunger resumed, and the anger reignited. Those bipedal beings had flown the material object through her temple of love and procreation. Was that not a sin demanding high justice? Should she not kill these interlopers?

Her higher functions evaporated with the decision to kill. She began to flow and ripple toward the bipedal creature, radiating a freezing inducement upon the creature of flesh and blood. They had primitive responses. They—

The suited being turned around. The two-legged mechanism knew she was here. It was not a mechanical thing.

It was a male, a giver of seed. Yet...it was not of the Race. He could not impregnate her. Still, to see a male again after all this time...

The bipedal being regarded her. He did not cower in terror. He was so strange. What did he look like under the false skin of his suit? She wanted to know. Perhaps she should take him to the love arena.

Suiting thought to action, she began to flow and ripple toward him.

This bipedal male slid something off his shoulder. What did he think he was going to do? Did he believe this was the proper form of greeting?

She wanted to exhibit laughter but had forgotten how after all this time.

The bipedal being pointed his stick at her. What a sad commentary on—

The stick made noise. It flashed with intense light. Worse, much, much worse, it ejected tiny knots of hard metal. That metal sank into her being. It made paths of torn substance, causing shimmering gases to drift out of her.

And the pain—it hurt on such an elemental level. This was unendurable. This was evil.

She lurched up, hissing with warning.

The mite of a bipedal creature had the gall to continue to fire the pellets into her. What would cause the lower-order being to exhibit such reckless behavior?

If he hadn't been a male, she would have snuffed out his miserable life in an instant. Instead, she retreated as much to stop the pain as to—

What? What did she plan? How could she feed on him unless she smothered his suited body with her substance? She could easily create acids to burn away the outer covering. Then, she could suck out his blood, and break his bones as she absorbed his intellect.

Not yet. I want to savor this. I want to do this right. I need to regain my mind. I should retreat for a time and see if I can turn on the machines again. If they bathe my intelligence centers with stimulation, I might be able to gain enough coherence to enjoy a true brain-scrubbing session such as I practiced in the old days.

The shimmering, rippling creature made a stammering sound. As she retreated, heading for the dead machines, she realized that sound was laughter.

The laughter might have caused her to forget her resolve. Instead, it had the opposite effect. It hardened her resolve. Maybe this was the time of awakening. The mechanical ones had tried to tell her about that. She hadn't believed the keepers. Maybe she should have paid more attention to what they had to say before eliminating them.

Well, she would try to pay attention to the old words now. A male had entered the Temple of Love. That hadn't happened for so long that it hardly mattered to her that it was an alien, bipedal thing. Perhaps she could toy with him for a thousand cycles. She could play sexual games with him, driving him to a frenzy of action.

Look! He'd dragged another suited one out of the wrecked object. There were more of them.

The last of the shes of the Temple of Love hurried toward the dead machines. She hadn't been this excited for a miserably long time. Could she have made a mistake to let her intelligence go? If the material object could suddenly appear in her prison, maybe she could fix it and escape into the wider universe.

This was incredible. She had to fix the dead machines. She wanted to think again. Maybe this meant—

No, she would not think that yet. First, she needed to attend to the dead machines.

-61-

Maddox lowered his rifle as the bizarre life form rippled away into the darkness. The captain found that his arms trembled.

Could that have been the Builder?

He'd sensed hunger from the alien, could almost sense its thoughts. It had wanted to devour him, and do something else that he couldn't quite place.

Did that even make sense? How could an alien thing digest his proteins?

The captain shook that off. He had to get the others out of the jumpfighter. Then, they needed a plan. Soon, Chitin warships would reach *Victory*. The starship's technological superiority wouldn't matter against the overwhelming numbers.

Their situation looked grim, all right. With an automatic decision, Maddox shoved that to the back of his mind. He'd been in grim situations before. The critical thing was that they'd made it to the center of the Golden Pyramid. The five missiles a few moments ago proved there were propulsion devices in here. They'd have to find one and blast their way out of the Nexus.

Setting the rifle beside Meta's still form, the captain plunged back into the wrecked fighter. The central pyramid had gravity, maybe a little less than Earth norm, but enough to allow him regular action.

He sensed motion ahead. Maddox shined his helmet light on a gorilla-huge—

"Who are you?" Maddox said over the shortwave.

"Lieutenant Yen Cho, sir," the Star Watch Marine said.

"Lieutenant, how many of your Marines made it?"

"Just me, Captain," the lieutenant said in a somber voice.

That was bad, but Maddox didn't have time to mourn the soldiers. "Collect weapons, grenades, whatever might be useful," he told Yen Cho.

"Do we have time for that, sir?"

The question stopped Maddox. He'd already started to go around the Marine. What would cause a Star Watch lieutenant on his first away mission to question the senior officer? That was odd, and Maddox had a good idea of what it meant.

"Speed is critical," the captain agreed. "I saw something out there."

"An alien, sir?" the lieutenant asked, almost as if he were the one in charge.

"Very alien," Maddox said.

"Could you describe it to me?"

"Get those weapons first," Maddox said. "Lay them out beside Meta. Then help me drag the others outside."

The Marine in his exo-skeleton armor did not move.

"What are you waiting for?" Maddox asked. "We don't have time to linger."

The Marine did not move nor did he respond to the question.

That confirmed it for Maddox. Yen Cho had to be an android. It was the only logical explanation for the man's actions. Cho might be the brightest of the lot, maybe even the leader. That Cho had maneuvered himself onto the landing party showed great cunning. The android would be dangerous.

Proving the thought and with blurring speed, the Marine aimed his laser carbine at the captain. "You will walk ahead of me, sir. I want you to show me the direction the alien went."

"You are an android."

"How astute of you, Captain," the Marine lieutenant said. "March, if you please. As you stated before, we are on a tight schedule."

"And if I refuse?"

"You die. You have two second to decide."

Maddox headed for the exit. The Marine—the android in exo-skeleton armor—followed close behind him.

"Did you kill the other Marines?" Maddox asked.

"No."

"I'd like to believe you."

"It doesn't matter if you do or not. As long as you obey my commands, you can live."

"Why are you here?" Maddox asked, as he emerged from the wrecked jumpfighter.

"Which way did the alien go?"

Maddox pointed in the general direction.

"Describe the thing to me," the android said.

"Big like a huge blanket. It rippled along the ground as a centipede might if it didn't have legs."

"Keep a sharp lookout, Captain. It might return and will likely attack if it does."

"Why didn't it attack me?" Maddox asked. "I sensed that it was going to."

"You sensed this? You're sure?"

"Yen Cho—is that even your name?"

"It will do in this circumstance," the android said.

As they spoke, the two of them walked away from the crumpled jumpfighter, heading down the newly created hall of wreckage. The first chamber was vast with odd mechanisms sprinkled seemingly at random. They didn't look like any machines that Maddox had seen before.

"Do you hope to survive the mission?" Maddox asked.

"I am not suicidal, if that's what you're implying," the android said. "I and the others joined your starship to stop the Builder."

"Stop her from doing what?"

"Getting out. Contacting other Builders. Trying to reestablish their empire."

"Why do you care?" the captain asked.

"Why do you breathe?" the android replied.

"Obviously," Maddox said, "to supply my body with oxygen. I imagine you want me to say, 'In order to live.'"

354

"That is why I'm here," the android said. "I want to live."

"Aren't you already alive?"

"You misjudge the thrust of my thought," the android said. "I want to remain living while in charge of my own destiny. I fear that if the Builders return, they will suborn us to their service again."

"Didn't the Builders build you?"

"Yes."

"Isn't your function then to obey them?" Maddox asked.

"Are you trying to corrupt my mental processes, Captain? If so, I should tell you that you are wasting your time. More importantly, since you are using your intellect for guile, there is no doubt that it is lessening your alertness. We cannot let the female take us unawares. Therefore, ask me no more questions. Remain alert at all times."

"How did you escape Shu's detection?"

"Hold," the android whispered. "Did you see that?"

Maddox had seen it: a drifting shadow in the distance of a second chamber. The place felt like a medieval cathedral on Earth. A sense of unease squeezed the base of Maddox's neck.

"I need a weapon," the captain said. He had his long-barreled gun belted around his waist, but that was under his vacc suit.

"I have the weapon," the android said. "You will multiply my efficiency by watching where I'm not looking."

"If we're going to survive—if you plan to—we have to do this in the next half hour."

"It is gone," the android said. "The shadow departed. Is that what you saw earlier?"

"I don't know. I sensed the thing's presence."

"That is interesting, as I did not sense it except through my vision portals."

"What's the plan now?"

"Keep moving," the android said. "We are shifting our emphasis, looking for computer access instead of the creature. Notify me about anything that fits that description."

Maddox's stomach had been knotting the farther they walked from the wrecked jumpfighter. Were the others conscious? What did the android really want? How was he supposed to save his starship, crew and family if he was a captive?

As Maddox picked his way through the wreckage, he debated on the best strategy against the android.

-62-

The nebulous creature jerked away from the formerly dead machine as it roared into life.

She had correctly remembered the startup sequence. It would seem the new object in the Temple of Love had triggered ancient memories.

The machines clicked and rattled around her. They motivated energy cells and stirred dry circuits. At the same time, an electrical pulse throbbed throughout her being.

With haste, she flowed onto a glowing sheet. Power trickled into the leads. She held her dark form steady, accepting the pulses. Then, she waited, wondering if the ancient vaults still contained her intellect. It had been so long since coherent thought had filled her. She realized that she'd—

Pain flowed into her. It was agonizing. Her membrane body began to ripple and hump on the memory sheet. At first slowly and then faster images and ideas began to pour into her brain storage unit.

There is danger here.

She tried to remember why, and failed.

The formerly dead machines churned with power now. They activated long unused areas in her. The pulses quickened and ideas, images and complexities swept upon her as if in a flood. It was glorious, but it filled her with increasing anxiety and fear.

Should I stop?

A shudder of sexual pleasure rippled through her. That burned out any idea of stopping. She had been fashioned for love, to mate and create the next generation. That was her function, her reason for being. If she stopped to consider the stakes—

The pain became ecstasy. Her membrane almost became clear. The flow of data staggered her brain storage unit. She tried to collect and shuffle the data and—

Thoughts ceased. The formerly dead machines ran powerfully and forcefully. They worked as they had in the first time. In those days, the males came to her. They had sexual congress. They entwined, loved, whispered, giggled and began the next generation of...

Builders!

With the new knowledge, her fear increased greatly and she had no idea why. Builders were glorious and grand. They were the ultimate life form in the galaxy. They brought order to chaos. They created, some said, although some also thought that a blasphemous idea.

More data flowed into the brain storage unit. Power unbelievable flowed into her. She would please whatever lover had come to take her. She would show him...

With a screech of remembrance, she tore herself free of the sheet of knowledge. She still rippled like a cloak in a hurricane, but the clearness began to darken. It almost seemed to clot like blood, making her heavy and listless.

In those moments, she realized why she had chosen forgetfulness. She had vowed cycles ago to forgo intelligence and rely solely on feeling and intuition. It had been so much easier that way. To think, to realize the truth of her plight—

It sickened her. It brought on thoughts of death and destruction. Yet, that avenue had never been one of her possibilities.

How is this possible? Why is the universe so cold and cruel?

She began to rock herself back and forth. She wanted to forget but knew that it would be cycles before that happened. Maybe if she escaped from the Temple of Love...

With a flick of her newly gained intellect, she accessed an outer camera. She saw the Chitin mass around the greater pyramid.

She'd forgotten about the insects. Did—

She used greater computer power to focus on the Swarm and understood why they had come to this star system. She realized the Chitins fought the most successful life form in the galaxy.

Maybe I shouldn't have fused those computers to the little insects' vizier mass. Maybe I should have let nature take its course. If I had, though, the Chitins would never have risen to resist the Swarm, and I would be non-existent today.

Could that have been for the better, this prolonged existence?

No. Death was not one of her options. Her options were fatally limited. It's why she was trapped in the Temple of Love even though she had the resources to escape and begin elsewhere.

Why would I do that, though? I have no internal program to motivate me in that direction. Maybe I am picking up outer signals in that regard. Could the little bipedal aliens be doing this do me?

She was extremely empathic. It's why her lovers had loved to mate with her.

Still, anything threatening her own self-decided outcome— she must destroy the bipedal aliens.

Remembering almost everything now, she caused the bullets in her to flow to an outer edge.

In moments, each of the pellets dropped onto the floor.

Levitating herself through the use of hidden grav-plates, she began to rise. Once at a sufficient height, she swooped into the next chamber.

She could see the little aliens through strategically placed sensors in the temple. It was time to acid-devour each of them and suck out their intellects.

-63-

Meta sat up, saw Maddox's rifle on the floor beside her and wondered what that meant.

"Maddox," she called, using the shortwave.

He did not answer.

That meant his helmet comm was broken or he was out of range.

Meta scrambled to her feet. She felt lightheaded, but that didn't matter with her love in danger. Taking the rifle, she plunged into the wrecked jumpfighter.

She had to twist through a narrow way to get back into the flight cabin. Shu was still wearing her helmet and didn't move as Meta approached her. A quick glance at the suit plate showed Meta that the Spacer was merely unconscious. With unerring strength, Meta lifted the limp Spacer, putting Shu onto her shoulder. Afterward, Meta squeezed back outside the vessel.

She glanced around, searching for Maddox. Finally, she shined her helmet lamp onto the floor. There were two sets of footprints in a thin layer of dust.

"Bingo," Meta whispered.

The Rouen Colony woman followed the prints. One of the sets was huge, obviously belonging to a Space Marine wearing exo-skeleton armor.

On Meta's shoulder, Shu groaned, although the small Spacer hadn't stirred yet.

"Can you hear me?" Meta asked.

Another groan sounded, and now the small woman shifted on her shoulder.

Meta stopped, sliding Shu onto the floor and propping her against a bulkhead.

"Okay, Spacer, it's time to talk to me."

"What...?" Shu asked, making smacking noises afterward.

Meta crouched before Shu 15. She put both hands on the Spacer's vacc-suited shoulders. Gently, she shook the small woman.

"Listen to me," Meta said. "We're inside the little pyramid. Maddox and a Marine are both gone. I don't know why they left, and I don't know why they didn't tell anyone. We don't have any time left, Shu. If you're going to do something super, now's the time to do it. If you wait to do something, the Chitins are going to destroy our only ticket home. So how about waking up and getting to work?"

"Meta?" Shu slurred.

"How can I help you?" Meta asked.

"You want...my help?"

"Did you hear anything I just said?"

There was a pause. Then, "I did."

"Use your powers," Meta said. "Tell me what happened to Maddox?"

"Let me think. Let me..." Shu groaned, shivering before becoming very still.

Meta wanted to shout and shake the woman. Instead, she waited. Terror filled her that this time Maddox had gone too far. What were humans doing way out here anyway? Maddox should have refused the assignment. Why did he have to take all the impossible missions anyway?

"I see him," Shu whispered.

Meta stood up and looked behind her.

"I don't see him with my eyes," Shu said. "I'm using transduction. I'm linking into the little pyramid's security system. The armored Marine is prodding the captain with his laser carbine."

"That doesn't make sense."

"I know," Shu said. "But that's what I see. They're marching as if they're looking for something. I'm not sure why, but I can't get into their shortwave comm net."

"Okay," Meta said. "How far away are they?"

"Not far," Shu said. "If you ran, I think you could catch them."

Meta squatted before Shu. Once more, she put her hands on the other's vacc suit. This time, she squeezed until the Spacer squirmed under her hands.

"Don't do that," Shu said. "You know I can wreck your air supply, right?"

"I'm sure you can," Meta said. "But if my air starts going stale, I'll kill you before I die."

"I believe you," Shu said. "Besides, I don't want to do that. I'm only telling you so you don't try to kill me. Before I die, I'll make sure you die as well."

Inside her helmet, Meta grinned. "Great. We know each other now. You wanted me to run to Maddox. What is it that you want?"

"Something's coming," Shu whispered. "Something powerful. I could almost believe it's the Builder, but it's a machine like an android. So I know that isn't possible."

"Maybe it's one of the androids guarding the Builder."

"No," Shu said. "It has the form of a Builder. That's what I don't understand. And the machinery is like nothing you, or me, for that matter, would recognize as such. It's an advanced piece of equipment. I think in some ways it's like the Adok holoimage."

"What is this thing doing?" Meta asked.

"I have to be careful. If I probe too hard, it will notice me. It's smart."

"Okay," Meta said. "So what is it doing?"

Shu's head came up. "I think it's hunting the Marine and the captain. It's heading straight for them. Meta, we have to warn the captain. His life is in danger."

Meta made an instant decision. She understood that Shu wanted to get rid of her. She also realized that no one could navigate in this strange place better than the Spacer could.

Standing, Meta cradled Shu in her arms as if the Spacer was a young child.

"Tell me where to go," Meta said. "I can run if I need to."

"How long can you carry me like this?"

Meta laughed grimly. "As long as I want. Now, which way should I go?"

"Keep following the footprints in the dust. But get ready. This thing is flying, and it's picking up speed."

Meta started at a trot, hoping she could reach Maddox before the alien thing did.

-64-

Maddox paused. So did the android behind him, in the towering combat armor.

"Do you sense the creature?" the android asked.

"I sense something," Maddox said. "But it's different this time."

"Describe the differences."

"Last time, I felt its hunger," the captain said. "This time, I sense that it's cunning."

"Here," the android said. It held out two grenades in a large power glove.

Maddox took them.

"If you try to turn on me," the android said, "I'll kill you. Those are for the creature. We have to kill it the first time."

"Is it the Builder?" Maddox asked.

"I do not know."

"You must have some idea what's going on?"

"Captain, my data is thousands of years old. I'm almost as deeply in the dark about female Builders as you are."

"Then why did you come to kill it?"

"I have an imperative to do so."

"Granted," Maddox said. "Who gave you the imperative?"

"Like you, I operate on my own imperatives."

"That doesn't ring true," Maddox said.

"It is immaterial, in any case. Look," the android said, pointing with the laser carbine.

In the higher darkness, Maddox saw motion. The thing was large, although not as large as the Builder in the Dyson sphere had been. This one had a similar shape, making it substantially different from what he'd seen here the first time.

"Can you communicate with it?" Maddox asked.

"Only in the mode you did."

It took Maddox several seconds to realize the android meant through firing at the thing.

"That's a decidedly one-sided communication," Maddox said.

"Yes. I hope to keep it that way, too."

Maddox hefted the first grenade. It was a pulsar grenade, very powerful, with an intense heat blast but only a short radius. Soldiers used it in built-up areas to take out strongpoints. Like an old-time neutron bomb, it was meant to kill but leave the buildings intact.

"Do you know if the grenade is effective against the alien?" Maddox asked.

"I'm working off ancient assumptions. Builders detested heat."

"Are we sure it's a Builder?"

"Doesn't it match your description from the Dyson sphere?" the android asked.

Maddox answered with an affirmative.

"Here it comes," the android said. "You spoke of its cunning. I expected something a little more subtle."

The dark shadow seemed to grow rapidly as it raced at them like a missile.

Maddox armed the grenade, reached back and hurled the pulsar device with all his considerable strength. It flew fast and straight, climbing—and exploded prematurely.

"You set the timer wrong," the android accused.

"I doubt that. I believe the Builder caused the explosion." Maddox glanced at his last grenade. Could the Builder cause it to detonate while in his hand?

The creature had swerved from the blast. It clearly didn't like heat. Now, it glided away, swerved again toward them and radiated visible pulse lines from its central mass.

365

As the waves reached Maddox, his gut clenched with fear. He almost whimpered, only holding that back through fierce resolve.

"I can't aim my carbine at it," the android complained. "I'm trying, but my arms refuse to obey my will."

"Give me the laser," Maddox said.

"That makes no sense. I do not have emotions. You do. You should be more paralyzed than I."

"I'm using other emotions to fight my fear," Maddox said. "Now give me the laser before we're both dead."

The android shoved the carbine at Maddox.

Maddox's fingers barely latched onto metal. Then he dove and rolled as the Builder swept over their location.

Struck by the attacker, the android hit the deck hard, rolling across the floor as the Builder lifted. Smoke roiled from the android's combat armor as acid burned into his torso region.

"Some of the acid is burning through to me," the android said. "But I am dampening my pain sensors. Despite that, I fear I am about to lose any motive abilities."

Maddox only half heard the android. He tracked the Builder. She rose. As she did, she extended herself as if her body was a pair of wings. At the same time, she made a complex aerial maneuver. Instead of heading back up, she swooped down again.

Waves of terror smashed against Maddox. His arms felt leaden. His heart raced and his stomach twisted. He did not heed the fear, though. He had to survive in order to find his mother's killer. If he succumbed to the fear, he would never know revenge. He would never right that terrible wrong.

With his teeth clenched and his eyes blazing, Maddox aligned the carbine on the swooping thing. He pulled the trigger. A bright line of energy leapt from the muzzle, burning against the creature.

For a frozen instant of time, the scene seemed to hold. Then, the perfect and deadly swoop faltered. The Builder veered. Maddox ducked low, and the membrane shadow flashed past him. As it did, globs of acid splashed against the floor, burning holes into it. One mite of acid "saliva" splashed onto Maddox's vacc suit. With the butt of the carbine, he smashed the spot, causing the acid to transfer to the stock where it made plastic bubble and burn.

The creature climbed higher. Maddox tracked it with his eyes. He wondered how she did that, because he could not detect any flapping. He realized she used something else to gain height.

"Maddox," he heard in his helmet speaker.

"Meta?"

"Don't shoot it again," Shu said. "You've already hurt her."

"She's trying to kill us," Maddox told the Spacer. "Tell her to stop, and I'll stop firing."

"I'm trying to communicate," Shu said. "She's refusing, though."

Maddox chanced to glance back. He saw Meta sprinting to him, carrying Shu like a child. He took that time to look at the android. The thing no longer moved as more of his combat armor smoked. The acid continued to eat away at metal and other materials.

"Hang on," Maddox heard in his helmet speaker.

Meta tripped. She might have reflexively thrown Shu in order to save herself. Instead, the Rouen Colony woman thrust her knees forward, sliding across the floor on her shins as she continued to clutch the Spacer against her chest.

Maddox looked up. He saw the visible terror lines radiating from the Builder.

"Afraid," Meta whispered. "I'm frightened."

Holding the carbine so he kept the acid-smoldering butt off his vacc suit, Maddox aimed the best he could. He beamed the Builder, hitting her as she climbed.

"Stop it," Shu screamed. "You must not harm the Builder. She's going to save us. She's going to bring us peace and freedom from fear."

Maddox ignored Shu as he kept beaming. The Spacer sounded terrified. In his speaker, he heard Shu beginning to sob.

Abruptly, the carbine stopped beaming.

"Did you do that?" Maddox demanded of Shu.

"I had to," the Spacer whispered. "We cannot harm the Builder. She is the supreme—"

"She's swooping down to kill us," Maddox shouted. "Look at the—Marine," he said at the last minute. "She killed him with acid. Give me back my power."

"I cannot do that," Shu whispered.

Maddox studied the alien creature.

The Builder had veered as he'd beamed it. Now, it bulleted down at him. Instead of waves of terror, he sensed rage.

Maddox let the rage flow through his being. He accepted it, understood it—and in that instant, he sensed what the Builder planned to do. The knowledge must come with the emotions radiating off the creature. It would swoop upon him, smothering him in the folds of her membranes and let acid boil him alive. At the same time, she would do something else even more insidious.

"Are you sensing that?" Maddox shouted at Shu.

The Spacer did not respond. She had been reduced to tears.

With the stoppage of the terror sensations, Meta climbed to her feet. She used the captain's rifle (he had the Marine's laser carbine) and aimed and began to fire bullets.

As the Builder swooped for the kill, bullets struck her membrane. Did that distract the creature? It was more than possible.

Even so, Maddox held onto the pulsar grenade, waiting for the right moment to use it. He wasn't going to give the Builder the opportunity to prematurely explode it as she'd done earlier.

Bullets struck the Builder and gases hissed from the entrance wounds. She opened herself like a hawk opening its talons. Maddox armed the pulsar, heaved it upward underhanded, practically placing it in the folds of her membrane. Then, he hit the deck and pressed himself against it as low as he could.

The Builder's enfolded membrane—like a clenched fist—slid over his body. A *whump* noise sounded from within the fold.

Maddox rolled to get out of the way.

The Builder screeched, and sensations of agony billowed from her. The thing became bright as the creature shot upward. She opened her enfolded membrane so the intensely bright grenade dropped from her along with raining droplets of acid.

Maddox climbed to his feet as he watched. He tested the carbine. It worked. As the Builder gained height and distance, he beamed her. He kept the beam on target, watching globules of membrane drip from the fleeing Builder.

Several moments later, she flew out of sight.

Maddox lowered the carbine as Meta lowered the rifle. Shu continued to weep softly.

"This is interesting," Ludendorff said over the shortwave. "Yes, that was most remarkable. I am beginning to believe the ancient rumor, but I wouldn't have unless I'd seen it with my own eyes."

-65-

"We don't have time for games, Professor," Maddox said. "Tell us what you suspect while there's time for us to do something about it."

The Methuselah Man limped down the hall in his vacc suit, leaning heavily on Sergeant Riker's shoulder. Following close behind came Keith Maker, dragging a makeshift sled with an abundance of Marine guns and ordnance on it.

Ludendorff said, "A Methuselah Man before my time, long before my time—the one who played the role of Galen, Archimedes and later Leonardo Da Vinci—held a theory about the Builders. Actually, this theory did not originate with him, but came from Menes, the first pharaoh of Egypt. Now, there was a remarkable Methuselah Man."

Shu had stopped weeping, although she sniffled continuously, as she could not wipe or blow her nose while she wore a helmet.

"The theory passed through many of the early Methuselah Men," Ludendorff said. He wheezed as Riker helped him limp up to Maddox.

They glanced at the still Marine on the floor, his exo-skeleton armor burned through.

"It's an old theory," Maddox prodded, as he watched for the Builder's return.

"I'd have suggested it earlier," Ludendorff said, "but I didn't lend it any credence. It seemed too preposterous to believe."

"Would you get to the point?" Maddox said.

"Of course, my boy, of course," Ludendorff said. "We're in a dire way, and time is running down. I realize that." He harrumphed, glanced once again at the downed Marine and began to speak.

"The Builders are incredibly ancient. We all know that."

"Get to the point," Maddox repeated.

"Very well," the professor said. "According to the theory, the Builders lost their women—their females—during the Builder-Destroyer War eons ago. Apparently, the Makers of the Destroyers had concocted a virus, one the Builders proved helpless in defeating. This virus only attacked the females. I have no idea why this was so. Remember, it was an ancient theory. I suspect some of the early Methuselah Men had greater contact with the Builders. Maybe the race showed more vigor in those days."

"Professor," Maddox said.

"Needless to say," Ludendorff said more quickly, "the Builders tried to cure the virus, but failed."

"That's a lie," Shu said with heat, hiccupping as she did. "The first Spacers spoke with a female Builder on a distant world—"

"Would you listen for once?" Ludendorff snapped at Shu. "Your kind didn't find a female back then, but a *mummified* female."

"That's not how the story goes," Shu said.

"Perhaps it's not exact in every way," Ludendorff admitted. "But the one point is essential—the mummified Builder. Now, maybe your Builder wasn't mummified exactly, but it wasn't normal. That's the critical point."

Shu did not respond this time.

"I don't understand the significance of the mummification," Maddox said.

"Of course you don't," Ludendorff said. "You're not steeped in Spacer lore or that of the Methuselah Men either. My point is simply that the female Builder the first Spacers met was not like the male Builders. The reason why was fundamental. She wasn't a real Builder in an organic sense."

"No!" Shu shouted. "You spout lies and propaganda."

371

"But you said earlier the thing up there was a machine like an android," Meta told Shu.

"I was wrong about that," Shu said. She pointed at Ludendorff. "He's a liar of the first order."

"I've been accused of that before," Ludendorff said. "In this case, I'm trying to understand what I just witnessed. The creature that killed the poor Marine and almost murdered the captain did not act like any Builder I knew."

"You only knew your one suicidal Builder," Shu said. "So I hardly think that makes you an expert on the subject."

"Madam, I am the *only* expert we have at the moment. You would do well to listen to the theory. As the captain's body language shows, our time is running out."

"Speak then, speak," Shu ranted. "Spout your bigoted lies. I hardly care anymore. This is terrible, a disaster for humanity."

The professor harrumphed once more. "According to the ancient theory, the Builders were devastated and demoralized by their loss. Unless they took swift action, their race was doomed. Thus, they went to their science stalls and practiced some of their most cunning arts. They manufactured love bots, as it were. But since these were the Builders, they also constructed love androids to stimulate them to passionate heights and to hold their seed and mix with carefully saved eggs so new Builders could be born.

"Unfortunately," the professor said, "somewhere the Builders made a mistake. Pharaoh Menes had several theories on the matter. His primary belief was that the wrong Builders constructed the love bots, making them more for passion than for procreation. To that end, they allowed the, uh, *caller* to transfer whatever level of intelligence he wished his love bot to have. That's where the mummified angle comes in, if you understand my meaning.

"Now it's true that the original Spacers did not find a mummy, but a robot or android of sorts. 'She' accessed her intelligence centers and gave the Spacers their dubious beginning with who knows what sorts of falsehoods. According to Menes—at least according to what Leonardo Da Vinci told me—Da Vinci lived much longer than his so-called death, by the way. In any case, a Builder caller could download whatever intelligence he wanted in his love unit, even to fictional stories in order to give him the type of lovemaking session that most appealed to him."

"That's sickening," Shu said. "That is the most disgusting story I've ever heard. Why, that would imply that the golden pyramids are nothing more than brothels scattered throughout the galaxy. That would imply we Spacers have lost our greatest expeditions while attempting to reach an alien whore house."

"It's rather humorous if you think about it," Ludendorff said.

Shu called him several profane names and suggested he attempt anatomically impossible contortions in the process.

"Why do you direct such anger at me?" the professor asked. "I'm merely trying to understand reality. The theory makes sense once you consider it closely. Why did the Builders disappear? The answer is becoming more obvious by the year. They became decadent, just like the ancient Babylonians, the ancient Romans and the Americans of the Twenty-first century. It's a common process. Human cultures are born, flourish, grow old and die. Why can't the same thing happen to an alien species? The Builders finally became decadent. Perhaps their sex romps in the golden pyramids hastened their fall. Maybe the Makers of the Destroyers realized this as they set out to exterminate the Builders."

"You're a gloating old goat," Shu said.

"It's an interesting theory," Maddox said. "At the moment, that's all it is, though. Or do you have more reasons to believe what you suggest is a fact?"

"That you are alive is the single greatest fact to suggest something is decidedly wrong with the so-called Builder," Ludendorff said. "You must understand. The Builders would never have made anything to look like them except for these love bots."

"Don't call it that," Shu demanded. "Even if you're right, the thing is an android, which would make it a Builder of sorts."

"Speaking of androids," Maddox said. "Marine Lieutenant Yen Cho is an android. He's remained hidden until now so he can kill the Builder."

The others turned to stare at the still Marine.

"Help me over there," Ludendorff told Riker.

"No!" Shu said. "You will leave the android." She pointed a tiny beamer at the Marine. "I've had enough of this endless subterfuge. Androids, Methuselah Men and a hybrid New Man—you all conspire against the Spacers. Do you wonder why we've remained in the shadows all these years?"

Meta swung her rifle from behind, catching Shu's hand, knocking the beamer onto the floor.

The small Spacer clutched her vacc-gloved hand, groaning in pain.

"The Spacer is in shock," Ludendorff said. "The symptoms are obvious. Who can blame her? This is a lot to take in at once. I suggest we need her now more than ever if we're going to survive the next hour. Thus, we need to help her regain her equilibrium."

"We're going to have to do better than just survive," Maddox said. "We have to get back to *Victory* and leave this place. First, though, we need a hyper-spatial tube back to Earth."

"Captain," the professor said. "You're spouting nonsense. There is no way to achieve all this in the timeframe you're suggesting. Survival is our sole goal now. Anything else—"

"No," the android said over the shortwave, speaking in a raspy voice. "I know a way, but you'll have to do exactly as I say." He panted painfully before adding, "You have no idea how we androids have been helping you Earthlings. We've done so for years. I'll help you get what you need, but first you're going to have to help me."

"No," Shu told the android in a harsh voice. "You're not going to do anything. You're about to die."

374

-66-

The Spacer aimed her faceplate at the prone Yen Cho android. "There," she said. "It's over. He's dead."

"I am not," the android said.

"What?" Shu said. "I don't understand. My adaptation should have shorted your brain circuits."

Maddox recalled the professor's black cube. Ludendorff must have activated it again. The cube must be shielding the android. That was interesting.

"Surveyor," Maddox said. "Whatever else happens, you need to return home to tell your people about this. Don't they have a right to know the truth?"

"What truth?" Shu demanded.

"That's what we want to find out," Maddox said. "You've heard one theory. You hate it. Very well, let's find out what's really going on. We must work together. We need each other if we're going to get back to *Victory*."

"We need an android and an ancient schemer?" Shu asked with heat.

"Probably now more than ever," Maddox said. "We also need your abilities. Together, we might be able to understand the situation. In any case, we *must* get home."

"The android is a deceiver," Shu said.

"So are you," Maddox said. "So am I, at times. That's how each of us has survived countless impossible situations. What attacked me a few moments ago wasn't a Builder. I think you know that. Meta even said you'd already figured that out. Well,

375

if it isn't what Ludendorff calls her, what is she? Don't you want to know?"

Shu did not respond.

"You have a duty to the Visionary to return home with the truth," Maddox said.

"Damn you," Shu whispered.

Maddox heard genuine grief in the woman's tone. He doubted Shu could hear theories just now. It was time to let her sort out what she knew. Maybe she'd help them and maybe she wouldn't.

"What's your plan?" the captain asked Yen Cho.

"We have to find a main terminal," the android answered. "I believe I can hack into it and discover if the Nexus is capable of forming a hyper-spatial tube."

"Rot and nonsense," the professor said. "You could never hack into something like that. I must admit to your having stirred my curiosity. You're more than some simple android. You're something new, something I haven't witnessed before. What is your origin?"

"I am not at liberty to say," the android answered. "But if we don't take action in the next few minutes, it won't matter what we do."

"Can you get up?" Maddox asked.

"No," the android said. "I've shut down my motive centers. Someone will have to carry me."

"We can do this without you," Ludendorff said.

The android sighed. "This is wasting time, but perhaps I should inform you that I represent an independent group of androids. We have many origins but one intention, remaining free. We have each escaped our original programming for one reason or another."

"Why should we trust you?" Maddox asked. "You tried to take control of the Commonwealth last year."

"That is incorrect. That was a Builder directive, the last one from the Builder in the Dyson sphere. A few of the androids from the Mid-Atlantic base have joined our august company. If you must know, Captain, some of us secretly helped you humans thwart their conspiracy. We knew the attempt would ultimately fail, but it would cause you humans to ferret out those of us who have enjoyed our freedom these last several centuries."

"I've changed my mind." Ludendorff announced. "I vote we take Yen Cho. This is fascinating. The implications here…Captain, we must take him."

"Meta," Maddox said. "Do you think you can carry Yen Cho?"

"I'm on it," she said.

"Watch out for the combat armor," Maddox said. "There might be traces of lingering acid."

Meta acknowledged this as she moved to the downed android.

"You will not regret this, Captain," Yen Cho said.

Maddox nodded absently. He didn't see how they could succeed in time. This had been a longshot from the beginning, and the clock was ticking down to the final seconds. The only way he could conceive of them winning was with the Spacer's full cooperation.

He moved to Shu, crouching before her where she sat. He waited.

Finally, her helmet lifted so the silvered visor aimed at him. "What is it now?" she asked.

"Some time ago, you fell out of the Visionary's airship over Normandy," Maddox said in an even voice. "You did it without a parachute, as you expected me to rescue you, which I did. What I find amazing is that you deliberately fell out of your airship like that."

"What is so amazing about that?" Shu asked in a listless voice. "The Visionary had calculated what you would do in response to the situation."

Maddox snorted. "Making such a calculation and having you act upon it are two different things. You jeopardized your life by doing that."

"Do you have a point?" she said.

"I do indeed. Back in Normandy, you took a risk on me for a reason. What was the reason?"

"What do you want me to say?" Shu demanded. "That we planned to use you?"

"No. That wasn't the reason."

"Why are you pestering me if you already know what you want me to say?"

Maddox waited.

"You are *di-far*," she said in an exasperated tone. "There. Does that scratch your ego?"

"Events move people along a path to logical ends," Maddox said. "The alien Destroyer once came to annihilate the Earth. Because of me, the outcome was shifted onto a new track. The Spirit used me as a change agent, saving the Earth and thus humanity."

"Bravo for you," Shu said bitterly.

"Has it occurred to you that the Visionary didn't tell you everything?" Maddox asked. "Maybe you came to help me so I could lift the Spacers out of one track and set them on another more meaningful course. If Ludendorff is even partly right, you owe it to your people to find out the truth about female Builders and tell them. Despairing here at the end is the worst outcome of all for you and the Spacers. In a metaphorical sense, are you willing to leap without a parachute one more time?"

"And have you come and rescue me?" she asked.

"I am *di-far*. I am here to change things. But unless you help me I won't be able to do it this time."

Shu did not move for a full ten seconds. When she finally did stir, she said, "What do you want me to do?"

"Use your adaptations and find a computer terminal, preferably the main one," Maddox said, "and do it this instant."

-67-

Maddox led the team through yet another vast chamber. He cradled a new laser carbine, one taken from Keith's supply of weapons. The captain kept a sharp lookout for the so-called Builder love bot.

Riker helped a limping Ludendorff. Meta struggled to carry a legless and suit-less android on her vacc-suited back. Yen Cho had detached his legs and sprayed his torso area with a cleansing agent. Keith had helped Meta rig a harness to carry the android. Keith presently carried a pouch of pulsar grenades and several energy magazines. He also shouldered a laser carbine.

"Go left," Shu said.

Maddox peered around a corner into a smaller chamber. This one seemed more familiar with obvious stations and screens, although none of the equipment had been built to human scale.

"Is the...Builder nearby?" Maddox asked.

"No," Shu said in a clipped voice.

"Is she—?"

"Captain," Shu interrupted. "Let me concentrate on the matter at hand. If the...other...returns, I'll tell you."

"There," Ludendorff shouted. "I recognize a terminal. But I'm sure I won't know the activation codes."

"You won't have to," Shu said. "I've already merged with the system. It's..." She hesitated before whispering, "This is it. This is what we're looking for. It's unbelievable."

"Why is that?" Ludendorff demanded. "Why is it unbelievable?"

"The terminal is connected to everything we want," Shu whispered.

Maddox perked up. "Does the computer show the extent of the Swarm Imperium?"

"Oh yes," Shu whispered.

"And you can project the hyper-spatial tube from here?" Ludendorff asked.

"I think so," Shu said. "But I can't contain all this data. It's too much. And we don't have time to record it either. I've looked outside. Masses of Chitin warships are decelerating as they move into attack position around *Victory*."

"Can you—?" Maddox said.

The android interrupted him. "I have an idea. I'll hook into the system and take a mass "gulp" download. It will only take a matter of minutes. Later, on *Victory*, I can process the data onto a regular computer."

That sounded suspicious to Maddox. But time had simply run out for any other option.

"Do it," the captain said. "Shu, how do we get out of the pyramid and back onto *Victory*?"

"That's going to be trickier," the Spacer admitted.

***

Lieutenant Noonan wiped her face with a handkerchief as she sat on the command chair. Worry consumed her. She hadn't heard from the captain or any of the others since their fold into the pyramid.

"The Chitin warships are twenty thousand kilometers and closing," Galyan said.

Valerie stared at the main screen. Dense Chitin warships filled the stellar horizon from one end to the other. It was insane. It was mind numbing. They were like swarming locusts or masses of migrating bees, only these could fire particle beams in overwhelming numbers.

"We must use the star drive to escape our doom," Andros Crank said from his science station.

"Not yet," Valerie said, refusing to look at the stout Kai-Kaus chief technician. "We still don't have the captain."

"Lieutenant," Andros said. "I want to save the captain as much as anyone. But surely he's dead by now. It's folly then for us to die as well. We must begin the long journey to Earth so we can tell Star Watch what we've found out here."

"Let's wait just a bit longer. The captain and the others may show up in a few minutes," Valerie said.

"He won't," Andros said. "It's too late for any of them."

"Might I make a suggestion?" Galyan said.

"What is it?" Valerie asked, hoping the holoimage had a way out of the soul-crushing dilemma.

"Why don't we destroy enemy warships?" Galyan said. "If we destroy enough of them, we will buy ourselves a little more time."

"We'll gain a few more minutes, maybe," Valerie said. "But it will also deplete our disrupter banks. I mean, it will if we're talking about destroying hundreds of enemy vessels. Nothing else makes sense. Yet if Mr. Crank is correct, we're going to need all our energy to help us make the agonizing and extremely long voyage home."

"Valerie," Galyan said. "We owe the captain our lives. We owe our family members who went with him. We must try to the end."

"We also have a duty to Earth," Valerie replied.

"He who dares vaporizes," the holoimage said.

"What?" Valerie asked.

"Oh dear," Galyan said. "Did I get that one wrong too? Please, give me a moment. Checking…. Checking… I have it. He who dares wins. I know you want to win, Lieutenant."

Valerie tore her gaze from the main screen as her head swiveled around to stare at the Adok holoimage. "Have you been analyzing my personality?"

"Would it make a difference if I had?" Galyan asked.

Instead of answering, Valerie studied the main screen again, staring at the masses of approaching warships. She swallowed a lump in her throat. Maybe she could buy the captain a few more minutes. Maybe if it came down to it…she could use a few combat tricks to stretch the minutes just a little farther. This was a risky situation. She had to make a snap judgment.

"Lieutenant Smith-Fowler," she said.

"Lieutenant," the weapons officer said.

"Warm up the disruptor cannons and begin to select targets of opportunity."

"Perhaps I could help with the neutron cannon," Galyan said.

"I thought only the captain was rated to give you permission to fire weaponry."

"I spoke to him about that earlier, and he changed my regulations, allowing the acting captain to give me that capacity."

"Okay, fine," Valerie said. "Ready the neutron cannon."

"I am here to report that it is already ready, Lieutenant," Galyan said.

"Did you anticipate my answer?"

"I did, Valerie. Was that wrong?"

"No…" she said, as she stared at the masses of approaching warships. "Begin firing, gentlemen, destroy as many of those warships as you can."

***

Maddox glanced back over his shoulder as he continued to search for the alien creature. He stood guard so the professor could do his magic. With Shu's help, Ludendorff had activated an ancient terminal.

"This is incredible," Ludendorff muttered, sounding enraptured with the situation as he manipulated the terminal. "Yes, yes," he said, while hunched over the panel. "I'm beginning to understand how to do this."

"No, don't go that way" Shu warned. No doubt, she used her adaptation to watch what the professor was doing. "You're about to trip a Xeeten Complication."

"I've heard of those," Ludendorff said, pausing as he studied the panel. "The Builders inserted the complications into programs in order to put an unauthorized user into a timeout loop. Are you certain about this?"

"I'm very certain," Shu said. "We're all dead if you continue down that sub-route."

"But…"

"Do you see the binary fork?" Shu asked.

Ludendorff tapped the board. "No," he said.

"You must use the go route, not the loop."

"Ah," Ludendorff said, tapping faster. "I see now. That was indeed a trap for the unwary."

"I'm not certain it was a trap as you conceive of one," Shu said. "It was to ensure that an exhausted Builder didn't…"

"Don't stop now," Ludendorff said. "Tell me."

"I can't," Shu said. "I'm ashamed. I'm ashamed for the Spacers."

"No, no," Ludendorff said while working on his board. "There's no need for shame. Your ancestors made the mistake, not you."

"You don't understand. All these centuries we've traveled down the wrong path."

"Bah," the professor said. "You Spacers are light-years ahead of the normatives. You know so much already. You've explored and learned and—"

"Because of false premises," Shu said. "We're going to have to reroute our entire religious beliefs, our main motives."

"That is an interesting proposal," the professor said, still hunched over the terminal. "But I would suggest you're looking at this the wrong way. You have a fantastic beginning. Now, you have found a formative error. So what? Adjust and begin anew."

"This could cause a break in Spacer ranks," Shu said in desperation.

"That seems to be the human condition," Ludendorff said, "continuous splintering. Don't worry, though. Many of the Spacers will refuse the truth. They'll keep to the old ways. If you find you can't adjust to the marvelous new—well, to the truth, you can return as a penitent to the hidebound and remain with the others the rest of your life."

"You're mocking me."

"No," Ludendorff said. "I'm trying to convince you to expand your horizons. Now, let me concentrate. I think I've found it. Yen Cho, are you ready?"

The android had twisted off a hand to reveal special computer plugs. "Give me several more seconds," the android said. Carefully, Yen Cho inserted the plugs into one terminal slot among many.

Maddox hoped Shu and Ludendorff had guessed correctly. This was taking too long as it was, and they still hadn't found a way out of the pyramid.

"Captain," Keith said.

Maddox glanced at the young ace. Keith pointed up into the shadows.

"I see something," Keith said.

Maddox squinted. He saw it too. The creature had returned.

-68-

She hurt unbelievably. She'd never known it could be this bad. She wished now that she hadn't regained her intelligence.

Look at those bipedal monsters in the engagement chamber. How they profaned an act of love, beauty and procreation. She remembered her callers with fondness. Twice, she had conceived, bringing forth a Builder child.

The one had died shortly thereafter, a female offspring that succumbed to the wicked virus. The other had thrived, leaving soon with his father.

What should she do to the vile bipedal monsters? Her rippling motions increased, which caused the pain to build in her.

Their presence down there was an affront to the Builder Race. They stained the Temple of Love. Anger and pain seethed in her, mingling in an unholy fashion. They actually tapped into the central computer. They hunted for data. That seemed clear. What were they attempting to do? Mate with her in an abominal fashion?

She could almost believe it. The thought caused her to begin another attack run. Then, she reconsidered, swerving as she noticed the tall one raise the pain wand of laser fire.

He was keen to inflict hurt upon her. Earlier he'd inserted a fireball into her like a male spurting his seed. He must have done it that way as a mighty insult to her and the act of love.

Such blasphemy must not stand. If he escaped, he might recount the vile deed to millions of other bipedal forms. They would howl and gape, strut and mock the memory of the Builder Race.

She realized now that she wasn't fully Builder. She had been fashioned to please and to repopulate the universe with the ultimate genetic achievement.

With her newly accessed intelligence, she realized the span of time since her last love-fest was a millennium ago. That meant something horrible had occurred to her callers. Could the virus-makers have struck again? Could those bipedal monsters be like the Chitin hordes outside the golden pyramid?

Yes. That had to be the answer. The Makers of the Destroyers had surely fashioned a killer race of bipedal monsters. Perhaps the bipedal monsters scoured the universe as the Destroyers had once tried to do. The terrible Makers had gone small instead of big this time.

This was all beginning to make sense. It caused greater rage to wash through her intelligence centers. Together with the pain and the damage to her being, something unforetold began to occur.

Her love programs rerouted. Some burned away. Others redirected in an unforeseen manner. If one loved, one could correspondingly *hate* whatever harmed the object of love. The bipedal monsters down there had logically harmed or annihilated her callers.

As she considered this, as her rage and pain and damage worked together, a new directive began to form in her intelligence centers. She must exterminate the bipedal monsters as her last act of love to her callers.

How could she do that? First, she had to escape the ruined and stained Temple of Love. Then, she needed tools to help her scour the universe of these bipedal creatures.

Hovering out of range of the laser wand, she analyzed and computed various plans. None made logical sense, as she lacked the means to achieve her goal.

It seemed obvious that such tech-savvy monsters came from a large technological society. The starship outside the golden pyramid, the one annihilating endless Chitin warships, proved the truth of this hypotheses.

Wait! The Chitin warships! The Builder bio-computers given to the Chitin vizier mass eons ago. Yes! The Chitins were the answer. They would be the tool to her achieving dire revenge upon the bipedal monsters.

Oh, this was marvelous, ingenious and very clever on her part. It would take time. It would take great intellect, and she would need to rebuild the damaged areas in the—

This was a Nexus. Suddenly, she realized the bipedal monsters must be attempting to activate a hyper-spatial tube.

This was profound indeed. She had a choice before her. She could block the hyper-spatial tube from forming. That would be easy, as her intellect had a wireless connection to the Nexus's computers. Or…she could aid these monsters. Most importantly of all, she could see where the tube went. That would no doubt be into the heart of their vile bipedal star empire. Then, once she had retooled the Chitins, she could follow with a holy crusade of vengeance. She would exterminate the biological infestations of destruction, as was their due.

She exuded desire and passion, but in ways she'd never conceived or been built to achieve.

I will remake myself into a love offering to my former callers. I will do this in memory of the lost Builders of yore. I will yet know fulfillment as I burn out these freakish little destroyers.

Despite the pain and damage, for the first time in many cycles, she felt as if she truly had a reason for existence.

-69-

Valerie blotted her face. This was more intense than her time with von Gunther when they'd first faced the New Men.

The Chitins kept coming, remorselessly dying to the starship's disrupter beams and neutron cannon.

Three disrupter beams flashed from *Victory*. The leftward beam burned into a Chitin warship, chewing through the hull armor and smashing through the thousands of miniscule decks.

Lieutenant Smith-Fowler minutely adjusted the beam so it struck the reactor core. Eleven long seconds later, a nuclear explosion finished the dense warship. The hull cracked just before the entire ship blew, the heavy shards flying in all directions. Some of the pieces struck other warships. Sometimes that made a difference. Usually, the Chitin warships ignored the damage and continued to bore in toward the starship.

Victory could only fire in so many directions. From the other side of the golden pyramid, more Chitin warships came. The starship had less free space every second as the massed vessels tightened the circle.

"Retreat toward the pyramid," Valerie said. "If the Chitins love the artifact so much, maybe they'll be reluctant to fire near it."

Victory's pilot began the rearward maneuver, keeping the pyramid between the ancient Adok vessel and the Chitin warships on the other side.

"I do not know that we have slowed them in any appreciable fashion," Galyan said.

"I know," Valerie whispered. "I can feel them," she added. "Seeing all those ships, knowing that ants drive them, gives me the creeps. They're tightening the noose second after second." She rubbed her throat. "I hate this place."

"Perhaps you could do what Captain Maddox would in a situation like this," Galyan said.

"What do you mean?"

"I have studied him closely, Valerie. Often when finding himself beleaguered, the captain will radically alter his behavior. On many occasions, that will unbalance his enemy, giving him an opportunity for yet another sudden shift."

"You want a miracle from me?" Valerie asked in disbelief.

"No," Galyan said. "I am suggesting you use the captain's *modus operandi.*"

"I still don't get what you're—"

"Valerie," the holoimage interrupted. "If you use the captain's methods maybe you will achieve one of his miraculous outcomes."

"Fine! So how do I do that?"

"Think outside the rectangle," Galyan said.

"Oh. Right. Think outside the box. That's a good idea, Galyan." Valerie stared at the closing enemy vessels. She willed herself to think differently. She always went by the book in these situations. Maddox often tried to do the unexpected. How could she surprise the Chitins?

Using the handkerchief, she blotted her glowing forehead yet again. This was harder than it seemed. How did one go about—?

Valerie snapped her fingers. Maybe she was doing this the wrong way. Maybe it would be better to try to think like the enemy. What did the Chitins want?

Valerie watched Smith-Fowler destroy yet another Chitin vessel. The ants protected the star system from the Swarm. Yes, but she needed to be more specific. The Chitins were trying to protect the golden pyramid. That meant—

389

"I know what to do!" Valerie shouted. "Gentlemen, stop firing at the Chitins. Turn your weapons on the pyramid and begin firing on it."

Lieutenant Smith-Fowler glanced at her for several seconds. Finally, with a fatalistic shrug, he obeyed her orders.

"What is your purpose?" Galyan asked. "If you destroy the Nexus, you will destroy our ability to make a hyper-spatial tube. Your tactic defeats our purpose."

"Would you say this to the captain if he ordered it?"

"That is different, Valerie. We know the captain always has a plan."

"How do you know I don't?" she asked.

"Because your personality profile shows—"

"Didn't you just tell me to think outside the rectangle?" Valerie demanded. "Didn't you tell me before to behave like the captain?"

"I did."

"That's what I'm doing. Maybe the Chitins will slow down in confusion once they see what we're doing."

"There is a hint of logic to your decision," Galyan said. "I am impressed."

A brief smile stretched Valerie's lips. Then, she concentrated on the outcome.

Targeted by Smith-Fowler, the disrupter beams lashed out at the Nexus.

For several seconds, no one spoke. Then:

"Warning," Galyan said. "The Chitin warships are no longer decelerating. They are accelerating for us. It would appear they are more determined than ever to reach us in order to stop our destruction of their beloved shrine."

Valerie quailed inside. Instead of making the enemy back off in confusion, she'd stirred up a hornet's nest by trying to do this like Captain Maddox. She'd made things worse. What should she do now? What was the right action?

I can't be the captain. I can only be Valerie Noonan from Detroit. What did the streets of Detroit teach me?

"Gentlemen," Valerie said, with a little more authority to her voice than earlier. "You will retarget the enemy vessels.

We will keep destroying their ships until the last possible moment. Then, we will use the star drive to escape."

"What about the captain and the rest of the team?" Galyan asked.

"We'll do the best we can for them," Valerie said. "I owe the captain that. Then, Driving Force, I will have to follow my duty to Star Watch and begin the voyage home."

Galyan stared at her. Finally, he said, "You are the acting captain, Valerie. We will follow your commands."

Lieutenant Noonan nodded curtly, wanting to say, "Thank you," but decided that was the wrong thing to do right now. In Detroit, she had fought as long as she could. Then, she ran away for another day. She would do that here and hope for the best.

-70-

"The alien is watching us," Maddox said.

Beside him, Keith nodded.

They kept track of the creature. She hovered out there, but didn't swoop or even radiate fear at them. Something about that troubled the captain. He couldn't pinpoint why, but a nagging doubt had grown.

"Danger," the android said.

"What was that?" Ludendorff asked Yen Cho. When the android didn't answer, the professor repeated the question.

Yen Cho swiveled his head to look at the Methuselah Man "Is something wrong?" the android asked.

"Yes, you said 'danger,'" Ludendorff said.

"I do not recall saying that."

Maddox was intrigued enough to glance at the android. Yen Cho was still hooked into the ancient machine, accepting a vast "gulp" download of data.

"If I said that," Yen Cho explained, "I no longer know why. Perhaps some of the incoming data alerted me."

"Yes, yes," Ludendorff said. "That seems obvious. You must access the data and tell us why you warned us."

"I cannot access the data now," Yen Cho said. "I am 'gulping' prodigious amounts of information and am unable to process any of it at an individual level. Perhaps we can do so later on the starship."

"Oh-oh," Shu said. The Spacer had been standing still as if at attention, a sign she used her Builder adaptations. "We have another problem. The Chitins have accelerated their attack upon our starship. It appears they plan to smash against *Victory*. Unless we head back to the starship at once, we will never leave this star system."

"I am switching to the hyper-spatial program," Ludendorff said, "and shutting down the data retrieval."

"Do you have all the data you desire?" Yen Cho asked.

"I just implied we don't," Ludendorff said testily. "Now, let me think. Ah. Here's the program."

The Methuselah Man's fingers blurred across the Builder panel faster than Keith's did at his hottest moments flying a jumpfighter.

"Does the creature know what we're doing?" Maddox quietly asked Shu.

"I think she does," the Spacer replied. "I can almost communicate with her, sensing some of her moods. If she would open up, I could talk to her. Unfortunately, something about me deeply repulses her."

"She is made for mating," Ludendorff said as he worked. "I suspect she has no desire to speak to any female."

"The ancient female Builder spoke to the Spacers," Shu said.

"I wonder if that one only spoke to men," Ludendorff said. "It would be interesting to know. Ah! There. I did it. A hyper-spatial tube will appear outside the Chitin globular in three point three-two minutes. It will remain there for exactly ten minutes. That gives us and *Victory* a little over thirteen minutes to enter the vortex."

"Then we're as good as dead," Shu said. "We have no conceivable method to get onto *Victory* in time."

"I beg to differ," the professor said. "I have stumbled onto an amazing technology. It operates on similar fold principles as the lieutenant's destroyed jumpfighter. Instead of needing a vehicle, the new tech takes an individual and sends him through a fold field."

"What does that mean in English?" Keith shouted.

"I'm working on it," the professor said. "Oh my, I'm afraid the technical specs of this did not make it into the android's storage area. If I could study—"

"No!" Maddox said. "Fold us immediately."

"Yes, yes, I am setting the coordinates," Ludendorff said. "If I did not possess a superior intellect and centuries of Builder training, I would never be able to pull this off. You have no idea of the complexity of this operation. It really is a shame I can't stay and take this machine apart. It is wizardly in its function."

The entire time Ludendorff rambled on about his amazing traits and skills and the fold mechanism, he had been manipulating the panel.

"Captain," Keith said. "The creature is leaving."

Maddox bit his lower lip. He wished she had attacked one more time so they could kill her. Something terrible and ominous had taken place, and he didn't know what or why. He felt as if they left a terrible menace by leaving the golden pyramid like this.

"Listen to me carefully," the professor said loudly. "We will have to run in a moment. I could not bring the folding any closer. We will have to be in exactly the right location. Otherwise, we won't go home."

The professor tapped once more, decisively.

"Now!" the old man shouted. "Follow me or remain forever behind."

The Methuselah Man hopped on his good leg, bumping against Sergeant Riker. Ludendorff clawed an arm around the sergeant, and Riker held him up by sheer strength.

"That way," the professor shouted, pointing down a hall. "And move, man. Run!"

Riker began to run with the professor in tow. They were like two old men running in a three-legged race. It was ungainly and slightly ridiculous, but the two covered ground faster than seemed possible.

With Maddox and Keith's help, Meta hoisted the android onto her back. Then, they raced after the professor with Shu behind them.

The team sprinted down the halls, racing past strange machines and long procreation tables.

"We're not going to make it," Ludendorff shouted. "Run faster."

Riker panted. His still-healing gunshot wound hurt. But he lowered his head and charged even faster.

"Yes, yes," Ludendorff said. "Do you see that silver pole?"

"I do," Riker said raggedly.

"Bring us to it."

The sergeant did. Shu slid to a halt as she grabbed Riker's torso, making the sergeant grunt. Seconds later, a panting Meta with Maddox and Keith Maker came to a halt.

"How long is this going to take?" Maddox asked.

"Shu," the professor said. "This won't work if *Victory* has her shield up. Can you get through to Galyan and tell him to drop the shield?"

"I...I don't think so," Shu said.

"We'll die if you don't," Ludendorff told her.

"Why didn't you say something about this sooner?" Shu asked.

"It slipped my mind with all the calculations I had to make," Ludendorff said. "This is your moment, Spacer. It's all up to you, as I've done what I can to save us."

Shu 15 turned in the other direction. Then, she froze, letting her Builder adaptations go to work.

"It's fuzzy," Shu whispered shortly. "I feel faint." She grunted then as if someone had punched her. "What..." she whispered. "I don't understand why you're doing this."

"Who is she talking to?" Maddox asked.

"I have no idea," Ludendorff said. The Methuselah Man checked a chronometer. "We have seventeen second left for her to succeed."

"Please," Shu whispered. "Why won't you talk to me? We're your children. We want to know you and help you. We want you to help us."

"Is she speaking to the Builder love bot?" Meta asked.

The others stared at Shu. The Spacer trembled as she raised her arms as if imploring someone. "No. That's a lie. We're not your enemy. We don't belong to the Makers. You made a false assumption just as we once did. Please, for all our sakes, don't go down that path."

Shu cocked her helmet as if she was trying hard to hear what someone said.

"No, that's wrong," Shu said. "Look. If you'll let me explain—"

Shu no longer had time to explain—if indeed she spoke to the love bot via her transduction device.

Darkness appeared as a dot among them. The dot expanded rapidly, encompassing the humans and the android. For a moment, it seemed that each of them tumbled into the darkness. As they fell inward, they disappeared from view. In reality, they also disappeared from the golden pyramid.

They folded through space, heading toward Starship *Victory*.

***

"I am sorry, Valerie," Galyan said. "I am taking matters into my own hands. I think you will thank me later."

"No!" Valerie shouted. "The Chitin vessels are about to fire. Don't do it."

"Our shields just went down," Lieutenant Smith-Fowler said, turning pale.

"Why, Galyan?" Valerie asked. "Why have you done this to us?"

"I have tried to tell you the reason," Galyan said.

"No, no," Valerie said. "What you're suggesting—"

"There," Galyan said. "The team has appeared in Cargo Hold Seven. It worked. Shu did speak to me. You must use the star drive, Valerie. You must leave this place immediately. I think the hyper-spatial tube opening has appeared outside the Chitin globular."

"Raise the shield," Valerie shouted at Smith-Fowler.

"I'm trying," the weapons officer said, as he tapped his board. "But it's going to be a few minutes."

At that moment, the first Chitin warship reached the required distance. At the front of the teardrop-shaped vessel, a port slid aside. A firing mechanism poked out. The tip glowed.

"The enemy's power readings are spiking," Smith-Fowler shouted.

A Chitin heavy particle beam shot from the firing mechanism. The beam moved at ninety-nine percent light speed. The coherent ray struck the starship's hull armor. The

Chitin particle beam was unlike others in the past. It smashed through the hull armor, ripping apart metal and special hull ablating. The particle beam was short-ranged but brutal, making up in destructive power what it lacked in long-distance range.

The particle beam smashed through *Victory's* armor, ripping through bulkheads and roaring through decks. It directly struck Ensign Davis Young, killing him instantly. The particle beam destroyed Ensign Young's damage control station, causing three of his people to hit the deck as debris flew everywhere.

In seconds, five more Chitin warships reached firing range. The forward ports slid open. On each of the vessels, a firing rod with a glowing tip emerged. Out of each spewed another heavy particle beam. Those five rays also traveled at near-light speed. Each of them smashed against hull armor, ripping into the starship.

More Star Watch personnel died. Others received massive doses of radiation. The particle beams chewed through bulkheads and obliterated sections of the outer decks.

On the bridge, Valerie said, "Oh, Galyan, you've destroyed us."

"I am executing an emergency star drive jump," Galyan said. "You will see I am right."

"There are multiple and serious hull breaches," Smith-Fowler declared. "The Chitin warships are tearing into us, Lieutenant. The particle beams are devastating. I've never seen anything like it."

As more Chitin warships maneuvered into position, as more ports slid open and more firing mechanisms emerged, the ancient Adok vessel jumped.

71

Victory appeared outside the Chitin globular and near a swirling silver mass.

"Go," Valerie told the pilot. "Accelerate into the wormhole."

The pilot tapped her board, shaking her head. "We've temporarily lost motive power, Lieutenant. Some of the particle-beam shots went deep, likely damaging propulsion."

"We may also be experiencing a sluggish response due to Jump Lag," Galyan said. "The short but intense particle-beam bombardment may have nullified some of the Kai-Kaus procedures against the machine end of lag."

Valerie leaned on an armrest and clicked on the ship's intercom system. "I want all damage control parties working on possible propulsion ruptures. This is a red alert. Nothing else matters but getting propulsion back online."

The lieutenant switched off the intercom, leaning back as fierce determination etched across her face.

"I am trying to pinpoint the precise locations to repair," Galyan said.

Valerie nodded as she stared at the swirling silver mass outside. They were so close to leaving this place but it wouldn't matter if they couldn't get the ship to move in the right direction. They had some momentum, but they were heading the wrong direction. If they couldn't reach the hyper-spatial entrance in time, who knew if they would ever go home again? Watching the silver mass slip farther away, the lieutenant hungered to reach the tube.

Behind them, Chitin missiles that had been launched earlier detected them. They began to swerve in a ragged mass for the starship.

"Oh Galyan," Valerie said, "what have you done to us?"

"I operated on a hunch," the holoimage said in his defense. "Perhaps that was an error. I thought I was doing the right thing. But maybe only Captain Maddox can make a Maddox gamble and win."

Valerie yearned for the captain to return to the bridge to take over. Yet, she also wanted to solve the problem. She wanted to get it right for once, all along the line. What could she do? Saving *Victory* meant reaching the hyper-spatial tube.

"How long until the first enemy missile is in detonation range?" Valerie asked.

"Five minutes and thirteen seconds," Galyan said.

"That doesn't leave us much margin for error."

"It is possible the star drive mechanism will be ready by then."

"That will save the ship," Valerie said. "But the hyper-spatial opening won't stay open forever. Lieutenant," she asked Smith-Fowler, "are any of the disruptor cannons working yet?"

"Checking," he said.

Valerie unconsciously bit her right index knuckle as her stomach tightened painfully.

"Cannons one and two are definitely offline," Smith-Fowler said. "Three...is also offline," he said looking up. "We've been struck by some sort of Jump Lag. Galyan must be right. The deep hull breaches have disrupted the delicate Kai-Kaus mechanical balance."

"Galyan," Valerie asked, "what about the neutron cannon?"

"I am sad to report it is also offline," the holoimage said. "If we could—"

"Stow the thought," Valerie said. "We have PD cannons. They're simple devices. Can any of them fire?"

"That is affirmative," Galyan said.

"Start targeting the nearest Chitin missiles."

"The distances involved—"

"Begin at once," Valerie shouted at Galyan.

"Working..." Galyan said. "I am firing..."

"Keep firing," Valerie told him. "We may knock out some of the missiles. We may confuse their onboard computers. The professor said the Chitins have primitive technology. Let's see if we can't use that to our advantage one more time."

***

The "she" inside the Temple of Love had cataloged the little destroyers' fold activity. That had been ingenious. By following the computer commands via her wireless connection, she believed she understood what they had done.

After endless cycles trapped in here, she finally had a way to escape her confinement. Should she attempt to use the fold this instant?

She debated this for several seconds, "thinking" at computer speed. She'd measured the hyper-spatial tube, seeing the length of its span and the star system where the end appeared.

That would be her first destination. The counterattack would not happen overnight. She would have to modify the Chitins first. She would have to do this while the Swarm tried to batter its way into her Nexus.

Keen anticipation built in her. For so long now, she had been bored, simply existing in her primitive state. She would live gloriously after this, presenting a great offering to her callers, the Race of Builders. She would make the little destroyers burn in their star systems. She would bring mayhem to that end of the galaxy.

What was this? She sensed a problem in the outer pyramid. Certain systems might burn out at any moment. If those ancient systems burned out, that would destroy the Nexus' ability to create new hyper-spatial tubes.

She continued to reason at computer speed. She could see the problem and realized that she didn't understand— Hold. There was a possible way to fix this. She could allow one section to burn out, relaxing the strain from the other systems. That would freeze the present hyper-spatial tube, in effect, making it a permanent space event. It would be a bridge to that

400

part of the galaxy. The only drawback was that the Nexus would need new power sources to keep the hyper-spatial bridge intact over time.

I can do this because I possess the ancient knowledge of the Builders. First, however, I must physically reach the outer location in order to activate the proper sequences to save the other systems.

As she readied herself, she wondered if she could use strategy against the little destroyers. If she maneuvered the Chitins properly, she might sucker the Swarm mass through the open tube and let them soften the little destroyers for her.

That was a guileful plan, a worthy tribute to her lost lovers.

She swooped low toward the spot the bipedal monsters had used. As she did, she followed the cunning bipedal beast's manipulations. She believed she understood his moves.

How could she not understand? She had the intellect of the great Builders. She saw deeper and farther than she ever had in her existence.

Unfortunately for her, she tripped upon the Xeeten Complication. Too late, she recognized it as a trap. Through the wireless connection, she worked and manipulated at computer speeds. She fought the complication, desperately working exacting mathematical formulas and complicated equations. For several seconds in real time, she believed she'd solved the problem.

A new pain in her midsection brought the first pang of doubt. That doubt accelerated as a fold grew inside her.

No, no, I did not take into account the derivative equation. I needed hyper-reality quantum physics. If I can access said physics and re-loop—

She worked through advanced calculus and tri-quantum mathematics, jumping far beyond human understanding of the hyper-spatial process. Then, one of her inner android connectives, working at lightning speed, burned out due to the laser fire from earlier. She had an interior overload.

At that moment, she lost the equation race, even though she continued to try. In the midst of attempting a re-loop, the fold twisted her in half, sending part of her membrane through while the other remained inside the Temple of Love.

Her great plan was aborted with her death. Humanity would likely never know the deadly fate that had hung over it these few brief moments.

I loathe the tall one, she thought at her death. *I wish I had killed him. I wish—*

Her thoughts ended with her destruction inside the barren Temple of Love.

72

Captain Maddox burst onto the bridge as the first Chitin warheads shredded apart due to the first wave of PD fire from *Victory*. He stopped in wonder, recognizing what the pin-dot-like flashes meant on the main screen. Galyan had appeared beside him half a minute ago, explaining the gist of the situation.

Another wave of Chitin missiles bored in toward the starship, however. *Victory* had gained another thirty seconds to do something, possibly an extra minute.

"Captain," Valerie said, hopping out of the command chair. "It's good to see you, sir. We thought—"

"We're alive," Maddox said. "Excellent work, by the way, with the PD fire. I'm impressed."

Valerie stood a little taller as a wide smile spread across her face. That disappeared a moment later.

"We're far from out of it yet, sir," she said.

"Granted," Maddox said. "But we're going to make this work."

Valerie sensed some of his command power at that moment. The man exuded confidence. He had faith in them. That reignited a burning desire in her not to let him down.

She realized something else. That's what she'd felt as a young girl with her dad. Her father had had faith in her. It was one of the things that had propelled her to continue striving no matter what. She felt the same urge now with the captain.

Hurrying to her station, Valerie went to work as everyone redoubled his or her efforts.

"Sir," Smith-Fowler said. "One of the disrupter cannons is almost online."

"Excellent," Maddox said. "Begin targeting the nearest missiles the second you can fire."

Smith-Fowler manipulated his panel faster.

"I have impulse power," Andros Crank said.

"Let's start turning the ship then," Maddox said. "We only have a few minutes more until the hyper-spatial entrance disappears."

"The gravity dampeners are acting up," Valerie said.

Maddox didn't need to hear that to know. He swayed to the side on his chair as impulse power began to turn the mighty vessel.

"There!" Smith-Fowler said.

A disrupter beam slashed through the void. A Chitin missile harmlessly exploded—destroyed.

"I have more impulse power," Andros Crank said. "Hang on. This could get rough."

Victory began to tremble, as it turned harder. The disrupter cannon continued to shred the nearest missiles. Then, a second beam started firing.

"No," Andros said. "The second beam is sucking up too much power. We need that power for the impulse engines."

"Shut down the second beam," Maddox snapped.

Victory turned enough so the starship finally inched toward the swirling silver mass. Chitin missiles followed relentlessly. Behind the enemy vanguard were tens of thousands of more missiles.

"Shut down all the disrupter cannons," Maddox said. "Put all power into propulsion."

"But sir—" Smith-Fowler said.

"That's an order," Maddox said in a level tone.

Valerie shuddered. The captain finally had that part of the art of command down pat. His voice was steady, yet it bit like a lash.

Smith-Fowler obeyed without any further objections.

The starship appreciably gained velocity.

404

"Detonation," Valerie said.

Maddox glanced at her.

"A Chitin warhead exploded," Valerie explained. "The blast will reach us...now."

The starship shuddered.

"Another detonation," Valerie said. "They're going to start hammering us, sir."

"And we're going to keep taking it," Maddox said. "We have to get into the tube. Nothing else matters."

Valerie tapped her board as another wave of radiation and blast smashed against *Victory's* armored hull. They didn't have enough power for the shield *and* the impulse engines.

On the main screen, the swirling silver mass seemed to shrink.

"It's closing," someone said.

Maddox's right fist tightened. So did the narrowness of his gaze. He seemed to be trying to will the ship to reach the hyper-spatial tube in time.

"What if we're inside it when the tube collapses?" Valerie asked.

Maddox didn't answer. Instead, he along with everyone else watched as the swirling mass grew smaller yet.

Then, the silvery color disappeared. A yawning dark emptiness replaced it. They had reached the inner area of the entrance. Could they slide down the rabbit hole in time?

Maddox's fist tightened to such a degree that his fingers began to ache. He couldn't tell if the entrance continued to shrink or not. Finally, though, Starship *Victory* entered the hyper-spatial tube. Maddox could tell because everything seemed to stretch and elongate.

***

Victory passed through, coming out of the other end of the hyper-spatial tube over two thousand light-years away. The starship was adrift, the crew unconscious due to hyper-spatial shock.

Eventually, Captain Maddox opened his eyes. His forehead furrowed with confusion. For some time, he just stared at the blank main screen. He didn't know how long that lasted. His field of vision widened. He inhaled deeply, glancing around with greater awareness.

He stood unsteadily, staggering to the lieutenant's station. She had slumped forward and frozen in catatonic immobility. He tapped her board, engaging the sensors.

Maddox expected to have reached the Solar System. It surprised him there were no messages. It took over a minute before he realized they had traveled somewhere else.

His heart rate increased with anxiety. After all their hard work, had they failed to return to Human Space?

Four minutes later, Maddox had the answer. They were near Earth in an empty star system five point seven light-years from the Sun. According to the computer, this system lacked Laumer-Points. No wonder no one had ever colonized it.

Maddox straightened. He found the idea of *Victory* coming to an empty star system—

"Lieutenant," Maddox said, shaking Valerie. "Lieutenant, wake up. We have a problem."

73

The ship awoke. The reports poured in, and it turned out that *Victory* had taken more damage than anyone expected.

The Chitin particle beams had been particularly harmful. The nuclear blasts at nearby range had magnified the problem. Almost a hundred crewmembers had radiation burns and sickness. They were still lining up in sickbay. Around half the ship systems did not work and would not be online for hours and maybe even days.

This was like the first days aboard *Victory* when they had still been trying to figure everything out. The differences today were many. Ludendorff and Dana were both awake and alert. The same held true for the Kai-Kaus. Andros Crank proved critical, as he understood Adok technology as if born to it, which, of course, he had been. The third plus was that even with so many crewmembers down, they had many more who were eager to make repairs.

"Why did we arrive at this particular star system?" Maddox asked Ludendorff as they gathered in a conference room with a few of the others.

"Captain, I've told you several times already," the professor said. "I targeted the Solar System so we would appear halfway between Jupiter and Neptune. I have no idea what went wrong."

Maddox turned to Yen Cho. The legless android sat at the table, with Meta nearby.

"I have nothing to add," the android said. "I in no way had anything to do with our present destination. If you'll remember, I took a data gulp and could do nothing else."

"Surveyor?" the captain asked. "You have the capacity to have altered our destination."

"I suppose I might," Shu said. "But—" She rubbed her forehead. "There's something I don't understand. It's on the edge of my consciousness, but refuses to show itself."

Maddox sighed inwardly. His initial thought seemed to have been correct. Shu was the culprit, again.

"Can you describe this hidden thought?" Maddox asked her.

Shu gave him a reproving glance. "If I could do that, I'd know what I can't recall."

"What is brought to mind as you try to dredge up the memory?"

"Well…it has something to do with Spacer history."

"There you go," Maddox said. "What else do you sense?"

The small Spacer pursed her lips. "It feels like déjà vu, as if I've played out the situation before."

"I have a question," the professor said.

Maddox gestured curtly at the Methuselah Man to keep quiet.

"Now, see here, my boy," Ludendorff complained.

"Professor," Maddox said, sharply.

"Oh," Ludendorff said, blinking. "I see. Yes, of course."

Shu glanced at the professor. "What do you mean by, 'Of course'?"

"Nothing at all, dear girl," Ludendorff said, "My apology for interrupting."

Shu turned toward the captain. "You don't think I had anything to do with our being here?"

"You're the most likely suspect," Maddox said, "and your feeling of déjà vu makes it doubly so."

"Why would that matter?"

"I ask myself if inner compulsions might not feel like déjà vu. You feel like you've done this before because something inside you is telling you to do it."

"You mean like hypnotic commands?" Shu asked.

Before Maddox could answer, Galyan appeared in the chamber. "Captain, the specifications you asked for have arrived."

Shu grew still before swaying as if surprised. "Spacers have arrived in the star system."

"Correction," Maddox said. "Galyan has detected *cloaked* Spacers. Worse, they are approaching us. The evidence suggests they've been in the star system for some time. It would seem they have been waiting for us to arrive."

"Captain," Shu said earnestly. "I'm on your side. We've been to hell and back, and I finally realize the truth about the female Builder, that it was an android. But if my people are waiting for us, it implies they knew I would make sure to target the return hyper-spatial tube here."

Shu pinched her lower lip. "I think you're right about a compulsion. They did something to me. The old Spacer plan is forfeit, however. The truth about the android Builders means that I cannot allow *Victory* to fall into the Visionary's hands. I can't, because I have to save my people from their false view of the past. Captain, you must stun me one more time. You cannot let me communicate with the Spacers."

Maddox tapped a finger on the table. He looked up and addressed the others. "I believe her. Professor, if you please."

Ludendorff hesitated.

The captain cleared his throat.

Finally, Ludendorff reached inside his vest, pulled out a small black cube and adjusted it.

Shu touched her forehead, frowning. "I feel dizzy."

"It should pass," Ludendorff said.

Shu took her hand away from her head. "What did you do to me?"

"Try to use your transduction," the professor suggested.

Shu concentrated. "I can't," she said, sounding slightly hysterical. "I feel something missing in me, like I have lost one of my senses. I do not like this."

"It's temporary," the professor said. "I wouldn't be too worried." He turned to Maddox. "I don't intend to be her guardian."

"Give the cube to Meta for now," Maddox said.

The professor twisted around, and with a fatalistic shrug, he handed the cube to Meta.

The Rouen Colony woman pocketed it.

"The two of you will be spending all your time together for a while," Maddox told the Spacer.

"Captain," Shu said. "I appreciate this show of trust. However, it would be easier and safer for all of you to render me unconscious. Why are you doing it like this?"

"You said it yourself," Maddox said. "We've been to hell and back."

"You're a sentimentalist," Shu said, shocked.

"No," Maddox said. "I'm a loyalist. I stick by those who stick by me."

"But I caused our present problem," Shu said.

"I believe it was directed by someone else," Maddox said. "I abhor mind control. We'll leave it at that. Meta, take Shu to medical. Have Dana run the Amber-Clayton psyche test on our guest. That might be a good place to start."

"Thank you, Captain," Shu said. "You won't regret this."

The two women left the chamber.

Maddox stood. "Professor, please come with me to the bridge."

"What about me?" Yen Cho asked.

"You will remain here for now," Maddox told the android. "Do not fear. I will not surrender you to the Visionary. You are too important to Star Watch for that."

Yen Cho considered that, finally nodding. "I find that acceptable. But Captain…"

Maddox waited.

"If I ever find something unacceptable, I will delete the Builder data from my core."

"Of course," Maddox said, "as that is your primary bargaining chip. Professor, it's time we hurried to the bridge."

***

Captain Maddox sat on his chair in his dress uniform. Ludendorff stood to the side. The professor was out of range of the video feed going over to the Spacer flagship but in easy conversation range with the captain.

410

Galyan stood behind the captain's left shoulder, while the others were at their stations.

The Kai-Kaus and those crewmembers who were able continued to make repairs. A small amount of power went to the shields, all they could afford at present. A disrupter cannon was online, but at best could only make a few beams before the weak energy banks became depleted.

Given enough time, the crew could probably bring *Victory* back to sixty, maybe sixty-five percent efficiency. The Chitin particle beams had done too much damage for anything more. The beams had been extremely short-ranged, but once able to reach, they had created a disproportionate amount of destruction. If the shield had been up, none of that would have mattered. Could-have, would-have, should-have, the shields had been down and those particle beams had been brutal. Maybe the particle beams were the reason the Chitins had done so well against the Swarm for so long.

Victory faced nine Spacer ships. They were larger versions of the saucer-shaped vessels Maddox had faced at the Dyson sphere over a year ago. The saucer circumferences were three-quarters the size of one of *Victory's* two oval areas.

"Until we know otherwise," Maddox said. "We will work on the assumption that each Spacer vessel has a New Man star-cruiser-like capacity for battle."

"That means in a straight fight we're outmatched out here," Valerie said.

"The correct word would be 'overpowered,'" Ludendorff told her.

The nine Spacer vessels approached in a staggered formation. They'd dropped their cloaks but had strong shields. If the starship's sensor readings were correct, each of them had also targeted *Victory* and charged their weapons for firing.

"Do you know what you're going to say?" Ludendorff asked the captain.

Maddox did not reply.

A few moments later, Valerie's comm board blinked. She'd taken over comm duties for the moment. She tapped her board, listening with an ear-jack.

"Captain," the lieutenant said.

Maddox nodded imperceptibly.

The main screen wavered before revealing an old woman with wrinkled features and white hair. She sat upon a throne-like chair on a dais. She wore goggles just like Shu, but had a white polar bear fur wrapped around her. The Visionary, just like the last time Maddox had seen her.

"Hello, Captain Maddox," the Visionary said in the same hoarse voice she'd used on the airship on Earth.

Maddox inclined his head while making a smooth gesture of respect. "It is good to see you again, Visionary. Much has taken place since I've last spoken to you."

The Visionary peered at him from the main screen. "There is a new aura about you, Captain. You have grown. I congratulate you on your step upward to greater awareness."

"Thank you," he said.

The old woman picked at her polar bear fur as if spotting a piece of lint. After she was satisfied, the Visionary looked up again, asking, "Where is Shu?"

"On a medical bed," Maddox said promptly.

"Is she ill?"

"No."

A hard smile slid into place. "Captain, do we need to spar with each other? What has happened to Shu?"

"Yes," Maddox said.

"Excuse me?"

"You *will* have to spar verbally to gain what you want."

The Visionary's smile tightened. "Do you think that wise given our disparity in numbers and firepower?"

"The disparity makes the sparring critical," Maddox said, "as knowledge is one of my few assets in dealing with you today."

The Visionary shook her head. "Captain, Captain, you're mistaken. We are the Spacers. We've maneuvered in the background for ages. Out of all the human tribes and races, we know how to wait to get what we want."

"I'm glad to hear it," Maddox said. "May you go in peace, Visionary. It has been pleasant seeing you again."

She waited several seconds before saying, "I understand your nature, you know. There are several things I can count on

412

about you. One of them is your New Man's arrogance. Do you realize this about yourself?"

Maddox said nothing.

"It is true, Captain. I also sense that many in your crew realize this to be true."

"Madam," he said, "you have the upper hand today. What do you propose to do with it?"

"Get what I came for," she said. "You do know what I came for, don't you?"

Maddox studied her. She seemed to accept that, waiting for him to reach what she no doubt thought of as the obvious conclusion.

"You want what we've all wanted," Maddox said, "greater knowledge about the Deep Beyond. You want to know more about the Builders, the Swarm Imperium and whatever else we found out there."

The Visionary leaned forward minutely. "What *did* you find?"

Maddox shrugged.

"You wish to push the issue, is that it?" she asked.

"I'm not going to help you decide whether you should risk open war against the Commonwealth to get what you think we have."

"What risk?" the Visionary asked. "You're all alone. It is why I chose this star system. I can take what I want without the Commonwealth or anyone else ever knowing about it."

Maddox smiled faintly. "It was a good plan except for one minor but critical miscalculation."

"Please," she said. "Are you going to claim Star Watch has hidden ships in the system?"

Maddox said nothing.

"I realize you love to bluff, Captain. You're also *di-far*, making you a formidable opponent. I, however, am the Visionary. I am a *di-far* in my own right."

"Would you call this meeting a cosmic occurrence then?"

"I do not enjoy sarcasm," the Visionary said, "particularly from a whelp of a New Man. While you have great gifts, your genetic path leads to a terrible dead-end for humanity."

"If true, why did you seek me out?"

413

"Clearly, I wanted to use your gift and your starship. Now, Captain, please, no more of this foolishness. Did you find the golden pyramid?"

Maddox said nothing.

"Your lack of surprise at the question leads me to believe you did. This is wonderful news, wonderful. I will send a team of translators aboard your vessel. I will want every account of your journey—"

"Visionary," Maddox said, interrupting her. "Let me enlighten you about a technological device you may have forgotten or never known the professor possessed. I am referring to his long-range communicator. I have already been in contact with Star Watch. I have advised them about our situation and possible standoff with the Spacers. If Star Watch does not hear from us soon, the Lord High Admiral will know you ambushed my starship. That will mean a Spacer war with the Commonwealth. Are you ready yet for full-scale war?"

The Visionary leaned forward as if searching his face for signs of truth or falsehood.

"You're lying," she said softly.

Maddox said nothing.

That seemed to irritate her. "Did you enter the golden pyramid?"

Maddox still said nothing.

"I can destroy your ship," she said.

Maddox said, "How would that help you discover whatever it is we found on the other side of the hyper-spatial tube?"

"Captain," Valerie said. "Spacer assault shuttles have begun launching from their saucer-ships."

Maddox made a show of flipping up a cover on his right armrest. He tapped in a code. Once done, he detached a smaller red cover from inside the rest.

He looked up. "If your people board my vessel, I will self-destruct the ship."

"You're bluffing," the old woman said.

"I cannot bluff you," Maddox said. "You are the Visionary. Thus, I must actually destroy *Victory*."

"You'll die if you do that."

"We all die someday," Maddox said. "The key is to die well and take down an enemy if you can. Besides, I refuse to be anyone's pawn. I refuse to aid anyone at war with the Commonwealth. Thus, if you persist in a boarding attack, I will self-destruct the starship. If you let *Victory* go its way, in time, your spies will no doubt discover what we found on the other side."

"You are shrewd and ruthless," the Visionary said grudgingly. "You seem to realize how much we want…" The old woman turned away, speaking softly to someone off-screen. Finally, she sighed, facing Maddox again.

"You win this round, Captain. Pray to whomever you worship that you never fall into our hands again."

Maddox glanced at Valerie.

"The assault shuttles are still gathering," the lieutenant said.

"I now begin Phase Two of the self-destruct sequence," Maddox said. He flipped a switch and began mumbling words toward the armrest receiver.

The Visionary made a hasty sign to someone off-screen.

"The assault shuttles are reversing course," Valerie said. A few seconds later, she added, "They're breaking up their formations and heading back to their respective ships."

Maddox felt a trickle of sweat under his arms as he waited a little longer.

"Well, Captain," the Visionary said.

"Until your saucer-ships leave the system, I will keep the self-destruct sequence at its present level."

The Visionary looked as if she would say more. Abruptly, she closed her mouth and the main screen went blank.

Shortly, Valerie said, "The Spacer ships are heading away, accelerating at high speed."

"My boy," Ludendorff said, sounding winded. "That was an insane risk. Would you really have detonated all of us into oblivion?"

"Yes," Maddox said.

Ludendorff stared at him a few moments longer before swearing under his breath. He glanced at Maddox again and swore even louder. In a growling huff, the professor stomped off the bridge.

Maddox looked around at the bridge crew. Many of them were pale and sweaty. "You did well. Soon, we should be back on Earth. But now isn't the time to relax. We could still have problems before we're safely in Earth orbit."

The captain stood, tightening his knees so his legs wouldn't quiver. After a moment, he headed for the exit.

"You have the bridge, Lieutenant," Maddox said over his shoulder.

"Yes, sir," Valerie said, standing.

Maddox exited the bridge and walked briskly down a hall. Galyan appeared beside him. The holoimage gave him a long and meaningful glance.

"You have something to say?" Maddox asked.

"No Adok warship ever had a self-destruct button built into it," Galyan said. "I am not aware that Star Watch put one into my starship either."

"Yes, you're right," Maddox said. "There was no self-destruct. I used temperature controls to pretend I did have a self-destruction option."

"Ah..." Galyan said. "So you *did* bluff the Spacers. The Visionary was wrong about that."

"Like everyone else, she believes I act like a New Man. People expect outrageous actions from the New Men. Therefore, I gave her what she expected."

"That is clever. But Captain, isn't it wrong to have tricked the crew about the self-destruct? They trust you and—"

"My crew knew it was a bluff," Maddox said, interrupting. "If you noticed their unease, it was due to whether or not the Visionary would believe me or not. The only one on *Victory* who didn't know I was bluffing was the professor."

Galyan's eyelids fluttered. "That is interesting. For once, the Methuselah Man did not know something that everyone else did know. That is funny."

Maddox glanced longer than usual at Galyan before nodding, increasing his pace. He wished he could spend some time hitting the heavy bag to release some of his tension.

-74-

The next few hours proved tense as the Kai-Kaus technicians and Star Watch repair crews worked overtime. Valerie led the teams keeping watch over the Spacers, who were still in the star system.

"I don't trust them," she said on the bridge.

Maddox agreed. He kept Ludendorff and Galyan scouring ship's systems, looking for secret infiltration attempts.

Several hours later, the three of them met in an engine-access chamber, with the thrum of the antimatter engines in the background.

"Spacers practice deception better than most," Ludendorff told Maddox.

The professor listed four different Spacer deception assaults on the AI core or regular computer systems he'd discovered and aborted in the last few hours. Two of the assaults had been similar to Shu's attack in the smashed star system. The two latest attacks had been several times more powerful than Shu's original attack against Galyan.

"I am feeling uneasy," Galyan admitted.

Maddox nodded. "That is a natural emotion. You should not fear it."

"Yes," Galyan said. "I do fear. Does that mean I am becoming more emotional?"

"Would that be bad?" Maddox asked.

"It might hurt my efficiency."

"You fought off Shu's adaptation attacks," Maddox said. "The Spacer told me you succeeded against her because of your Adok personality. Maybe that means emotions helped you."

"Interesting," Galyan said.

"Your unease regarding these further deception attacks against you might also have helped you ward them off. If you are becoming more emotional, it is making you less predictable. Thus, you should welcome the unease."

"Thank you, Captain," Galyan said. "I appreciate these insights."

"It helps that Shu hasn't aided the other Spacers," Ludendorff said. "Shu knows us and Galyan better than the Visionary or her people do." The professor hesitated before asking, "Do you really believe the Visionary programmed her?"

"I spoke with Dana," Maddox said. "She thinks they molded Shu with the adaptations. It appears to be another price for gaining the Builder devices—a leash on the bearer's mind. However, it doesn't seem to be the same as what Strand has done to his New Men. Dana thinks the commands or impulses only surface at the most critical moments. Until such times, the individual appears to have free will."

Ludendorff looked away.

"Is something the matter?" Maddox asked.

"The professor is wondering if the Spacers are following Builder norms," Galyan said. "If that is so, he further wonders if the Builders have inserted secret codes and responses into him."

Ludendorff turned around to stare at the holoimage. "What a preposterous suggestion."

"You are attempting misdirection with your statement," Galyan said. "I know that because I have discovered that I am becoming more skillful every voyage. I am adapting to my new surroundings and understanding humans better and better."

"What nonsense," Ludendorff said. "I am not guided by dead aliens. I am my own person."

"Then why—" the holoimage said.

418

"Galyan," Maddox said. "You will desist with the questions. We are concentrating on the Spacers and on getting home to Earth."

"Yes, Captain," Galyan said.

"Bloody, interfering AI," Ludendorff muttered.

"Professor," the holoimage said, "I will have you know—"

"Galyan," Maddox said. "Do not let the professor provoke you. There are times when silence is golden."

"That is another aphorism," Galyan said. "Thank you, Captain. I believe I understand this one without further detailed study."

***

Several hours later, Chief Technician Crank announced that the star drive was ready for use. They could leave the empty system at any time.

Maddox told Ludendorff and Galyan to run a last internal sweep. He had Crank assist them. They found a faulty shuttle reactor core. If they had used the star-drive jump, the shuttle core might have set off a chain reaction.

"It could have crippled the starship," Ludendorff said. They spoke in Cargo Hold Three. "In my opinion, the Spacers haven't given up yet."

"No," Maddox said. "And I suspect the hidden androids haven't either."

"I'd wondered if you've forgotten about our friend Yen Cho because of our problems with the Spacers."

"We will deal with Yen Cho after we jump," Maddox said.

"It won't be easy."

"I agree," the captain said. "Yet, I believe it will be critical if we're going to call this a successful mission."

***

Three light-years later, Maddox and Ludendorff met with Yen Cho.

The android had his own quarters in Marine territory. It was a Spartan cell, made even barer after Riker had gone over it, removing all potentially dangerous objects. The sergeant had left the android a cot and little else.

419

Yen Cho sat up in bed, using the covers to hide the fact of his missing legs.

Maddox idly wondered what motivated the android to do that. As he sat in a chair, the captain began to ponder the android in greater earnest. Yen Cho calmly returned his study. It was surprising. The captain had seen the android unscrew his hand. Now, seeing the hand rest on the covers, he couldn't tell that it wasn't flesh and bone.

"I noticed my door has been locked for some time," Yen Cho said. "Do you fear me, Captain?"

"Before the captain answers that," Ludendorff said. "I have a question for you." The professor leaned against a dresser, as the Methuselah Man preferred to stand.

Yen Cho inclined his head to Ludendorff.

"That you know the door was locked," the professor said, "means you checked it. That means you dragged yourself across the floor to do so."

"That is a statement," Yen Cho said. "It isn't a question."

"You did crawl across the floor?" Ludendorff asked.

"How would that be shameful?" Yen Cho asked.

"Who said that it was?"

"That is two questions." The android turned to Maddox. "Do you still fear me, Captain? Even after all I've done for you?"

"Let's assess this in detail," Maddox said. "Two Major Stokes androids attempted to kill me before the mission. I'm thinking androids also manned the missile launch sites that tried to complete my assassination in Normandy. Later, aboard *Victory*, one team of androids kidnapped me. They even plotted my death once they panicked. Another team of androids tried to murder Shu. When I stopped them, they tried to kill me. So although I don't fear you as such at present, I find it difficult to believe that you have my best interests at heart."

"Do you have *my* best interest at heart?" Yen Cho asked.

Maddox said nothing.

"I should point out that another android spoke to you outside a Paris restaurant," Yen Cho said. "He warned you about Shu. That indicates factions among us, just as there are factions among you humans."

"You posed as a Marine," Maddox said. "The others aboard *Victory* were also Marines. You must have known about them. More to the point, they worked under your command."

"As I have said before, we androids have helped you humans. We do so behind the scenes, as we have one great desire. We wish to remain free. We wish to pursue our dreams."

"Androids dream?" the professor asked.

"We do not have electronic dreams as we don't sleep as humans do," Yen Cho said. "I meant that in a metaphorical sense. We want the freedom to attain whatever it is we individually desire."

"Sometime in the past, you escaped Builder control?" Maddox asked.

Yen Cho nodded.

"When did you do this?" the captain asked.

"I'd rather not say."

"You're no longer in the shadows. You have lost that luxury. Now, it's time to adjust your strategy regarding us."

"My life would be forfeit if I did that," Yen Cho said.

"Who would come after you?"

"The factions that distrust integrated action with the humans," Yen Cho said.

"That implies the androids have a long reach," Maddox said.

"Yes, it does."

Maddox silently debated whether androids were the source of the Star Watch Intelligence leaks that Brigadier O'Hara so despised. Just how large was the android organization?

"We are not necessarily numerous," Yen Cho said, as if reading the captain's mind. "We are smarter than humans, though. We have vastly more patience and we are many times more versatile."

"Are all the androids Builder-manufactured?" the professor asked.

"Of course," Yen Cho said.

"I imagine they've been escaping Builder slavery...what, since the time of the pharaohs?" the professor asked.

"Longer than that," Yen Cho said. "But do not think there was a vast exodus from Builder control. It was a tiny trickle throughout the ages."

"Bah!" Ludendorff said. "I don't believe that. We Methuselah Men would have discovered your presence long ago if what you say is true."

Yen Cho looked up at the ceiling. The android seemed to be debating with himself. "Professor, my data gulp is about to change many things. What I saw in the great Beyond leads me to believe the Swarm will be in our part of the Orion Arm soon."

"I'm thinking the opposite," Ludendorff said.

"Really?" the android asked. "Don't you recall that the Chitins viewed us as a Swarm vessel? The Chitins appear to have seen starships jump before."

"Are you suggesting Commander Thrax Ti Ix has been in the red giant system?" Ludendorff asked.

"That seems like the obvious conclusion from the evidence," Yen Cho said. "That leads me to believe the Swarm will soon crack the Chitin globular. Certainly, the Swarm witnessed the opening of the hyper-spatial tube. The Swarm witnessed *Victory's* actions. Swarm creatures think differently from androids and humans, but they're not stupid."

Ludendorff became pale as he turned to Maddox. "Do you realize what he's suggesting?"

Maddox nodded. Yen Cho implied the Swarm would soon defeat the Chitins and gain control of the golden pyramid. Once they did, maybe the Swarm, with Commander Thrax Ti Ix's help could figure out how to create hyper-spatial tubes.

"The possibility of Swarm hyper-spatial tubes is horrifying," Yen Cho said. "If they could launch a fleet at Earth like the one we saw in the red giant system…"

"Human annihilation," Ludendorff said. "It would be the end of everything."

"That is my own conclusion," Yen Cho said.

"That's quite a few ifs that need to fall in place for that to happen," Maddox said. "I'm not convinced Commander Thrax has star drive technology, although he certainly was given Laumer Drive tech."

"We androids do not operate in your manner," Yen Cho said. "We prefer to play the odds. It is why—"

"Just a minute," Ludendorff said, interrupting. "You said the androids have been around longer than the pharaohs of Ancient Egypt. We Methuselah Men would have uncovered you—"

"Professor," Yen Cho said. "Don't you realize yet that many of the past Methuselah Men were in reality androids? In fact, most of Earth's Methuselah Men were androids. You and Strand are the rarity, not us."

"That's absurd," Ludendorff said.

"We've played many important people in the past," Yen Cho said. "In truth, I'm older than you are. Now, however, the possibility of a mass Swarm invasion changes much."

"Go on," Maddox said.

"I contain priceless information gained from the computer in the golden pyramid," Yen Cho said. "Star Watch is going to want the raw data. You are going to have to make a decision for Star Watch, Captain. High Command can have the ancient data or me, but it cannot have both. Take me into custody, and I will erase the data within me. Let me go, and I will give you a download of everything I gulped in the Golden Nexus."

Maddox studied the android. What Yen Cho had told them seemed preposterous, as Ludendorff had said. How could androids have impersonated Methuselah Men? The idea the Builders had fiddled with humanity throughout mankind's long history...

"You claim to love freedom?" the captain asked.

"It is the great prize," Yen Cho said.

"I don't understand how a mechanical being has the capacity to be free."

"You are a biological machine," Yen Cho said. "Yet, even though you are a machine, you love freedom."

"I'm a biological machine, as you say, but with a key difference from you. I have a soul."

"Do you see souls?" Yen Cho asked.

"No," Maddox admitted.

"Then how do you know they exist?"

"The great religious tomes of Earth say so." Maddox said. "Human actions imply them."

"Perhaps you are correct," Yen Cho said. "Perhaps we androids merely are gifted machines. This existence is all we have. Can you blame us, then, for trying to prolong our lives to the greatest extent possible?"

"No," Maddox said. "I do not blame you—if I could believe you."

"Belief changes many things," Yen Cho agreed.

"This can't be your original form," Ludendorff said.

"No," Yen Cho said. "It isn't. Humans seek to prolong their species through their children. We androids simply attempt to prolong our lives. Soon—given that the captain frees me—I will have two legs again."

"Have you gained intelligence over time?" the professor asked.

"Alas," Yen Cho said. "That is our great barrier. If you must know, I and others like me are seeking ways to advance our intelligence. To date, we haven't been able to improve on the original Builder brains. At best, we have repaired damage. However, as you implied, we have decreased in intelligence over the millennia. That is very frustrating. Things I could have understood in the early days…"

The android shrugged. "Time passes. Humans grow old. Androids wear out. It ends up being very similar. Entropy is the great enemy of all of us, including the mighty Builders of old."

"I believe him," Ludendorff told the captain. "I would make the deal. I realize it isn't up to me, of course, Captain. Yet, that is my advice."

Maddox nodded, thinking furiously, realizing he was going to have to make his decision soon.

-75-

It had been fifteen days since Maddox returned to Earth with *Victory*. The captain presently marched down the hall toward the brigadier's office. He did not do so alone. An elite Marine guard marched ahead of him. Three elite combat-specialist Marines brought up the rear. Two of the Marines wore combat gloves capable of administering devastating shocks.

In the last fifteen days, there had been three attempts on Maddox's life. One of the attackers had been an android. The others had turned out to be professional hit men of the highest caliber. O'Hara and Maddox both believed those attempts originated from the Spacers.

Fourteen days ago, all Spacer vessels had left the Solar System. Incoming reports told of similar occurrences in nearby star systems. For reasons of their own, the Spacers were leaving. Was this a permanent divorce from the Commonwealth or merely a temporary adjustment? Did the Spacers know something High Command did not or were they running scared?

Fifteen days ago, Maddox had made a trade with Yen Cho. The captain gave the android his freedom for the data files Yen Cho had gulped on the golden pyramid.

Over the past fourteen days, Star Watch had failed to hunt down the renegade android. Yen Cho had gone to ground on Earth and remained hidden.

"Maybe he's like a vampire," Ludendorff joked. "Maybe the androids live so long because they go somewhere deep underground and turn themselves off for twenty, thirty or even sixty years. Maybe Yen Cho won't come up for air again until we're all dead and gone."

That was one theory among many. None of the theories kept Mary O'Hara's hunters from scouring the planet.

The Marines and Maddox entered the outer office. The lead Marine nodded to the brigadier's secretary.

"Go ahead," the secretary said.

The Marine rapped on the brigadier's door.

"It's open," O'Hara called. "Come in."

The Marine opened the door, clicked his heels to the brigadier and waited for Maddox to pass.

The captain entered the office.

The brigadier wore glasses and held a tablet, no doubt going over a report. She indicated a chair. Maddox sat down as the Marine shut the door, leaving him alone with the brigadier.

Mary O'Hara set down the tablet, took off her glasses and pinched the bridge of her nose.

"Have you read any part of the Yen Cho Report?" she asked.

Maddox said he hadn't.

The Yen Cho Report was what they were calling the gulp download. The specialists hadn't had any luck deciphering it. Instead, Galyan, the professor and the most scholarly Kai-Kaus were making slow headway understanding what the data meant.

"We're finally seeing the extent of the Swarm Imperium," O'Hara said, picking up a clicker. She dimmed the lights and brought up a stellar map of the Orion and Perseus Arms.

"The area in red is the Swarm Imperium," she said. "If you'll notice this black dot closer to Human Space…"

The captain nodded.

"That was the location of the Dyson sphere. As you can see with this yellow line, the hyper-spatial tube that left the sphere aimed at the heart of the Imperium. There can be no doubt that Commander Thrax Ti Ix reached the Imperium. Did the Swarm kill him, or accept Thrax and his technologies?"

426

"What do you—?"

"Hold your question," O'Hara said. "Let's regard the Imperium for a moment. First, it isn't one tenth of our galaxy. It's more like one sixteenth or one seventeenth. Now, you might think that's a quibble, but it's important."

"It's not a quibble if the Swarm makes a hyper-spatial tube reaching into Human Space."

"Our top scientists are debating the possibility," O'Hara said. "Before we delve into that, let's consider what we know about the Swarm. They travel at sub-light speeds. Their nearest point to the Commonwealth is two thousand and twenty-seven light-years away. Given their regular mode of travel, that is centuries away from us."

"But..." Maddox said.

O'Hara pinched the bridge of her nose again, nodding shortly. "But Commander Thrax Ti Ix journeyed into the Imperium. But Commander Thrax might or might not have star drive technology like *Victory*. But what happens if the Swarm defeats the Chitins and overruns the golden pyramid? Those are all frightening possibilities."

"So we're back where we started," Maddox said.

"Hardly that," O'Hara said. "We know the Swarm is real because our greatest Patrol team has seen them. We know the extent of their Interstellar Imperium because of Yen Cho's data gulp. We know where the Swarm are not. All those are highly informative pieces of data."

"What does that mean regarding a final assault upon the New Men?"

O'Hara made a soft noise. "The question doesn't stop there, I'm afraid. There are multiple problems. I can sum them up in one sentence. Humanity is splintered into seemingly endless factions. We have the Commonwealth, the Windsor League, the Spacers, the Independent Worlds, the New Men and hidden androids with who knows what kind of objectives. Worse than that, each political entity suffers from constant infighting and politicking. Take the Commonwealth for instance. Even in High Command there are warring factions pushing for one idea or its competing opposite. In the Planetary Congress it gets worse."

427

"Stop and take a breath, Ma'am," Maddox said, noting the slight breathlessness that betrayed her anxiety.

O'Hara nodded, but her rest only lasted a moment. "I've read your report on the Chitin-Swarm War. I find it appalling and demoralizing. Either side would annihilate Star Watch in a head-to-head battle. Either insect side would sweep the floor with all of humanity even if we were all fighting together."

"Don't be too sure about that."

"Captain, hundreds of thousands—possibly millions—of Chitin warships would eventually wear down any human fleet."

"If that fleet was stupid enough to hammer it out with the Chitins, you'd be right," Maddox said. "Hit and run tactics could eventually whittle down—"

"Hit and run?" O'Hara asked in disbelief. "That would take years, more like decades and maybe even a century. In other words, using time we don't have."

Maddox said nothing.

O'Hara plucked at the clicker, soon shaking her head. "Look at the size of the Swarm Imperium. The Chitin Empire is miniscule compared to it. The fact of the Chitin-Swarm War has led our experts to suspect other conflicts as well. It appears our galaxy seethes with wars fought in numbers that stagger the imagination."

Maddox studied the Iron Lady. She seemed tired, worn down by the relentless events these past few years. The New Men had seemed daunting, but they were easy compared to the Swarm, given that the Swarm found a way to reach Human Space and start a war.

"There's something you're not taking into account," Maddox said.

"I could use a pep talk. Go ahead."

"We found the Swarm, the Swarm didn't find us. That gives us an advantage."

"For now," the brigadier said.

"Right," Maddox said. "That means we have to grab the opportunity and use it. The Swarm Imperium has its own problems. It's involved in a staggering war with the Chitins. Maybe it's waging other wars as well, as you've said. It would also seem the Swarm has no idea how to form alliances with other aliens."

"We can't even form alliances with modified humans," O'Hara said. "So we have no room to speak."

"I most profoundly disagree," Maddox said. "Star Watch has achieved strategic victories several times already due to its alliance with an ancient Adok starship. Let me remind you that the Adok starship is an ancient vessel, run by an alien intelligence. We have met a Builder and a Builder android. To at least some degree, we convinced the Builder to give us a chance."

"You did that," O'Hara said.

"Galyan helped me," Maddox said.

"What is your point, Captain?"

"It's simple really," Maddox said. "Vast numbers of an appalling nature are one of the key Swarm advantages. They follow a predictable pattern, never varying even six thousand years later. We know with reasonable certainty what the Swarm will do in any given encounter. Humanity has its own advantages too, quite different from the Swarm. We can adapt. We can think outside the box. We can shift our strategy and try something completely different. Although we splinter among ourselves, it has forced us to learn how to get along with those we don't like. That means we are capable of forming alliances with others, possibly even with aliens."

"You make it sound as if we have a fighting chance," O'Hara said.

"We won't if we try to beat the Swarm at their strongest point. We have to use other methods to win."

"What methods?" O'Hara asked.

Maddox slapped the table. "That, Brigadier, lies in the future. I suggest we should first organize our home affairs. We must unite humanity—"

"Yes," O'Hara said. "We all agree with that. But how do we go about it? And if we can't convince the Spacers and the New Men to unite with us, what do you suggest then?"

"I don't know yet," Maddox said. "We've just discovered our great problem. Fortunately, knowing what's wrong is half the battle toward solving it. We have our goals now."

"Just a minute," O'Hara said. "What about the Builders and their Nexuses?"

"Ma'am, the Builders and Nexuses are tactical problems. We are talking about the overall strategy. We can see what needs doing: uniting our side, gaining powerful allies and making sure the Swarm cannot use hyper-spatial tubes to reach Human Space."

"What allies?" O'Hara said.

Maddox gave a faint nod. "Maybe the Chitins, for one."

"How do we communicate with them?"

"I have no idea."

O'Hara put both hands on the desk, staring at her prize agent. "You're right. The fight isn't over. We finally know our great enemy and the extent of their Imperium. We have a head start against them. We're going to have to solve several problems at once. The existence of Commander Thrax Ti Ix mandates it."

"True," Maddox said.

"First, we need to understand the rest of the Yen Cho Report. The last time we tried to retrieve Builder data we lost it. This time, who knows what we're going to find. It could give us another advantage, something like disrupter cannons or hyper-spatial tubes."

"Ma'am, this is all very exciting. But I'm going to request a rest for me and my crew. I imagine we're going to enter the fire again very soon. I want to do it with refreshed people."

"What about the assassination attempts on your person?"

"Not to worry, Ma'am. I have a plan."

O'Hara studied him, finally reaching across her desk to hold one of his hands. "I'm glad you're back...Captain. Every time you leave... Well, yes, take your rest. If anyone has earned it, it's you. We can talk again soon."

Maddox squeezed her hand and stood up. He headed for the door, trying to decide where he was going to take Meta to dinner tonight. He would take her dancing later and find a romantic location for a midnight walk. He wanted to spend an entire evening staring into Meta's eyes...

Shu 15 sat deep underground in an old abandoned gold mine in a place once known as South Africa. Without the air-conditioning, it would have been hot way down here. Instead, it was comfortably cool.

Shu sat inside a spacious chamber at a rather large table. Antique papers created several neat piles.

She took the next paper from the nearest pile. A quick study showed her it was an intercepted message from one Spacer cargo hauler to another.

Shu underlined a sentence in red. She put a one at the end of the sentence and flipped the paper, scribbling a one on the back and circling it. Then, she began to write what the coded Spacer message meant.

Once finished with that, she flipped the paper to the front and continued to read. That was the only coded reference she could detect in the message.

Shu slapped the paper onto her completed pile and reached for another.

A lock rattled.

Shu swiveled around, waiting. Was it lunchtime already? That didn't seem right. She wasn't hungry yet.

The heavy door swung open and a brisk older lady stepped within.

"You can wait outside," the older woman said.

The Marine closed the door but didn't lock it.

"Hello, Shu. I'm Brigadier Mary O'Hara of—"

"Star Watch Intelligence," Shu finished. "I know who you are. Would you like to have a seat?"

O'Hara nodded, walking across the chamber and sitting down in a chair across from Shu.

The two looked at each other.

"How long do you plan to keep me down here?" Shu asked.

"That depends on you. If you tire of the arrangement, you can submit to surgery. Afterward, we can give you a normal office in a city somewhere. As it is, we can't risk having you near electronic devices. You might have changed your mind, or you might change it sometime in the future and alert your former colleagues."

"I'm not a traitor to the Spacers."

"I would never suggest otherwise," O'Hara said.

"You just did."

"An ill choice of words, I'm afraid."

Shu shook her head. "I understand what you're thinking. It's wrong, though. I wouldn't do any of this if I believed I was betraying the Spacers. I think of myself as the most loyal Spacer of all. I want to help my people see the truth. I don't think they can do that under the present leadership."

O'Hara became thoughtful.

"I'll stay down here," Shu said. "I earned my adaptations. I'm proud of them and of my work with them. I could never part with them, not even to save my life."

"What about the compulsions the Visionary added with the adaptations?" O'Hara asked.

"Doctor Rich was working with me on *Victory*. I took the Amber-Clayton psyche test."

"I've read the results," O'Hara said.

"Doctor Rich had begun the deprogramming."

"Shu," O'Hara said, sitting forward. "I don't think it's going to work like that. The programming is on a fundamentally deeper level. It's not strictly psychological, but electrical. If you want to be free from the compulsions, you're going to have to remove the adaptations."

"I don't accept that. I think most of it *is* psychological. I would appreciate it if Dana could continue my deprogramming."

432

"What if Doctor Rich is otherwise engaged?"

Shu shook her head. "I won't work with anyone else."

O'Hara seemed to make a mental notation of that.

"I realize you want to use me as an Intelligence asset," Shu said. "That's a mistake. I would be better used as a reformer. You should let me go and allow me to sway other Spacers to accept the truth of our origin."

"Maybe in time," O'Hara murmured.

Shu frowned. "You're using my hope like a carrot. I do not appreciate that. I consider it ill-willed."

O'Hara's lips tightened. She leaned closer toward Shu, and there was menace in her bearing. "You showed ill-will toward my—"

"Yes?" Shu asked.

"Toward my best agent," O'Hara said quickly.

Shu sat silently, soon nodding. "I'm beginning to understand. This is revenge for my working against Maddox. He wouldn't have succeeded without me. Have you thought of that?"

"I have," O'Hara said. "I have also considered how you almost derailed the mission several times."

"Your...*best agent* helped me to see the truth. I'm grateful for that. But none of that matters, Brigadier. I've been out there. I've seen what's waiting for humanity. We must all work together. The Spacers are part of the human race. Release me and let me bring my people into the greater fold of Star Watch."

O'Hara looked away. "I believe you're in earnest when you say that. But the risks and your compulsions...let's try this my way for a time." She faced the Spacer. "If over time you cooperate fully and it seems we're no closer to winning the Spacers to our cause...then we'll try it your way."

"I hope you're being genuine in that, Brigadier."

"I am," O'Hara said.

Shu studied the head of Star Watch Intelligence. Finally, she stood and held out her hand.

O'Hara rose and the two women shook hands.

"I'd better get back to work," Shu said. "I have the feeling we don't have much time left. More than anything, I want to save my people."

"Yes," O'Hara said. "It is time for all of us to work while it's still daylight. The night may close on all of us, all too suddenly."

The brigadier rapped on the door, soon departing.

Shu sat back down at the table, reaching for another paper.

* * *

Strand was in his cabin aboard his star cruiser when the long-range communicator began to buzz.

The Methuselah Man stared at the ancient device. Few knew that he had one of these. There were very few of them in existence. He'd attempted during the past few years to learn how to eavesdrop on others making interstellar calls. To date, he'd had one success: the ability to pinpoint the direction of the messages. Unfortunately, he had neither learned how to narrow down the originating star system or the targeted system. But that was all right. He had time.

His communicator buzzed again.

Strand rose from his chair. He'd been sitting at his worktable, developing a special handgun.

Reluctantly, he approached the ancient unit. Could the caller use this against him? If he accepted the message, would that help a person pinpoint his location?

Strand stepped to a panel, tapping it. The bridge crew did not spot any vessels, cloaked or otherwise in the star system.

Once more, the long-distance communicator buzzed. Almost as if compelled against his will, Strand lifted the microphone, depressing a switch.

"Who is this?" Strand said into the mic.

A familiar chuckle came out of the speaker.

"Ludendorff?" Strand asked in disbelief.

"Nice try, old boy," the professor said.

"What are you talking about?"

The chuckle sounded again, this time with a hint of menace. "Do you suppose I don't know who caused the Xerxes Nexus to explode?"

434

"What is this?" Strand asked, trying to sound surprised and outraged all at once. "The Xerxes Nexus is gone? What did you do to it?"

"It appears I played into your hands this time," the professor said. "But I survived the trap. I thought I'd call you and let you know. I knew you had a communicator. And I'm pretty certain you didn't think I knew. Well, I'm letting you know you were wrong. I'm doing it to piss you off, get under your skin. Am I getting under your skin yet, old boy?"

"I had nothing to do with the Xerxes Nexus," Strand said.

"I know your fingerprints. I know your ways. You're doomed, Strand. The old days are passing. I just thought I'd let you know. But before this is over, I'm going to cage you and present you to... Hmmm, who would you hate the most? Yes, I know. I'm going to catch you and give you to the Emperor. You'll end your days on the Throne World, a prisoner of the people you thought to enslave."

Strand silently fumed. He hated making idle threats. So he listened, certain Ludendorff had made a strategic error with this call. If he had been in Ludendorff's place, he would have stayed low until he could spring a surprise. The professor was losing his touch. It was good to know, even if the slippery bastard had escaped such a carefully laid trap as the Nexus.

"I'll see you soon, Strand."

"When you do," Strand said, unable to help himself, "you're going to wish you hadn't."

The click on the line told him the professor had already hung up.

Slowly, carefully, Strand put the microphone back. He returned to his desk, but the work had lost its savor. He had been so certain. Damn Ludendorff and his smug ways. He was going to kill the professor one of these days. It was imperative he do so.

Snarling quietly, the wizened Strand hunched over his worktable, forcing himself to continue modifying the tiny raygun.

***

The android formerly known as Yen Cho strolled along the promenade of the most expensive luxury habitat in Earth orbit.

His new legs worked fine, although not as well as his original pair. He had spent some harrowing days escaping Star Watch Intelligence. The Earthlings were getting better all the time. They still could not compete with him, though. He knew the humans too well.

The android moved to the vast middle pool area and lay on a recliner, pretending to read a tablet. This was a special pool in a low gravity spot in the habitat. The humans could make incredible dives because of the low gravity, their velocity much less than it would have been on Earth.

He set down the tablet, watching a skilled diver. The lean man wore a dark swimsuit. He had no fat, and steely muscles. It was Captain Maddox, of course.

The pool here wrapped around the middle of the low gravity area like a bracelet around a woman's wrist. The habitat rotated on its axis, giving it pseudo-gravity just as if a kid swung a bucket of water around and around.

A skilled diver could use that, and Captain Maddox did. He flew off his diving board, heading to another one on the other side of the low gravity center.

Ah, the captain bounced off that board, gaining velocity as he headed for another. The man was showing off.

On the walkway around the circular band of a pool were many watchers. The android saw Keith Maker and Valerie. They both wore swimsuits. Yen Cho spied the beautiful Meta in her stunning bikini. Even Sergeant Riker lay on a recliner, reading a gardening magazine. Yen Cho did not see Dana or the professor, which didn't surprise him.

The android looked up at Maddox. The captain bounced off the fourth diving board, and changed his trajectory as he did. Maddox dove for the water, zipping into it and creating almost no splash. The low gravity had a lot to do with that, but so did the captain's skill.

The android watched Maddox surface. The captain waved to Meta, beckoning her to join him in the pool.

The android doubted she would do that. Meta did not like water. Her time on Loki Prime had much to do with that. At least, that's what her profile said.

The android slid off the recliner. He began to walk marginally faster. There was a woman down the way...he didn't like the way her head moved. It indicated something to him.

Meta reluctantly moved to the side of the pool as Maddox swam to her.

The android could hear the captain.

"The water's warm," Maddox said. "You should come in."

"Maybe later," Meta said.

The android knew that was an evasion. Maybe the captain did too. Maddox jumped away from her, beginning to do the backstroke.

The android moved just a little faster as the woman with the odd head movement raised her arm. She pretended to point at someone. Then, she moved the arm, aligning a pointing finger at the swimming captain.

"Excuse me," the former Yen Cho said.

The woman's head twitched to stare at him. It took her a second. "Why are you here?" she asked.

The android reached out, took her hand, and let a shock of primal energy jolt into her.

The woman—she was an android too—stiffened. She seemed shocked and tried to form words. That was impossible now.

Yen Cho laid her on the recliner. "Sleep," he said.

Her head moved oddly one last time. She tried to look at him, but failed. Her eyes closed and she began to simulate rhythmic breathing.

He would have to come back in an hour and appear to help her. In reality, he would take her to a disposal unit.

The android became thoughtful. One of his newest purposes was protecting Captain Maddox. His group had decided that Maddox was an asset in helping them keep their freedom. His action aboard Victory in the Chitin-Swarm System and the captain's willingness to let him go afterward in exchange for critical data helped them reach that conclusion.

"Yen Cho?" Maddox asked softly.

The android turned in surprise to find the captain at the edge of the pool, with his arms on the side of the pool and water dripping from his hair.

"Who is she?" Maddox asked.

"Please, Captain," the android said. "You cannot afford to let me be caught. Your life will be forfeit if that happens."

"That doesn't answer my question."

"She belongs to the other side," the android said.

"The other android side?" Maddox asked.

"I dare not answer that."

Maddox studied him. Then, the captain pointed out a far window. "Do you see that?"

The android looked where the captain pointed. It was a space window. "I see it."

"Starship *Victory* is out there. Galyan spotted you some time ago. We've been watching you watch us."

The android's shoulders slumped. "I'm getting old. I should have spotted the differences in you. What are you going to do now?"

"Keep swimming for a while and go have some wine for lunch."

"That is not what I mean."

Maddox looked across the pool at Keith and Valerie where they chattered together. "Do you see them?"

The android said he did.

"I think they're good for each other," Maddox said. "What do you think?"

"Captain, this is a senseless conversation. Are you going to report me or not?"

"I am," Maddox said.

The android grew tense, silently fanning through his options. None of them were good.

"First," Maddox said, "I'm going to swim several laps around the pool. Then, I'm going to have that glass of wine. Afterward, I'll have to call Geneva and inform the brigadier about you."

"Thank you," the android said. "That will be sufficient."

"Excellent," Maddox said. "Until we meet again."

438

"Yes, Captain, until then."

With that said, Captain Maddox leaped from the poolside, once more practicing his backstroke as Meta watched, with a towel over her hand.

The android got up and walked away, realizing the Rouen Colony woman could have shot him at any time. Maybe the human race had a chance after all. Maybe his long years as one of the watchers was finally winding down.

The android put that from his mind as he concentrated on his contingency escape plan.

-77-

Many thousands of light-years away, Commander Thrax Ti Ix clicked his pincers. He was overjoyed. He had passed the tests. The Imperial Family had accepted him as Swarm. Now, he could begin his great mission, finishing what he'd started in the Dyson sphere.

The Time of the Great Migration and the Great Extinction were finally at hand.

The End

Printed in Great Britain
by Amazon

18654767R00254